Man of Iron

Published by
Elpis Productions
Flat 4, 3 Victoria Road,
Lenzie
Glasgow
G66 5AW

ISBN 978-0-9569031-0-5 Paperback

Man of Iron

Robert Watson

Elpis Productions, Lenzie, Glasgow, Scotland

Chapters

Chapters

Man of Iron

PREFACE

This fascinating novel, based on fact, follows the life of the world-famous Christian Reformer and leader of the Protestant Reformation in Scotland, John Knox. It outlines his brave character, his little known, harrowing, time as a French galley slave, his years of exile in Geneva with John Calvin, in Lausanne and Frankfurt, his return in 1559 to preach again in St. Andrews Parish Church in prophetic fulfillment, and to lead the dynamic Scottish Reformation a year later.

Read of his fiery preaching and equally fiery interviews with Mary, Queen of Scots, a sad, disturbed, and turbulent figure, who contrasts with Knox's rock-solid trust in the face of adversity in a trustworthy God, who is always in control.

The story brings to absorbing life the spiritual revolution which transformed the Christian Church in Scotland to return her to its Biblical roots and justification by faith alone in Christ. Just as Wallace, her first great son, also a man of iron wrenched her national independence from the tyrannical overlordship of the King of England, so her second great son plucked her spiritual independence from the tyranny of the Papacy and, founding it upon the knowledge born of free inquiry, bequeathed it as a priceless heritage to his race. Where the spirit of the Lord is, there is freedom.

The faults of Knox were the faults of his age, but his virtues were the virtues of all the ages, an unflinching courage, an absolute disregard for self, a noble patriotism, a keen sagacity, a love of the Bible, and a deep, tender, and reverent faith in "things unseen and eternal." He even had a foundationary vision for universal education. John Knox was truly a man who neither feared nor flattered any flesh. Scotland owes him a great debt for the Protestant Faith.

John Knox's House, The Netherbow, Edinburgh

CHAPTER ONE

THE CONFUSED TUTOR

A slightly below middle-sized man, broad of shoulder, with coal-black hair and beard surrounding a face of full, reddish, cheeks, narrowish-forehead above grey-blue eyes set deep beneath heavy ridged brows, was slowly traversing the green sward of the village of Giffordsgate on the edge of the county town of Haddington in East Lothian, some seventeen miles from Scotland's capital.

His head was down, and his long, high-ridged, nose and full mouth, with the upper lip somewhat thicker than the lower, were pulled together in the manner of one in some personal pain. He was not a particularly distinguished-looking man, and in fact an observer could have been forgiven for thinking that Master John Knox, tutor to the children of the Lairds of Longniddry and Ormiston in East Lothian, a mere nervous young man of faltering words, as was revealed in his plea to God in the beginning.

"Ah, Lord God, look at me! I cannot speak, for I am a child. But the Lord God said unto me,' Say not that I am a child, for you shall go to all that I shall send you to, and whatever I shall command you, you shall speak. Be not afraid of their faces, for I am with you to deliver you," saith the Lord. Then the Lord put forth his hand and touched my mouth. And the Lord said unto me, "Behold, I have put my words in thy mouth. See, this day have I set you above the nations and over the Kingdoms to root out and pull down, to destroy and to throw down, to build and to plant. Therefore, gird up your loins, and arise, and speak unto them all that I command you. Be not dismayed at their faces, lest I break you in pieces before them. For, see, this day have I made you a pillar of iron, a defended city, and brazen walls against the whole land, against the Kings of Judah, its priests, its Princes, against the people of the land, and they shall fight against you, for I am with you to defend you, says the Lord."

With a sigh John Knox closed the book and slipped it into his tunic. Hard words they were, bold words, powerful words, and hadn't Jeremiah gone on to be condemned as a traitor to his people for telling them of the condemnation of the nation by God? This would be seen in their being taken away into captivity by the pagan Empire of Babylon for Israel's sins, terrible sins of turning to the same pagan worship of the Baalim and Asherah on the green high places.

It wasn't only Israel who came under the condemnation of God, but also Pharaoh Hophra, King of Egypt, who would be given into the hands of Nebuchadnezzar, King of Babylon, and of course there was the eventual deliverance of Israel, which the Scots tutor knew was the sure hope of God's people. Was this to be Scotland's fate too? He himself had a delight in abstract thought and dialectical disputation, which even in that age of vain ambition and quick-tempered violence was recognised throughout Europe as typical of Scottish scholarship.

He had priestly orders even back in 1540, but had not followed it through and done clerical work as an apostolic notary in Haddington, East Lothian's county town. He gazed over to where the great outline of the ancient Abbey of St. Mary of Haddington reminded him of how ecclesiastical scoundrels enriched it with lands, titles, and other benefices. It had been founded by Ada, mother of King Malcolm and William the Lion, and dedicated to the Virgin Mary. He sighed, when he recalled how it had taken many years imprisonment in England to teach King William the Lion the error of impetuosity in foolishly invading England with insufficient forces only to be defeated at the Battle of the Standard.

Finally, due to King Richard the Lionheart's need for enough money to finance the Crusade from England to the Holy Land, King William's Scottish nobles had been able to ransom his freedom at last. Men learnt wisdom the hard way often, Knox thought to himself, for the remainder of William the Lion's fifty year reign had been one of a great and wise Christian King of Scotland. In fact the Scottish emblem of the Lion Rampant in its fiery stance derived from William the Lion, who had been laid in state in Arbroath Abbey with a magnificent stone lion beneath his feet. He sighed once more. It had a great history, this town of Haddington, and he mustn't allow these negative thoughts to affect this greatness. Corruption could always be defeated.

He started to wander back through the village of Giffordsgate to the sparse lodgings where he had left his pupils, Francis and George Douglas, the sons of Longniddry, and Alexander Cockburn, the son of John Cockburn of Ormiston, slaving intently over their copies of Virgil. On a sunny summer's day it was the last thing that young blood, active for games, wanted to do. Knox almost felt sorry for his youthful charges, as he looked wistfully out over the fat farmlands of East Lothian.

There was no finer land in the Kingdom and no finer farmers, and as for the county town of Haddington, there was nothing more permanent, with its long, wide, main street, and grey houses appearing as if they would last for eternity. Never having been over in France, he could not say, but Knox had been told that the French influence could be seen in the form of the town squares, like those of Normandy. The border towns of Kelso and Jedburgh had certainly seen the same influence from France. France's long and passionate love affair with Scotland was something John Knox had to acknowledge, but its present representative, ruling from the mighty castle of Stirling, was a figure he certainly did not trust, Mary of Guise-Lorraine, their Queen Regent. The vibrant new faith, which had been espoused by Calvin and Luther, was filtering through from the Continent, but it would never take root as long as this French woman was in power. When Jamie V had died, his widow had, instead of returning to her beloved France, remained on in Scotland to protect her new born child's inheritance, biding her time in the hope of better times, like a good politician.

What would the child, Mary, turn out to be like? Could any good thing come out of Linlithgow Palace? He crossed the little bridge over the Tyne, which divided Haddington, heading for Samuelston hamlet nearby, where he had left his three pupils diligently working at their Latin. His liking for Latin had been great when a boy at Haddington Grammar School, and by sixteen he had advanced so much in his academic studies that he had left at that early age for Glasgow University in the steps of his parents' great hero, John Major, the mighty scholar and teacher of Theology and Philosophy, who had attended that same Haddington Grammar.

Yes, John owed great deal to his father, William Knox, and his mother, a Sinclair, faithful and loving parents. But what would they have made of the religious and political turmoil that was beginning to afflict this poor land of Scotland, a Scotland on the edge of Europe, but a Scotland still the backdoor for an ambitious French King to enter England,

Old houses at Giffordsgate, Knox's birthplace, near Haddington

an England he coveted? A whelp barked in the sun from an open doorway, and he nodded shyly at the villager there. John Knox longed for life of study, and to be able to cross the sea to attend one of the great centres of learning in Germany, Marburg, Nuremberg, and Heidelberg. The religious storm clouds were gathering thick and black over Scotland, and he did not wish to be caught in them. Ah, the red sandstones of St. Mary's looked so soothing and reflected beautifully on the waters of the river Tyne by the glowing sun.

He hurried on to the cluster of houses that was Samuelston. No doubt his three budding academics were chaffing at the bit, toiling over the tortuous journey of the Trojan hero and his band to fulfill their destiny in Italy and the eventual establishment of Rome. Ah, Rome, now there was an irony! Ancient classical Rome or the Rome of Popery? The boys heard the crunch of Master Knox's shoes on the gritty path, and their fresh faces lifted eagerly at his entrance.

"I'm just finishing the passage, Master Knox," piped up Francis Douglas, at fifteen a year older than his brother John. "Why is it that Aeneas the hero, keeps meeting up with people and things that hinder him on his journey?" "It's just a story!" broke in Alexander Cockburn smartly and a little self importantly. "No, no, it's not just a story, my boys," said John Knox gravely. "It's just pagan mythology, you must remember, Francis, but if pagan writers can show that jealousy and other human sins can hinder the destiny of its heroes, how much more can it happen in sinful real life."

Virgil tells us the famous story of Aeneas, the Trojan hero, only second as a warrior to the great Hector, after the fall of Troy, and how he was to lead the remnant to found in Italy the city which would eventually become ancient Rome. But to some, like the landed gentry of Longniddry and Ormiston, Knox was just another Lowland academic and man of the people. Among the people of East Lothian he was likely to live and die an obscure dominie. For John Knox, born at the beginning of the tumultuous sixteenth century was always more temperate in action than in speech, and now of all times action was called for. He put his hands below his cloak for the Bible kept secreted in a pocket of his tunic, one of many smuggled into Scotland acting as ballast alongside other varied cargo, such as the loads of red pantiles brought by the merchant vessels from the Continent to the Fifeshire villages of Ansthruther, Dysart, and Crail.

The printing press of Guttenberg, a famous inventor and citizen of Strasbourg for much of his life, had begun to revolutionise the dissemination of knowledge, not least through the Scriptures, which had been deliberately restricted by Holy Mother Church and become a closed book to the common man. Along with the lack of guidance from God's Word had come the moral corruption that was inevitable.

Knox was now fingering through the pages of Scripture, which crinkled crisply, looking for his favourite prophet, the one they called the weeping prophet, Jeremiah. He felt so much like the ancient Israelite prophet who was the unwilling instrument at first of God's trumpet of truth to the nation, which had left the God of their fathers. But Jeremiah had not been like one of the gods who tried to prevent Jupiter's will because of jealousy. Their gods were fallible, unlike ours.

"What did the goddess Juno do, Douglas?"

"She sent a storm to wreck the fleet, Master Knox, by making Aeolus, the god of storms and winds, loosen his bag of wind. But Neptune stilled the sea and waves, and defeated her wily schemes."

"Correct, John. What else?" "Venus made Dido fall in love with Aeneas and persuaded him to stop in Carthage, where Dido was Queen. The Carthaginians became the great enemies of the Romans," responded the teenage Alexander Cockburn. "But Aeneas later sailed away to Italy to fulfill his destiny, and when he looked back he saw the sad Queen Dido burning herself to death on the shore of Carthage, because she loved Aeneas so deeply. But he had to fulfil his destiny. We all have destinies too, don't we, Master Knox?" The boy Cockburn was so earnest, and John Knox was touched, for he loved his pupils.

"Aye, young Cockburn, life is full of sadness, and terrible things, boys. And aye, we *maun dree our weird*." He lapsed into the well known vernacular phrase for pursuing one's God-given destiny. He often wrestled, even thus early in his Christian path, on the difference between Divine Providence and *Atropos*, one of the three pagan Fates, the one which could not be avoided. "Now, my young laddies," Their tutor continued, settling down in his chair," if an unbeliever like Virgil could see how the wiles of the enemy can try to prevent the fulfilment of the heroes of mythology, who are not true to history, how much more the Devil will hinder the Christian.

God tells us in His Word to put on the complete armour of faith He gives us to withstand the fiery darts of the enemy, the world, the flesh, and the Devil himself. You must hold up bravely the shield of faith! The Devil would put temptation in your way!" Knox had begun to preach to the boys before he realised his voice had risen to a high point. The three pupils' mouths were by now wide open in surprise. The fieriness of their normally sedate tutor had startled them totally.

"What's going to happen to the Protestants, Master Knox?" enquired Francis Douglas, who now lowered his head, almost ashamed of his outburst. "My father says that the Reformer, George Wishart, is in deadly danger from the Church! They say he is a heretic! My father says that the Church burnt another heretic years ago in St. Andrews before I was born! Why do they do such terrible things?"

"Aye, Francis, his name was Patrick Hamilton, a hero of faith, who met such an evil end, even though he was of noble blood, the nephew of the Earl of Arran, Lord James Hamilton, by his father, and related to the Duke of Albany and to King James himself by his mother! None lifted a hand to save him till the flames licked up over his blessed face!" Knox's anger had returned. "Why was he burnt alive, Master Knox?" asked Francis faintly, his young eyes clouded by a troubled mind and the hint of a tear, as he mirrored the others. "What could he have done that was so wicked?" "He did no wrong, lad, but the Archbishops of St. Andrews and Glasgow, the Bishops of Dunkeld, Brechin, and Dunblane and their underlings condemned poor Patrick Hamilton of Lutheran heresies, that pilgrimages, purgatory, praying to saints and for the dead, are not taught by God.

There are many other teachings, but the thing which matters most is that he taught what the Bible teaches, that by faith alone in Christ are we made right with God. Good works do not make a man good, but a good man does good works, as an ill man does ill works. I am afraid that the Church has departed far from God, my boys," Knox nodded sadly to himself.

"Aye, that's what my father says too," piped up Alexander Cockburn, but why?"

"Boys always ask the questions that most adults don't want to, awkward questions too. My opinion is that men fair like power and controlling their fellows, and the Church is made up of sinful men, controlling others." Their tutor was about to continue on the same sad but realistic theme, when a rapid, loud, knocking at the door arrested his speech, and at a sign from Knox, little Johnny Douglas rushed eagerly to the heavy oak door and pulled at the iron rung.

They had not many visitors other than the elderly lady, in the Samuelston hamlet, who brought them their dinner and evening meals from a house nearby. This was clearly another person. In a moment the lad returned with an armed man, his cuirass emblazoned with the escutcheon of the arms of the House of Ormiston. He was perspiring, and had pulled off his helmet, as much to cool his head as to show respect for his Master's tutor.

"Master Knox, my Lord of Ormiston has ordered me to escort yourself and your charges to the safety of the House of Ormiston. There has been a plot to assassinate George Wishart by the Cardinal's agents! Sixty armed men were waiting in ambush to kill him between Montrose and Kinnear in Fife, where it had been deliberately and falsely reported that his friend lay dangerously ill. But the Lord God gave Master Wishart forewarning by miraculous knowledge that they were waiting for him on the road, and he and his escort returned to Montrose."

"Will the Cardinal's wickedness reach new depths?" Knox's eyes sparked with a new ferocity few could have guessed at. "Gather your scripts and books, my children. We will accompany you, my man, at once. I dinna trust the Sherrif of Haddington, for the Earl of Bothwell seems to run wi' the hares and hunt wi' the hounds."

"Ye're right, Master Knox," growled the veteran soldier. "In my time Bothwell has twice been imprisoned by his late Majesty for treachery, and once banished from Scotland. He would have betrayed us into the hands of the English even, if he could. He must have used magic to inveigle himself into the good graces of Mary of Guise."

"Fetch the horses frae the stable, Francis! We maun take refuge in your father's Castle."

"We could aye hide in father's yew tree, sir!" quipped Francis, not aware of the seriousness of the situation. "Master Wishart had a hale congregation hidden underneath it yince when he was preaching for twa hours!"

"Och, aye, the famous ancient yew!" smiled Knox. "It is not a tree favoured by this impatient age for its slowness of growth. Yet it will grow in many soils, and, remember, boys, nothing in this life will come quickly and easily that's worthwhile. These things are worth waiting for. Now, ye rascals, lets ride for the safety of Ormiston Castle!"

His students were soon astride their steeds and with wild shouts were quickly ahead of their tutor, for they were all expert riders. Within an hour they had ridden into the hamlet of Ormiston and passed its simple cruciform Mercat Cross. Shortly its Castle appeared a large, round, tower, within protecting walls, as were the gardens, stables, and servants' quarters.

Not far off stood the mighty yew tree, stately and proud, its deep, dark, green, leaves, contrasting with its vivid red berries and tough, dark reddish-brown, knotted, bark. Knox knew that some yews were reputed to go back to the time of Christ, so that he looked at this strange tree with almost a hint of awe. Its spell was broken when my Lord Ormiston rushed out enthusiastically to meet them, delighted and relieved no doubt.

"Master Knox, my worthy friend, you have brought back my bairn, and you, Francis and Geordie Douglas, Longniddry's lads! Beaton's treachery is so great that he would inquisition and imprison even children! I'll send for Longniddry. Godly Master Wishart is expected any moment from Ayrshire, where he has been making a preaching round of the nobility and gentry there, and has had a great reception, I hear!" Ormiston's cheeriness was infectious and Knox was encouraged. "He will be exhausted after travelling so widely through the south-west, preaching the Good News in Mauchline, Ayr, and Galston!

I have heard on good authority that Alexander, the Earl of Glencairn, is now firmly with us, on the side of the Protestant cause! Amen to that!" John Cockburn was like a little boy in his joyous abandon, more than his son, so full of faith. In the new Reformation of religion in Scotland and all the incredible transformation it would bring in the life of the nation, untrammeled by control of men's souls. It was as if a new horizon with a golden prospect had been opened to his spirit. The spirit of prophecy birthing in John Knox enabled him to share in that fresh vision of faith, as the dead hand of institutionalised religion had fallen away from him forever. His shackles were off, and now John Knox was free.

CHAPTER TWO

THE ASSASSINATION

Agroup of five men were gathered in a clandestine meeting in an upper room of a turret on the corner of Market Street and College Street in the historic town of St. Andrews, the ecclesiastical capital of Scotland. It was the last day of May, 1546, and the winter storms, which normally battered the rocky shores of the Scottish town most dedicated to her patron saint, had long blown themselves out.

The air was so quiet that even the lap of the North Sea on the harbour wall, around the base of St. Andrews Castle, and even along the broad, sweeping, shore of the West Sands, could be heard, and was even welcome as a familiar sound as a relief from nervous tension. For truly the five men foregathered were on desperate business, and could have wished for any kind of sound to cover their voices and the comfort of nature's constancy.

The tinkle of a lute and the sound of a not infrequent roisterer, drunk in his cups, were not unusual, for the example emanating from the chief occupant of the Castle and Cathedral, Cardinal Beaton, was one of debauchery and moral corruption. Cynicism was the mode of the day and that of the people of Scotland of all classes. Services were sparsely attended, and it was whispered that, if it had not been for the Godly influence of such as John Major, Doctor of Divinity at the Theological College of St. Mary's at the University, and John Annan, Principal of St. Leonard's College, things might have been more hellish than divine. Norman Leslie, the heir of Lord Rothes, William Kirkcaldy of Grange, James Melville of Raithe, Peter Carmichael of Balmode, and John Leslie of Rothes, uncle of Norman, were all set on radical change.

"There is no going back, I tell you! Cardinal David Carmichael, the instrument of the Church of Rome, is a Scottish Borgia! I have talked with merchants, who have traded with Italy, and they have brought back the most horrific tales of the corruptions of the family Borgia. It was not for piety that Rodrigo Borgia was elected Pope Alexander the Sixth! It was safer; it was said, to be Rodrigo's pet dog than his son! How he poisoned all who got in the way of his advance to the seat of the Pontiff, and family came to control the highest positions in the Roman Church, is one of the world's most wicked stories! As for David Beaton, he has the flavour of an Italian Renaissance tyrant, statesman and inquisitor! He lives sumptuously, and acts ruthlessly. He has seven bastard children. I have seen women of the night from the town still going into the Castle under the cloak of darkness, led by one of his bodyguards."

The speaker was a grizzled and aggressive man, John Leslie of Rothes, an old soldier, experienced in the ways of the world, a world he did not approve of at times. "Keep your voice low, Uncle John. Beaton has spies in the town ever since the death of Wishart. These Observant Friars are well-named, for they seem to be everywhere and observe everything. They are the spoiled favourites of the late King James and his second wife, that French woman! Would that he had never married again, but the Stuarts were ever a thrang race!" Young Norman was a rationalist, though committed to the Protestant faith. He was a more cautious man than his uncle, wary of being carried away.

The fledgling Protestant faith must be nurtured closely and sensitively. "Beaton well kens that the death of that worthy man will have caused the deepest anger, even amongst those who are not Godly, for all men of good conscience admire a brave man."

"Brave man? Brave man? George Wishart was an angel of God! I remember one of the friars taunted him as he passed between a line of those clerics on his way to the stake, to pray to our Lady, and he simply told the mocker to tempt him not. Some of his last words I will never forget, before the bags of gunpowder exploded around his blessed body and the flames of the fire reduced him to ashes." The eyes of John Leslie, a Fife man as tough as the weather, which challenged all those who lived in that raw but fertile land, had the glint of religious zeal and a touch of fanaticism in them now. "Christian brothers and sisters do not be offended at the Word of God on account of the tortures which you see prepared for me. Love the Word which publishes Salvation, and suffer patiently for the Gospel's sake." Leslie let out a groan of sorrow mixed with anger. "For preaching that Gospel, I am now to suffer, and I gladly suffer for the Redeemer's sake. Should any among you be called to account for persecution, fear not those who can destroy the body, for they cannot kill the soul, but fear he who can cast the body and soul into hell. Most falsely have I been accused of teaching that the soul sleeps after death until the last day, and its resurrection. I truly believe that my soul shall sup with my Saviour this very night!"

"You have memorised Wishart's last speech, I see, Uncle John." There was a tinge of awe in Norman Leslie's voice. "You do not memorise the words of a friend, Norman. They are imprinted on your soul!" declared James Melville, an earnest individual if ever there was. "George Wishart was my friend ever since his days as a schoolmaster in Montrose. I recall his heartbreak when his beloved Elizabeth died from the plague on the eve of their wedding, but it only steeled his determination to follow the Saviour gladly and restore the truth to this land."

"Aye, Mary of Guise will soon have Scotland a Province of France! Look at the latest additions to the Palace of Linlithgow! They have made it similar to a Chateau on the Loire! It's well seen that it was built for the child Princess Mary to be born there." Leslie of Rothes almost spat out the words. The Queen Regent, Mary of Guise, was widely unpopular, not least for her French ways and quick temper, and influence, even to the country's architecture, dress, manners, and domestic manners even.

"Don't forget that it was in the Palace of Linlithgow that the good Sir David Lindsay wrote the 'Satire of the Three Estates'". I laughed loud and long at the discomfiture of the clergy. All their bastard bairns were exposed to the public gaze, as was naked nepotism of appointing these infants to Bishoprics! Lindsay was ruthless. Its six years since and I cannot believe that he has escaped unscathed, for Lindsay was unremittingly scathing of the Church!" It was William Kirkcaldy of Grange, who had fiercely interjected, another bold youth like Norman Leslie.

"I believe David Lindsay is truly for the Reformation, and will join us if we make a stand." "Maybe, maybe," it was Peter Carmichael of Balmadie, who was a kindred spirit to John Leslie, a spiritual pragmatist in all things. "The Kingdom of Heaven must be taken by storm. We must be rid of this corrupt Cardinal! Cut off the head, and the body will wither! Those of us who are bold must lead those who are less bold."

9

"Kill the Cardinal? Surely not?" Norman Leslie paled and his lips trembled as he spoke. "Death only begets death. Have you never heard in Scripture that the blood of the righteous cries out for vengeance? First it was Patrick Hamilton, and now it's George Wishart, who will be next? The smoke of their burning still reeks the streets of St. Andrews! Did not the Godly Ehud plunge his sword deep into the stomache of the fat Moabite tyrant, Eglon?" Peter Carmichael's anger was rising like a tide of hatred. "Lower your voice, Peter! Remember that the Observant Friars are around, and some of them are very observant," Norman Leslie warned, going to the window to peer out from the corner of the curtain down upon the darkened street. Some late night revellers were carousing along College Street, heading for South Street and no doubt another hostelry. Their minds were on conviviality, far from plotting, deceit, and desperate measures. "It'll be a sword in the belly from the Palace guards that we'll be getting! But, anyway, which of us is corrie-fisted?"

Like many of the Reformers, Leslie was steeped in the Scriptures of the Old and New Testaments, and that was why they were revulsed by the corruptions of the Roman Catholic Church, which had succumbed to the power of this world and its attractions. He knew well the Book of Judges, of when the Israelites had done what was right in their own eyes and so fallen away from the Lord. They knew how Eglon, the King of the Moabites, had, with the help of the Ammonites and the Amalekites, captured Jericho, the city of palm trees. So he had gained control over Israel and its people.

For eighteen years the Moabites were subject to Eglon, King of Moab, until they cried out to the Lord for help. He raised up a man to deliver them, Ehud, son of Gera the Benjamite, who happened to be left-handed. The Israelites sent him to pay tribute to Eglon. But Ehud made himself a two-edged sword, just fifteen inches long, which he fastened in his right hand underneath his clothes. Now Eglon was a very fat man. When the tribute had been brought forward by the men accompanying him, Ehud requested to have some words in private with the King.

"I have a word from God for you," he said, and prayed fervently within that his plan would not fail. Eglon fell into the trap, unsuspecting. Eglon rose and dismissed all his attendants, and the two retired to sit on the roof chamber of the Moabite King's summer palace. When the Moabite came close to him to hear his special word from God Himself, Ehud reached below his cloak with his left hand and drew his sword from his right side to drive it into the King's belly. The haft had gone in after the blade, and the fat closed over the blade. So Ehud had not drawn the blade out but left it protruding behind in his bloated body. He had then gone out onto the porch and fastened the doors. Ehud made his timely escape before the servants finally unlocked them. Hurrying away to the hill country, Ehud the bold made an exultant announcement to his assembled fellow Israelites.

"Follow me, men of Israel, for the Lord has delivered your enemy, the Moabites, into our hands!" Roars of triumph thundered through the air.

"*Jehovah Jireh! Jehovah Nissi!* The Lord is our Provider! The Lord is our Banner!"

Down the Israelites poured into the valley, and seized the ford over the Jordan, thus preventing help from their other enemies, the Amalekites and the Ammonites, and on that day they slaughtered ten thousand fighting men of Moab. No one escaped. The Moabites had become subject to Israel, and peace reigned in the land for eighty years.

"Left handed, or not left handed, Ehud was God's instrument of righteousness to kill his enemies, and so are we! Eighty years of peace are more than enough, I tell you, for the Protestant Reformation to gain ground and take root. The ideas of Luther and Calvin have been brought over from Germany and Switzerland by the trading vessels, packed with roof pantiles as ballast. Bibles were hidden among the red pantiles, which now roof our Fife fishing villages, and their teachings must be given time to take root, or rot again! Brave Patrick Hamilton and gentle George Wishart have been taken from our midst, but we must take up the cudgels, and carry on the work of the Lord!

There was a man, who followed Wishart, even carried a powerful sword, a certain tutor from Haddington whom I noticed. He is rather small, broad of shoulder, and has a quiet dignity and authority about him. He is a man of learning, but, although he seems very content to be a tutor to the sons of Longniddry and Ormiston, I believe in my very heart that this man Knox is destined for greater things. He is a slow- burning flame, just waiting to burst forth and, like the Burning Bush of Holy Writ, he will not be quenched. He carried the sword for a short time to protect Master Wishart, hardly the sign of an academic, but a man of action."

"With such an example, let us prepare for the taking of the Castle tomorrow!" Leslie of Rothes was like a mastiff, straining at his leash. "We have the arms."

"Tomorrow?" Norman swallowed nervously. Are we ready?"

"*Carpe diem*! Seize the chance, say I, Norman! One hundred men are engaged in working on the walls to strengthen them against attack from the sea. The masons are already toiling early in the morning and they lower the drawbridge to let the stone carts lumber over it, and the drawbridge is the only entrance from the landward side. Aye, it is now or never, my friends! Aye?" The elder Leslie glared around inquisitorially at the others. A moment's silence followed, pregnant with meaning, and then all five men grasped hands in an unbreakable bond, and they prayed. Just then the bell of St. Leonards tolled, and the question arose in their minds, for whom it tolled.

At six o'clock in the morning of the last day of May the deed was done. The seagulls were already crying out their mock alarm at the sounds of the masons labouring, about a hundred in number, the plotters estimated. They were beginning their work on the ramparts of St, Andrews Castle, and the cartfuls of stones were rumbling over the drawbridge. Despite the hour, the first visitors to the Cathedral were arriving, not to worship in the main, but to transact business, such as legal discussions and even merchandising. The spirit of devotion was not primarily in the minds of the majority, and the group of plotters, now sixteen in number, led by Norman Leslie, had no problem in merging with the crowd.

They were known to some of course, and exchanged greetings, while trying to contain their excited breathing. If their attempt to take the Castle was a failure, then death would, without doubt, be their lot. Slowly and as unobtrusively as possible, the little cluster of Fifeshire gentry worked their way towards the Castle drawbridge. They gathered in knots of twos and threes around the Castle rock and the Cathedral Churchyard. At last, glancing surreptitiously around, they placed their feet on the structure, just as a cart clattered by. Rough, sandstone blocks jutted awkwardly at angles from the vehicle. They waved casually to the unsuspicious workmen, hoping that their weapons had remained hidden beneath their cloaks.

"Ye are nae feart o' attack, are ye, my man?" joked John Leslie to the man, who appeared to be the supervisor. "Is that why you are shoring up the ramparts?"

"One never kens, sirra. These are unsettled times, what with the 'Rough Wooing' by King Henry's English and the burning of the heretic Wishart. There is a lot of sympathy for these fanatics, ye ken? The Cardinal has even heard that there is an English plot on his life!"

"Och, aye, that could be so," answered one of the group drily.

"These Protestants are springing up like mushrooms after the overnight rain!" said the supervisor worriedly. Leslie of Rothes nodded his agreement, thinking to himself how quickly the man would find this out literally. He again steeled his nerve and his grip tautened on his concealed sword, as he and the other four wandered on casually into the courtyard. The porter looked a little suspiciously at them. Norman Leslie approached him boldly.

"Is my Lord Cardinal awake yet?" As he spoke, a signal was given to the well over a hundred men, who had been waiting in hiding outside the walls. They poured over the drawbridge in a deluge. The terrified workmen were paralysed, totally bemused. But the porter started to shout out the alarm to the sleeping guards. Carmichael of Balmudie rushed over and seized the porter, struck him on the head with the butt of his sword, and threw him into the moat. All was confusion amongst the occupants of the Castle now, for the actions of the assailants were swift and efficient. They took the guardhouse, seized the keys, and soon were masters of the fortress.

Under the leadership of Kirkcaldy of Grange they ejected the workmen and some fifty of the treacherous Cardinal's attendants from the Castle. Cowed, they went like sheep, and Kirkcaldy and Norman Leslie stayed to guard the postern gate and courtyard, while John Leslie, Peter Carmichael, and James Melville continued with the grim task ahead. What animated their savage breasts was a mixture of hatred for a religious tyrant and a conviction that they must remove this man Beaton, a major obstacle in the path of God's Reformation in Scotland. They had prayed to the Lord of Hosts for success. They that shed blood by man shall their blood be shed.

By now the Cardinal had been awakened by an overpowering, strange, fear that his last hour had come. His thin, sanguine features, dark eyes and black, pencil-thin, moustache could indeed have been the features of an Italian Renaissance patron and, while he had at one time gazed down at one time in bigoted fanaticism upon the blazing pyre, which horribly consumed the body of the heroic martyr, George Wishart of Montrose, now he gazed down from a window in his luxury chambers on the Courtyard below at a scene of hostile, armed, men, in a frozen panic. He sped back to his inner rooms, bolted the door, and ordered his chamber boy to heap up heavy furniture against the door.

A cold sweat gathered on the Cardinal's brow. His red biretta stood him in no stead now. Still in his underclothes, with a silk cloak thrown over him, Beaton seized the sword which he always kept in his chamber. All men of the Church must use the weapons of this world on occasion, and he prepared to face the door and his opponents beyond it. No longer did the authority of his office protect him. A battering ram smashed against the door and threatening voices could be heard.

"Who calls there?" Beaton cried.

"Leslie!"

"Which of the Leslies? I shall have Norman in. He is my friend, I know."

"You shall have those who are here, for you will have no other!" replied the elder Leslie in scornful harshness at the coward behind the door and continued with Melville and Carmichael to crash their considerable shoulder force against the oaken woodwork, which quivered visibly.

"Will my life be safe?"

"It could be that we will save your life, in the same way that you spared the life of George Wishart!" Leslie shot back.

"Nay, swear to me by Christ's wounds that my life is safe, and I will open the door to you," responded the Cardinal fearfully.

"Bring fire from the kitchen, and we'll burn this door down!" Leslie was incensed at the delay. Within, the Cardinal in a cold sweat rushed to where a private stair lay behind an awning, but, when he stumbled down the steps, he was to eventually find William Kirkcaldy of Grange standing grim faced at the exit. Inside information had told the attackers that this secret escape route existed. With a strangled cry Beaton ran back to his bedchamber. The hammering continued and the door began to splinter. The despairing Cardinal shrank back in his chair and cried out for his life.

But for a short time he reasserted his authority, and when the threat of fire being brought became likely, he told his trembling chamber boy to open the door. Nervously the lad unlatched it, and, when he saw the terrible look on the faces of the assailants, he fled down the corridor. The Reformers stared at the Cardinal, who had taken hold of a huge old sword, and they realised that they had come to kill the most powerful man in all Scotland, Cardinal of the Order of St. Stephen, Papal Legate of Paul III, and Lord High Chancellor of Scotland. For a moment Beaton took courage at their hesitation, and challenged his would-be murderers.

"I am a priest! Would you kill a priest, a man of God?" But, even as the very words issued from his prim mouth, it slackened into a look of despair, and he turned pale as his gaze travelled from face to face, and mercy could be found nowhere in their features. For a long second the three murderers stood still, and then rushed on the prelate. John Leslie drove an armpit dagger into him. Peter Carmichael followed up with his sword, but James Melville of Carnbree, filled to the brim with a religious zeal struck up their weapons with a long, thrusting sword.

"This sacrifice is the work of God," he spoke in a quiet, but deadly solemn tone," and as such ought to be conducted with becoming deliberation. It is the vengeance of the Lord." The wounded Cardinal cowered before them, shrinking into his body. "It is for you to repent for all your wicked sins, Cardinal," Melville continued quietly, "but especially for the merciless murder of poor Master Wishart, the blessed instrument of God for the conversion of these lands of Scotland to the true faith of Scripture. His death, which you watched with open pleasure, seated at your ease on silken cushions, now cries out for vengeance, and we are sent to inflict this deserved punishment from God. Remember that the stroke I am about to deal is not the mercenary blow of a hired assassin, but that of a most just retribution." He then ran his weapon into Beaton's chest, already stained with blood. "Die, cruel papist!" cried Melville.

"I am a priest!" The dying Cardinal's last words were strangled in their utterance. "All is gone!"

Even as he expired, he bells of St. Andrews began to ring out their alarm over the waking town. The majority of the citizens were confused with the turmoil, but the Provost and the Town Guard were already alert to the attack on the Castle. By now the drawbridge had been pulled up, and so, when the Town Guard approached the bridge, it was a stand-off situation.

"We wish to see the Cardinal at once! You are rebels against the Church and the Regent." The Provost shouted from the safety of his armed guard. For a moment time stood still for all of them. Then, those watching from outside saw, horrified, something being pushed over the wall of the fore tower, till they realised that it was the dead body of the Cardinal, hung by his arm and leg. A huge sigh went through the crowd. It was a sigh, not of sorrow, but of an indefinable emotion, more of fear than anything else. To some it was an act of sacrilege, to others it was a just vengeance and to most it was as if a whole new era had begun. The defenders were not about surrender, and they shouted their defiance.

"Return to your Jezebel of a Regent, that Mary of Guise, and tell her that a hypocrite and tyrant has died, and that a Reformation from papacy has begun this day in Scotland that will never be destroyed! The pure Protestant faith of Christ will spread over this land from this time on!" It was young Norman Leslie, who had cast aside his initial abhorrence at the thought of murdering the Cardinal, and was now seized by an overwhelming spiritual zeal.

The pent-up emotions of the Reformers had burst forth now, which had been stored up by the memory of the agonising death in the flames of martyrdom of Wishart, Patrick Hamilton, and the priests, friars and others, who had turned to the old truth rediscovered, Sir Duncan Simpson, gentleman, Robert Forrester, priest, Friar Killore, Friar Beveridge, and Thomas Forrest, Dean of Dollar, all of them burnt upon the Castlehill of Edinburgh almost ten years before. The Protestant Reformation had begun in earnest, and political and military nerve had become allied to religious enthusiasm and doctrinal conviction of the need for change. A milestone had been reached in Scotland's history and faith, ironically by the shedding of blood. An ancient seer would have been happy to forecast that a torrent of blood by God's grace would not result, contrary to expectations.

"Well, William, our Rubicon has been crossed, and the die is cast. *Iacta alea est!*" said John Leslie grimly to young Kirkcaldy of Grange, as they watched from the battlements the Town Guard, Magistrates, and motley members of the population of St.

Andrews retire reluctantly from the Castle walls.

"What shall we do with the body of the Cardinal?" asked Kirkcaldy with a scarcely-veiled apprehension.

"What else but throw his stinking carcass into the hellish depths of the bottle dungeon? Where else did they consign our beloved George Wishart to spend four long weeks of darkness without sign of sun or moon or stars? But he had the light of the Gospel to illuminate his soul. But Beaton had darkness, and still will have in the world to come, so it won't make any difference to our former Cardinal!" Carmichael's irony was consistent with his character. "I think we will be under siege for a long time to come, and so, unless we want to be stunk out by his rotting carcass, we had better salt the Cardinal. He'll make excellent Primate beef, eh?" Peter laughed at his own crude joke, but none of the others joined in. The full significance of their deed had just come home to them, and the deadly danger to them all. Mary of Guise would not rest until she had avenged the murder of her favourite prelate, and she had the potential power of the might of all France to back her up.

The distasteful task of salting the corpse of the Cardinal was quickly completed, and it was carried to the sea tower, the deep chamber cut into the rock on which the Castle of St. Andrews was built. Above the sea, which pounded ceaselessly upon the same rocks from which the dreadful bottle dungeon was constructed, the cell descended twenty four feet down into the inky blackness. No light entered the dark depths except through the narrow grating at the top.

It narrowed to fifteen feet at its bottom, which had also been rounded to make it difficult for the wretched prisoners to sleep, or even rest. Its filth had besmired the brave George Wishart, and when he was taken up by rope to answer the charges of heresy before Beaton and all his proud, mocking, court, the guards, full of sympathy for the man who had won their admiration by his indomitable spirit, washed and fed him in their quarters. Wishart's eyes, accustomed to darkness for a long month, had been blinded almost by the sudden, piercing, daylight. These same guards had been struck by the deep faith of a man, whose psalm-singing had penetrated up to them, while on duty. The bottle dungeon may have been rightly called the *oubliette, as* in its murky depths any unfortunate resident would be forgotten by men, but he was surely not forgotten by God, nor did forget Him.

"Lower it down then," said Carmichael brusquely. "It is well named the *oubliette,* for soon the evil Cardinal will be totally forgotten! We must look to the holding of the Castle, not only against the Provost and the Town Guard. They will be enraged. It is the Regent who will come from Edinburgh with the Lords of the Council and a force large enough to defeat us, if they have sufficient artillery. We must get as many to join us before the Regent comes, but will they have enough courage to join us?"

"They will come, I am sure," broke in Kirkcaldy of Grange eagerly. "We have made the vital first step. My father, brother, and three uncles are ready to join our cause, and your family, the Melvilles of Raith, can be counted on, can't they?" He looked almost accusingly at James Melville, who turned red with unrestrained wrath.

"Aye, ye ken they will, Kirkcaldy!" He threw back the verbal challenge. "And forby there is a Balfour of Montquhanny, his son, the Laird of Pittendreich, and others. The

Lothians and Fife are for the Protestant faith!"

"We have sufficient food for a month, and the well there has a lasting source." Norman Leslie pointed towards the deep well in the centre of the courtyard parade area. The Castle was truly a natural fortification, built upon a high promontory of rock projecting out into the North Sea. The Ocean side was especially built to resist approach or bombardment from the sea. Not only was the prison and the bottle dungeon situated there, but the kitchen tower. The Castle walls formed a part of the protection of the harbour. On the mainland side, the Castle was cut off by a deep ditch, so that the approach was only by the great drawbridge. Behind that was an arched entrance to the Castle precincts. The foretower at the entrance was four stories high. A great wall extended completely round the Castle area, encompassing the large courtyard. The continuing improvement of the defences that the workmen were engaged in, when John Leslie had first led his band in to murder, was all for the purpose of strengthen its ability to withstand a lengthy siege.

"We will need to act promptly before heavy artillery can be placed on the vantage point on top of St. Salvator's College there. They could crush us from there and from the Cathedral there." Norman Leslie pointed to the famous old College nearby. "I vote that we send an urgent message to John Rough to bring us the Lord's blessing as chaplain. Unless the Lord build the house, they labour in vain that build it. He is God's man, the one for us, I am sure. Though he used to be chaplain to the Earl of Arran, John Rough has left that turncoat's service."

"Aye, Arran is nothing but a self seeker. He sought the Regency, but was bought off by the title and lands of Chatelherault in France! He is but a lickspittle of France, he and that Mary of Guise, a right pair!" Peter Carmichael spat scornfully from the ramparts, and minced around in mocking caricature of a Frenchman. "They follow in footsteps worthy of them! Beaton, they say, forged the Royal Will to seize the Regency. I saw his whore, Marion Ogilvy, in town yesterday. Oh that I had put my poignard into her!"

"Cease that talk, Peter Carmichael! God will avenge her immorality. Remember that this is the work of God we are on, for the whole of Scotland's blessing!" James Melville's face was lit up with a vision, as he gazed out over the green Lomond Hills of Fife that rose near Loch Leven, and to the North he caught sight of the Sidlaw Range beyond Dundee. In a land of panoramas it was not quite a magnificent scene, but it was at least beautiful blend of land and sea as viewed from St. Andrews Castle. But the true vision that James Melville and his comrades saw was one of the heart and spirit, which would sweep across Scotland for God's Reformation of religion.

There was no scene worthier of this vision than the resting place of Scotland's patron saint, Andrew, whose bones were brought from the distant shores of Patras in Greece. It mattered not to the Reformers whether the saint's three finger bones, arm bone, and knee cap rested there or not. It was not for nothing that the English vulgarly jeered that the Scots acknowledged no other Saint. God had blessed St. Andrews in the past, so much that Frenchmen, Dutchmen Flemish, and English came to the town to pray, in fact the whole world it seemed, and God would bless her again.

THE SIEGE

For about a fortnight there was an uneasy peace between the town and the Castle. Supporters of the besieged Reformers filtered in, to the number of about a hundred and forty, including women and children. The Castilians now began to take on both the form and soul of one great family of the Protestant spirit, so that, when on the morning of the tenth of June a group was seen approaching the drawbridge, the nerve of those within had been steeled to the strength of an Andrea Ferrara blade. John Leslie called down to the Provost, who had stepped out with a soldier carrying a white flag of truce.

"What is your message, Provost? Have you brought us our flag of surrender, or have you come to realise that God is with our cause and that the Church of Rome has departed from the truth and is no longer the Church of Christ?"

"Far from it, Leslie!"

"If you are under the impression that we are going to surrender, you are blinded by the Godless arrogance that afflicted your late Cardinal!"

"More than that, Leslie!" answered the furious Provost, reddening and holding up a parchment. "This is a summons for treason passed under the Great Seal, citing all conspirators and those who afterwards entered the Castle to appear before the Parliament of Scotland in Edinburgh on the 30th of July!"

"Well," laughed John Leslie," That gives us about a month and a half to walk there, all of us! That should be sufficient, even for the children. Begone, Provost, and your minions, before you and your followers go to meet your Maker, and that you may not like!" He lifted up his musket, as did others posted along the wall. The Scottish Parliament at this time were without warships, and, therefore, unable to control the sea, so that weapons could be smuggled in by fishing boats in barrels, as if they were salted herring, in the same way as Bibles were in fact. God in his humour was using both contrabands.

"You refuse at your peril, Leslie, and all of you, Norman Leslie, Peter Carmichael, William Kirkcaldy, and you James Melville, are condemned as guilty of treason, and forfeit your lives. Soon the Earl of Arran will march upon St. Andrews." He looked up from the sealed document in his hands, as if his authority resided in the official paper. "Turn before it is too late!"

"So be it, so be it!" cried John Leslie, his lined countenance fixed in a firm conviction that brooked no weakness. "God is our refuge and our strength!" But his look belied that conviction, once he had turned away to confer with his fellow Reformers. "But can we hold out without the help of England and her soldiers, my brothers? I would not beg from that tyrant in London!" Henry VIII, for all his seeming to outlaw the Pope's authority from England and to embrace the Protestant faith, horrified the Scots by his wicked life, his convenient divorce from the Spanish Princess, Katharine of Aragon, his procession of spouses afterwards, and their certainty that Henry's religion was a sham.

Hadn't King Henry been awarded the title of Defender of the Faith by the Pope for his Theological Treatise against the English Protestant Reformers?" I refused to be tempted in the past by King Henry's offer of even a thousand pounds to assassinate the Cardinal!"

"We must not reject help from whatever source, John," broke in Norman Leslie.

"We know that no one will be better pleased than Henry VIII to see an obstacle to his designs, like Beaton, put out of his way. Yet we do not need to subject Scotland to his dictatorial hand by accepting assistance against the Queen Regent's party, the party of France. The Lord would have us as wise as serpents, even though we are hardly as harmless as doves." He laughed grimly. "Henry is not our friend, for we cannot forget *The Rough Wooing'*. Many of my closest friends suffered from the widespread devastation and burning of the Border country right up to the Lothians and Fife by Henry's vicious troopers, all in an attempt to enforce a marriage of himself to that Mary of Guise, when she had already been promised to King Jamie! Why anyone would want to marry that French shrew totally perplexes me! I hear that the King's second wife, Jane Seymour, died just before he tired of her. No, they are not easily forgotten or forgiven, Henry VIII's sins, but although he is not our friend, he need not be our enemy."

So it was that the Castilians resigned themselves to a long siege. Soon the Regent and the Earl of Arran, whose son had been appointed to command the Scots Guards as a sop when denied the Regency, arrived with sufficient troops to crush the puny garrison of one hundred and fifty, but a fact in the form of the almost impregnable walls of St. Andrews Castle prevented that happening, and they had no siege engines or artillery. In vain Mary of Guise pleaded for assistance from her native land, her voice and hands raised in a religious passion back in her headquarters at Stirling Castle. To her the death of Cardinal Beaton was not cancelled out by the horrific burning of the gentle tutor of Montrose. Beaton had been her favourite, sufficient of the Renaissance Continental to delight her Court parlours.

But the French had made a Treaty with the English, which left Boulogne in English hands. As the summer wore on and the cold winds from the North Sea blew bitingly and the foaming waves battered the base of the Castle walls, the besieging forces of the Regent became discouraged and, leaving a token force, they withdrew for the winter.

One day, through the thick misty haar that was accustomed to envelope the Fifeshire coast, a lookout espied a small group of riders approaching the drawbridge. They appeared friendly. When the alarm was raised, Kirkcaldy of Grange peered down through the mist to see the passport of a white flag. But it was the figure at the front of the party who aroused his surprised interest.

"Why, unless I'm mistaken, that man there is Henry Balnaves of Halhill! What can a lawyer, who has done the work of the Lords of Session, and who has accused us of rebellion and treachery, want with a truce, and why does he come in secret? However, my father did have some confidence in Balnaves, and used his expertise in some estate wranglings."

"Aye, but he is a man experienced in statecraft and European ways is Balnaves, so let's gang cannily," advised Melville. "He has raised himself up to distinction by rare talents. When he returned from studying in Europe, which men o' pairts like he always seem to do, it was no time before he was appointed an Advocate and then even a Lord of Session. We shall need care in dealing with such a man, as wily as he is. No doubt he has been influenced by their Papist ways on the Continent and the superstitions they practise there. See, he signs upwards to us for a parley. This haar drapes us like a shroud, it's so thick! I can hardly see beyond the drawbridge!"

"There are no rich pickings here for legal vultures, Balnaves!" shouted Peter Carmichael. "Go back to that spineless Earl of Arran and tell him the answer is still the same Scotland wants to see the end of French control, and, more important, the end of the idolatries of Rome, and her unscriptural Masses and images!"

"I have come here not from Arran, but on my own account," Henry Balnaves called back, his voice echoing somewhat through the sea fog, which swirled in banks round the Castle walls. "I and my friends have come under cover of this Heaven-sent mist to join you and your cause. Why else would we come in such weather, unless it was to take your Castle by craft, and clearly we are not!" His lawyer's tone had sufficient irony to drive it home.

"What then?" called Melville of Raith.

"I have already said that I wish to join you. The Lord our God has convinced me of your cause and its righteousness. Too long have I been silent. In Paris I was touched by God's spirit and the early ideas of Leclerc the Lutheran Reformer, whose convictions of how a man is made right with God only by unadorned faith, had filtered through from Erfurt and Wittenberg! There was a sincerity in his voice that impressed the defenders, but they could not be sure. The Devil had a cunning way about him, and who better to use than an advocate.

"Enough of these foreign names, Balnaves!" snapped the elder Leslie. "We are concerned here with Scotland and her freedom from the trammels of Rome and her superstitions! We wish to serve the living God in the manner of the Scriptures!" "That is my desire too, from my heart. The death of Wishart was the turning point for me."

"Why did you not join us before?"

"It was well nigh impossible for me, for was I not one of the Court of Session, which had been involved and convened to answer the turmoil caused by the death of the Cardinal?"

"It is true, it would have been difficult to join our band," admitted Norman Leslie.

"Will you have me into the Castle, or must I remain freezing out here in this fog forever?" Balnaves' impatient lawyer's tone came through again, annoyed that they doubted his sincerity.

The leaders agreed to lower the drawbridge, and within it took little time to be convinced of the genuine turnaround in the beliefs of Henry Balnaves. They soon saw the great advantage of such a sharp legal mind on their side for the negotiations ahead with the Regent of Scotland, the Earl of Arran, who had called a temporary armistice. Balnaves had a mind hones to sharpness by studies abroad for years, which had raised him up to be a Lord of Session. But a great danger presented itself before negotiations of any sort arose, with King Henry of England, if they could get a message to him in London. Balnaves would be the ideal Ambassador, though it still grated on their spirits to have to beg help from an evil English tyrant.

But one day Carmichael was patrolling the cellars to find any hidden stores, when he heard an indistinct scraping and crushing sound. It seemed strange, for there was no one around. He listened carefully, ear to the ground, unsure of its source. Soon he was drawn to a corner facing out beyond the moat. Bending down, Peter Carmichael lay down upon the dirt floor. There it was again; the clink of metal on earth and rock, and again it came. There was no mistake. His heart froze, as it dawned on him what it was, an underground mine working to make a tunnel. Their enemies were digging a mine to attempt to force an entry into the Castle through the solid rock! He rushed out from the cellars, crying the alarm.

"They are engineering an underground mine to capture the Castle!"

"The cunning fox, Arran! What shall we do?" John Leslie was full of anger.

"Let us see what we can from the battlements first of their workings," advised Balnaves wisely. "Let us find the direction of this mine."

Sure enough, they sighted activity in the town, men going out and in of one of the Merchant Houses nearest to the Castle. Could it be that they were digging in the garden hidden behind its walls?

"That lying scoundrel, Arran! Trust a Hamilton! An armistice indeed, by the Lord, just so that they could tunnel within our walls!" The elder Leslie was incensed.

"Two can play at that game!" cried William Kirkcaldy of Grange.

"What do you mean, William?" asked young Norman curiously.

"I mean that we should make a counter-mine to meet theirs, and stop their advance. After we drive these human moles back, we shall block it off forever!"

"A much easier way would be to make a sally and destroy the entrance and kill a few in the process," said Peter Carmichael fiercely.

"Are you so blind that you can't see the glint of armour in the midst of the townhouses, ready at the drop of a hat to cut us into pieces?" Leslie senior's irony was unnecessary.

"If you don't trust in the arm of the Lord, then you should leave those who are the true soldiers of Christ to fight the fight of faith!" A dark fanaticism stared out of his fixed eyes, but his challenge only aroused the ire of Leslie.

"Are you daring to doubt either my faith or my courage, you religious fanatic?

"It is blindness and arrogance like yours which will bring our Protestant faith crumbling into ruins before it is born!"

20

In a moment Carmichael had drawn his sword and would have driven it into the older man, had not the younger Leslie and Kirkcaldy of Grange quickly pinioned his arms behind his back.

"Is this what we captured the Castle for, and took God's vengeance on Cardinal Beaton for, so that we can murder one another? This is the same old story of Scotland and her stupid feuds for so long, fighting and snapping like curs amongst on another!" Kirkcaldy's voice was breathless, as he held onto the violent Carmichael. "Aye, my father told me that once a hundred and twenty Murrays were burnt to death in Monzievaird Churchyard by their enemies, the Drummonds, and the rivalry between the Crichtons and the Maxwells caused a spectacular riot in Dumfries! Are we going to repeat the tragedies of history?" Norman pleaded with the two men.

"How many remember the causeway affair in Edinburgh between the Douglases and the Hamiltons in our fathers' times?" Kirkcaldy scanned the crowd which had gathered on the battlements, when they heard of the fracas. There was a general shuffling of feet and lowering of heads among them. "So let us be up and doing, and get started on the counter-mine then!" He looked round again, not least at the two antagonists, Leslie and Carmichael, who now remained silent and convicted. Suddenly with a concerted shout of defiance, most dashed fiercely down from the ramparts in the wake of Kirkcaldy of Grange.

But frustration awaited them, for after days of patient digging and burrowing, trying all the time to pinpoint the exact position of their enemies' tunnel, they found the sounds of their workings receding. They had made a mistake and tunnelled above and beyond it.

"This is useless and a waste of precious time!" Peter Carmichael's nerves were fraught. "Have we asked the Lord's guidance? I feel the Lord's displeasure at the crude jesting, the unseemly language, and immoral lives of some of those who have joined our cause. They have come for selfish reasons. They just wanted to get their hands on the wealth of the Cardinal, which is well known. They will but bring dishonour to our faith! Again, I say once more, Master Rough, whom we have elected as our chaplain, is too weak an instrument to lead us, a frail reed who will bend and break when the storm comes." Once more the look of religious zeal suffused the dark eyes of Carmichael. "John Rough is a holy man, liked by us all, but not strong enough in Theological debate with the expert advocates of Rome."

"No, no, that's not true, brother Peter! Master Rough is the man to deal with our opponents, and to lead the cause of the Reformed Kirk! He is able to debate with the best that St. Andrews can throw against us, even the great John Major himself!" It was the earnest young Kirkcaldy calming things down, while the diggers in the tunnel paused wearily for breath. The dust in the confined space choked them.

"It is simply too that we have made a mistake in our earthly guidance, a very earthly, not heavenly. For a while I have noticed that the sounds of the workings of our beseigers has been getting fainter. Remember too that they will have the help of pit ponies to cart away the rubble, so they are making faster progress than we are no doubt!" "Let us continue the search for their workings. They cannot be too far off." The younger Leslie encouraged the others.

But the second attempt was also unsuccessful, begun like the first within the narrow vaulted space between the two curtain walls on the south side. The doubling up of the defences had of course taken place prior to the Reformers' capture of the Castle. But the third shaft opened in the ditch to the east of the great foretower, which had itself been strengthened against mining by the construction of a sloping base, met with singular success. Their enemy could be heard, and as each hour passed and the defenders laboured, sweating profusely in the dimness, lit only by two flickering oil lamps, the sounds of the approaching force drew closer. But they were not to meet before another error for a while caused them to mine a gallery too far to the east. The elder Leslie was astute enough to stop them wasting any more precious time and they desperately rerouted in a south-westerly direction. Their desperation too was shown in the cramped dimensions of the tunnel they were excavating. The cursing of the less saintly caused anger among the more Godly.

To load the rocks and rubble day after day and trail it back to the surface in baskets in the manner of human donkeys took its toll on their constitution. But at last Kirkcaldy of Grange, who had led by example, held up his hand for silence. The clink of axe and shovel ahead of them was distinct to all. A thin curtain of wall lay between them. With whispered instructions he sent back for fresh reinforcements from above and weapons to force home the attack.

When all was ready, at a given signal some workmen suddenly started to smash through the wall. Shortly it gave way and the oil lamps revealed a panic-stricken enemy, who were totally taken by surprise by the counter-mine. With a fierce yell they clambered through the ruins and set upon the Regent's workmen, who, when they could, for most were exhausted, turned to flee. For the most part the Castilians let them go, for their chief intent was to seal up the mine

Soon the dust had settled and they were able to see that the tunnel made from the town was much more spacious and further back had finely-chiselled steps cut into the rock, descending from its entrance. But the defenders withdrew quickly in case soldiers were sent in from above. Back at the break-through point they set to work with an urgency to block up the aperture, piling up as much loose debris as they could gather and then back to the surface for more material, which had been hacked out previously when excavating the tunnel. At last they ceased their feverish activity. They had been afraid that the enemy would return before the tunnel was effectively sealed up. But in fact the soldiers of the Regent were dispirited by now, and in many cases only half trained. Scotland had been weakened militarily. *The Rough Wooing* had taken a heavy toll.

For a while there was an uneasy peace, or at least no active hostilities, and free intercourse was allowed between the Castle and the town of St. Andrews. By December an 'appointment' was arranged that there should be no further hostilities until an absolution had arrived from Rome and the Pope for the murder of the Cardinal. It was with total distrust that the Castilians had agreed. By now the late Cardinal had been succeeded by Archbishop John Hamilton, the brother of the Duke of Hamilton and Earl of Arran, now the Regent.

"How do you think that we are so foolish as to believe the word of an illegitimate brother of the Regent?" said the elder Leslie to the others. "What too does the absolution from a Pope mean in our beloved Scotland, where we have repudiated the authority of Rome?"

"We must be wise as serpents in dealing with our enemies! St. Paul advocates this at all times. Remember that we must win the whole countryside to the Protestant faith, and to do this, we must be seen to be men of peace and reconciliation! The absolution of the Pope is still seen as the visible hand of God fulfilling the pardon for penitents, although God is concerned with the unseen and the hearts of men."

"I know."

"I still do not like it," growled Peter Carmichael. "Rome's ways are subtle and devious; her priests corrupted by power, how much more the Pope! Let us not forget the reasons for our being here, the departure of Rome from the simple Gospel of faith in our Lord Jesus Christ alone. Images, indulgences, purgatory, the Mass, and the Papacy itself, are all departures from Scripture. We shall wait and see the answer from Rome. I am sure there will be a snare hidden somewhere in the answer! Rome will never forgive the killing of a Cardinal. Meanwhile, I vote that we send a trustworthy messenger to Henry of England for assistance, tyrant though he be, while liberty is yet allowed." He gazed around the circle of leaders.

"The winter is setting in, and our supplies are low. We need money for food, horses, and arms, just in case......." Carmichael's dark eyes left the rest unsaid. They all knew the struggle was over and difficult times lay ahead.

"I shall go," A voice said quietly. It was the voice of the lawyer from Fife, Henry Balnaves of Halhill. "You ken it is my natural gift to negotiate. I have the mind of a lawyer and know the thoughts and intents of men's, hearts, as if a mirror had been held before them. King Henry is old, and, if reports are true, likely to end his dissolute life soon. The Earl of Somerset will succeed during the minority of the young Prince Edward, who has been brought up and educated as a true Protestant. I know the spirit of Somerset and his hatred of anything French. You must let me be your ambassador. There is no one else suitable.

Most of you here in leadership are more fitted to the pulpit or the field of battle than the Court." There was a buzz of discontent and even anger among the group at this newcomer to their cause, in whom some as yet had not placed full confidence. But at last the majority saw the sense of the plea, and a message was lodged with the Fife man to the English Court, pleading for help. He would play the French threat card, although the then King of France, Francis I, was an old style gallant, who possessed a romantic dream to control the north of Italy and the Duchy of Milan, and was less concerned with extending the French Empire to include Scotland and even England.

It was planned that Balnaves and a small band of riders should slip out from a side gate in a mist -shrouded January night and ride south unnoticed, but for some reason it was a milder than usual January and ideal conditions for their break forth did not prevail for some weeks. By then word had filtered through that Henry VIII had succumbed to the evil and intemperate life he had latterly lived. He had died lamented by few.

"So much the better," exclaimed Henry Balnaves heartily," though it is sad to see what depths a man of great intellectual talent and learning can sink to under the debauchery of power wrongly used!" He sighed in the way of a man familiar with the ways of the world only can.

It seemed an interminable month of waiting for the garrison before they knew if the power of England was to support the Protestant cause. They knew that Mary of Guise was alert like a vixen for when a more militant French policy would thrust experienced troops into the Scottish scene and nip the Protestant flower in the bud before it could blossom. It was a vital time, probably a new French ambassador would be appointed by then.

The countryside around St. Andrews was quiet for the moment, with the Regent's troops withdrawn to Edinburgh and Stirling. Master John Rough, their chaplain, had even been able to debate with John Annan, the Principal of St. Leonard's College, in the Parish Kirk of St. Andrews, but he had usually come off worst, as he was unable to match the Professor's rhetorical skill in academic things. Annan had championed the ancient cause of Rome as the Eternal Church, they claimed, established by Christ on Peter as the first Pontiff. Inexperienced in debate, the holy John Rough, sincere and gentle, had withdrawn to the Castle with the promise that he would renew the debate.

But encouragement came one blowy February day, when a lookout on the foretower gave a shout, and pointed to a weary group of horsemen beating furiously up the coastal path.

"See, it is Balnaves and the others! They have returned at last!" Sure enough mud-spattered and exhausted but in good spirits, the lawyer brought good news.

"Somerset is with us! See, here is one thousand and sixty pounds, half a year's pay to maintain a garrison of eighty able men in the Castle and forty horsemen to keep the countryside around St. Andrews under control. Forby, though the Princess Mary is but a child of four, Somerset is keen to follow the desire of King Henry to marry her to the young King Edward-to-be. We do not have to act like the Trojan horse to our beloved Scotland, like my Lords Glencairn, Cassilis, Maxwell, Fleming, Douglas and his brother George Douglas.

They bought their freedom after the Battle of Solway Moss by selling their souls to Henry, pledging themselves to advance the English cause and to help that wicked King achieve dominion over the Kingdom of Scotland, should the young Queen die, in return for pensions of English money! I spit on their base treachery! No, we are seeking a free Alliance, which will advance our faith as Protestants! Sir Ralph Sadler, the English ambassador, assured me that young Prince Edward has been conscientiously nurtured as a Protestant, and already has revealed an aptitude for languages and Theology."

"But we must not run before we can walk," advised the gentle Master John Rough, their faithful chaplain. "The very creatures of Nature teach us that that weak and pliable man, Hamilton, our worthy Regent, has reverted to Rome like the self-seeker he is, and he is not likely to change his coat again!" The minister was unusually animated.

"I believe Arran has thrown in his lot with the French with the promise of the little Queen in marriage to his son. At the travesty of an investiture at Stirling's Castle, Annan bore the Crown, Lennox the sceptre, and Argyll the sword, while behind them all, hindering God's work of Reformation, stood Mary of Guise like a spider watching over the future of her child. I tell you, many a battlefield has to be fought on by the Lord for his servants before our Protestant Reformation is victorious and vindicated throughout Scotland!"

For a moment the others were silent as the prophetic mantle fell on John Rough, and awed them deeply. "It is time for the Lord's leadership and for God's man to lead us, and I feel he will come soon!" Rough blinked for a second as if returning to reality. "But the Lord's blessing will not follow us, if the sins of certain of our company are not brought to account, for they swear, blaspheme, and complain continually. They have joined our cause for the wrong reasons, greed and power. While you have been absent, Balnaves, I have had to chastise some for their loose behaviour among the women of the garrison." He looked pointedly down into the Courtyard at a rough-looking individual, who was swaggering across it with a sneer on his face, but when he became aware of Master Rough's stare, he looked away in the manner of unrepentant guilt.

"It is inevitable in prolonged periods of close confinement, Master Rough," Henry Balnaves replied, attempting to allay the fears of the chaplain. "Be not concerned, for we shall tighten our discipline."

"Aye, some of the bolder spirits, who have ridden into town and into the countryside around, have behaved indecently, and, when we have admonished them, they have laughed in our face and almost challenged us to be rid of them. They know fine that we need their arms." Master Rough's indignation was strong, and his soul outraged.

"Well, we can now exert some control over whom we allow to be included in our garrison with this thousand pounds!" He patted a heavy pouch beneath his cloak. "We maun be more careful and discerning as to who are truly on the Lord's side."

Indeed discipline improved, but the stalemate continued right through the beginning of the year, and conditions also deteriorated. Illness began to spread. Many found the skin of their bodies had become cold, and their faces had a drawn and withered look. Muscular cramp gave them severe pains, and, though the well continued to supply everyone with fresh water, for some reason their thirst became devilishly intense. Superstition arose that the devil was abroad. "Every hour I draw water from the depths of that well to quench this raging thirst, and I still cannot satisfy it!" groaned James Melville, a speck of doubt now appearing in his eyes, which up to that time had shown a look of certainty.

"I have never felt like this before. A sleepiness comes over me in the midst of the day, and I am troubled by diarrhea. Almost everyone is affected." His voice rose in a kind of panic. "Has the spirit of that evil Cardinal come back to haunt us? Perhaps it was wrong to leave the body in the bottle-dungeon?" The carcass of Cardinal Beaton still lay pickled in a barrel at the bottom of the dark shaft. Melville shivered, and it was not just from sickness.

"Be calm, James," soothed his chaplain. "The Lord will keep us safe in the palm of his hands. He is our rock and fortress. We fight not against flesh and blood."

But a hammer blow was to fall at the end of March with the news that Francis I had died and his son, Henry II, a militant Roman Catholic and imperialist, had taken the throne of France. A remote promontory in the north of Europe now mattered in political affairs. A new French ambassador, Sieur D'Oysel, was appointed, and French influence increased rapidly. England bided her time, unwilling to actively defend the fledgling religious revolution. But in the midst of this time of despondency for the garrison, a tired, dusty figure of humble appearance arrived with three young lads in his care at the Castlegate. He begged admittance. Shortly after Kirkcaldy of Grange hurried to John Rough's apartment.

"Master Rough, John Knox of Haddington has come to us with the sons of the Lairds of Longniddry and Ormiston, to whom he is tutor! They seek refuge. They are weary from being hunted from one hiding place to another, and Knox has been advised by his students' fathers to seek the protection of our walls. But I must say that I am not impressed by this timid tutor. He looks as if he would flee away at the sight of a mere bat! I thought you said to us that he had been a priest and was a man of character?"

"He has come at last." A quiet glow came into John Rough's gentle orbs, as he ignored the question as unnecessary. Though he said nothing to young William Kirkcaldy, he believed the man of the hour had come. But he did not know that that hour had still to appear on a distant horizon, and many hard struggles had to be gone through first.

CHAPTER FOUR

FRENCH GALLEY SLAVES

The hunched figure of the tutor of Haddington ushered his three pupils across the drawbridge, already thrown down, into the protective embrace of St. Andrews Castle like some fussy mother hen. Alexander Cockburn of Ormiston had insisted on it, and John Knox was in no position to gainsay him, nor did he wish to. He was weary of continual flight from the Regent's minions.

He had come a long way from the time when a fierce rush of anger had instilled in him the courage to take up the great sword he possessed as bodyguard to the Preacher of Montrose. But what could be done against the powerful forces of civil authority and a proud and repressive Church? Already he knew the self-seeking of the nobility and their greed for the Church's riches and property.

Wishart's last speech before his death on the funeral pyre still lived in his mind, imprinted there forever. The closing sentence had been repeated three times by Wishart.

"O thou Saviour of the world, have mercy on me. Father in Heaven, I commend my spirit into Thy holy hands." His words before that had been equally memorable. "I am to suffer for the true Evangel and for Christ's sake I urge you not to be offended at the Word of God because of my torments. Consider my face. You shall not see me change my colour. I do not fear this grim figure and I pray that you won't, if any persecution comes to you for the Word's sake, and not to fear those that slay the body but afterwards have no power to kill the soul. Some have said that I teach that the soul of man should sleep till the last day, but my faith is sure that my soul shall sleep with my Saviour this night before six hours have passed." Then the gracious Wishart had prayed for his accusers and murderers.

"I beseech you, Christ, to forgive them that have condemned me to death ignorantly this day." George Wishart's loving gaze would never be forgotten by John Knox. It contrasted with the hatred of his enemies, especially Beaton, who had seated himself sadistically on a luxurious couch beside a window in the bishop's Palace to overlook the terrible execution. The proud, triumphal, sneer that exuded from his saturnine features was ignored by the angels in Heaven, Knox was sure, in preference for the beatific countenance of the martyr. It had been such that the hardened executioner himself had actually asked Wishart's forgiveness before he set fire to the heaped pyre. The victim had kissed the axeman's cheek with the final words.

"Lo, here is a token that I forgive you, my heart. Do thine office."

"We are bound to be safe in the castle, sir," piped up Johnny Douglas. Knox's mind was drawn back to the present. "These walls are so huge that they make my father's tower of Ormiston's tower look tiny!"

"Safe we may be, Johnny, but you will still have to study your Latin text. We are about to examine Horace's Odes and Georgics, and you will need to work harder. I have noticed that your Grammar is weak, my boy." John Knox hid any amusement he felt, for he took education very seriously and was dismayed at the ignorance abroad as well as the widespread beggary.

Beggars, vagrants, and vagabonds of every kind swarmed up and down the countryside, and the rags of misery flapped everywhere, in stark contrast to the wealth of the Church. If a Reformation was to take place, it would have to address this problem, he determined. But he already suspected that the motives of some of the nobility were mixed and the glint of greed was in their eyes. But any further anxious thoughts were brushed aside by the joyful embrace of Chaplain John Rough, who had scurried forward eagerly to greet John Knox.

"Master Knox, at last! I have longed for this day! My, you are pale with weakness!" Indeed the ruddy complexion that was surprisingly the tutor's normal colour had faded into a sallowness, which could be laid at the feet of the life of the hunted.

"The Lord restores our health to us when He wishes. He heals all our diseases and renews our youth as the eagles', the Psalmist tells us. He is Lord of all. I understand, Master Rough, that an appointment has been made to await an absolution from Rome for the just death of that evil man, Beaton" Knox's usual calm look took on a fierce aspect. Beneath the academic was a militant character.

"Ah, yes, but it is Easter, and we are still awaiting word from Rome I do not at all trust the Regent or Rome's answer when it comes! They will never forgive us."

"Never trust Papal seed. Blessed are those who trust in the arm of the Lord! Cursed are those who trust in man! The Papal See is an invention of man and the desire of man for power. By their fruits you shall know them, and, as time passed, corruption has set in, as sure as night follows day. Only the Gospel and the Word of God are incorruptible. The Roman Church count there to be seven Sacraments, while Scripture tells us there are only two, the Lord's Supper and Baptism, and the Mass is an Idolatry to any who study the truth of the Bible. They tell us that the Sacrament of the altar is the real body of Christ and his actual flesh and blood!"

"Aye, the Bible is to be understood spiritually and not carnally, and so the Mass is wrong, for Christ once offered Himself for sin on the cross, and indeed will never be offered again, for at Calvary He put an end to all sacrifice forever. But how did the light first dawn on you, brother John? However, I do err in not looking to your care; my dear heart, for you and your pupils are tired and hungry. Forgive me; let us gang to your quarters." Rough affectionately wrapped his arm around Knox and with his other gathered the three boys ahead of them. Knox replied, as they made their way into the Castle.

"It is my delight to tell you that I can trace my enlightenment by God from the time when the preaching of Thomas Williams, one of the Blackfriars, touched me. He was a man of sound judgement and doctrine, who increased my spiritual knowledge to such an extent that four years ago my eyes were opened and I stood up for the Reformed faith." Knox, encouraged by the friendly comradeship his older brother in the faith, closed his arm around Rough's frail shoulders. He was among friends now. "And there I have cast my anchor, no matter what........."

So it was that John Knox gained in confidence and in the respect of the

Castilians. Rough's observant eyes followed him closely, his movements, attitudes, and words, as he tutored his noble students and intermingled with the garrison people. In such a close-knit community there was a transparency about every member, those whose life was holy, and those whose character was ungodly. God knew everything about everyone, Knox mused. Rough continued to debate with Principal Annan of St. Leonard's College in the Parish Kirk, but almost always came out badly bruised in the theological cut and thrust. But the honest soul of Rough had been impressed with the gifts of John Knox as a natural preacher and born controversialist, and so in a spirit of humility he requested the help of Knox's pen in composing his sermons.

"Principal Annan is a rotten Papist, Master Rough, and it is long overdue that the whole stinking edifice was brought down round him! We cannot stop crows nesting in an old, lifeless, tree, but we can chop the tree down." Knox readily acquiesced in composing much of Rough's messages. In addition, he led studies in the Gospel of St. John every morning for the garrison, but, secretly when he retired to rest, Knox prayed with anguish over the godless state of many among the hard-swearing, blaspheming, members, who were more interested in freedom from the smothering control of the Church than in genuine religion. He longed for a pure and holy people. But at last he could hold back no longer, and burst out one day in a zeal for the Protestant cause.

"I beseech you, Master Rough, to allow me to preach in St. Andrews against Principal Annan! He takes refuge all the time behind the authority of the Church of Rome, a false and spurious authority, flimsier than a spider's web. But let him distinguish the true Church from the false, and deal with the living Word of God! I will defeat him with that, which is sharper than a two-edged sword." It did not take much to allow him to preach, for John Rough was easily persuaded.

Word spread like wildfire that a new contestant for the Protestant people would hold forth in St. Andrews, and so the following Sunday the parish Kirk was packed with both the common folk and the dignitaries of the University and Church. Even the great John Major was present, the philosopher supreme, aged and ailing though he was with but a few years to go. Knox was thrilled that he was there, and had to quieten his nerves.

The atmosphere was tense, as all were aware that, despite a temporary truce while the garrison waited in tight suspense for the Papal absolution, which everyone with the slightest sagacity knew would never come from Rome without a precondition, and that a crisis was coming. There was no room for neutrality. The common people who could not either obtain a seat or afford one were standing on tiptoe. This distinctive, dark-haired and bearded, man with the deep-set eyes was relatively unknown, but his reputation for a rock-like faith had been published abroad through word of mouth, which travelled faster than the swiftest horseman. Principal Annan and John Knox now faced one another from two opposite lecterns.

"The authority of the Church condemns all heretics and Lutherans, and renders all disputes unnecessary," Annan launched forth, continuing with his self-confident approach, from head to toe an academic.

"Christ established His Church upon St. Peter, to whom He gave the keys to Heaven, the power of binding and loosing, Master Knox." The congregation waited, tensely wondering what would be the response of the unknown preacher.

"The Synagogue of Satan and the Pope of Rome, the Man of Sin!" The crowded audience gasped at the man's incredibly bold words, bold beyond belief. Normally they would be enough to sound his death knell, to bring him to the stake. "If you are willing I can prove that the Church of Rome has degenerated further from the purity of Apostolic times than the Jewish people from the Law of Moses when it consented to the death of Christ!"

"How dare you blaspheme against Holy Mother Church, Knox?" Annan's face was a veritable mixture of shock and disbelief. "Our Church holds Salvation from above through the administration of Baptism and the Sacraments!"

"The Salvation from Heaven is through faith in the Lord alone and not through any sacrament! And which of the Sacraments do you mean? There are only two, Baptism and the Lord's Supper."

"Blasphemy!" burst out Annan.

"Not blasphemy, but God's Word. For too long I was the Pope's knight. We ought to obey God rather than man. I now acknowledge myself as a miserable sinner before God."

"You say that the Mass is an idolatry? How can you say such a terrible thing?" Annan's features were nearly apoplectic.
"We deny that the Sacrament of the altar is the real body of Christ in flesh and blood. I repeat, in case you are short in understanding," Knox's tone was cutting. "The Scriptures are to be understood spiritually and not carnally, and so the Mass is wrong, for Christ once suffered for sin and will not be offered again. He put an end to all sacrifices, and our sins are all forgiven!"

"But our Lord said, 'This is my body and this is my blood.' "

"Our Lord Jesus Christ, to whom be all praise, was speaking symbolically, so that we are to celebrate His Supper in memory of Him. Clearly it is a commemorative meal."

The face of Principal Annan was contorted, as his emotions rose up to a boiling point from deep in his bowels. With huge difficulty he repressed his extreme anger and decided to change his tack.

"What about marriage? Is it not a Sacrament? What about the celibacy of the priesthood, is it not ordained of God? I have heard it whispered that you Reformers deny the holiness of celibacy?" The air was thick with spiritual battle in earth and heavenly places and the audience were exhausted as they followed it. They strained their necks, craning to hear every word, like starving birds out to catch every crumb.

"I think marriage is a blessed bond, ordained of God and approved of God, and free to be enjoyed by all the sons of men, but your priests abhor it and abstain from all marriage, as if God forbids it, which He does not. The marriage bed is undefiled, says the Bible. In the meantime your priests take other men's wives and daughters! You vow chastity and do not keep it!"

The congregation was in an uproar, and with difficulty the vergers restored order. The supporters of the Reformation gave enthusiastic cheers mixed with some disbelief at Knox's unexpected success, while the Papist party was outraged at the sheer audacity of the rebel priest. It took several minutes before the relative bedlam died down, and again the congregation listened with bated breath.

"Do you deny the authority of the Holy See of Rome and that of its Bishops?"

Annan fell back once more on the authority of Rome, the bedrock of his blind belief.

"While men still have believed that Christ established a Vice Regency at Rome with the power to define doctrines, enact decrees, and command the obedience of men, the Reformation of Christendom is hopeless, indeed impossible. Some minor abuses might be corrected, but the great tree would still be left standing, and what though some of the branches were lopped off, they would grow again. It was some time before brother Martin Luther was able to perceive the truth and then to strike at the root of the tree. Brave Patrick Hamilton and George Wishart saw this but not very clearly, as through a glass darkly.

They fought against the darkness, and gave their dear, precious, lives, but it is for me to grasp the vital truth. The whole system of the Papacy is manmade, a tradition of men, and as such bound to corruption from its very roots. It must be plucked up and the life-giving Gospel of our blessed Christ planted in its room!" A deafening silence reigned over the whole audience, the entire Congregation awestruck by the very idea. The basic authority of Rome had never been really questioned before as not being from God. Now the whole foundation was accused of being suspect. Within many present a light was dawning. "When Peter confessed that our Lord was the Christ the Son of the living God, the Lord then said that this was the Rock on which He would build His Church and the gates of Hell would not prevail against it. Peter was not that Rock, but a sinful man, who later denied our Lord three times."

Principal Annan was now beside himself, and choked, spluttering over his words. He looked around towards the Regent's Party for assistance to guide him. This was a very different opponent to the less astute Rough. This Knox was a dangerous man. Annan signed to his supporters that he didn't want to continue the debate. An end was called, and the people streamed out into the streets of St. Andrews on fire with a religious zeal and religious gossip, perhaps the latter more than the former. People were people the world over.

Nevertheless, a major work had been done and crossroads reached. John Knox was wisely closely surrounded by his supporters, who ushered him out, guarded by them all the way back to the relative safety of the Castle. This quiet tutor was a precious commodity now. It was a week or so later that a deputation came to Knox, composed of Rough, Balnaves and Norman Leslie. They were clearly nervous, and Henry Balnaves had a challenge in both his eyes and his voice.

"Several of us have become aware that you are a man of uncommon gifts and that God has given them to you for a purpose. We would press upon your conscience the duty of taking up the public office of protagonist and preacher to the garrison. We are convinced that you are the spokesman for the Protestants in Scotland! You have proved it by your speech against Annan that you have an extraordinary ability as a contestant for the Protestant, Reformed, faith. We urge you not to resist the call of God!"

The lawyer's demeanour was deadly serious, as he and the others intently watched Knox's reaction. The latter, however, lowered his head in a self- deprecatory and self-conscious embarrassment, afraid of all that was entailed. His longing for a quiet life of study in Germany at the new Protestant seats of learning returned with renewed force.

"My gifts are for study and the classroom, not for the heavy responsibility of the life of the preacher. I tell you, you are mistaken." His grey eyes avoided theirs, as if wishing to escape the light. "There are others more suited, more able, and more zealous for the cause." His voice was weak and trailed off, and no one was persuaded. A battle was going on within him, and the internal struggle was tearing him apart.

"No, no, John, you are the man!" It was like the mantle of Nathan the prophet had enveloped the holy John Rough, who now urged their suit. "The fire and power of your words in St. Andrews Kirk defeated the arguments of Principal Annan in a way that I could never do. I beseech you, be our preacher and leader under God!" Rough's self-effacing spirit touched the soul of John Knox. How could he refuse?

"But I cannot do it! I will fail you!" Tears of pain, as real as physical pain, sprang into his eyes." I cannot preach to the people, I am a teacher, a priest unto God, as are all true believers, and my vocation is to work to tutor young people, to communicate the Gospel in writing. I will not run where God has not called me." Knox tried in vain to convince them, and himself also.

"Brother, you shall not be offended, if I tell you that I have been charged by this garrison to say this in the Name of Jesus Christ, the Son of God and in the Name of God Himself. I charge you not to refuse this holy vocation. As you are concerned to increase God's Kingdom, edify the brethren, and comfort men, who are oppressed by a multitude of troubles, accept this call to the public office of preaching!"

"But I-I-I will fail you," mumbled Knox once more, miserably.

"Never! You fused reason with theology and a passionate logic!" John Rough held his colleague Knox firmly by the shoulders and gazed squarely into his eyes, where tears started to appear. Knox drew his hand across his face to hide his emotions.

"I-I –ask you to excuse me, for I must seek my room and go to prayer for God's advice and wisdom," Knox half-stuttered, and hurried off, his shoulders bent under an invisible load.

That was the last any of the garrison saw of him for three days. The trio of Leslie, Balnaves, and Rough said little, alone with their thoughts, afraid of the future, for these were desperate times. At last Knox appeared, his features refined by prayer and fasting, with many tears shed. Clearly he had come to a decision, for no longer were his shoulders hunched but straight as a lintel.

"The Lord has spoken to me clearly through His Spirit and through his Word! From this time forward I am called to preaching, and am certain of the Divine origin of my calling, for it runs counter to every inclination of my heart's desires." For a moment strong emotions threatened to burst forth in the blue-grey eyes beneath the ridged-brows, but John quickly reasserted his control. Rough embraced him, as an Elijah, an Elisha, while Balnaves and young Norman Leslie gripped his hands with dignity and fervour. They all knew that many trials lay ahead, but surely God's hand was with them?

It was as the summer was drawing nigh at the beginning of June that it became to the garrison that something important was happening in the town. From the ramparts people could be seen scurrying around and figures entering and re-entering the Town Hall. News had come. Soon an Embassy under the Provost's desired to speak with the Castilians' leaders. He and other officials of the Church and University decked out in their finery, resembled peacocks, and, as he looked guardedly down from the Castle Wall, Knox was reminded of the words quoted from the speech of the Lollards of Kyle, those brave pioneers, who had earlier in history questioned not only the beliefs and practices of Rome, but also the arrogant oppression of the lower classes by the nobility.

"Where then was the gentleman in the Garden of Eden, when Adam dug and Eve spun? Jack was as good as his master then?" These were words of biting rhetoric that secretly delighted John Knox, and, had he but known it in a prophetic way, he would frequently employ against his enemies. But the Provost was speaking.

"We bear an offer of absolution from the Pope himself." The Provost called out, preening himself with an assumed dignity. "Open up to a deputation, which I shall send with a copy of the absolution."

"*Timeo Danaos et dona ferentes*. I fear the Greeks, especially when bearing gifts." Knox quoted the famous line from Virgil's classic quietly to Rough beside him. They may have something to offer us, but be sure there will be a catch, a conditional clause in their document that leaves us exposed to the Pope's condemnation. Be assured, brother, that Rome will never forgive us either our rebellion or the death of the Cardinal. Also be sure that they wish to enter the Castle in order to see the condition of our garrison and just how long we can survive. No, let us send a party out under a flag of truce and examine the terms of the document." Rough trusted the wisdom of Knox implicitly and so it was agreed that Henry Balnaves should lead a small group out to parly. It was as John Knox had forecast. There was a catch in the Latin text of the document. The practiced eye of the experienced lawyer caught the phrase, *Remittemus peccatum irremissibile.*

"We shall remit the irremissible sin," he muttered to himself under his breath. "Ah, there is the catch, they are forgiving the unforgiveable. How can that be done?" But he did not allow his suspicions to be obvious to the Provost and his officials, or the Regent's men, nor did he hint that famine, plague, and disease were taking their toll on the Castle's inhabitants. "We shall withdraw to consider the Papal statement," he informed the impatient Provost.

"Do not delay too long," growled that worthy. "You have the Pope's promise. You see, it is quite safe to surrender the Castle."

"Ah, yes," answered Balnaves non-committedly, but refused to give an unconditional surrender. "Give us time to consider, Provost. In the thoughts of a number, there is wisdom." Back among the garrison, John Knox congratulated the Fifeshire lawyer on his tact."

"Aye, how typical of the double-dealing and equivocation of Rome! They pretend friendship, and retain the right to remove it, if it suits them! If we surrender, it will be playing into their hands."

But the end was to come in a way that left the Castilians no choice. They had contemptuously dismissed the Regent's terms, but on the last day of June a guard on the Foretower cried out excitedly.

"Ships on the skyline, a goodly number."

"Are they for us, ore agin' us? I cannot make out their pennants."

The garrison rushed to the walls, women and children too. Many families who had supported the Reformation in Scotland and befriended George Wishart in his preaching, had joined the Castilians by this time, and they had suffered for it. Could this be the relief at last England had promised would come? Their eyes strained toward the horizon, where the unknown sails filled the scene. At least twenty large galley vessels could be seen now. Too sadly their hearts dropped, the pennants at the mastheads were not what they had hoped for. They were not the lions of England or the Cross of St. George.

"It is the fleur de lis! They are French!" John Leslie's words almost choked n his throat.

"God's will be done," said Knox quietly. "Today we shall celebrate the Lord's Supper, and trust in the arm of our God."

Soon the mighty fleet of twenty one huge galleys swept, sails billowing, into St. Andrews Bay and anchored offshore. The Castilians watched grimly, as a long boat pulled ashore, with a black-bearded, long-haired, figure seated self importantly in the stern, clearly the Fleet's Commander. The Scots would regret his acquaintance. In due season, that night the Lord's Supper in the Bible fashion was celebrated in the Castle chapel, held in a tense but reverential quietness.

For some it was the first time in the simplicity of the Reformed faith after the Mass. The rye bread was broken into rough, uneven, pieces, and a watered-down claret was passed around in silver tassies. The presence of their God, whose body had been broken in agony for them. God the Son was very real to them all, young and old. Some of the celebrants, who had been habitual cursers and had attached themselves to the Reformers for selfish reasons hoping to get their hands on some of the wealth of the Church, were present, though they did not participate. They had been warned by John Knox of God's condemnation on their unholy lives.

No longer was the host offered up by a priest in a repeat sacrifice of what was achieved once and could not be repeated, and no longer was the holy cup drunk only by the priest. In fact the very word priest had been banished from among the Reformers, as their pastors and ministers were to rightly take their place. The silver flagon reached Sir David Lindsay, whose caustic pen had written *The Satyre of the Three Estates,* exposed the corruption of the Church, the Court, and the Government. His frequent visits during the respite in the siege had made him inclined to cast in his lot with the Reformers.

"There is no power here but the power of God. The power of man is banished," he observed with his penetrating insight.

"We shall soon, however, need that power of man, I fear," he added significantly.

"Aye, never have I seen such a fighting force as the French fleet, but we cannot turn our backs on the fledgling work of the Reformation. We must discover the power of prayer."

Sure enough, word came that the French commander, Leone Strozzi, demanded the surrender of the Castle, which they immediately refused. But their confidence was quickly smashed. With increasing trepidation they saw the huge cannon being brought ashore from the French vessels and wheeled to the walls towers of the Abbey and St. Salvator's College. They were then dragged to the highest vantage points overlooking the Castle. Their fears were realised, when the cannon balls started to smash into their walls. For the following three weeks the cannon played on their target with deadly effect. Depression set in, as the inevitable loomed.

"No help is coming from England!" "Kirkcaldy of Grange complained bitterly.

"We must make the best terms we can, and trust in the mercy of God and men"

"Cursed are those who trust in men, William," said John Knox fiercely. His words were to prove only too true.

Kirkcaldy of Grange was sent out with a flag of truce. He found the French Commander was surprisingly an Italian.

"I am Leone Strozzi, Commander of the Fleet of His Most Illustrious Majesty, King Henry II of France." His ebony-dark eyes glinted in a manner not without some humour.

However, something about his oily, brown, complexion and slightly clipped, but controlled, accent, struck William as not only other than French but untrustworthy and dangerous. The man's French was impeccable, as was Kirkcaldy's, which was why he had been chosen to negotiate. French was still the language the Court, the upper class, and the educated attained to. The beautiful tones of French often made up the songs of the lute and cither in noble households.

"But you are not French?" Kirkcaldy had enquired politely, aware that he must not give unnecessary offence. Strozzi's gold-braided green velvet coat spoke of sartorial elegance.

"Ah, si, Signore Scozzese. I am from *la bella citta di Firenze*, of the noble Florentine family of Strozzi! My grandfather, Filippo, known as 'The Elder', commenced the construction of the wonderful Strozzi Palace in Firenze-you should see it! My father Gianbattista, opposed the Medicis and their tyrannical ways, and led the Florentine exiles to freedom, *La Liberta,* it ees so important!" The Italian's obvious pride, as he gesticulated expansively with his hands, suddenly changed into an explosive indignation." But when he was captured, my beloved father committed suicide so bravely rather than give in to Medici torture and the stake, like the bold Girolamo Savonarola, a true martyr for his faith." Kirkcaldy bit his lip and let the Italian continue. He noticed Strozzi used the word his, not my. The Scot had no knowledge of Italian history and was in no mood for a lesson.

"To think that Lorenzo the Magnificent was once a great man and patron of the Arts. But to my story, my brother, Piero, and I fled to France. He became a Grand Marshall of France, but poor Piero was mortally wounded before Thionville in action. But I, Leone, entered the Order of Malta, and have become, as you see, a Commander in the French Navy." Strozzi spread his broad hands and stared expressively at the Scotsman opposite, as young Kirkcaldy sat spellbound somewhat by the colourful character before him. He was rather out of his depth. To negotiate was difficult. "So what are we to do, my Scotsman? Surely you realise that it is impossible to hold out against our Fleet? Our batteries will smash your walls to little pieces, and have already begun."

"We demand a surrender with honour, for we but stand for our freedom of faith and conscience as Protestants, to practise our Reformed faith in Scotland. We already have the pope's absolution for the death of Cardinal Beaton, not that we much store by that." The Scot laid as thick a sarcasm as he could. "We have had our Protestant martyr, Monsieur Strozzi, George Wishart, burnt cruelly before our very St. Andrews Castle! Cardinal Beaton watched it without pity in his heart." He had raised his voice and watched the other closely for his response.

"Ah, *si*, the Papal absolution," Strozzi coughed politically, inferring it was not worth the paper it was written on. He clearly didn't have much regard for the Church of Rome." In Italy we know all about the Pope's absolution," he added dryly. "As for me, I am a simple soldier. If you will surrender, here are the generous terms. The lives of all within the Castle will be saved, men, women, and children, English as well as Scots. They shall be transported to France, and, if they are not content with the conditions offered by the King of France to remain in service and freedom there, they shall be safely conveyed at the King's expense to any other country of their choice, except Scotland." Leone Strozzi sat back in his chair in the house of the Provost, elbows on the table, fingers of both hands cupped around one another. Young Kirkcaldy was immobile, struck silent with the offer, a more than generous one, if exile was to be seen as preferable to imprisonment and death. Could he trust the suave, smiling, Italian, whose eyes were, nevertheless, hooded, as he regarded the other narrowly?

"We shall consider your proposed terms very carefully," Kirkcaldy answered shortly.

"Don't take too long," said Strozzi equally shortly, and the Scot thought for a moment the mask dropped.

"We have no option," groaned the elder Leslie later. "They will blow us to smithereens with their cannonades. The plague is eating into the lives of the weaker ones, and for the sake of the women and children any more suffering would be a sin against God. What would God have us do? David, a man after God's own heart, yet said, *Against Thee only have I sinned and done wrong in your* sight, brethren we can worship that God freely on the Continent according to the dictates of our conscience? We have the choice to do so, wherever we please. There are Reformed congregations in Amsterdam, Hamburg, Geneva, and Frankfurt already, I hear. My spirit tells me to opt for Amsterdam. We Scots have often fought alongside the Dutch, and our young men of education have studied at the University of Leyden." Leslie sounded sure of his words.

"But can we trust the Italian Strozzi?" Kirkcaldy struggled in his mind. "I am aware that the Reformation will go on, whatever. What God has begun He has brought to fruition. God will raise up the men for the moment. The Bibles, which have been brought from England in secrecy, could have been given cartloads. But what of our future? Will such good men as you, Master Knox, yourself, Henry Balnaves, and your worthy self, John Rough, be lost to the Protestant cause and the work of God in Scotland?"

"Be not over-concerned," responded John Knox, a fervent light in his eyes. "Better a live dog than a dead lion! We live to fight in a future day. God has His special-chosen instruments. Perhaps it is the light of the Gospel from Europe which will set fire to the torch of faith here in Scotland." He gazed like a seer across the cold North Sea's stormy surface to the misty mainland of the Continent beyond. Some ancient Celtic soothsayer might have named it second sight, but to a follower of the Christian way it was a prophetic vision. "Let us accept their conditions, allowing for all the women and children to be free to depart to homes where they will be given needed succour. Though hearts will be broken by separation from loved one day they will be re-united again."

So it was that, trusting to the word of Leone Strozzi, the Reformers surrendered to the French, though their hearts were heavy. But they were shortly to be disillusioned. As they said goodbye to the wives and bairns, and were boarding the French galleys in the parties into which the hundred and twenty active men were divided, they noticed the large number of slaves shackled to the benches and oars. John Knox estimated that there were close on three hundred galley slaves on the vessel to which he and others were assigned, the Notre Dame. But still the Scots were initially treated fairly well, with accommodation in the cabins just sufficient, and their severest grief was when the horizon closed on the familiar coastline of their native Scotland. Would they ever see their land again, and when?

During the voyage to Rouen, where they would winter according to Commander Strozzi, John Knox suffered as he watched the agony and miserable conditions of the galley slaves, as they laboriously hauled the long, sixteen foot, oars back and forth in a machine-like movement to the monotonous beat of a drum. It was a life of unutterable horror and designed to break a man's spirit so that he might play false to his convictions. From stern to stern there was a platform, known as the *coursier*, along which the officer and crew moved from one end of the vessel to the other.

The benches were fixed at right angles to the ship's sides, and to these benches were chained from four to six slaves, who sat on these without the slightest change of position by day, and slept under them by night, absolutely without shelter in all seasons of the year. Strozzi spoke of them without the least compunction or compassion, and something in his demeanour made John Knox apprehensive. His suspicions were aroused, and he sensed in his spirit and instincts that all was not well. The Officer in charge of the slaves was called the *Comite,* he was told, and he moved along the *coursier* whip in hand, applying it to the back of every wretch who showed signs of flagging at his oar. Knox noticed that special punishment was meted out often to the fierier spirits. He shivered involuntarily, as he saw one galley slave flogged into insensibility, and turned away to gaze at the pale faces of the two Leslies, Peter Carmichael, and a certain James Balfour.

The other leaders among the Castilians had been divided into groups and put on different ships of the French fleet. The drawn look on the faces of the four, which had been etched on them as the shores of Scotland disappeared below the horizon, had now become even more pronounced. A feeling of foreboding enveloped John Knox. He was certainly unafraid to die, as were the others, he was sure. But what of the stripling faith of the Reformation, would it survive without their vital leadership? He knew that in the Border country the Reformed faith had been set alight by local preachers, and helped to ignite by the faith from across the frontier with the auld enemy. Knox's sense of the destiny of God, however, was severely tested.

"What would I give to have a set to with him that has that whip!" growled the fierce Carmichael; who had been so prominent in the assassination of reprisal on the Cardinal." The coward is without mercy, when he is in control. But you take note that not one of these officers or even crew members dare venture down below at night into the slave quarters, Master Knox." It was pitch black just then amongst the oarsmen, and the tutor of Haddington could imagine what might be possible under the cover of darkness, if any of the persecutors were tripped and a shackle chain quickly drawn tightly round his neck to throttle him. His end would be violent, vicious, and swift. No doubt there would be reprisals, but, if it happened, the hatred that filled the hearts of the slaves would be somewhat satisfied, and of course the Captain could not afford to lose many oarsmen.

Leone Strozzi continued with his mocking air, but no longer did he look John Knox or any other Scots in the eye. His words and attitude were offhand in their tone, if not contemptuous.

"Remember, if you do not like the French way of life, and I myself find it as an Italian quite congenial, you are welcome to seek a safe haven in another country of Europe. You have much trade from Scotland, I believe, with the Low Countries and to the Baltic States of the Hanseatic League. So maybe you would feel more at home there, eh? *La belle France* will of course pay for you all to travel there. You do not wish to end up like these galley slaves there, do you? There are always dangerous pirates and Barbary *corsairs* raiding our shores, you know. These wretched slaves are enduring purgatory before their time, eh?" Strozzi laughed blasphemously, but his eyes were hooded. Indeed, Strozzi's sarcastic mockery echoed hollowly in Knox's ears, and all too soon the coastline of France hove into sight.

"Lo, my friends, there lies Rouen! She is the ancient capital of the proud Duchy of Normandy, as you probably know," he pointed from the bridge." It is a turning point on the Seine. You will love Rouen, I'm sure, but then you will have no choice, for none of you will have any choice, for you are not going any further." Leone Strozzi and his nearby officers guffawed, but it was no longer the laughter of mockers, but of masters. The Scots gazed at one another in fearful alarm.

"But you gave your solemn word of honour in the surrender terms at St. Andrews that we would all go freely to whichever country we desired! Our desire is to go to the Low Countries and Amsterdam especially!" Norman Leslie was not normally aggressive, but had lost all his equanimity. But before more angry words could be exchanged, the Scots' arms were cruelly pinioned behind them, and at the point of the sword, dagger, and musket, fighting and struggling they were trussed up with powerful ropes.

"Now, you will be glad to know that your compatriots in the other ships are at this moment being seized and bound like Scots turkeys!" Strozzi was back at his mocking best, but his eyes were cold and distant now, no longer interested." Our galleys are badly in need of fresh fodder for oarsmen. Some of those below are getting old and broken down, but we will give you excellent free gifts, good, strong, serge jackets and fine, cropped, haircuts! We can't have the lice living off our good galley slaves, eh?"

"You cowardly scum! You have broken your sacred word, and I curse you to Hell forever! God's judgement is on you!" Peter Carmichael's fiery temper would have seen him tear out Strozzi's throat, if four burly soldiers had not held him in check.

"Don't worry; your friends in the other ships are receiving the same special care," Strozzi's staccato accent grated in John Knox's Scottish ear." Look at the Tower of Rouen Cathedral, raised through the abstinence of the faithful from indulging in the luxury of pure butter! It will become a familiar sight to you, when we return to winter here every year. You will come to experience what these good French Catholics felt like, for butter will not be part of your future diet." John Knox saw the tall Tower rising beside the spire of the Cathedral before he and the four others were hustled down below.

Soon, shackled and chained in the depths of the ship's bowels, depression settled over the spirits of the others, but Knox attempted to encourage them.

"Do not give up hope my brothers. Prayer is an earnest and familiar conversation with God. We can declare all our miseries and get all His support and help in our adversities. We can laud and praise Him for all our benefits. God will not cast away a perfect man; neither will He help the evil doers, till He fills your mouth with laughing and your lips with rejoicing."

"Well, you lead us in prayer, Master Knox," requested James Balfour quietly and sincerely. There in the darkness the five gathered round to kneel before the God of love and light, who would surely deliver them from a life of slavery. Even as he sought God's face, the dreaded sound of the drumbeat, by which the oarsmen took their time, could be heard along with the hated command of the *comite* sounded out to give further motivation.

"Lord," he prayed fervently," You, in your good time will deliver us. Victory is ours and the battle is the Lord's. It is not for martyrdom that we are here in this accursed French galley, but for the glorious good of Scotland and the Protestant faith! God will give us the ultimate victory. These vestments of spiders' webs shall not abide the forces of the wind of the Lord. We trust in Thee, our Lord Jesus Christ and Redeemer!"

But the words of the man of Haddington, for all their confident sound and the temporary encouragement they brought to his companion Scots seemed to echo hollowly against the French vessel's planking. A life of tortuous slavery in a French galley ship stretched ahead of them. His vision for the Protestant Reformation in Scotland seemed a wispy dream that was turning into a nightmare.

IN DESPERATE PLIGHTS

Contrary to what the prisoners had been told, the French fleet did not remain long at Rouen. Soon the vessels were on their way, and word spread that they were to winter on the Loire at Nantes. But what Knox and his companions of the Notre Dame did not know was that the principle Scots gentlemen had been taken off and incarcerated in Rouen Castle, the fortresses of Cherbourg and Brest, and the infamous island stronghold of Mont St. Michel. Knox and the others were confined on board the galleys, bound with chains, to pull hour after weary hour the heavy oars and be exposed to all the indignities with which the Papists were accustomed to treat those whom they regarded as heretics.

The sardonic Italian commander, Leone Strozzi, John Knox was never to see again, but he missed him infinity less than he did his faithful and good friend, the eloquent and clever lawyer from Halhill, Henry Balnaves, whom John deeply respected. Balnaves had been regarded as a real danger and threat by the French, who recognised his wide knowledge of European politics. As yet the former tutor was an infant in these things. Knox they saw merely as an upstart preacher of heresy, and no threat to their ambitions to unite Scotland and France through the marriage of the young Princess Mary, now five years of age, to the youthful Dauphine of France. If the French leaders had possessed the eye of the seer, they could have seen how wrong they were.

Even the notorious Mont St. Michel's fastness was not to hold the four brave Scots, young William Kirkcaldy of Grange, Peter Carmichael, and the Leslie brothers, forever. Yet the four could have been forgiven for the deepest despair they felt, as they were frog marched across the long, sandy, causeway at low tide to the almost impregnable fortress high up on the ancient, volcanic, rock thrown up by primeval forces. At high tide the treacherous causeway would be entirely covered by water. They were forced over a strong, wooden, footbridge to the *Porte de l'Avancee*, the only entrance to the Castle ramparts.

A second gateway led to an inner gatehouse, flanked by two bombards or stone-throwing cannon, which had successfully resisted Henry V's forces, when all of Normandy had been overrun by the English armies. A final inmost gate, the rather ornate *Porte du Roi*, the Gate of the King, had a portcullis and battlements. As they were roughly shepherded through it, Peter Carmichael could see the carvings of sea shells and salmon, the emblems of the Abbey and the Town of Mont St. Michel, inscribed above. This formidable fortress was an ecclesiastical bastion in fact, with its garrison maintained by the joint support of the King and the Abbot.

"We have as much chance of escaping from here, as has that salmon of coming to life and swimming to the sea," growled the usually aggressive Carmichael, but now hopelessly depressed, as he pointed up at the colourful carvings.

"Come, Peter, my brother in Christ, do not abandon hope! Nor faith, and remember that faith is the substance of things hoped for and the evidence of things unseen. God has not abandoned us, as indeed He has not left Master Knox, James Melville, Henry Balnaves, or the Leslies there!" Kirkcaldy, vibrant as ever, glanced over at Robert and William Leslie, to see how they were affected. Their relatives, Norman and John were with Knox in the galleys.

"Yes, I believe that we shall survive," said Robert quietly.

"Aye, for how long? Yonder's our future home," Carmichael growled again, unconvinced, nodding in the direction of a steep, broad, cobbled street, which stretched upwards towards a great pile of Gothic and Romanesque buildings, all structured one upon another, culminating in a magnificent, soaring, spire, pointing heavenwards, as if to reach the celestial spheres. He had a grudging admiration for the flamboyant delicacy of the spire.

But the reality was that this was their Abbey prison. Carmichael turned to look back at the miles of mudflats cut across by the Couesnon River, at whose muddy mouth rose the towering granite mound of Mont St. Michel. Some of the mudflats could be extremely treacherous quicksands at low tide, and at high tide the waves would come roaring in, until they lapped around the base of the Abbey mound. Before the four Scots Protestant prisoners could dwell on their predicament, the platoon of brutal French soldiery pushed them up the long *Grande Rue* to their dismal prison, prodding them painfully in the back with their halberds. Carmichael reacted angrily and was cruelly smashed in the face with a halbert butt.

Meanwhile the *Notre Dame* was ploughing southwards through the choppy waters of the Atlantic towards Nantes, and the harsh life of the oar was making its mark on the bodies and spirits of the Scots. Knox was glad to find that his good friend, James Balfour, was next to him at the oar, which had six unfortunates pulling painfully at it. At the top end of the oar, where the maximum force would be exerted, John noticed that a brown-skinned, clearly of Arab origin, was positioned there. The Scot guessed that the man was likely a captured Barbary corsair.

The Barbary pirates operated out of the North African ports, like Tangiers, Tripoli, and Algiers, and were a common threat to all the major European nations. Their merchant shipping was a frequent prey to these vultures of the seas. The *corsair* had no sense of mercy and justice, and, though destruction had been vented on their fleet, the problem was almost insoluble. The harbours on the African coast, where they sought refuge and had their fortified castles, were too shallow for the larger European vessels of France, Spain, and the Italian States to enter. But this particular sailor had been less fortunate. The Scots preacher observed that the Arab had strong, sinewy, arms and an air of acceptance, even surrender, about him. The man seemed to be uttering some strange words repetitively to himself.

"He has given up hope entirely, James," John Knox concluded and touched James Balfour with his elbow and nodded in the direction of the Arab galley slave." Let us pray that we ourselves never reach that stage in our hearts. Hope deferred makes the heart sick."

"Perhaps his religion, that of the Mussulman, makes him too readily resigned. I have heard that their God teaches them that nothing can be done in this world to change what is meant to happen to you, especially the darker things. I jalouse that our captors have deliberately placed our Mussulman friend at the end of the oar, for he is not only strong, but he has also accepted his slavery as from God."

41

"Aye, you are absolutely right, Balfour. I thank God that our faith is a Heaven apart and that our God, though He rules all things by a Heavenly decree, yet He brings light out of darkness and will not suffer us to be governed by it. The future can be changed by prayer!"

"Sometimes I do not understand God and His inscrutable purposes," groaned Balfour.

"Ah, Jamie, He is the Lord, who works all events in our lives for good to his children, even this! Have faith, brother!" He seemed to feel the coarse rubbing of the canvas shirt against his soft skin and the humiliation of the close-cropped haircut, though he uttered words as if to deny it. The serge jerkin possessed a hood, which he could pull over his head in times of cold and rain.

They had been pulling for some days now, and John Knox's constitution, while strongly enough built, was not accustomed to such exertions of an extreme nature. The aching pains were a continuous agony throughout his joints. Perhaps his body could acclimatise to the unending stroke of the oar? But as yet the one- time disciple of George Wishart and chaplain to the Protestant garrison of St. Andrews Castle was not adequately prepared for this new chapter in his life. He sought refuge in the comfort of Scripture and the starkly honest words of the Royal Psalms.

""*How deep I am sunk in misery, groaning in my distresses, yet I will wait for God; I will praise Him continually, my Deliverer, my God. I am sunk in misery, therefore will I remember Thee, though from the Hermons and the springs of Jordan and from the hills of Mizar deep calls unto deep in the roar of thy cataracts, and all Thy waves and all Thy breakers pass over me.*" Knox intoned Psalm forty two, which he had learnt from a child. How real the words were to him here in the depths of a French galley in the heart of the North Sea." *The Lord makes His unfailing love to shine forth alike by day and night; His praise on my lips is a prayer to the God of my life.* The challenge and contradictions of the words give hope, even to a galley slave. My dear brother, the serpent has only the power to sting the heel and to trouble the flesh, but not to move the spirit from adhering to Christ," he encouraged James Balfour.

"Aye, let pray so, but it is fair sore on the flesh," muttered Balfour.

The *Notre Dame* drove on through the tossing waves, and the Reformer felt the grim irony of the vessel's name, when he totally detested what he considered the blasphemous title given by Rome to the holy Israelite maiden, Mary of Nazareth in Galilee. How much had the religion of ancient Rome seeped into the Roman Catholic Church, just as had the religion of ancient Egypt under the Pharaohs and the gods of Greece been absorbed into Rome?

The sacred mother and child associated with Isis, the wife of Osiris and daughter of Horus, the highest of the Egyptian deities, was originally the goddess of the earth and the moon. Her worship had been introduced into the Roman Republic and the Empire later. The temple of Isis at Rome had stood in the middle of the Campus Martius and priests and servants of the goddess were introduced. Many of the Reformers, including Knox, believed that the worship of the Virgin Mary was but that of Isis dressed up in Christian clothing. As he tried to sleep, as much as his over-exhaustion would allow lying cramped under their bench every night, little did John Knox know that his anger against the falsehood of idolatry would soon be given full vent.

Just after their arrival at Nantes a priest came on board and the chant of the *Salve, Regina,* imploring the help of the Virgin Mary floated over and down to the Scots prisoners below. But it was as if an invisible sign had been given to the Scots Protestants in the different galleys that had now arrived back in the Loire from their voyages, and to a man they deliberately covered their heads with their cap and snoods. Enraged, the French officers strode along the coursier, and threatened the Scots with torture, if they did not give the acceptable signs of reverence for the Virgin. The comite whipped his lash wickedly over their heads and backs, like the deadly tongue of a serpent.

"You will become true worshippers, you cursed heretics, and give adoration to our Lady, the Queen of Heaven!" shouted the *Arguesyne* of the Notre Dame raging at Knox, the more so that he recognised in him the Protestant equivalent of a priest. At a command a sailor jumped down among the galley slaves and thrust between them a wooden image of the Virgin Mary, gloriously painted in deepest blue, red, gold, and white.

"Handle the figure of our Blessed Virgin and give her the kiss of adoration, you heretical scum!"

"I will not even touch it, for such idols are accursed!" Knox cried in outrage.
"But you will," The officer snarled at him, and thrust the image once more into John Knox's face. Just then some of the other prisoners rattled their chains violently in support and in protest. Distracted, the officer turned away to restore order with the assistance of the crew. Knox then seized the hated image from where it lay on the bench, and standing up, threw the painted figure with disgust over the side into the Loire.

"Let our Lady now save herself! She is light enough, so let her learn to swim!" All the Scot's pent-up hatred for false religion and the broken promises of the French was centred on the piece of useless wood. His anger and fierce irony could have been that of Elijah on Mount Carmel before the priests of Baal. The other prisoners, less bold, were aghast and waited in trepidation for the violent reaction of the cruel guards.

Strangely enough, when the panic-stricken officers, in superstitious fear that their idol might be lost to them and bring a curse, had with difficulty retrieved it from the waves, they seemed unusually subdued by John Knox's audacity, and from then on the prisoners were saved from subjection to such acts of Popish worship and idolatry. But they, nevertheless, continued to resist all attempts, direct and indirect, to induce a change in their Protestant convictions. They stubbornly refused to acknowledge the celebration of the Mass and the chanting of the *Salve, Regina.* Their spirits were satisfied with the Last Supper as a Feast of Remembrance and sanctified the Lord in their hearts.

The same steely determination strengthened Norman Leslie and the Laird of Pitmilly, David Monypenny, in the Castle of Cherbourg, when they too were ordered to attend the Mass and they refused outright.

"The Captain has the power to command our bodies, but he has no power to command our consciences," said Leslie sternly.

"I have the power to compel you to go where I lead you," replied the Captain of the garrison.

"We will not refuse to go any lawful place with you, but to do anything against our conscience; we won't do, neither for you nor for your King!" Leslie, like Knox, would not be moved.

"Will you not attend the Mass?"

"No, and if you compel us, we will disrupt the service, and everyone will know that we dispute the doctrine."

None of the hundred and twenty nine Scots in French hands had compromised their Protestantism when the Fleet left the Loire and sailed for Scotland to guard her coasts against the threats of English attack. But Knox's health was beginning to weaken under the continued strain of the unceasing labour over the oars, exposure to the freezing winds and rain, the malnourishment of an insufficient diet, and the blasphemous swearing of not only his French captors but also his fellow captives, had a draining effect on him. He had formed a deep friendship with James Balfour, and they sought to comfort one another in their terrible situation, which saw little of light for the future.

When one was in despair and his heart despondent, the other lifted him to the comfort of Christ. It had seemed, as day followed day, that the beat of the ship's drum, the huge strain on their back and shoulder muscles, the blistering and callouses on their hands, the smell of their own and others' stale sweat, and the mockery of their French masters, would all never end. Chained by the neck in couples, compelled to row for ten and twelve hours day and night without a rest, goaded by frequent strokes of the whip, closely packed at night on little straw mats, gnawed at by rats and mice, for John Knox and the Scots it was all the most terrifying experience of their lives.

"Do you think we shall ever gain our freedom once more?" Balfour, in a low mood, asked his friend. He had an idea that they were near home and off the Fifeshire coast, and to be so near and yet so far was an unbelievable strain. Knox was by this time suffering under an extreme fever, and, though he had a sweating and high temperature, his French masters refused to relieve him at the oars. There was a hospital on board, but only when a galley slave had collapsed, did the *Arguesyne* permit his senseless body to be dragged away. In a twisted way James Balfour felt convinced that, if John Knox had a prophetic gift, it would be shown for certain if he could reveal it, especially when he was in this valley of Achor.

"I know that God will deliver us from bondage," John answered with an authority in his tone, as he raised his weary frame from the oar during a brief respite when the ship anchored off their beloved native land. He almost breathed her freedom and the tang of the heather hills made him sick with longing. His shoulders shook with the ague and his bleary, red-rimmed, eyes strained to discern recognisable landmarks. A relatively light east coast haar blurred the outline of the land. But James Balfour's eyes were sharper and he suddenly pointed excitedly.

"There, John, can you recognise it?"

"I ken it well," murmured Knox weakly, following his outstretched finger to where an unmistakable Kirk spire poked its proud top through the mist, appearing like a beacon of hope to the two men." For I see the steeple of St. Andrews Parish Church, where I first preached a sermon and glorified God, and I know that I will not die till I have preached and glorified the name of God again in the same place."

His features, emaciated by his months of slavery, had taken on the set look of an Old Testament prophet. His thoughts had dwelt during many dark nights on the life of suffering of Jeremiah, the weeping prophet, whom he most admired in the panoply of God's heroes." Even though we are forgotten galley slaves, forsairs, as they call us, abused and treated like cattle, one day it will be different, James Balfour, I promise you on the Word of God!"

Knox felt the exhilaration, which came from the source of being convinced unwaveringly that he was the chosen instrument of the Lord, who would not put him aside till his purpose was fulfilled in him." The interests of religion were advanced in Bible times by the exile of Joseph, Daniel and Moses, you will recall?" John Knox turned and his blue-grey eyes bored into those of Balfour. The latter's faith was uplifted for a moment. Little did Knox foresee that at the end James Balfour would desert the faith of Christ and die a violent death in a foreign land. Like all men, the prophet of God was limited in his knowledge.

A day later, still off the Fife coast, John was to be comforted by an event, symbolical in itself, that the enemy did not have the upper hand always. The fleet had sailed down the coast until they reached the island of St. Colm's Inch and the picturesque village of Cramond near Scotland's capital. A lookout announced a warning that an English squadron was in sight. A panic seized the French, who had been so confident up till then. The *comite* on board became so alarmed that his lash whipped out over the backs of the galley slaves, but merely as a threat to provoke them into instant action. It was vital that even oarsmen be in the best condition possible.

The weather was calm and the day fair, so that they skimmed over the waves. But the English vessel was much swifter, and soon gained on them. They came within range of their cannon off Inch Colm's sandy spit.

A furious cannonade followed them, while the galley slaves, restricted by their heavy chains, could only say their prayers, for, if fatally hit, they would inevitably go down with their ship. Eventually, being outgunned, the French vessels started to draw off, even though one English vessel had taken fire. But, as they withdrew, one French ship which Knox had already noticed was that bit grander in bulk, and more numerous in guns, and crew, had suddenly gone aground on a rock near Inch Colm through the sheer negligence of the crew.

The name of *The Cardinal* adorned its prow, and it flew a scarlet red ensign along with the blue and white fleur-de-lis. Even as the Scots watched fascinated, one of France's fairest vessels foundered and became stranded. Knox and the other slaves were unable to resist a resounding cheer at the disaster which had befallen the enemy ship. *The Cardinal* without doubt would fall into the hands of the English. This lifted their spirits more than any medicine, for they had come to hate all things French, not just their Roman Catholicism.

"God is showing that the land of Scotland will bear no Cardinals!" John Knox shouted out in triumph to all who would hear. His sardonic words were a welcome release from the internal as well as the external sufferings of himself and his compatriots. The Cardinal was stuck fast, and its crew could be seen throwing themselves in panic overboard, as the English fired flaming arrows onto her deck in a relentless hail.

Soon The Cardinal was completely ablaze, and the English vessels contented themselves with ringing her in a victory formation, while the Notre Dame and the rest of the fleet retreated in abject depression to the shelter of Inch Colm. To the dismay of the galley slaves, the Captains and crew abandoned their ships, carrying all the muskets they had, and even wheeling their cannon onto land.

There they dragged these guns to a nearby fort in French hands, where they clearly intended to make a stand against the English forces. Knox was almost overwhelmingly tempted to pray for deliverance by the Protestants of England, for it was to England, which had seen the birth of the Protestant Reformation, that his beloved land must look to for salvation from the French oppression. But he knew in his spirit-man that the time for their release was not yet. His body shrank and shuddered, however, when sure enough the English vessels made no sign of pursuit.

The French had had a fright, and John was not long in noticing that their captors' behaviour was not so arrogant now. The Reformer caught an occasional glimpse of the Captain or Patron, and his lieutenant, the Arguesyne, strutting nervously along the bridge. A sharp lookout was kept for the English ensign of St. George.

When the September winds began to blow, John Knox's fever began to abate. But a painful wrench on his strained emotions was soon to hit him, when the French commander decided to separate the fleet, with some ships remaining to stay on guard off Scotland, and the others to return to winter in Rouen. They also separated the oarsmen. The weaker ones were to be taken back to recuperate in France for the winter months, at which time the mountainous seas made sailing hazardous for the open galleys. When the comite sent strong sailors down to unshackle their fetters and remove some to a different galley, they laid forceful hands on Knox. He had some last words of affection and encouragement for the others.

"We are to be separated in the body, but not in the spirit. The Lord God Almighty is our gracious commander and not the Captain of this vessel. He will see us and our cause through to the end. The counsel of Satan has been to stop the wholesome wind of Christ's Evangel from blowing upon the hearts of men. Be not concerned for me. Our merciful Father has here provided some rest for me in the midst of these tempestuous storms, which winter is beginning to arouse. I will pray for you."

A last longing handshake between the comrades was wrenched apart, when the preacher was hauled away by the sailors. But it was really a time of rest and recuperation for Knox on board his ship anchored upstream on the Seine in Rouen harbour. This time he had a much closer look at his surroundings than previously.

The harbour teemed with people of every kind. Rouen was a centre of great trade in cloth, foodstuffs, and implements. Once more his eyes were drawn to the famous Tower of Rouen Cathedral, the flamboyant *Tour de Beure*, raised from the subscriptions of those who had purchased false indulgences to allow them to eat butter during Lent. He grimaced to himself at the misguided attempts to please God and placate their own uninstructed consciences. Surely God had already forgiven them and accepted all who had faith in Christ?

It was at this time that the Scots were taken aback by the laxity which their French taskmasters now had towards them. They had not long tied up in Rouen Harbour, when they had bunches of hay, rye grass, and thin branches thrown down amongst them onto the deck.

"If you will not attend the Mass, sing the *Salve, Regina* and believe the true Faith, you Scottish heretics, at least you can earn a living and add to your upkeep." The *comite* growled at them." These are the materials to make baskets and mats, and, if they are good enough, they can be sold to the local people in the harbour market for a few francs." His cynical accent grated in Knox's ears. "If we have to pay for provisions for your whole winter's quarters here, you may be sure that it will be just ship's biscuits, and some of our worst, moulded, meal! But if you earn many francs, your diet will improve, I promise you! You have my word." Knox doubted if his word had the slightest value.

But most of the oarsmen were eager to accept his offer, sick of the miserable, continuous fare of dry biscuits, beans, and oil, often covered with mould and holed by weevils. Knox made a sign to the comite that he wished to speak with him.

"I am grateful for your offer to supplement our fare, but I would want to request paper, pen, and ink to write down some of my beliefs and thoughts. I would be most thankful to God for this."

The *comite* stared at him askance and tapped his head, as he smiled over at some of the sailors. He looked closely at Knox again to see if he was serious, but, nevertheless, after a long, searching, gaze, turned away to converse with the *Arguesyne*, the vessel's lieutenant. Later, to the preacher's surprise, parchment, a quill pen, and a rather chalky ink in a bottle were brought to him. His prayers had been answered, he shouldn't have been surprised.

It was vital, he had decided, that he pen a *Confession of Faith*, faithful to the Bible, for the fledgling Protestant Faith, just as Martin Luther had set out his *Ninety Five Articles* pinned to the door of Wittenberg Cathedral. He had to prepare for the future, for when he assuredly would return to his native land. Knox longed for the winds of Scotland, her trees, her hills, the villages and hamlets of East Lothian and its long, brown, fields, and not least the good, strong, Scots, accents. Little did he know that his exile would be long. How he hated the French posturings and arrogance! The spire of Rouen Cathedral could not be compared in his mind with the memory of the square tower of St. Mary's in Haddington, supporting its open-crown spire so alike to St. Giles in Edinburgh. St. Mary's had been known for long as the *"Lamp of Lothian"* , though he knew, if truth be told, that it really referred to the ancient Abbey nearby, commemorated by a hamlet still, where light and truth once shone forth prior to the corruption that had set in.

So, while his fellows busied themselves in the construction of mats and baskets, Knox applied himself with furrowed brow to compose *Confession of Faith*, in which were set out the centrality of faith in Christ alone without works of penance, the Bible as God's inspired Word without adding the traditions of men, the blasphemy of images and idolatry, and the falsehood of the doctrines of the Mass and the Papacy. One day Scotland would be independent of Rome and the Pope. The tree must be cut down, so that the rooks could not settle in its branches. It was his conviction that one Mass was more dangerous than a thousand enemies.

The whole atmosphere on board the vessels in Port had changed, and Knox was allowed to write away unhindered. In all honesty the French regarded the Scots preacher as slightly mad, but he was little worried by it. Was not the prophet Jeremiah thought to be insane, when he walked through the streets of ancient Israel with a heavy yoke over his shoulders? Amazingly, one day another missive reached Knox. It had already been opened and examined firstly by the ship's Captain of course, who was most disappointed that it was not a plan to audaciously escape, but it was merely a Theological Treatise that baffled him with its deep Biblical terms.

What warmed Knox's heart, apart from the deep satisfaction with its contents, which were on justification by faith, was that its author, his old friend, Henry Balnaves of Halhill, was still alive and well, imprisoned in Rouen Castle. There the Fife lawyer, like Knox, had been afforded the freedom to transcribe his thoughts and had turned to Theological exposition. Knox found it a very well-balanced Treatise and annotated it in the margins, as well as dividing it into Chapters. His spirit was uplifted by Balnaves' work, and he tried to communicate with all his might that encouragement to his companions.

Some time later a second letter reached him. This time for some reason inexplicably it had not been opened, probably because, he surmised, the bored French thought it was another religious tract. This was most fortunate, and he saw the hand of God in it, for it was from the four Scots imprisoned on the Abbey fortress of Mont St. Michel. They were chafing over their close confinement in their island prison. Again Knox marvelled at the freedom to write given to them.

It was just as well that their French captors were not conversant with the broad Scots, for the four sought his advice on whether they should attempt to escape or not. Should they trust that in God's due time they would be released? The French, whether in the galleys or prisons at St. Michel, Brest, or Cherbourg, had indeed relaxed their restrictions, allowing the prisoners to communicate, confident that escape for these foreigners, so far from home, was impossible.

As he pondered over his reply, happy once more that responsibility was thrown upon him, as the sense of leadership of men had grown on him, John Knox was sure that, if escape was possible, it should be taken, and he signified so to them. God's sovereign will would be effected, but the Lord expected his servants to play an active part. So in his reply he recommended that they should do what they could, on condition they kill no one. The assassination of Cardinal Beaton was a just retribution for the evil martyrdom of George Wishart, whose loving, strong, features still appeared before Knox's eyes, especially when the sweat and pain were greatest at the oar. But this was a different matter. He felt stimulated to continue with the difficult Confession of Faith.

Winter had now arrived, and the harsh winds from the Atlantic swept inland, but the Scots were comparatively warm, protected from the storms, sheltered up the Seine.

John's health had somewhat recovered. Meanwhile Mont St. Michel saw the fierce-tempered Peter Carmichael becoming more and more strained in his nerves, as he continually stared moodily out of his cell window across the mudflats towards the green Normandy countryside. The broad flats were yet bare sand and mud, before the swiftly-flowing tide arose over them. These flats were treacherous for any late traveller to the Abbey Mount.

"Ye ken, when I first clapped my eyes on this great lump of rock and saw the spires of their Benedictine Abbey pointing out of the sea, my heart missed a beat. Aye, it did richt enough! But now the loneliness of this island of rock has gripped me like ice, and my heart longs for the bonnie Lomond Hills and the Howe o' Fife!" Grange's youthful face gazed over sympathetically into that of the older man.

"Aye, I too am sick of this rock, and these Benedictines with their silent ways! I almost welcome the guards and the clatter of their weapons and feet on the cobblestones, and even, God forgive me, their swearing! If God had meant us not to speak and for Nature to be silent, why did He give us songs to sing and birds to listen to?"

"The beat of the Ocean's waves on these walls outside day after day rings in my ears, even in my mind! It's driving me mad! We are going to die here, I tell you! How could God allow such a sad ending to all our hopes for Scotland's Reformation?" Carmichael's bitterness seemed to seep through the whole prison cell.

"Let us not abandon hope, Carmichael!" pleaded John Leslie." I gathered from one of the guards, who has a smattering of English, that Christmas Day is almost upon us, and something tells me that this is our opportunity to make our escape, I don't know how."

Now it happened that there was a strange half- Spanish boy who brought their food and who was of a garrulous nature, and who began to show a real friendliness. He had an over-excitable spirit, and he would roll his eyes around wildly, as his mind switched from one subject to another, so that the Scots did not trust this strange boy. But he did not seem to help them. Kirkcaldy of Grange alone of the four attended the Royal Court at Edinburgh and Stirling, where that language was commonly in use. The lad gabbled away to him, while delivering to them their stale and boring fare, and the other three watched as Kirkcaldy's features registered his fascinated interest in the boy's words. They heard the words 'Festa' and 'Epiphania'

At last he turned to his compatriots.

"You are hardly going to credit this? The lad says that the Feast of Epiphany, or the Twelfth Night since the birth of our Lord, is very close, and on that night the guards get very drunk! He's sure that if we truly want to escape, Epiphany is the perfect time!"

"But what good is that to us, even if the whole of Mont St. Michel is drunk?" Carmichael snapped angrily.

"The thing is, Peter, that Hernando - that's his name, he is half-Spanish, half-French - can steal the key to our cell, and lead us over the salt flats. He kens when the tide is out."

"I don't know," muttered Robert Leslie." I don't trust the boy He is a half breed. I think he is unstable."

"I think so also, but Hernando tells me that his French father is a cruel man, and his Spanish mother has died. So he has very little love for France and the French. He will surely guide us across the Normandy countryside. He is our only hope!"

"Aye, I miss the yorlin's early morning song and the taste of the hindberries in late summer," said William Leslie longingly." Not to forget the pipin' o' the throstlecock." His Scots' soul was filled with nostalgia.

"If we gain our freedom, there will be time enough to listen tae a thousand birdies!" retorted Carmichael." Epiphany is the manifestation of our Blessed Lord to the *Magi* from the East, and a sacred occasion! But it seems that the Roman Church is as corrupt over here as it is in Scotland. For I have seen muckle examples of their drunkenness here," he said scornfully." The common people laugh at the clergy."

"Perhaps the invisible Deity will make His servants invisible?" Robert Leslie's attempt at humour met with a silent response.

"Unbelief will open no doors, Leslie. Only hope and faith will do that. We maun stand together, Robert, and need no worldly jesting."

But the doors did open a few weeks later when the Holy Feast of Epiphany saw the guards celebrating in their usual carousels. The young Hernando with a scarcely-disguised excitement came with their evening meal one day and then produced the key. The sound of carousing could be clearly heard resounding round the Abbey confines, making a mockery of its sacred purpose. To the prisoners the imposing monastic solitude of Mont St. Michel seemed irretrievably broken. They wondered why the monks did not put a stop to such drunken behaviour. The lad had brought with him a whole bundle of what looked like rags in a bag. He had obviously the confidence of the guards, whose minds were too stupefied to suspect anything anyway. He threw them down, and pointed to the Scots, speaking volubly.

"He is saying that we have to dress in these clothes to be disguised as beggars," said Kirkcaldy of Grange.

"I still don't trust this madcap boy further than I could throw a farthing." Robert Leslie expressed his continuing unease.

"Remember Master Knox's words, Leslie! Don't be afraid. Such fears proceed not from God's Spirit, but only from a blind love of self. A good enterprise should never be stopped through a fear of the consequences, which are entirely in the hands of God. He also said that we have to avoid any killing. We have only to overcome the guards, and they are certainly drunk by now." Leslie was much more likely to trust the advice of Kirkcaldy of Grange than that of Carmichael. It was a clear moonlit night, which boded ill for their escape through the Abbey confines and across the treacherous causeway

Quickly they assumed the beggars' clothing and silently unlocked the cell door. The drunken singing had by now died down, and subdued, slurred, mouthing of favourite

French ditties could be heard, as they tip-toed into the *Salle des Gardes*. The four could not believe the utter helplessness of the soldiers. They were totally inebriated, and it was a simple matter of tying them up and bundling them into the guardroom. When the monks arrived in the morning, they would simply conclude that the guard had over-indulged and were sleeping it off.

Guided by Hernando, the escapees slipped through the Aumonerie, the Gothic vaulted hall with a central row of pillars, which served as a dining room and almonry for distributing to the poor. Passing the open shaft by which provisions were hauled up to the refectory, they glided down the ninety steps of the *Grande Degne*. They scarcely stopped, even for the superb view of this combination of natural and man-made beauty in the moonlit scene below. Then, with all-out speed they ran for their lives along the Grande Rue, expecting an alarm cry any second, out through the *Porte de L'Avancee* and the *Porte de Roi*, this time without the slightest glance up at the carved shells and salmon, and out into the exposed causeway.

Freedom at last, was their inner cry. Dressed as beggars, they would avoid suspicion, as mendicants were common throughout Europe. Hernando and even Kirkcaldy of Grange would make any communications necessary, as they made their careful way across this rural part of Normandy towards a seaport. Prayerfully, there they would throw off their disguise and obtain a trading vessel for England or even Scotland. When countries were on a war footing, merchants still carried on their personal dealings and transactions. As for the boy, Kirkcaldy told the others that he longed to journey to Spain, his mother's homeland.

Meanwhile, on board the *Notre Dame* still esconced snugly in Rouen harbour, Knox continued to endure the saying of the Mass on stated occasions, though his whole conscience revolted against what he saw as its false teaching. He rejoiced that the Lord Jesus Christ had given his precious life once at Calvary. When the *Salve, Regina* was sung on Saturday nights in adoration of Mary, Knox alone adored the Christ, who died for him. All the Scots slaves doggedly continued to deliberately cover their heads with their hoods. His beard, which had been shaved and his head close-cropped when first chained to the oar over a year and a half before, had grown again, but not near the eighteen inches he had been proud of at St. Andrews.

Though still weak from periodic bouts of fever, and his constitution not as strong as many of his companions at the oars, many of whom were thieves and murderers, yet his spirit within remained unbroken and he clung to the unalterable conviction that he was the chosen instrument of God. The Lord would not put him aside until his purpose was fulfilled in this world of sin. By now the French had given up trying to convert any of the Scots back to the ways of the Church of Rome. Even the whole situation of exile, seemingly under the grinding heel of the enemy, made him feel that they were as the children of Israel in slavery in Egypt, and caused him one day to write in his journal.

"These are things that appear to be of no great importance, and yet if we rightly consider, they express the same obedience that God required of his people, Israel, when they were carried away to Babylon."

He detested the close presence of the criminal element around him, who were hardened to the Gospel as well as the harsh toil. He prayed continually for Scotland and the Revolution of religion there, groaning to himself in the darkness of night, as he beseeched God for his faithful friend, Balnaves, shut in Rouen Castle, visible through the January mist, which enveloped the town.

Knox had served his second spell on the high seas off Scotland's coast, and he sensed that mighty things were happening in his homeland, as the English and French battled for control. He saw French troops being ferried ashore onto the Lothian and Fife coast, but naturally information was not being volunteered to the galley slaves, who were treated as if they were automatons. Knox was content to wait God's time to be free and continued laboriously over his annotation of the Treatise by Balnaves.

He gathered from a letter that the Scots lawyer had been singled out for Theological examination by special, well known, experienced Roman Catholic Theologians of France. They had debated with Balnaves, who had confounded the Catholic clerics with his sharp answers. He stood firmly for Protestant doctrine until they finally left him alone in their frustration. Knox rejoiced, when he read it, and penned a note of praise to his compatriot. He took the opportunity too to scribble a note to those at Mont St. Michel, whom he had not heard from for some time. Sometimes the French delivered the epistles, sometimes they didn't.

"Some of us the Lord will liberate by one means or another; others must abide for a season upon His good pleasure," he wrote to cheer their hearts.

In fact at that very moment a great search was being made of the whole Province of Normandy for the four escapees, as in freezing winter weather they hid in forests and caves, and slept in ruined farmhouses and haylofts, as soldiers passed closely by. They suffered great weariness, pain, and hunger, seizing what livestock they could, erratically guided by the strange laddie. Paradoxically, it was the equable Leslies who began to lose faith and to curse God, while the normally hot-tempered Peter Carmichael revealed a rock-like faith. Such was human nature.

"Ach, damn this whole escapade! This is absolute misery! Where is the God we are supposed to believe in?" William Leslie complained bitterly, shivering in his meagre clothing." This wee rascal is deliberately leading us astray!"

"Have faith in the Lord, Leslie. We will soon reach the coast, and take ship either for the Low Countries or England," Carmichael retorted sharply.

But, ironically, Leslie's words were fulfilled that night, as they slept fitfully in a cold, dark, wood near the coast, and found in the morning that the boy, Hernando, had disappeared with the money Grange had hidden in his coat lining, when first imprisoned.

"He has gone, the laddie, and my purse with him! But what I fear is that he will describe us to the authorities and betray us. I suggest that we divide up and go our different ways, and even change garments, if we can steal some." Carmichael's words were sound, and without argument they agreed to separate. Secretly Kirkcaldy was glad, for a spirit of bitterness had overcome the Leslie brothers. He thought of the darkness that had inexplicably enveloped King Saul of Israel. He had become yesterday's man. Who could search the depths of the soul of man? William Kirkcaldy had seen too much of the corrupt nature of some of Scotland's self-seeking noblemen to fall into cynicism. But just now he preferred the dependable strength of Carmichael to support him.

Sure enough, Kirkcaldy and Carmichael made it to the Port of Le Conquet, still dressed in their beggars' garments, where they attempted to pass themselves off as poor sailors. Helped by Grange's French, the two travelled from Port to Port for thirteen weeks, until they took a vessel trading to the west of England. The Leslies reached Rouen too, but though they survived, nothing was heard of them again, and they were like Demas, lost to the Protestant cause, if not to the cause of Christ. Years later rumour filtered through that they had left the faith and lived selfish lives. But those who were faithful out of the St. Andrews garrison were to meet their beloved chaplain again.

"*Arranque! Arranque!*" The dreaded words sounded out like a whiplash. The command to row faster still echoed in Knox's ears, even though the fleet had been in Rouen harbour for two months. The raucous, international, language of the high seas, the bullying, the taunting, and the insults were continually present.

"You heretic scum, you blasphemers of our Lady, you are content and happy enough here, safe in harbour, weaving your stupid, little, baskets and mats, which the even stupider people are willing to buy from you. But be sure of this, the spring will come round again, and then you will know the weight of the oar and the lash! How many of you will survive this time, and how many will end up being thrown overboard as useless carcasses? Be sure that you will pay for blaspheming the Holy Virgin and the divine, sacred, host, you dogs!"

The eyes of the French quartermaster resembled dark arrows directed at John Knox in particular, full of spiteful and ignorant bigotry. The Scot tried to ignore him and concentrate on his writing. He refused to let his French persecutors think that they were trampling on the Scots, and, most of all, crushing the true faith. One day the Lord would vindicate His Word, and trample on his enemies. He did not seek martyrdom but victory, so he bore it stoically, when the *comite* kicked him viciously and remarked sarcastically to another something about 'the crazy scribbler'.

'*There are two kinds of vocation,*' Knox wrote down meticulously, summarizing one of the chapters in Balnaves' Treatise.' *One called by God, as with the apostles and prophets, without the authority of man, and another, where one man calls another,* as Paul called Timothy and Titus to be bishops.' Aye, he agreed with the Theology of Balnaves. The long periods of loneliness, dependant on the Lord alone, had added a steel to his character that was needed. It was with a firm feeling, therefore, of God's Sovereign plan rather than surprise that the news came that some of the prisoners were to be exchanged for Frenchmen in the hands of the English.

Joy flooded the hearts of the Scots. Their liberation had come. But their hopes were dashed, as January passed without their shackles being removed. Hope deferred made the heart sick. Yet one day in February it was all the more welcome, when the *Notre Dame*'s Captain addressed the crew through an interpreter.

"I have good news for all among you who are Scottish, for a Treaty has been signed at Boulogne with the English, and hostilities have ceased. The English have agreed to withdraw from your country, you will be happy to know." His eyes were blank to hide his real feelings." But the best news of all is that your beautiful little Princess Mary has married our young Dauphine at a great ceremony in Paris! Scotland and France are now one country! You should be grateful for this inestimable privilege! Our Dauphine leaps for blitheness, they say. As a seal of our Union and of our good favour, I have agreed to exchange some of you heretics for good, worthy, Frenchmen, who are in the hands of these English pigs!"

In the midst of the excitement and joy at leaving this hellhole, Knox's heart sank at the terrible prospect of a marriage between the future crowned heads of France and Scotland. He had a cold premonition that a time would come when the Princess Mary of Scotland would be a thorn in his side and that of the Reformers. If the French Captain had expected the Scots to greet his announcement with a response of joy, he was soon disabused, as a sully, stony, stare of distrust met him. Most found it hard to believe, after so long at the oars. Yet the Captain's words were borne out as true shortly after, when John Knox and Alexander Clerk of Balbirnie were freed along with several others. The rest would be freed later.

As they were bustled ashore, Knox turned his head to gaze back anxiously to where his friend, James Balfour, who had been his faithful companion through many, dark, months, still sat chained to his bench oar. A silent, caring, message passed between their eyes. They would meet again back in Scotland, but no longer as friends in deepest adversity but as bitterest enemies, for Sir James Balfour, as he was to become, would not remain faithful to God. John Knox would have been grateful for the prophetic gift was not his then. He did not know that James Balfour was to become a blasphemer back in Edinburgh, governed only by ambition. At that moment his heart was taken up with gratitude to God for his freedom from a life of terrible slavery. His spirit sang and his soul looked forward in eager anticipation to all that the Lord would lead him into and do for him in His Divine Plan.

MINISTRY IN ENGLAND

W hen John and the other Scots returned to England, they found the Reformation in a good state if a little precarious in its future and that it was with the death of Henry VIII that their liberation was due to the young, precocious, committedly Protestant, King Edward VI. But it was Archbishop Thomas Cranmer, who was the key to the future of the fledgling faith, the man who had played the cautious cleric during the treacherous times of the tyrant Henry, when sincere Christians with a desire for the purity of the Gospel trode a narrow line with the madness of the King. Cranmer sent for Knox immediately on his landing, though the Scot was still suffering from his privations, having lost much weight, but he brushed aside any offerings of rest above the barest necessary. He determined that he would talk little during the rest of his life about his sufferings aboard the French galley, for what was it really for a disciple of Christ, who had promised nothing else?

He could not but be impressed by the tradition of centuries offered by Canterbury, the ancient Saxon capital of Kent, on the river Stour, which the Romans had named *Durovernum Cantiacorum*, but had long since changed to *Cantwarabyrig,* the old English fortress of the men of Kent. This was no other than where King Ethelbert almost one thousand years before had welcomed Augustine's mission from Rome to England. Were the effects of that mission for good or for bad, Knox wondered? The minute he met Thomas Cranmer, he had a good impression of a Godly, sincere, man, whose serious features yet displayed an uncertainty and lack of the fire and power, which he himself had now attained through the strength of God. Would a spell in the galleys have broken Cranmer? John Knox dismissed the unworthy thought as soon as he conceived it. Archbishop Thomas Cranmer was after all, the first Protestant Archbishop of Canterbury, adviser to King Henry VIII and now the youthful Edward VI.

"Ah, Master John Knox, welcome in Christ's Name to you at last! I have heard so much of your brave ministry in St. Andrews before your sinful betrayal with your compatriots for the Reformation in Scotland! How much you must have suffered at the galley oars?"
"The Lord is able," answered Knox tersely, lowering his head, and keeping his own silence.
"I understand," replied Cranmer sympathetically, after a significant pause." But what is Scotland's loss is England's gain, at least for the moment. Master Knox, we are desperately in need of educated ministers all across land! The clergy in England, it is sad to say, are generally ignorant and sunk in superstition. Earnest preachers must be sent forth immediately. I and the Privy Council wish you to be one of those to preach sound doctrines in the remotest parts of the Kingdom." Archbishop Cranmer stopped, and closely scrutinized Knox's reaction.

"The Lord has surely called me to preach, but just where that would be?" responded Knox cautiously. He was wary of falling from one bad situation into another by an unwise move, but he did realise that one of Scotland's great hopes was England.

"I am admittedly proficient in Latin, Greek, and French, but since when did education qualify a man in the service of the Lord?" The Englishman winced under his plain speaking but he perceived and valued the Scot's sterling qualities. Cranmer was essentially a scholar who lacked a single-mindedness and a strong, fanatical, spirit. He obeyed reason rather than instinct, always learning and never ashamed to admit it. Knox saw that Cranmer was a man of a humble spirit, and almost felt ashamed of his words, but not quite.

"I recognise your need for caution, good Knox, and I agree that the gifts and calling of God are without repentance, but as a child I was taught by a marvellous, severe, and even cruel, schoolmaster, and it has not only instilled in me a permanent pliability and even an uncertainty," Here Thomas Cranmer paused and looked around his clerical chamber decorated with murals and tapestries of Biblical and sacred scenes, as if the walls had ears," but also an admiration for an academic knowledge and sound grasp of Theology.

Over twenty years gone by, when the wellsprings of the Reformation were springing up with the teachings of the blessed Martin Luther, I gathered with a group of other scholars at Jesus College in Cambridge to discuss the Theological problems raised by the new way of thinking of Luther's revolt. They called us *'Little Germany'*," he laughed lightly, but became deadly serious again." Among them was William Tyndale." They were both silent, as they remembered the great Reformer's terrible sacrifice for truth among the flames in Belgium." So it is that I have invited such as Peter Martyr and Martin Bucer of Strasbourg with others from Germany and placed them as Protestant professors at Oxford and Cambridge." Under the young King Edward England had indeed become a magnet for foreign Theologians. All Knox's doubts were beginning to dissolve under Cranmer's persuasive power.

"I have never sought high office, Master Cranmer, but I believe God equips his servant and I know that there is a battle ahead with many enemies and many dangers."

"Thomas Cromwell, my predecessor, once told me that the Popish knaves would have my eyes and cut my throat before I could do something about it. Oh, well, it hasn't happened yet," he concluded with a shrug. It was the nearest Cranmer got to an encouragement.

"Where will you send me?" asked Knox, persuaded at last. Secretly he rejoiced at this new door opened to him by the Lord." The French have broken their word, and therefore, I am no longer bound by the vow not to return to Scotland."

"No, it is to Berwick-on-Tweed, our tough, border, garrison, town, that I intend sending you to, near enough to your native land to feel familiar, far enough to be safe." Archbishop Cranmer gazed appealingly at this firebrand Scot, sure that he would be just the person to touch the hearts of the hard, English, garrison, soldiers. Thomas Cranmer not for nothing had alone of the fierce, inconsistent, Henry VIII's advisers retained the King's goodwill. Henry had even foiled three elaborate attempts by his enemies to convict him of serious heresy. The corrupt monarch had been slightly amused by and awed by the incorruptibility of his servant and his clemency towards others in trouble. He cared for the man in front of him too.

"I accept the call, Archbishop Cranmer," Knox was happy, and the other was relieved

It was months later, when, much to his amazement, John Knox's preaching had been attracting large crowds, with many changed by his bold and convincing earnestness, in the tumultuous border town, continually on guard against marauding Scots, that John Knox noticed during his services at Berwick a large lady, who attended regularly at the Lord's Table, served in the Reformed manner, with the elements remaining just the same bread and wine. She was not irregular even on weekdays, and was totally intent on his sermons. Her demeanour was so very serious, not a smile shown, as if hanging on his very thoughts, afraid to miss some teaching or a vital pearl of truth.

She seemed to drink in the Reformed doctrines thirstily which Knox expounded fearlessly, disowning the Papacy and its unscriptural claims, encouraged by the outspoken words of the young Protestant King, Edward VI, and his right hand man, Archbishop Thomas Cranmer, though he detected in Cranmer just a little weakness and indecisiveness. The situation required no compromise with Rome. No piece of religious plaster must be stuck over the gaping wound that claimed to be Christendom. It must be sliced off like branches, so that the rooks could not roost in them.

"All worship of God that has been invented by man, and not commanded by God, is idolatry!" he thundered from the tiny pulpit in the small parish Church of Berwick, and even the battle-hardened soldiers of the garrison blinked." What a blasphemy that

Christ's sacrifice can be repeated by a priest saying words! Vain trifles profane our Sacrament. Should the Mass not be used to pray that our toothache be taken away, or our oxen should not be sick?" His invective was thick with irony." In the Papistical mass the congregation gets nothing but the priest's duckings, noddings, crossings, turnings, and upliftings, which are only a profanation by the devil of the Lord's true Supper. Now duck, nod, cross, as much as you like, they are nothing but your own inventions! What we need is the light, grace, and purity of the Holy Spirit!" Bishop Tunstall of Durham, who had come to hear this wild newcomer, winced visibly. Cuthbert Tunstall was a dissembler and hedge-sitter, who preferred compromise and reconciliation with the religion of Rome, and not confrontation. Knox now turned his attention back to the congregation present.

"Christ did not offer us the sacrament as spectators, but for all to eat and drink! What comfort that Church has taken from us, that the mere sight of it should be considered sufficient! Where there is no sacrifice, there are no priests with the power to sacrifice. All true Christians are Kings and Priests, a Royal Priesthood, a holy nation, and daily offer themselves a living sacrifice to God, which He finds most acceptable, the crucifixion of our selfish desires!" Even amongst the irreligious as well as those committed to the new faith, there were gasps of amazement at the boldness of his words." We are justified by faith, and faith alone!" His strident Scots tongue rang out across the north English congregation, making a deep impression.

But at the sermon's end he sought out the Lady's identity. He found out that she was Mrs. Elizabeth Bowes, the wife of the Captain of Norham Castle, Sir Richard Bowes. Norham Castle stood nearby high on the banks of the lovely Tweed. In fact he was met by the Lady herself waiting after service one Sunday, anxious to meet him, but clearly nervous. Her tone faltered, breathing quickly, as she introduced herself.

"Good Master Knox, would you permit me to introduce myself and to say how blessed it is to hear the riches of the Gospel expounded so clearly! I am Elizabeth Bowes, and my husband is Captain Richard Bowes, Lord of Norham Castle yonder. He has much influence and many men, but, I'm afraid, has little conviction of the work that is being done by God in England now. My brother-in-law is Sir Robert Bowes, Warden of the Marches. I am the co-heiress of Roger Aske of Aske." The Scot was confused by her presence, and when she curtsied to him and held out her hand to him, he honestly was a little intimidated by this large woman with the serious, fixed, gaze, as if she was trying to draw out of him what her very soul vitally needed. But yet he was strangely drawn to her.

"The praise of God is my chief intent, Madam, but it was said of Jesus that he grew in favour with God and man, so it is heartening to hear you say so." If he had felt a little tension at first, John Knox now felt positively scared by her next words.

"How heartening it would be, if you would accept my invitation to come and preach to my family in Norham Castle. I have fifteen children." John Knox drew in his breath sharply." And I should love all of them to hear the life-giving words of the Protestant faith." But here she hesitated, and a cloud descended on her broad features, and her great bosom sagged." My husband, Richard, is solely concerned with the safeguarding of the frontier against the Scots, so that he may not take kindly to you. He is also convinced of the rightness of Roman Catholicism, and sees no reason for changing from the old ways. He disapproves of my attending your services, though he has not said so openly, and may regard you as a heretic." Her face was full of apology. Knox felt sorry.

"Be not concerned, Madame Bowes, for that would be no new thing to me," replied Knox, with an inner amusement almost. A picture of the Notre Dame arose in his mind, of his pain-racked, slavery at the oars. Involuntarily he looked down at his hands, on which the callouses, which followed the agonising blisters, remained still.

He said nothing, but he could yet hear the dreaded command, 'Arranque! Arranque!' followed by the ever-threatening crack of the whip. But he was now more at ease with this great lady, when he realised her great sincerity of spirit and seeking after the things of God.

"I am not come to bring peace but a sword, said our Lord, and to divide apart father and mother, brother and sister. Of two men at the plough, one will be taken, the other left. I would be most pleased to come out to Norham Castle on the invitation of your husband, Captain Bowes. It is to preach the Gospel to whomever that I am sent here. I hope that I do not have to kiss every one of your fifteen children, Madame Bowes! One will be sufficient." He allowed himself a touch of humour in an attempt to relax this so serious woman. He had found that the sharp-edged, humour in this North of England, as well as their rough accents, was not dissimilar to those of the Scots.

Not long afterwards the invite came, and John rode in a little trepidation the half dozen miles along the banks of the magnificent, rolling, sparkling, Tweed, rich in salmon and sea trout. The Castle stood on a knoll of a typical motte and bailey kind built by the Normans in a country still largely inhabited by Angles, Saxons, and Jutes at the time as a defensive domain. The Scot was wary of his possible reception, remembering their betrayal in St. Andrews. Sure enough, it was clear that Mrs. Bowes had been the sole influence in inviting the Scots preacher, and that it was against the wishes of her husband, who was surly and suspicious. Captain Richard Bowes was a military man essentially, short and peremptory in manner. Knox felt unmistakably then the hostile spirit emanating from the Englishman. John was sure he was fated to meet such men, and was reminded of the overbearing Governor of Berwick, who had not been over welcoming, but had to obey Cranmer's instructions.

"My spouse tells me, Scotsman, that you are preaching some fiery sermons, and bringing some new doctrines! I must tell you that I am for the old ways and the old religion. What has been good enough up till now is good enough for me! The intrigues of the Court in London, with their fops and gossips, who change their clothes and their opinions with the day of the week, are not for me, and the teachings of the hair brained theologians of Oxford and Cambridge are all far away, and so I leave the theological wranglings to others. Yet I do not care for heresy," he glanced sharply at Knox," Scottish heresy, or any other heresy, or for impertinent intruders." He hesitated, and thought better of pursuing it further, having already gone too far for John Knox's irritated spirit.

The nobleman turned to formally introduce two others, men of a noble and proud demeanour also." These are my brothers, who are dining with me and asked to meet you, Sir Ralph Bowes of Streatham Castle and Sir Robert, Warden of the Marches." The men stared with curiosity at the preacher, whose reputation had reached all parts of the north country by now for changing the manners and language of the Berwick garrison so much for the better that attendances at worship and preachings had increased to overflowing. Hard-bitten soldiers are touched by down-to-earth faith.

"Sir Ralph was knighted at the Battle of Flodden, a disaster for you Scots!" Captain Bowes gazed keenly at John Knox, clearly trying to stir up antagonistic feelings in the Scot's patriotic soul. Paradoxically, John saw a sympathetic light in the eyes of Sir Ralph, who had won his spurs on the field of Scotland's tragedy.

"The Scots should have won, Master Knox, they were superior in numbers and artillery. In battles of the past it was the victory of the arrow which won for England, but at Flodden field the English archers were lost to the action as soon as the armies became locked in conflict. It was the great eighteen foot German pike, normally so cumbersome, that led to the Scots defeat against our powerful, English, brownbill, as well as the foolhardy impetuosity of your brave, foolish, King James. If he had but remained on the heights of the hill nearby and not allowed himself to be taken in a rear action across the Twizel Bridge, who knows what would have happened?" The English knight spread his hands in a gesture of despair and resignation." What a slaughter, and so meaningless!" His sorrow was genuine and impressed Knox.

"Aye, Flodden Field was Scotland's graveyard," sighed Knox sadly. He did not say that his own father had died there." Men propose, but God disposes. Jamie the Fourth, ten Earls, three Bishops, eleven Barons, the Archbishop of St. Andrews, and other eminent men of God, Scotland's Treasurer, sixty eight knights and gentlemen, as well as ten thousand of Scotland's bravest blood, all gone to meet their Creator! But our King was warned by a prophet of God beforehand that he was not prepared and that disaster would follow, as night follows day. He chose to neglect the words of the prophet of God. Dark ends always happen to those who do not heed the voice of God. The Psalmist tells us that the secret of the Lord is with them that fear Him. They shall keep His Covenant." The mantle of the prophet seemed to have fallen on the stocky frame of the Scot and the steeliness in his voice now imparted itself to the entire Bowes family, who were quieted in the presence of a superior spirit.

Captain Bowes and his brothers looked askance at this strange Scotsman. Against the desires of their hearts they found that he commanded their respect. He had magnetism about him and exuded an authority, which drew their fascinated attention. But first Richard Bowes shared a sad post mortem to the terrible Battle.

"Lord Dacre found the body of your King of Scots on the field. It was carried here to Berwick town and embalmed, as befits a King. We honour royalty and nobility here, you should understand, no matter the nationality, my fiery Scotsman."

Captain Bowes bent his thickset eyebrows on this man, whom he secretly regarded as an upstart commoner." King James's body was then taken to Newcastle, and then to London town, where it was buried in the Carthusian monastery at Sheen. Although King James had been excommunicated for the part he played in the death of his father, James III, the Pope gave permission for our King Henry to bury him in St. Paul's Cathedral, --or so they say, for there is no evidence."

He looked at Knox with a spiteful glance." I have heard that when that profligate, Henry, sacked our monasteries for his evil greed, the body of the King of Scots was found lying wrapped in lead in an attic among waste timber and rubbish, or so I was told by my friend, the Earl of Northumberland, and I trust his word." He gave a sarcastic curl to his lips as he said it. Knox controlled his anger and hostility, as they threatened to erupt in his Scottish soul. It was a statesman-like control which was to stand him in good stead in an uncertain future.

But by now Mrs. Elizabeth Bowes was clucking with embarrassment and was ushering them into dine. Before that was an introduction of the fifteen children, and, much to Knox's relief, he was not forced to kiss any of them. As it was, most of her offspring were surly towards the alien Scotsman, but the exceptions were one of the boys, who responded cheerfully, and one of the girls, Marjorie by name, who turned out to be the fifth of the ten daughters. Her modest demeanour impressed him immeasurably. Although he was more than forty years old, John Knox had been limited in female acquaintanceship, and, if he was truthful, a shyness afflicted him in the presence of women, whom he found an attractive mystery.

The sternness of his life meant a loneliness that touched his soul at times and the impression had been forced on him that his peculiar destiny had cut him off from his fellow men. A constant companion with soft and gentle ways held a great attraction for Knox. As he gazed at the demure Marjorie Bowes, John Knox felt a tremor of magnetic excitement run through him, and he knew that there was something exceptional about this young woman. Surely this was the partner for him, unlikely as it might seem, from an English family, where the father and most of the others were openly hostile to him, with the notable exception of the mother, whom God had clearly touched and convinced of the desperate need of a radical reform of the Church from the false and distasteful teachings of Rome.

But the suspicion of the others was almost a tangible thing, "The trouble with the Scots is that they cannot even control their own side of the nation! Every little Baron has his own little Kingdom!" Sir Robert Bowes, the Warden of the Marches, himself fairly bristled with invective. "The Musgraves, the Elliots, the Kerrs, the Hopes, and the Armstrongs, and the rest of those thieving rascals! We mustn't forget the Armstrongs,

Norham Castle, Northumberland, home of Marjorie Bowes, John Knox's wife

the worst of the lot! They're a law unto themselves, and fair glad was I to hear how your King Jamie at last showed some good sense and lured that notorious rebel, Johnnie Armstrong, out of Gilnockie Castle to his own hanging! At least we can thank him for that, if nothing much else, like siring a daughter, which you could imagine!" He turned away to busy himself with the succulent veal and roast pheasant before him, as if aware of Knox's anger. John noticed that not only religion was something that figured highly in the affairs of the male Bowes family.

But the Scot was certain that the Lord meant him to be at Norham Castle that day, and when he gazed over at Mrs. Bowes, who could not do enough to attend to his needs, was bustling around like a mother hen, so that her husband was very irritated, and at the girl, who was an attractive, blonde, lassie about half his age, he was all the more certain. When it came to saying goodbye and he had not yet been asked to preach at Norham Castle, Captain Bowes made it abundantly clear that he would not be attending Knox's sermons at Berwick parish Church, but John was unconcerned. He knew that Mrs. Bowes was not one to be gainsaid by her husband, and that she would bring Marjorie with her.

Good news was soon forthcoming of a different nature. Word came from London that the Scot was to be given a new pastoral assignment in Newcastle and had been appointed one of the six new Royal chaplains to King Edward. Their duties included preaching at Court and itinerant work in places needing Protestant zeal. Knox was greatly enthused in his spirit, and he felt the warmth of God course through his body and felt the hand of God leading him on to an international sphere.

He travelled down to London with his confidence high, and, if he had been a fly in the Court of Edward, when Archbishop Cranmer was in earnest conversation with his youthful monarch, that confidence would have been further increased.

"This Scotsman, John Knox, your Majesty, has a most powerful nature, and strenuous intelligence, more aggressive than those of Bishops Latimer and Ridley, and even Hooper. Hooper has much zeal, but is ill-trained, and without Knox's power of fusing logic and passion to storm the hearts and minds of the audience. Latimer has a great literary bent, Sire, and buffoonery at times, but he has not the structure of the Scotsman, or his voice which would make the leaves on the trees tremble in its storm!"

"He sounds a very paragon of virtue, Archbishop. Surely the Scriptures tell us that we should beware when all men speak well of us? This man, Knox, must have his detractors, if he is truly a man of God?" The King, knowledgeable and steeped in the Scriptures already, leaned forward with curiosity.

"Oh, yes, he has his detractors all right, Majesty, like Bishop Cuthbert Tunstall, his superior at Durham, and some of the other clergy in the North, who are not over-keen on change. I am worried about Tunstall, for he will bend in a strong wind. They are angry at Knox, because he attacks the doctrine at every opportunity, and stirs up a veritable hornet's nest with his vigorous preaching. He does not seem to fear the face of man, Your Highness."

"That's the kind of man we need, Cranmer, isn't it?" The boy monarch broke in eagerly, his eyes seeking confirmation." I hate it when everybody around me always agrees with everything I say, and you know that they are hiding what they really think!"

For a second his pale face was full of genuine annoyance, and it led to a bout of coughing.

"Be careful, Majesty. You must remember what the doctors say. You are not to get upset and put a strain on your lungs. But what shall we do to use this fiery Scotsman to the best in the Lord's service, and our own?" he added.

"Bring him down to London to be one of my Royal chaplains," answered Edward in a spate of enthusiasm." We shall pay him an annual salary of forty pounds," he added with a theatrical flourish of generosity. Young Edward VI, though he had a body which was beginning to waste away, had a large and gracious heart. The King of England and Ireland for almost five years, and at merely fifteen years old, Edward was the tyrant, Henry VIII's only illegitimate son by Jane Seymour. Intellectually gifted, Edward's ability to grasp Latin, Greek, French, and Theology had astonished his elders, a distant reflection of that occasion when his own heavenly Master in the temple of Jerusalem had astounded the religious leaders of Israel.

As a boy, he had been hemmed in by powerful men. His ferocious father had decreed that during his son's minority the country was to be ruled by a Council of Regency. His uncle, Edward Seymour, the Duke of Somerset, had in actuality run the country till overthrown in 1549 by the unscrupulous John Dudley, the Earl of Northumberland. The King became the mask behind which Northumberland controlled England. But fortunately for the Protestant movement both Seymour and Dudley took measures to consolidate the Reformation. This agreed with the intense devotion of the youthful monarch to Protestantism. However, Cranmer was beginning to worry over the distinct appearance of consumption in the junior Monarch, who hitherto had been fairly robust. He now reminded Edward too that he should have to seek the approval of the Duke of Northumberland.

"Yes, yes, I know," responded Edward testily. Like all youngsters, he wanted his own way and quickly, until the reins were pulled up by a more mature and powerful hand." But I'm sure that Dudley will approve," he coughed again, revealing signs of the tuberculosis that was to consume him and end his life prematurely." But am I not the head under God of the Church of England, and so must administer it, as He deems fit?"

"Most decidedly, Majesty, most decidedly!" Cranmer was in haste to agree that Edward definitely had a potential for administration." But do you know that this Scotsman, whom controversy seems to attach itself to, is most obstinately opposed to kneeling at the Lord's Table?"

"Oh, that's not important, Cranmer. I'm sure it will not cause us any problems." The King dismissed it lightly.

"Maybe," the Archbishop muttered, unconvinced. Cuthbert Tunstall had written to him and complained again about the insolent Scotsman, which he had done often.

So it was that the Scot, unable to refuse the King's command, and, if he was honest, eager to move south into the hub of things, became one of the chaplains Royal. For a while all seemed rosy, and he looked forward to happiness in the land he had come to love, with the promise of marriage to his young Marjorie Bowes. Her mother's strong influence had been able to overcome the opposition and undoubtedly hostility of her husband, Sir Richard. John regarded it as a sign of the stamp of God's approval that such a difficult union should come to pass. But tension and conflict were beginning to surface. The matter of kneeling at Communion still troubled him.

"This smells of the idolatry of the Mass unmistakably," he voiced vehemently to the Privy Council at Windsor Castle, to whom he was summoned. Truth was at stake." If sitting was good enough for Jesus, it is good enough for us, is it not?"

"But of course Christ did not kneel," objected Cranmer, irritated at this irascible Scotsman, whom he admitted to himself he had let loose like a fox with his tail on fire into a field of corn. This Knox stuck like a burr too." If we were to follow the custom of the time in fact, we would eat lying down on the ground, as the Turks and Tartars still do!" He tried to sound moderately scornful, unwilling to start an argument." I urge you, sirs, to pay no attention to unquiet spirits, which only do what they fancy and never cease to cause trouble when things are settled and in good order." He hoped that Knox would not take personal offence, as he uttered these words." As you all know, we have drawn up the Forty Five Articles of Faith to govern our Church of England."

Not a few of the Council frowned at this, for there had not been universal agreement over it, and always in the background hovered the powerful Robert Dudley, the Duke of Northumberland, like a dark moth. In fact Dudley wished to see Knox as a bulwark against the power of Cranmer over the throne. He was happy that this strong-willed Scotsman was such an awkward character. Secretly Dudley had hopes that, if the King did not survive his illness, Lady Jane Grey would inherit the throne, but meanwhile he would play the balance of power encouraging the Church of England in its new-found freedom from the shackles of Rome.

For John Knox it was a heady period, to come from the despair of galley-slave to preaching before the King of England himself, and he continually had to seek the Lord God above for the humility that only comes from above in his private devotions. So, when he reached such a position of esteem one day among his clerical colleagues that he was offered the Bishopric of Rochester and the rich living of All Hallows Church in London, it was in a spirit of both nervousness and boldness that he refused the two. Privately he mused to himself that he chanced losing all that he had gained. The offence that might be given to the King, Cranmer, and the leading clergy might end his career forever and England's help for the cause in Scotland might be aborted without a second offer.

He sweated in prayer over his decision and knew that his conscience would allow him to do no other, a conscience informed by God's Word and Spirit. When the summons came to appear before the Privy Council to give an account of his inexplicable decision to refuse the great honour, his determination had become iron-hard. Humanly he trembled, as he stared at the assembled Lord Archbishop of Canterbury, the Bishop of Ely, the Lord Treasurer, the Earls of Northampton and Shrewsbury, the Lord Chamberlain, and the Royal Secretaries, who seemed to him to resemble some birds of prey with their hunched shoulders and expressionless eyes. Before he could dwell unhealthily on their thoughts, the Council spokesman rapped out an enquiry.

"Why did you refuse the benefice provided for you in London at All Hallows Church?"

"My Lords, I do not wish to give offence or to show that I am unaware of the honour afforded me." That was enough of a public apology, he decided, and stared back at the questioner." But my conscience witnessed to me that I might profit more in some other place than London." A low intake of breath was the response of the Council.

"Do you think that a Christian can serve the Church according to the laws and rights of the realm of England?" Silence descended, as the spokesman fixed Knox with his unwavering gaze.

"Many things need Reforming in the ministry in England, and without this no minister can discharge his duty before God. For no minister here has the authority to separate the leprous from the healthy, and this is a vital part of his office. But I will refuse no office, which might in the least promote God's glory and the preaching of Christ's Gospel." As he spoke these outspoken sentiments, the Scot was careful to keep hidden his even more radical thoughts.

He knew the worldly spirit and selfish motives of Northumberland, who wanted him to play the whetstone rubbing against Archbishop Cranmer's rock, and he knew with a certainty that he was not going to be either bruised or flattered into submission. His heart wasn't in controversy for controversy's sake, whether arguing with Cranmer, or kneeling at the Lord's Table or not. Politics were not his primary desire; he had now come to know in his inner being. As if to provoke him, the last question was deliberately designed so.

"Is it not a matter of indifference whether we kneel or not at the Lord's Table?" He saw the clear mischief in the eyes of the interrogator.

"Christ's action was the most perfect, and it is most safe to follow His example. The disciples did not kneel. Kneeling implies adoration. It gives the Papists the chance to say there is no difference between their Mass and the Holy Communion of the Church of England. Who can tell me that Christ did not sit at the Last Supper and that sitting is not a sign of dignity and true joy?" He looked slowly round the assembled dignitaries of the most powerful personages in England, who made up the Privy Council, and some of them quailed before his gaze. But he had stirred up consternation in others. Archbishop Cranmer was once more showing frustration, and a strain appeared on his refined features, as he saw the Church boat being rocked by this stormy petrel.

"Have we not been over all this before, Master Knox? Kneeling is simply reverence, and in no way implies superstitious adoration, as I have shown in the Forty Five Articles of Faith I have drawn up."

"Christ is not in the elements, Archbishop Cranmer, as we have established, so why kneel? Perhaps the Forty Five Articles need adding to or subtracted from?" John Knox's boldness amazed even himself. He never doubted that he was right, that his interpretation was correct, and that the burning power of the Word of God would smoke out falsehood and erroneous confusion. He was only too aware that he saw the world and also his own heart not so much under a steady, equable, light but by extreme flashes of passion, true for the moment, but not always true in the long run.

It was, therefore, imperative, that he be controlled and tempered by the authority of Scripture in the Bible, for passion was of a dangerous and unpredictable character.

But, as he gazed, grim-faced, at the Council, John Knox thanked God that passion was always better than the stifling dullness of sentimentality and bourgeois virtue that finds it most brilliant achievement to be respectability. He also thanked God that these men could not read his mind.

After much glowering and undercurrents of gossip, Knox's respectful declining of these preferments was accepted. He was much relieved, and looked forward to exercising his ministry in Scotland, as soon as the first opportunity occurred. Notwithstanding his numerous friends, he had a few enemies, who objected strongly to his views and two or three times more he was summoned to appear before the Privy Council, but so discreetly did he answer the charges against him that the Council refused to convict him. But then the thunderclap fell, which took matters out of his own hands.

The Reforming King of England, the fine youth, Edward VI, died on the sixth of March in the year of Grace, 1553, succumbed to the killing disease of tuberculosis. The new Protestant Church held its breath. Many feared, if Mary Tudor, Henry's Roman Catholic daughter by Catherine of Aragon, came to the throne, their future would be doomed. But the sick young King and his close adviser, the Duke of Northumberland, had decided on a device to set aside both Mary and her Protestant younger sister, Elizabeth, born to Anne Boleyn, one of Henry's wives.

They chose as the new Queen Lady Jane Grey, a quiet, learned, girl, firm in her Protestant beliefs, and very unwilling to get involved in power struggles. Her parents were ambitious for her, and, to ensure his own position, Northumberland arranged a marriage between Jane and his son, Lord Guildford Dudley, whom she did not care for in the least. But poor Lady Jane was a 'Nine days Queen'. Despite her religion, the majority of the English people knew that Mary Tudor was the rightful claimant, and, when she rode into London town in triumph to cheering crowds Lady Jane Grey's time was numbered and her nine days was ended. Dudley was executed, Elizabeth was sent to a semi-imprisonment in Woodstock, and poor young Jane Grey met a sad end on the executioner's block along with her husband. She was just seventeen.

"Poor lassie, she was but the pawn in other folk's ambitious schemes," Knox had commiserated to a friend. He had also endangered his own life by moving among the London crowds, trying to warn them of the dangers of a Roman Catholic Queen, but to no avail. A rebellion by Kentish gentlemen was put down with severity.

After Mary Tudor had ascended the throne, despite her assurances of freedom of worship for all at first, John Knox remained decidedly uneasy. Mary had said publicly that, though a Roman Catholic, she would not compel adherence to her faith, but he did not trust her. He felt the tension in the air that summer of fifty three, and it was not just the seasonal heat. Knox and other Protestant preachers had to restrict their language, and it went strongly against the character that God was forming in him. He was not permitted to use the words 'Papist' or 'heretic', and no one could preach without a special license from the Catholic Queen Mary.

The Scot knew in his spirit that a confrontation was coming, that it was the calm before the storm, and that underneath the surface this Queen was a raging Jezebel.

The last few days before Edward's death had been sad and a mistiness hung in the air was anything but mellow for the Protestants of England. A depression had set in, but Knox continued evangelising in Buckinghamshire around Amersham and other towns of the south of England. But then the crisis came in the autumn, when word arrived that Archbishop Cranmer and Bishop Hugh Latimer had been arrested and put in the Tower of London. The mask had finally come off, as the summer ran out, and real danger was alive. The congregations of French and Flemish Protestant refugees were expelled from the country by Mary. At first this did not arouse any animosity, since the contrariness of twisted human nature was seen in the fact that many English people felt a resentment at these foreigners' presence, whether Protestant or not.

Knox knew with a certainty that it was a precursor of evil things to come. It was no longer safe for him to remain in England. He had little thought that he would ever look longingly over to France. He had begun to see that the time-honoured obedience to the Sovereign, which the English Protestants accepted as their God-given duty, was a deception. In the midst of his fears and confusion, his thoughts were for Marjorie Bowes, his English love, and her devout mother, Elizabeth Bowes, back in the north, and he sat down to write a letter to them at Norham Castle.

Though large crowds had flocked to hear his bold preaching as he travelled through Buckinghamshire and Kent during harvest, when they gathered in the grain and erected the stooks of wheat, corn, and barley, and the spiritual seed sown by the Morning Star of the Reformation, John Wycliffe, now bore a rich harvest, yet he was somehow despondent about not only the survival of the Reformation, but also the remote chances of his marriage to Marjorie Bowes. His face puckered with annoyance at the scornful rejection of his proposal of marriage by Sir Robert Bowes, her uncle, whom he had arranged to meet in London. The English soldier had treated him with disdain, as if the Scots preacher's marriage into their noble family was an outrageous idea. John had barely kept his temper. Chewing his feather quill pen with anxiety, he wrote to Mrs. Bowes in despair.

'Dear mother, you well understand that I recently spoke with Sir Robert Bowes on the matter you know," He was so pained and frustrated that he did not even mention the marriage by word," as you requested, but his spiteful words have pierced my heart, so that my life has become bitter. I put on a good face with a sore, troubled, heart underneath. I do not care what country consumes this wicked carcass of mine.

If it wasn't that no unthankfulness of man will move me to cease being a blessing to Christ's congregation with God's strength for my weak body, I would not have England supply my bread for much longer. It will not be till the twelfth of November that I can come north to Berwick.

I am almost determined not to come. You know the cause. May God be more merciful to some than they're just in their judgement of me. My conscience is clear before God, who looks not at the importance of men."

With a sigh of exasperation he laid down his quill.

Time passed and no answer came. He wrote several other letters, but unaccountably again were unanswered. Worry set in, and determined to see the two women who meant more to him than anything in his life, apart from the Lord's work of Reformation, he set out for the north in November's mists under a cloak of secrecy. But disappointment awaited Knox, for when he reached Berwick and requested to see the Warden of the Marches; a messenger came back from Alnwick Castle, the key Border fortress, sent by Sir Robert Bowes.

"You are not wanted, Scotsman," The rebuff was harsh, almost physical in its force, and for a moment the stocky figure of John Knox quivered, like a stallion, which had been goaded, yet he was reluctant to leave, unless of his own freewill. It would have been easy for him to slip quietly over the Border to his beloved Scotland. It had been nearly six years since he had spent any reasonable time in his native land, and the fresh tang of the heather-clad hills seemed almost to penetrate his nostrils.

His homeland was calling. In addition, word had come that the Franco-Scottish authorities had abandoned for the moment the policy of harrying and pursuing the Protestants. But, as he sat on a bench outside a Berwick Inn, his hooded cloak pulled over his head to hide his identity, the vision appeared before John Knox of when eight years before the faithful George Wishart had gazed tenderly at his one-time bodyguard, while he was bound at the stake, and he had uttered the words pregnant with significance.

"One is enough for a sacrifice, brother John. Return to your bairns, and God bless you!"

No, he had to survive to lead the work of the Lord, for who else was there strangely it was a loyalty to England, not Scotland that consumed him. He must take flight, or death would be his lot. He must leave England now, and a week later with the assistance of urgent friends in London the Scot was on his way back to the Continent, where he had experienced not only the despair of slavery but also the great faithfulness of the Lord.

He crossed to Dieppe, a seaport on the Haut –Normandie region of France, lying on the English Channel north of Rouen. As his vessel approached Dieppe harbour, he thanked Almighty God for his narrow escape from certain death. He heard later that over three hundred were sacrificed in the flames of martyrdom in London's Smithfield in the furnace that had become England. It was truly a haven of safety for him. With the winter winds coming at the close of November had also come the icy blast of religious change and the return to the old ways of Rome.

The English Parliament had repealed the laws in favour of the Reformation and re-established the Roman Catholic Church. Those who chose might worship according to the Protestant manner until the twentieth of November, but after that they might do so at their peril. It was an undisguised threat. Many of the Protestant Bishops had been thrown into prison, others escaped beyond the sea. He was following their example. The last straw had almost come, when one day his servant, Patrick, had stumbled in, distressed and exhausted, and gasped out his bad news.

"I've been robbed o' my letters, Maister! It wis the Queen's men, but I managed to escape in the dark, when they were taking me tae jail! I'm sorry, Maister!" The Scots lad, whom he had taken into his service since his Berwick days, was downcast.

"Be not concerned, Patrick. For I have taken precautions." For safety he had used his mother's name of Sinclair instead of his own in his correspondence." But the noose is tightening," he had admitted. Fearing that this bad news would reach his new wife, John Knox had started out for Berwick-on-Tweed once more to prove to her that he was safe, for, aye, the one bright light in the darkness that was beginning to overwhelm Protestant England was that he and Marjorie had at last quietly married at Berwick, despite intense opposition. Here they were to be separated already for the Lord knew how long.

He had been obliged to take shelter on the road north along the coast, and now, heeding his faithful friends' advice, he was now gazing at the steep, white, cliffs, that bordered Dieppe's deep harbour mouth. As his vessel approached Dieppe harbour, he thanked Almighty God for his narrow escape from certain death.

He looked longingly towards the deep mouth of the River Argues leading into its harbour. Its Saxon meaning of 'deep' had given the town its name. It was truly a haven of refuge for him. He had been informed by a good source that Dieppe had been influenced a little by Protestant teaching. The French Kings in the past had realised the strategic importance of Dieppe, and granted it numerous privileges. A challenging vision of Europe as well as a vista lay ahead of the intrepid Scots preacher. He was in great need of a Barnabas, a son of encouragement. Had he but known it, he was to find that Barnabas in the historic city-state of Geneva.

THE MAN OF GENEVA

Though the Lord in the Scriptures had warned against flight in winter during a time of persecution, it was in the dark season that John Knox had finally sought refuge on the Continent of Europe. But, for that January, when the cold winds blew sharply over the Channel, John remained at Dieppe under the hospitality of the Protestant merchants, whose wealth kept the struggling Reformed Kirk alive materially. They welcomed English Protestant refugees with open arms, but they honoured the Scot for being one of the last to escape from Mary Tudor's tyrannical clutches, as she had imprisoned Cranmer, Hooper, Ridley, Latimer, and many Protestant clergy, and that, even as Mary had ridden through the streets of London to cheering crowds he had been bold enough to move among the people, warning them openly of the deadly danger that this Jezebel would be to England.

Even now Knox's anger and frustration boiled to the surface, as he shared with these Protestants of Dieppe the last desperate days which had led up to the Roman Catholic Queen's seizure of the throne. Before he had finally succumbed to the tragic illness from tuberculosis, which took his life, the young sixteen year old King Edward VI had tried with his influential adviser, the Duke of Northumberland's help on a clever means to set aside Henry's daughters and put Lady Jane Grey on the throne, but it had all unravelled before their horrified eyes. When the expected death of the young monarch had come, the gentle, unambitious Lady Jane had lasted so briefly, until the support for Mary had built up sufficiently for her to claim the throne. A Catholic Queen had returned to the throne. The nation, in the throes of the Protestant Reformation, held its breath. Everyone took it for granted that she should marry, for a woman could not rule alone. But confusion reigned as to who her husband should be. An Englishman would make her nobles jealous, while a foreigner would tie England to another power.

"She soon revealed that her true mind, though perhaps not her true heart, was set on King Philip of Spain," Knox said in conversation with the merchants of Dieppe." With this ungodly marriage she will soon be strong enough to restore the Romish faith. I tell you, she bears a Spanish heart under an English name. She even promised to the men of Norfolk and Suffolk to uphold the Protestant religion, and not to marry a foreigner! I pray that God will send a Jehu to execute His just judgement. She is a treacherous Jezebel and will not escape the vengeance prepared for her by the Lord!"

The merchants were a little frightened, if they were honest, by the vehemence of the fiery Scotsman. But his next words lessened their fears." But perhaps I am too hasty, and that violence against the Queen and the Catholics should be restrained. If I thought that it was right and that it had the support of men of assurance, I would put my very life at stake with a good conscience to see what could be done in these sad and dangerous times, but, seeing it cannot be instantly without great danger to others than myself, I will abide the time that God shall appoint! But of this I am sure, that this tyrant of England, Mary Tudor, and her fellow idolaters, who worship other than the true God in spirit, besides their condemnation and torment in Hell, shall also be plagued in this present life, unless they repent. We must love our enemies, but hate the enemies of our God and our faith!" His fervour was beyond human source.

"As Christians we must forgive injuries committed against ourselves, but not injuries against the true faith. Our public and private vengeance is different. Of this I am certain; as I am that my God lives! But," Here his brows furrowed and his eyes clouded over, as he looked down at his hands, still calloused and hardened from his year and a half at the galley oars," whether it is just to revolt or not, I am still uncertain."

John felt at home in this crossroads of Europe. There was always a ship leaving or arriving from Leith or some other Scottish port. Knox found that the Huguenot French Protestant influence had still widespread in French society, but mostly of the upper merchant and nobility class. He was warned to stay well clear of Paris and be very wary of trusting peasantry in the more rural areas, who were subject to Rome and loyal to these beliefs. But he was glad to be assured by the Dieppe merchants that, when the right time came, he could travel relatively safely through the French countryside on his way to Geneva, for the Scot had determined that his destiny lay with the great man of Geneva, the mighty Reformer, John Calvin. But for the next few weeks until the end of January the Scots Protestant preacher was content to remain among his friends in Dieppe and gather his thoughts.

He had already decided to complete his exposition of Psalm Six. It was a prayer of desperate longing from the heart of King David to the Lord for his release from the agony in his bones, the anguish of his soul, and the all-night weeping on his bed. May shame, dismay, and disgrace be on his enemies, and all those who do evil. The Lord would hear his cry for mercy and accept his prayer. But first he must write to Mrs. Bowes, Marjorie's mother, at Norham Castle. He must assure her, and dearest Marjorie of course, that he was safe, rescued from the furnaces of Smithfield. But would he ever see them again in this life? Europe was in turmoil. Mrs. Bowes had openly encouraged his courtship of her daughter, but her Catholic husband had been hostile to the end. No matter, he might die in exile anyway.

'Though it appears that in the beginning of this battle for truth, I have been a faint-hearted and feeble soldier, yet it's my deepest prayer that I may be restored to the heat of battle again. England and Scotland shall know that I am ready to suffer more than just poverty and exile for the Heavenly religion, of which God in his mercy has made me its simple soldier and witness.'

He felt, as he penned these words, the strong need to prove himself no coward. He could not have taken being thought that by those dear to him. It was true that he had not been foolish enough to put his head in the lion's deen by going to London town to claim his 40 pounds stipend last winter, but it would have been to court disaster. He would certainly end up in the Tower with Cranmer and the others. It meant he had landed in Dieppe almost penniless, with hardly a groat to his name. But God would provide, and already had through these gracious Protestant merchants. No, discretion was the better part of valour.

He was no good to the cause of God dead. Better is a living dog than a dead lion. He continued writing to Mrs. Bowes. *'There is nothing I would not give for the opportunity to preach a few sermons in England, I urge you not to bend with the wind and give in to pressure to attend Mass.'* They would suffer for it, and he could only pray for his friends. He at last brought the epistle to an end with what might be his final farewell. *'Beloved mother,'* (He already felt the Bowes were his family), *'since it is uncertain if we shall meet again in this earthly life, I fear I must take a last goodnight on earth from you.'*

By the beginning of February he felt in his spirit that it was the time to go and cross France towards the south-east border with the independent Swiss City-States to reach Geneva. It was not merely to find work as a preacher, but to meet the great man, Calvin, whose fame had spread through all Europe. The Frenchman's writings had a finely- honed touch to them, as if written with a Theological scalpel Scotland's faith, he was certain, was bound up with this man, John Calvin. Some of the generous Protestant merchants of Dieppe, who were Scots exiles, were prepared to meet his travelling expenses.

"Give yourself three weeks to cross France," advised one." These are the addresses of French Huguenot contacts, with whom you can bide on your route. Although things are still tense, the Huguenot party are quite strong in France, especially in the south –west, particularly amongst the nobility. But beware of trusting the peasantry, who are bound up in superstition. Speak as little as possible." Despite his nineteen months in the galleys, Knox's French was as yet not perfected." God go with you, Master John Knox, and use you in his great service!" The business-minded Scots merchant cleared a lump in his throat, as he grasped Knox by the shoulders.

So it was that John Knox slipped quietly across France, keeping his own counsel, and helped by Protestant friends, despite the occasional, suspicious glance, arrived at the high walls of Geneva, set above the beautiful, blue waters of Lac Leman. He was conducted through the narrow streets of old Geneva, and could not but admire its natural setting, with the magnificent, towering, Jura Mountains in the distance, still snow-capped even at times in summer. The air was like wine.

Soon the footsteps of his guide arrived at Number eleven Rue des Chanoines and the man knocked discreetly. Within seconds the door was opened by a man with a slight hunch. For some reason Knox did not take to him. There was something vaguely untrustworthy in his demeanour, which surprised him in a household such as Calvin's. He was yet to find that the man of Geneva, along with a rapier mind, had a trusting and loving nature above the average.

"Is Master Calvin at home?" enquired the guide.

"He is deep in study, I believe, and not to be disturbed." The hunchback was slightly surly." He has a Service at St. Pierre on the morrow and at La Madeleine on the following day." Strangely enough, the Scot heard the cries of happy children at play, as if to contradict the man's words, so that Calvin's study must have been deep not to have been distracted by the noise. It made him feel at home, though as yet Knox was childless.

"Will you tell him that there is a man arrived from Scotland desirous of speaking with him, the preacher John Knox?"

The hunchback looked at the Scot from underneath heavy eyebrows. He had never met a Scotsman before and was suspicion of all foreigners, but seemingly satisfied after his close examination of John Knox, who glared back at the servant. With a gesture to wait, he departed to return almost immediately, slightly chastened.

"Come in, come in! Master Knox is very welcome. Monsieur Calvin is anxious to meet him at once."

The man, to whom Knox was introduced, had his study in what amounted to an unadorned room with a bare writing desk, but it was the book-filled library cases which held his attention and impressed him. Here was a great man of letters, but a man of simplicity and hospitality, as John Calvin showed in his slightly-shy approach with hands outstretched, as if welcoming, and yet introverted. His voice had the French intonation, but the language was that of Christian love.

"My beloved brother in Christ, John Knox, at last we meet! I am overjoyed to have the fellowship of the brave Scotsman, who has suffered so much for the Reformed faith. Your torture, labouring in the galleys of France, must have been an agonising test to your body, mind, and spirit. To be chained to an oar and under the lash for so long must have been a terrible strain, but, thanks to our Lord Jehovah, He provides us with the means to bear it! To have recourse to prayer must have been a wonderful thing."

"It was, Master Calvin," exclaimed the Scot, as he returned the fraternal grasp of the Reformer, who was known throughout the Continent as the gug light of the Reformation, now that the peasant-born, ex-Augustinian monk, Martin Luther of Erfurt, had departed to his reward. He felt the thinness of the great theologian through the man's hands, to go with his spare, pointed, features, in which the dark eyes of the consecrated, as well as compassionate, man vied with that of the zealous preacher and expositor of God's Word. This was a man who led from behind for fear of taking any glory for himself and from his Master. Within minutes Knox knew that their hearts were knit.
"I had extreme need of prayer, when I and my fellow Castilians were subjected to severe sufferings and humiliations, after the perfidious Strozzi and his French masters treacherously broke their word to God and man to provide us with a safe passage to the Continent. A curse on all treaty breakers! They will be judged by the Lord! I will not say more than that the drudgery of endless rowing was a sore fight. Our taskmasters promised to set us free, if we renounced our faith. We had to attend the Mass and kiss an image of the Virgin Mary to gain our liberty. How can any Christian worship a blind, lifeless, image, against one of God's Commandments through Moses?

When anchored up the river Loire at Nantes a painted lady was thrust into my face for me to kiss, but, fortified by the Holy Spirit, I told my captors to trouble me no more, for such a useless idol was accursed, and I refused to touch it! Still they tried to push it into my face, but, when their attention was distracted, I seized the idolatrous thing and threw it overboard. Let the lady save herself now, she is light enough. Let her learn to swim!" He laughed lightly to justify his righteous irony, and Calvin accompanied him, as he clapped him on the back, brothers in truth.

"Elijah allowed himself to rightfully scorn the priests of Baal in their paganism on Mount Carmel. Their gods were either unable, or unwilling to answer their wild cries and beseechings to send down fire from the Heavens to set alight the pyre of wood. Were their gods asleep?" But, changing his tone, the man of Geneva became sollicitous again. The Scot was to discover that deep sincerity and a listening ear were the abiding qualities of John Calvin." Were you not sick with longing for your homeland of Scotland? For there are times, dear Knox, when I long with deep nostalgia for France, the poppy fields of Picardy, and the old bridge at Pont L'Eveque village, where I played as a child.

My grandfather, and his grandfather before him, was the boatman on the river Oise there. What strong things are our emotions! Oh, how I miss the deep, pealing, bells of Noyon Cathedral, my hometown. Noyon is not called for nothing the city of bells, belfries, and songs by its famous Choir schools in her great Cathedral, where Charlemagne himself and the Capetan Kings of France were crowned. I must confess that our trusty St. Pierre Cathedral Bell that we call *La Clemence*, impresses my heart and ears daily, and brings back sweet and joyous memories." His piercing, dark, eyes misted over for a moment, and John saw a tear.

"Indeed, once when our galley ship was sailing along the coast of Scotland off the lands between Dundee and St. Andrews, I recognised our whereabouts and the steeple spire of St. Andrews Parish Kirk, where God first opened my mouth to glorify Him. My heart and body were sick then, but my spirit prophesied that, no matter how weak I might be then, I should not depart this life till my tongue should glorify the Lord anew in the same place."

"The words of the prophet are subject to the prophet, and, be assured, brother, that God shall fulfil His promises."

"He has already partially fulfilled his promise, for after the Lord liberated us, He blessed my ministry in the wild, frontier, garrison, town of Berwick-on-Tweed, and later Newcastle. Many hardened hearts were changed and immoral tongues cleansed. I did not dare return to Scotland at that time, for I well knew that my enemies would pursue me there. The boy-King, Edward, was God's gift, his youthful mind so eager for truth, and to know the Scriptures, a child prodigy he was described as. How sad that he was taken from us so quickly!"

"Your Edward was really a rare flower. I sent a letter to him some time ago, and to Cranmer, exhorting them with all my heart to prosecute with fresh zeal the Reformation of the English Church by purging it of falsehood. To the King I sent the present of a little exposition of Psalm 78, of how much danger Kings and Princes are in, when the height to which they are raised, should dazzle their eyes and amuse them here below, while making them forgetful of the Heavenly Kingdom."

"After preaching the Good News in the north," Knox continued his dialogue, though he was fully aware of Calvin's contribution to the battle," The King did me the honour of appointing me a Royal chaplain. He even offered me the Bishopric of Rochester, but I refused it, for I cannot bring myself to consent to all the doctrines of the Anglican Church. Yet I am happy to say that under the hand of God I was instrumental in the composition of the Black Rubric as a vital part of the *Thirty Nine Articles of* the Constitution of the Church of England.

It opposes the doctrine of the magical changing of the bread and wine, and any hint of improper teaching, like kneeling at Communion. To destroy Rome's power, one must destroy the Mass! Such work brings enemies." He glanced up at the slightly taller man from under shaded eyelashes, and saw an unmistakable agreement." though I had many faithful friends in England, I had a few dangerous enemies, who tried to trip me up, but they never succeed. God gives wisdom.

Then there were some like the Duke of Somerset, the Lord Protector, uncle to

King Edward, whom I never knew was a friend or foe. He was for following the ways of Luther, subjecting the hierarchy of the Church to Kings and Princes, and attributing their authority to God. On his side Somerset had my Lord Archbishop Cranmer, Nicholas Ridley, the Bishop of London, a Godly man if ever I saw one, and the statesman, William Cecil, Lord Burleigh, who, unless I'm mistaken, is as clever and astute a man as politics could desire and deserve. Cecil would not miss the tiniest spider in the thickest forest. William Cecil is a survivor, and I am convinced that our paths will cross again, though, I have to confess, brother Calvin, that he reminds me of the Unjust Steward in the Bible parable, who safeguarded his future."

"Ah, yes, my Scottish brother, we have to remember that our Lord does not commend the Steward's dishonesty, but only his intelligent foresight. He made friends of his master's debtors before he lost his job. Here in our City-State of Geneva I and brother William Farel, whom you will meet soon, and both the Little Council and the Great Council believe that the Church and State are the inseparable faces of the same coin and God works through the Civil and Church Courts. But, as for enemies, it was ever so, John. Beware, when all men speak well of you. At least I cannot say that!" He laughed dryly, but there was no bitterness. If he was honest to himself, Calvin already found this blunt Scotsman someone a little awkward to handle, especially at this time when the struggle to control Geneva was still being waged between him and the licentious, luxury-loving, Libertines, who took high exception to the discipline Calvin had exerted Calvin's predecessor, and close colleague in the Reformation, William Farel.

All too clearly he recalled that dramatic confrontation in the *Bear Inn* on a cold and lonely night when John Calvin, a Frenchman from Picardy, fleeing with his affectionate brother, Antoine, and sister, Marie, from the horrific persecution of the infant Protestant Church in France, had stopped off in Geneva. They had been on their way to seek refuge in Strasbourg, that famous border city, half French, half German in its history and culture. But that had been John Calvin's date with destiny, when the flame-haired Farel of the fiery temper had stopped the man from Noyon in his tracks with a pointing finger and the words of a prophet. This latter day Samuel had challenged him to remain in Geneva and take up the reins of God's work there. For long, John Calvin, who longed wearily for a life of tranquility and study at such a place as Strasbourg, had pleaded his unsuitability, but all in vain. Farel, twenty years his senior, but a man of humility and vision, who had seen in this younger fellow-Frenchman the gift of leadership, had spoken words which even now as he conversed with the bold Scotsman, echoed in the brain of the Geneva preacher.

"May it please God to curse your rest and the peace, you are seeking for study, if in a time of such great need you withdraw from Geneva and refuse to give me help and preaching assistance here."

With such burning zeal the thundering words of William Farel had seared Calvin's mind and soul, and seemed like a curse from God Himself. It was as if God had stretched out his hand from on high to halt him, and so he had stayed. And now this provocative Scotsman had come to disturb his peace once more, but somehow, though inwardly he felt that Knox had much to learn and that he had better tread carefully with the volatile Scot, he knew with a certainty that here was a man who could be a rock in the building of the Protestant Faith, a man who would not compromise with Rome or anyone. Such men were desperately needed.

"But earthen vessels we are, all of us, and so it is necessary, Master Knox, that, when we see the errors in others, we forgive them. So it was that, when my enemies, the Libertines, had driven me out of this city by their sheer vindictiveness, although I was so happy in my new home of Strasbourg, when the Church of Geneva begged me with all their heart to return, I could not refuse God's manifest call."

"It shows your greatness, Monsieur Calvin, that you could change your mind." The Frenchman knew the man before him was no sycophant, and appreciated the compliment."

"*Merci*, Monsieur Knox. I had sworn that the death of a thousand cuts would not take me back to Geneva. But, pray, continue."

"Aye, just like when all things seemed to be going well in England, disaster struck when the Godly youth was taken from us to gain his reward above but to our great loss." Knox was downcast for a moment." But we must see it as God's beneficent will, as He does all things well. It was like a bolt from the darkness that snatched our bright hope and Morning Star of the Reformation, and set that Jezebel, his sister, Mary Tudor, on the throne. My flight at night was immediate, when the bloody work of persecution began." He was silent concerning the fact that he had been one of the last to flee England's shores and so had courted death." After a sojourn in Dieppe for a few weeks to gather my strength, I have come to Geneva to seek your Godly ministry and that of Professor Beza."

"Ah, yes, I must inform Theodore Beza that you have arrived, Master Knox, when he returns from a trip he has made to Neuchatel to see brother Farel. He is very close to William Farel. They often discuss Theology together, like two cats in a bag! Have you read Beza's New Testament translation from the original Greek? Come, my good friend, you shall find Geneva a new and welcoming home, if not quite New Jerusalem!"

"Master Calvin, you have already been a good friend to me, but I am very tired, and badly need rest and refreshment. I am also tired of lies and hypocrisy, and most of all political corruption." Knox's strained features and sunken eyes revealed the strain he had been under during the three weeks trek through France, taking refuge in friendly Huguenot farmhouses, and even the mansions of noblemen, but all the time uncertain who was friend or foe.

"It is what you must come to expect from our enemies." Knox noticed that Calvin used the possessive pronoun to include them both, and his heart warmed, for it had been a lonely life at the vanguard of the cataclysmic Reformation, which had engulfed nations, challenging all their preconceived ideas on the authority of the known Church.

"Poison has been used against the supporters and especially its leaders! A strong rumour has it that Luther was poisoned by his enemies in Germany, but the Lord protected him. Lies and hypocrisy are weapons which they will use at the least encouragement. What a perversion of the truth to accuse me of provoking the French refugees to take over the city from the Genevans! But God will honour those who honour Him. Come, let me introduce you to my faithful brother Goodman, whom you will like, but I forget myself, rest and refreshment first."

The next morning, refreshed by a satisfying, dreamless, repose, Knox gazed out from his bedroom window over the lovely Lake of Geneva, shining in the early morning sun. He could not make out the upper reaches of the mighty Alps beyond for a mist which hung draped like a curtain over the high peaks. But suddenly a breeze made an opening in the clouds, which parted and a world of grandeur was revealed to his awe-struck eye. Where before there had been a curtain of dull vapour, there was now to be seen a glorious array of mountains, with their gorges, rocks, and pine forests contrasting with the dazzling snows and flashing pinnacles. Verdant vineyards clothed the shores of the magnificent Lake and he saw other cities in the misty distance strung along its side. Lausanne would be one, which he knew had stood bravely for the Reformed Faith, but, like Geneva, was fiercely independent.

Aye, he had much to learn in this new arena of life, and not just the natural beauties of the broad, blue, Lac Leman, the Jura with their thickly clothed hillsides, and the snowy Alps, but in the world of the spirit a whole new vista had been disclosed, where the clouds of ignorance and superstition had been swept away. These had hung between so many people and the Bible, including those both who had struggled for a free conscience and an open Bible back in Scotland, and these citizens of Geneva. What sacrifices the Protestants of Geneva had undergone, he could only guess, and somehow his eye, as he gazed from the window of his lodgings high in the old city close to the magnificent Cathedral St. Pierre, was drawn to the high walls which surrounded the town, extending from the heights of the old part of Geneva across the river Rhone, which bisected Geneva. The walls stood for strength against the Savoyards and the rival city of Berne, but also for separation from the world and its worldliness.

Just then John Knox's meditations were interrupted by a servant, who came to say that Master Calvin had invited him to *petite dejeune* at the Rue des Chanoines. As they climbed the steep, cobbled street, the Scot felt the atmosphere of reverence, which seemed to exude from the quiet, orderly, citizenry. He felt at home in this place. There was something pure about this Geneva, which touched his soul with contentment. How it contrasted with the hard-swearing riotous, folk of Berwick-on-Tweed, when he had first arrived there, where nightly fights and daily aggression had led to stabbings and a continual atmosphere of fear. With the help of God he had changed things. But there was a definable calm about this self-contained City State, and it was no more epitomised than in the quiet authority of this man, Calvin, in whom reason seemed to have cooled his head, though as he was greeted with open arms by the Frenchman at his open door, he knew zeal warmed his breast. He had found there was no typical Frenchman, though generally more expressive than the Scots. So much had his previous feelings been provoked against all Frenchmen by the arrogant, cruel, and spiteful, even treacherous manner in which they had treated him.

"Welcome again, dear John. This time I shall walk with you round our fine city, which has cost us much precious, blood, and may cost more." A shadow passed over Calvin's thin features, responsibility for others never far away." There is much opposition to our party, and threats to my life. Not long ago I found a letter in my pulpit at St. Pierre, ranting and raving with madness. It said '*If you and Farel and Beza do not shut your mouths, and if you drive your enemies too far, you will curse the day we had skipped from the monastery. It called us renegade priests come here to ruin them.*' "Well," he laughed dryly," I was never a monastic brother nor a renegade priest, and that can be said of my beloved brothers, William Farel and Theodore Beza."

But we had best beware these mad men, who would cause trouble. The anonymous author of the wicked letter threatened that I would receive what happened to Monsieur Werly at Fribourg. My friends said it was just childish abuse, all bluster, but I cannot forget that Werly was killed when riots took place after the celebration of the Lord's Supper in a garden on Good Friday. Fribourg is a Roman Catholic city, which was once bound to Berne and ourselves in a Triple Alliance. But we have cast off any connection with Fribourg and even with Berne, which declared for the Reformation nearly twenty five years ago, has had her link with Geneva loosened. The Genevans are a fiercely, independent-minded people." Calvin showed a rare gleam of pride.

"Come, you will have a glass of our fine wine and some strong, Swiss mountain goats milk cheese. I am fortunate that the *Commune*, our General Assembly, which meets only twice a year, voted some barrels of wine as part of my stipend. It embarrasses me, for one major meal a day suffices me, and but a cup of wine. Yet, as we both know, the Lord wants us to enjoy all good things. He brings wine out of the earth to gladden men's hearts, oil to make their faces to shine, and bread to sustain their strength. I have already broken my fast." Calvin showed his guest into a modest dining room, where a gentle-looking woman laid the table.

"This is my sister, Marie, a faithful woman, who makes me proud. She has been true to the Lord, following me with my brother Antoine, when we fled from the bloody scaffold in Paris. We were heading for the refuge of Strasbourg, but troop movements made the direct route hazardous and we were forced to make a detour south through Geneva, and here was our destiny." A tinge of triumph broke the surface of the Reformer's disciplined manner.

The sweet-faced woman inclined her head respectfully to John Knox's greeting and smile. She was in fact his half- sister, but clearly the children were hers. Knox saw through the kitchen window a well-stocked vegetable garden in the rear of the house.

"Yes, Geneva is not all buildings. They are fond of their gardening. All the houses in our Rue des Chanoines, as well as those in the Place St. Pierre and the La Riviere have their productive plots, and even the poorer houses in the jumble of streets and lanes in the Lower City and across the Arve in the Saint Gervais district have their proud little vegetable patch. You see how they stand pressed together, like books packed on a shelf!" He laughed, and pointed with his thin tapering finger down to the other side of the divided city." Yes, we teach thrift in Geneva."

"A worthy attribute, which we Scots admire and try to inculcate. He, who never wastes, never wants. I have a vision for Scotland that, with the Lord's help, when our enemies are vanquished and the pure Gospel is restored, that we shall see an Elementary School in every parish and a Grammar School in every Burgh, where education will be open to all from the highest to the lowest, the richest to the poorest, when there will be a sense of individual worth, a conviction of spiritual independence and a notion of equality before God. Kings and Barons may still oppress and bully, but it will be known that there is a King of Kings and Lord of Lords, that there is One greater than Caesar, to whom the meanest cottar has direct appeal. There will be a new Scotland. One generation has been dumb and servile of soul, but the one to come will be out on the moorlands and mosshags singing the old hundred and twenty fourth psalm."

Knox's face had taken on the look of a visionary. Calvin gazed at him, impressed by the spirit that infused John Knox, the spirit of the prophet. He smiled within, for he recognised that spirit, and he quoted out loud the famous psalm.

"If that the Lord had not our right sustained,
when cruel men against us furiously,
rose up in wrath to make of us their prey."

Despite his French intonation and foreign metre, Knox was delighted to hear the Psalm he loved so much, spoken with such authority.

"Amen, so let it be! It's a worthy vision, my Scottish friend. Keep to the Word of God and be faithful to it, and the vision will be realised. Fight the enemies of the Lord with all your might. Last summer a wild and crazed genius came to Geneva, called Michael Servetus, though he was also known as Michael de Villeneuve. He was a slippery character indeed, a doctor of medicine, a native of Navarre in Spain. He was a madman, whose mind was filled with strange ideas. He sent me a flood of letters, when I was in Paris, provoking me with his blasphemous opinions, so that I could not help being furious.

Servetus called infant baptism a demonic monstrosity, and believed in freewill, which is a total falsehood, when we all know that the Scriptures teach that we are all controlled by the evil one until the light of Christ dawns on us. We are steeped in sin and born in iniquity, but praise God, Christ has redeemed us! The wicked Doctor Servetus or Villeneuve had wiled his way into becoming physician to the Archbishop of Vienne, but, when he was exposed, he was arrested and put in prison to be interrogated by the Inquisitor General of France, Matthieu Ory, at the head of a Commission. I understand that, like a snake, he retracted his statement of heresy, even denying that he had written them. The Trinity was denied by him, and he called the Father, Son, and Holy Spirit a three-headed Cerberus! For it was on the point of his being condemned to the stake by the Commission but he cleverly got hold of the key to the back garden, where he was imprisoned, and climbed the walls to escape. The Tribunal of Vienne burnt Michael Servetus in effigy along with his books. But what did this incredible play actor then do, but deliberately stop off in Geneva, putting his head in the lion's den, when travelling to Italy. He even had the bravado to attend my sermon in St. Pierre. The bold- faced of heresy is blind to its own danger often, and so, when Servetus was recognised, he was arrested."

"What happened then?" asked Knox, holding his breath in suspense, as if he already knew the horrific outcome. Had he not seen it enacted before in his own land of Scotland, a scene etched forever in his mind? It was an age of extreme belief.

"He was heard before the Syndics, who are the four leaders, who are elected each January by the Commune, our General Assembly, led by Monsieur Pierre Tissotas Prosecutor. He is a fair man, I assure you. But Genevan Law requires the accuser or his representative to go to prison for a short time until proofs of the heresy of the accused is produced. My brave young secretary, Nicholas de la Fontaine volunteered to go in my place, and would take no refusal on my part. At last Servetus stood before firstly the Syndics, and then the Little Council."

"What was the verdict of the Council, surely the condemnation of a heretic?"

"It was not just the danger from the man himself, but that my enemies, the

Libertines, who are still around unfortunately and have a strong influence in the Council of the Two Hundred, will use this confusion this wild man might arouse to attack me and my stand. They would reintroduce their immoral ways into our city, and re-open the brothels all over Geneva then Geneva will become a morass of corruption once more! Men like Perrin, Berthelier, and Vandel want to overcome all God's work and ours, but, glory to God the work of the Lord stands by His omnipotent power! What are man's puny efforts by comparison?"

John Calvin's face was more animated than Knox had ever seen, and it was not that of a blind fanatic but one who knew God's inner counsel." Servetus was condemned by his own words. He claimed almost beyond belief that the mantle of the Archangel Michael in Revelation had fallen on him! His spirit, voice, and emotions were those of a crazed man!" Calvin's pale features changed again with a slightly strained expression." He claimed he knew all the sixty signs of the power of the Anti-Christ and that already Heaven and Earth were moving against the Dragon! Already the Lamb who was slain was beginning to open the Books, which had been closed with the Seven Seals!"

"He was a mad Millennialist, this Spaniard Servetus!" Knox was shocked by the words of Calvin." Always when God is doing a great work, the Devil will come along in the disguise of a religious zealot, full of falsehood. What did he say of Jesus Christ?

"He quoted the Early Church Fathers, Tertullian, Irenaeus, and Clement, who talked about the Person of the Son of God. He believed that when Jesus was born he became the Son of God by adoption. He claimed that Christ existed only in the mind of God as an idea and not as a person, and that the title of Son of God was given as a man to Christ Jesus!"

"What a blasphemy! Did not our Lord say, 'Before Abraham was, I am,' and surely this is proof of the total oneness of the Father and the Son, and that the Son is from all eternity?"

"Without doubt the Trinity of God is a cornerstone in our faith, the Three in One and One in Three. But the twisted mind of Servetus knew no bounds in its wickedness, claiming that we believe in three Gods, even four! The essence which we call the ground of our being constitutes a fourth, he even said. His opinion was that, because we believe in three Gods in one, or four, which is of course impossibility, we are really atheists. To Michael Servetus in his madness God could be a stone, a flower, or a tree. He accused the Church of putting God in a box, like Simon Magus, and he insisted wildly that God was literally in all things."

"This is pantheism, and totally unscriptural, for God is outside of all creation!" Knox responded in protest." In the beginning God created the Heaven and the Earth. Without Christ, who is Co-Eternal with our Heavenly Father, nothing was created. Who else was the Word but our Lord Jesus Christ?" Knox was a mixture of bewilderment and anger, first at the incredible wildness of Dr. Servetus and then anger at the man's hatred towards the wonderful mercy of God." Do not the Scriptures tell us that proud boasters will come without understanding? This Servetus was one of these men, afflicted in his mind by Satan, the father of lies. The Consistory could do nothing else but condemn him for what was worthy of death, blasphemy. He was burnt at the stake there at a Champel, a scene near Geneva. I tried with all my heart to have the sentence changed to death on the scaffold, but in vain," John Calvin's white face was whiter with pain at the fresh memory, which yet haunted his dreams.

Just then his servant, the hunchback, Daguet, could be heard going to the front door from where an insistent knocking was audible.

"It is that presumptuous vagabond, Alberg, Master Calvin. He is but a wandering beggar if ever there was one, forever scrounging! He is an incorrigible rogue, living from hand to mouth, sniffing out money from those he can wheedle, dressing in others clothes. Alberg is just a dog, shuffling around, picking up the scraps from every corner, when he has more than enough for himself. He is just a confidence-trickster, I tell you, sire, and you ought not to see him." The man, Daguet, who was, it seemed, the general factotum around Calvin's house, still aroused an instinctive suspicion in Knox's mind, and his insensitive treatment of the beggar further confirmed that feeling.

"Oh, show him in, Daguet, and don't forget that our commission from our Lord is not to question the sincerity of the needy, but to come to their aid, for we do it to God Himself. We must never turn the poor away. The Lord never did, and St. Paul admonishes us to be imitators of him as he was of Christ. We can do no less, Pierre. Forby, I am amused by Monsieur Alberg. He's at least a merry trickster, and neither a straight-laced hypocrite, nor a hostile enemy like Perrin, or an openly immoral Libertine I confess, I do love the ingenious rogue."

A slightly dishevelled figure, with a threadbare cloak thrown around him, was shown in. But a lively spirit danced in his eyes and a confidence that contrasted with his poor appearance, for he looked a healthy enough vagrant. He stretched out his hands to Calvin in the familiar manner of old friends.

"It is so good to see you again, Monsieur Calvin. When was it now? My life is such a topsy-turvy thing that I never remember the important things from the utterly trivial ones!"

"Come away, you old rascal. It wasn't so long ago, I assure you, and I also remember clearly how, when I was in exile in Strasbourg, you came to me begging for money and you extracted twenty batzen from me. I could little afford it then, for I had to sell my very books and was almost entirely without funds." He laughed in the manner of one to whom worldly possessions are of little matter.

"Ah, yes, I recall it, and I'm entirely grateful, sir." His impish grin defied contradiction of his sincerity.

"Do you know that I had to borrow these twenty batzen from someone else, Alberg?"

"You are the very epitome of a Christian, Master Calvin," quipped Alberg cheekily. John Knox felt embarrassed for Calvin, but the latter seemed to delight in this light-hearted badinage. It was a justified relief from the gravitas of heavy theological study.

"And do you know, Master Alberg, that I still haven't got the money back? Geneva permits only a five per cent interest in usury, but it would amount to a considerable amount now."

"Is that so? I can't believe it! How could I be so remiss? I meet so many people, that's it. The Lord knows my weakness, too many friends and too little memory!"

"Really? You know, my brother Antoine tells me that you are nothing but a confidence trickster. Where are you sleeping, Alberg?"

"Under one of the bridges over the Rhone, Master. It is nice and warm and comfortable, and I have the choice of some furry boon companions. We can really get close to one another. In fact you might say we have to!" Even the serious-minded Scot, who had looked askance at this professional beggar, had to laugh along with Calvin and his secretary, De La Fontaine, who had joined them. Here was a shameless rogue indeed. Scotland was full of hordes of such mendicant vagrants, who thronged her highways." For the winds fairly whistle up through the bridges in winter from across Lac Leman and the high Juras," continued Alberg.

"And how do you eat these days?" asked the Reformer caringly.

"Well, if I am honest, Monsieur Calvin," The man had adopted a whine and a foxy look, which irritated Knox." The Libertines tried to buy my allegiance with free suppers so that I would help stir up a riot against yourself and the other French Protestant immigrants in Geneva, Huguenots I think they call them."

"Do not use that corrupted word, or even *Eidgenossen*, my man!" retorted Calvin sharply, his eyes flashing and Knox saw the other side of the famous Reformer.

"My apologies, Monsieur. Anyway, I refused their blandishments of course, especially of that rascal, Monsieur Perrin, and his acolytes, Favre and Vandel. I swear by the true God that I remained true to you, Master Calvin. I heard that these Libertines employ a mob, which insults you with jibes whenever you leave your house. Is that so?" Knox squirmed at the wheedling behaviour of the man.

"That's only too true, Alberg. But that is only the cost expected of a true disciple of Jesus Christ. But, come now, what do you really want? More money? Your motives are usually ulterior, you persuasive rascal!"

"Oh, sir, how can you say so? It is only a few crowns as a loan and see, I have a valuable box with me, which will be the guarantee of security for the money." He brought out a small box of an attractive-smelling wood from under his cloak.

"I was wondering what you had beneath your voluminous cloak, you vagabond. I guessed it might be a change of clothing."

"Oh, no, something much more valuable. I can't reveal what is in it, in case someone less worthy than your good self robs me of it."

"Really? It looks certainly an intriguing little box all right, Sandalwood, I surmise?" John Knox could not believe that Calvin would be so naive." Sandalwood is part of the wondrous creation of God. When burned, it gives off a glorious, sweet-smelling, aroma of incense, but truthfully it is our prayers which are the real incense to God."

"Oh, definitely sandalwood! Will you lend me those twenty crowns?"

"Most definitely sandalwood!" Knox enjoyed the light irony of the man of Geneva, for his own lip curled in distaste at the strong whiff which reminded him of his former life as a priest." So its twenty crowns you want? Are you sure that will do? I must be soft in the head as well as soft in the heart, as my brother Antoine often says to me. Wait here, till I get the money."

When Calvin was absent, the vagabond was distinctly uneasy in the presence of John Knox, and coughed and shifted embarrassedly, as the Scot fixed his fierce, penetrating, gaze upon him. The man from Haddington had less sympathy for such types than the man of Geneva.

"Here's the twenty crowns." Calvin's return was none too soon for Alberg, who had found Knox's stare unbearable." You may leave that Pandora's Box in the corner. When am I allowed to open it? I am sure it will not be my destruction, even though pagan mythology tells us that the world was ruined when Pandora's box was opened." He looked over at the Scot apologetically." We had to study about as much pagan philosophy as we did God's Word at that miserable College du Montagu in Paris. Their over-rigorous, misguided, regime and wretched food have still a bad effect on my constitution! You may not know the story of Pandora's box, Master Knox?" He enquired lamely, as if excusing any mention of superstitious, Greek, mythology.

"I am sad to relate I do, as my studying of the Classics was overlaid with such fantastic tales which cling to one's memory like leeches." The Scot's mind went back to his strict academic regime at Haddington Grammar and the Latin and Greek Master who dinned in verbs with military precision. Pandora had been the first woman on earth, sinful like Eve, after the Fall. When Prometheus had stolen fire from Heaven, Zeus in revenge had caused Hephaestus to make a woman out of the earth, who by her charms and beauty would bring misery upon the human race. Aphrodite had adorned her with wonderful beauty. Hermes bestowed upon her boldness and cunning, and the Gods called her Pandora, the all-gifted one, as each of the Gods had given Pandora some gift or power, by which she was to work the ruin of man. Hermes took her to Epimetheus, who made her his wife, forgetting the advice of his brother, Prometheus, not to receive any gifts from the Gods. Pandora brought with her from Heaven a box containing every ill, and when she opened it, and they all escaped, and spread over all the earth, Hope alone remained in the box.

At a still later period the box was said to have contained all the blessings of the Gods, which would have been preserved for the human race, had not Pandora opened the vessel, so that the winged blessings flew away." Aye, folk tales, though pagan, have a fascination always for the unregenerate mind, and even the fallen side of the regenerate," he added. He was only too aware of the spiritual battle within his own nature of good intentions and bad intentions.

"So when am I permitted to open this Pandora's box?" Calvin turned to the presumptuous beggar with a wry smile.

"If I haven't returned the twenty crowns to you within a month, the box belongs to you with all its treasures."

"I cannot wait, you rogue!"

"Thank you, dear Master Calvin! The Lord bless you a thousand fold! I might even treat my boon companions under the bridges to a hot meal." Alberg scuttled sideways through the door, and Knox breathed a sigh of relief.

"Au revoir, mon ami. Now, let us begone, my dear Scot. The City and Lake of Geneva call," said John Calvin.

CHAPTER EIGHT

WANDERINGS ON THE CONTINENT

Geneva had been founded and grown larger on the side of a hill in the centre of a natural basin between the Alps and the Jura Mountains, where the Rhone River met the lake of Geneva. The climate was tempered by the very presence of the Lake, while the Juras created a barrier that diminished the rainfall considerably. So It was unusual that a soft, dappled, day should by chance have been chosen by John Calvin for their walk down by the lakeside that misty morning. The buildings were grouped so closely together that Knox was taken aback, and the trees beyond them cast light shadows in the sun.

"These waters are most distinctly blue and translucent," The Scot observed in wonder

"Most unusually so, and another strange aspect to the Lake's waters are the *seiches,* when the whole waters of the Lake swim rhythmically from shore to shore." Knox could not but be entranced, as he gazed out over the broad, beautiful, waters. Although John Knox was essentially a man of the Word, his soul could be touched by the natural creation as now, and as he had experienced earlier when he arose." It is not as rich in fish as other Swiss Lakes, they tell me. Yonder," Calvin pointed out," you can see where the River Rhone enters the Lake the towns of Villeneuve, which belongs to Switzerland, and the town of St. Gingolph, which is in France. Over there across the Lake is the faithful city of Lausanne, which is still dependent overmuch on Berne in my view. But her Church, thank God, has broken free from the shackles of Rome and her false, human-based, traditions, and is like a sister to our own city of Geneva. Ah, liberty, my beloved friend, is like a precious jewel, but it is a dangerous one."

"Why is liberty dangerous, Master Calvin?" Knox was surprised and curious, as he pulled his unwilling gaze away from the hazy outline of Lausanne across the blue expanse.

"Christian liberty brings responsibility. It is a necessary part of the faith. That we have a good and clear conscience and that we act boldly and confidently without unneeded inhibitions. For what hampers action more than doubt? But it is misunderstood by such people as the Libertines, who use it as an excuse to do simply what they like, and misunderstood by the reactionaries also, who conceive that it will overthrow the established Government."

"Aye, I can comprehend that, for liberty is not physical, but spiritual, and I can foresee in Scotland that if there is a spiritual Revolution, there will have to be a safeguard against unbridled license. The Lords and Nobles of my homeland will have to be won over to the doctrines of the Reformation!" In his mind's eye as in a vision from the Lord he saw himself journeying round Scotland preaching at great houses, mansions, and castles to the leaders of his country, but not to them only but to the common people, who thirsted for God's Word.

They started to ascend from the lakeside to the southern part of the city, which

85

made up the greater part of Geneva, and he could not but be reminded of Edinburgh and her ancient Castle on the rock. Geneva was like a fortress, and possessed no suburbs, its walls rising up from the pastures and arable fields like cliffs from the sea. Danger of attack from her enemies, whether Northern Italians, French, or from other Swiss cities, had compelled the construction of a city restricted within the cramped, new, defensive, walls. The townspeople who passed the two walkers greeted Calvin with a polite reverence, but did not make a move to converse. They were too busy, it seemed, Knox noticed many who were clearly merchants, others artisans at their stalls, cobblers, tailors, pastry cooks, butchers, carpenters, stone-masons, barbers, and a few shops announced their owners as goldsmiths, printers, and apothecaries. It was an industrial scene. He had also noticed also strangely enough there were none dressed like nobility. He remarked on it to Calvin.

"There are some wealthy merchants, but no Merchant Princes in Geneva! The only Banking House we have is a branch of the Medicis of Florence. Our high society here is represented by the Cathedral Canons and the professional people who live in the vicinity of the Cathedral St. Pierre in the Upper City. Most of the citizens expend their energies in clothing, housing, and feeding our inhabitants, so that it leaves little room or time for luxuries and fripperies. But there are the exceptions, such as these men before us in the road." Sure enough, Knox had no difficulty in recognising those referred to, a knot of men dressed rakishly like popinjays, with an ostentatious feather sticking from their bonnets jauntily, sword hilts projecting from their hips, colourfully-brocaded cloaks and breeches of yellow and red adorning them Their demeanour exuded bravado and an arrogance, which contrasted with the serious behaviour and plain dress of the rest of the citizenry.

"These are some of the Libertine party, though, I am happy to say that I feel their power has been broken and is on the wane in Geneva, and these rascals are now the stump and waiting to be rooted out of the fresh, clean, soil of our great Protestant city! Don't be concerned at the spite the arrogant scoundrels will surely show to us as we pass by, my dear brother. It is but the dying hiss of the serpent!"

John Calvin's words were exactly fulfilled, for as the two preachers passed the group of openly mocking Libertines, their goatee beards fairly bristled with an aggression and their glinting eyes almost spat out venom of hate.

"A curse on you, Calvin!" One of the Libertines, clearly their leader, snarled at him.

"May the smoke of the funeral pyre of Servetus forever blacken your memory. May the spirit of Philip Berthelier haunt your nightmares! You are responsible for cutting him off from God! Instead of good, red, blood, you have milk and water flowing in your veins. Hypocrisy is your middle name!"

John saw Calvin's neck muscles stiffen and his face pale imperceptibly in his already pale complexion, as the name of Servetus was mentioned, and he knew that a painful nerve had been touched. But the man of Geneva refused to be affected, and carried on his way towards the old town and the Cathedral of St. Pierre at the top of the street, as if he had never heard. The Scot, though of a similar temperament, doubted if he could have resisted such a vicious insult himself.

"Sin is an illusion and salvation is deliverance from the phantom of sin! What we do is done by God, and what God does we do, for we are God!" Another Libertine called after them. Knox was totally shocked, not just by the tone of mockery, which filled their mouths, but by the utter evil and confusion of their words.

"You see what unlicensed men these are! What a disaster it would have been for Geneva, if they had gained control! These Libertines might have been freed from the paralysing spell of the Church of Rome and have breathed the intoxicating air of the new liberty of mind, but they have assumed a license, which brooks no restraint and which rejoices to plunge into orgies of mental dissipation."

"It is more than mental dissipation!" cried John Knox in the heat of his anger, forgetting that he was in the presence of the greatest theologian in Europe." It is utter blasphemy! Sin is an illusion?" Knox was beside himself, and his temper, always on a knife edge, was one of the few things that distinguished him from the calm man of Geneva.

"They have flung themselves from the prisons of the false traditions of Rome into the hedgeless fields of free thought! They claim they can just think as they please, and are a law unto themselves. I believe in the Ancient World they were called Sophists! The Libertines of Geneva have wedded free thinking, as they miscall it, to free living, and detest any control over their mind and morals, and have adopted a philosophy which merely harmonises with their style of life and, therefore, vindicates it. No church is possible under these circumstances! The Church is an organised body of men and women, dominated by one ideal and welded together by one defined faith."

Calvin's face had taken on a look of determination, and he stopped for a moment to glance back to where the group of Libertines had become embroiled in a heated argument with other citizens, who had taken exception to their abuse of the preacher of St. Pierre. John Calvin knew well that it was not his business to get involved in such personal confrontations in the street. The Consistory and other Courts of the city and in the pulpit of St. Pierre were where the battles were won. No, he mentally corrected himself a second time contritely, it was his business in the prayer closet and through the power of his pen, pouring out a stream of letters and encouragements to the crowned heads, princes, and leaders of Europe, that the real work was done. The pen was mightier than the sword. He continued with zeal.

"The whole religious future of Europe depends upon the formation of such a body, a united Protestant and Reformed Church of Europe, covering Switzerland, Germany, France, England, Scotland, Denmark, the Low Countries, Sweden, and, yes, even Bohemia and Transylvania, where the Lord has touched the heart of the Count of that land of forests." Knox was astonished at the breadth of the vision of this man. His own Scottish spirit, he confessed, could not see even beyond his own land and over into England.

"Who is Philip Berthelier?" He changed the subject, as they breasted the rise to approach Cathedral Square, and the deeply resounding peal of La Clemence began to ring out its magnificent sound." No doubt he was your enemy?"

"He was indeed my deadly enemy, a snake, and I shall never forget the occasion when God's hand alone prevented him taking my life. I shall tell you sometime, when it is convenient/." His mind went back to not long before; when in this very Cathedral before him he had stood defenceless in front of the Communion Table. Arranged against him were men, enraged to madness by his determination to prevent unholy men from partaking of the holy elements. His life had hung by a thread.

A silence had fallen over the vast Cathedral, which could have been cut by the sharp swords in the hands of these savage men facing him. He had lifted up the spotless white napkin to display the symbols of Christ's body and blood, food for believing souls. He had sought God's blessing on these simple elements, and was about to distribute them to the congregation. At that very moment there had been a violent movement among the Libertines present, as they attempted to seize the very bread and wine. Calvin had in defense covered the sacred symbols with his hands to protect them, and exclaimed in protest. His tones had rung throughout the Cathedral, echoing God's protest. He addressed their leader, Philip Berthelier.

"You may crush these hands of mine! You may lop off these arms with your weapons, and take my life! My blood is yours, you may shed it! But you shall never force me to give holy things to the profane and dishonour the Table of God!" His quiet eyes, full of the peace of God, had gazed out at Berthelier, and, as if an invisible power had flung back those who threatened him, after a seeming eternity Berthelier and his bullies had slunk away finally, cowed and abashed. The great congregation had opened a passageway for their cowardly retreat, condemned by the absolute silence around them. A profound calm had succeeded the event and the sacred ordinance was celebrated with a deep awe, as if the Deity Himself were visibly present in their midst.

Calvin shook his head imperceptibly to bring himself back to the present, as the two advanced across the Place St. Pierre, where a figure of impressive bearing had detached himself from a house on the far edge of the Square, which was dominated by the mighty Cathedral.

"Aha, here is Lauren de Normandie, at one time a great lawyer and mayor of my home town of Noyon! How blessed I am to have so many old and faithful friends give up positions and comfort in this world to come and share the burden of God's work here in Geneva! Do you know that Nicholas Cop, a learned scholar in the University of Paris, has come to live next door in the Rue des Chanoines?" John Knox was confused by the flood of foreign names and places, but avoided interrupting." Francois Bude has also left Paris to dwell here with his mother, two brothers, and two sisters, round the corner in the Puits Saint Pierre!"

Calvin was clearly a man who loved community, a man of the people. He now moved forward to greet the former mayor of Noyon, stretching out his thin arms, clad in his voluminous black gown, fur trimmed to keep out the early morning cold.

"Laurent, God bless you and your precious work here of publishing. You are a treasure from the Lord! The printing machine is vital. Sometimes I am amazed that you have come to our humble city to confer honour on Geneva!"

"Oh, come, come, Master John! If anyone confers honour on Geneva, it is surely you! I honestly do not believe that there can be found the like of you in this world. For who can count your ordinary and your extraordinary labours? I doubt if any man in our time has had more things of greater importance to listen to, to reply to, to write to! The vast amount and quality of your writings is enough to astonish anyone who looks at them."

He turned to John Knox, who saw the amused expression on the face of Laurent de Normandie, a man who resembled as much a patrician as it was possible in a city of middle-class merchants and artisans. It was obvious that Monsieur de Normandie was aware that he would embarrass Calvin with his extreme praise, but Knox knew he was no sycophant.

"He never ceases working day and night in the service of the Lord, and very much against his will he hears the prayers and beseechings of his friends on the very day, on which he gives himself some rest. Are you a stranger here? More than half the population is strangers, like myself in fact. They keep flooding in from everywhere, so many that the city will soon burst at its seams!"

"I am John Knox, a refugee from England for the truth of the Gospel." He thought it better not to mention Scotland yet." Mary Tudor tyrannises there from the throne, a misguided slave of Rome! But Scotland is my homeland, and there another she-wolf, the Jezebel, Mary of Guise, holds sway and imposes her will on the fledgling Reformation born to lighten Scotland with the illumination of God's Word!" Knox's eyes sparked off the others." When I left Dieppe I did not yet know the fate of my dear father in God, Archbishop Cranmer, and my beloved brothers, Latimer and Ridley. I fear for their lives and those of many Protestant brethren." The spark had changed to a tear, as his heart went out in longing for those in the furnace back home. But in a moment his anger had kindled, as he thought of the traitorous Bishop Tunstall nicknamed 'Dreamy Durham' for his lack of spiritual spine. He also remembered too well the sinister Duke of Northumberland, John Dudley, that unscrupulous noble, who hung around like a dark moth and shifted his loyalty according to the power stakes.

"Have faith, Master Knox!" The kindly Laurent tried to encourage the Scots exile." I foresee a better day coming, a rosebud in the east, when each man will be able to worship God, his Creator, under his own juniper tree, and the Bible will be the possession of all, from the baronet to the ploughboy." Normandie's features, normally so relaxed, had assumed an animated look.

"I thank you from my heart in the Lord's Name, sir. It is indeed the prayer of my heart, Give me Scotland, or I die!" Knox had been caught up too.

"Come along, meanwhile, my brethren," Calvin broke in," Let us attend the Cathedral's Service, for it is time for Choir practise under Louis Bourgeois. I have appointed Louis Master of Singing. Monsieur Bourgeois I have brought from France to form a wonderful Choir, which inspires us all! They give up four hours a week to the practise of the Psalms and the general study of Music." Again Knox hid the fact that he was taken aback by interest in culture." Monsieur Bourgeois has adapted and composed over eighty airs, many, I have to admit," and here he hesitated," from popular street ballads, and for a while this has worried me.

I thought the world might encroach upon our worship. We have had to guard against a frivolous spirit, which was so rife in Geneva and not allow that part of the Service to be an opportunity for purely sensual enjoyment." His sharp features brightened once more." Why, the Psalms of Clement Marot are sung so widely, a witness, my dear Knox, that there is a want in the heart of man.

My poor, late-lamented, brother in Christ, Ulrich Zwingli of Zurich, was sadly in error to omit singing from his public worship, to be substituted by mere responsive recitation. But he always was a willful firebrand, Zwingli, and his premature death at Kappel robbed our Reformation of a great mind. What a waste! Our weapons should be not carnal, but spiritual to the pulling down of strongholds. Brother Ulrich should never have taken up arms." But here again John Calvin's demeanour brightened with a soulful joy,

"Amongst all the things that give men pleasure and satisfaction is Music the chiefest, or at least one of the principal means, and we must be convinced that it has come from God's hand for this purpose. Why, even the lords and ladies have their favourite psalm, and King Henry of France has been known to chant the words *As the hart pants after the water* when he goes hunting! I wonder if it helped his pursuit?" Knox was amazed at this new side of a man, who up till then had been so sedate and sober. He continued his peaen of praise." Praise is simply sung prayer, my friend." Knox was all but caught up by his enthusiasm."

The Council of Trent has protested in vain against the tide of psalm singing. Even the Roman Catholic Church has sung their *Credo* and *Paternoster* to the tune of some drinking or love song, but we shall desist from that, thanks be to God! Let not the Devil rob us of the Psalms! Where else can we find the same warmth and passion to be infused into our Service of worship than from the Psalms of David, which the Holy Spirit dictated and gave to us? Then, when we sing, we can be certain that God has put the words in our mouths, as if He Himself sang within us to exalt his glory!"

The Scot was all but in awe of the complete eloquence of the man beside him, but abruptly checked himself." But we must always sing in the language known to us, for us French, and not in Latin, where for most they will sing without understanding, like some linnet, popinjay, or nightingale, which is a great mockery of God! But I forget myself, and am getting carried away. Let us to the enjoyment of the actual praise"

The bells were now sounding out sonorously across the high hill of Geneva, delighting John Knox's heart, for it was the call to worship, and he longed for the day when a similar summons would be sounded out by the bells of St. Giles in his beloved Edinburgh. But the cadences of the Children's' Choir as they echoed through the Cathedral were something the Scot could only envy. The Scots were not ready for such delicate sounds yet, he felt. But, even as they sat in the dim light of the Church, Knox's mind was on something of more concern to him just then.

Was it ever right for subjects to revolt against their established ruler? In his last letter to the Protestant Lords in Scotland he had touched on the delicate question of resistance to supreme Rulers. Soon after the marriage of their young Scots Queen Mary to the Dauphine of France, the Scots had begun to be worried by the designs of the French Court against their liberties and independence. It was not difficult to excite the resistance of the independent and haughty Barons of Scotland, accustomed at the best of times to yield but a very limited and precarious obedience, even to their own Princes. They had lately shown proof of this in their refusal to co-operate in the war against England, which they considered as undertaken merely in the interests of France.

Was he to seize this as an opportunity to inflame the irascible minds of the selfish nobility and get them to join themselves to the Earl of Arran, who desired the Regency? Knox was genuinely confused over the issue, and desired deeply to know the minds of the outstanding theologians of the Reformed Faith across Switzerland. The mind of brother Calvin, he knew, was very cautious on the subject. He felt in his inner soul that rebellion was *anathema*. Did not the Bible say that rebellion was worse than witchcraft? But was there a limit?

"I am troubled by this whole question of obedience to tyrannical rulers, and whether it is ever just to rise up and remove them, brother John." He questioned Calvin, when, after the joyful solace of youthful praise conducted by Louis Bourgeois in the sanctuary of St. Pierre, they had retired to the latter's quarters." The nobility are the guardians of the national liberties, but there are limits beyond which obedience is not due surely?" He sought Calvin's eyes, as if for a sign of agreement. The great man remained impassive. What was he to do with this irascible Scot, much as he admired him? Were they all like him, these Scots?

"Scripture admonishes us to be subject to the powers that be, John, for they are instituted of God, says St. Paul in his Epistle to the Romans. Recourse ought not to be had to resistance until matters are tyrannically driven to extremity. It is incumbent on you to be very circumspect in all your proceedings that your enemies might have no reason to allege that you or any of our Protestant cause are covering a seditious and rebellious design under the cloak of religion.

My advice to you is that by dutiful and cheerful obedience to all lawful commands, and by humble requests you should endeavour to recommend yourselves to the supreme authority and procure its favour in promoting the Reformed Faith." The man of Geneva had written many carefully-couched letters to the crowned heads of England, Poland, France, and Germany, and so he knew the value of statecraft." If your endeavours fail, you ought to make sure that the Gospel is preached, and the Sacraments administered to you and to your brethren." He glanced archly at the Scot to see how he had received his controversial advice. He could literally see the hackles rise in the Scot, but he knew that his heart was sincere to seek God's will.

"But, if attempts are made to crush us by violence, I believe it is lawful for us in our high station to stand up in defence of our brethren. For there is a great difference between lawful obedience and a fearful flattering of Princes. This would just lead to the destruction of a Commonwealth. As for the rule of women, Divine Law surely has said that at the creation of the first man and woman he was to have dominion over her and she was to be subject to him? Female Government was never permitted among the Jews. To promote a woman to bear rule, superiority, and dominion over a man in any realm, nation, or city is repugnant to nature, hostile to God, and most contrary to His revealed will, and even the subversion of equality and justice!"

This outburst of such audacious words struck even Calvin dumb for a moment, as he sought how to calm down this firebrand of a Scotsman. But Knox was to unknowingly open the way for John Calvin to be able to sidestep the issue of women rulers, remembering the viciousness of the Medici House in France. To unnecessarily antagonize Catherine de Medici was playing with fire." I would ask a favour of you, brother John," John Knox continued in full flow, caught up in his fervour." I wish to visit many of the Swiss Divines to confer on their Protestant theology, and to ask their advice on these points." Calvin was much relieved, as he had feared what the Scot's request would be." Would you give me a letter of introduction?"

"Of course, my dear friend! Heinrich Bullinger at Zurich is a close friend of mine and a valued colleague. He will be delighted to see you. He will give you sound advice on these matters," he exclaimed," perhaps more than me," he added." I would recommend the pastors of Lausanne, Neuchatel, Basel, St. Gallen, and even that awkward city of Berne, even though some of these proud Bernese still claim control over our independent Geneva! I shall furnish you with letters of good introductions to all of them." Knox never ceased to be amazed at the network of Europe-wide connections Calvin possessed. He was soon to find out that often he was closeted for long hours over his international correspondence, pleading the case of his persecuted brethren with all the kindness of his great heart and the eloquence that his ready, legal, pen could acquire.

With Calvin's introduction in his wallet, Knox rode through the mountain passes to the free city of Zurich, accompanied by his Geneva guides. The largest of the Swiss Federation, Zurich stood on a central plateau extending from the Alps to the German frontier, and, as the escort party and he rode along the shores of Lake Zurich towards where the city stood at its north end, John could not but admire the verdant hills that surrounded them on both sides of the Lake. It was now approaching spring, and, being a clear day, the snow-capped mountains of the Glarus Alps could still be seen to the southwards.

He looked forward with heightened anticipation to meeting Heinrich Bullinger, whose writings and theological interpretations had influenced the Protestants of England even more than Calvin. He had been only too aware that John Calvin been wary, too canny to commit himself to how far the persecuted people of England and Scotland should go in overthrowing the two women who tyrannised over them. Bullinger, he hoped and prayed, would be more assertive.

Knox sighed, as he let his eyes dwell on the hills around him, which reminded him of the Lammermuirs, the Pentlands, the Ochils, and even the small Lomond Hills of Fife, so gentler than the mighty Alps in the distance. It seemed so long since he had last seen his native land, apart from the nostalgic gaze he had often given across the Border country seven long years before. Seven was God's perfect number, so perhaps with God's help; it was time to return to Scotland? But how could he go back into the lion's den, the dangerous fires of persecution?

Calvin had told him that the burnings in London were horrendous and numerous. But he had heard in a rare communication from Scotland that the danger was now less there than at this time in England, and that several of the Protestant leaders had escaped the clutches of Bloody Mary Tudor and found a haven in Scotland, including William Harlaw and John Willock. These Englishmen had encouraged the brethren there, the missives said. But somehow he knew it was not time yet. His five years labouring in England had given him a discpline, which had stiffened his spiritual backbone and prepared him for his crowning work back in his dear land, of that he was certain. John Knox had no doubts of the righteousness of his cause under God.

He breathed in the sweet, Swiss air. Its freshness invigorated him, and he thought of Marjorie, his love back in Norham Castle, in England's northland and her mother Elizabeth. She and her mother were women, to whom he felt bound by a deep spiritual tie. Truly he longed to see them again. Would Sir Richard Bowes release both the women? Not only did he desire to marry Marjorie in God's sight, but the soul of Elizabeth Bowes had been won for the truth of God's Reformation. He knew well that she and her husband had become mutually alienated from one another and the marriage tie loosened radically.

The Lord of Norham Castle had become set in his Romish ways, maybe irrevocably, Knox knew from a year before. If Elizabeth Bowes was to leave her home at Norham Castle to follow Marjorie in her marriage to him, why should Sir Richard Bowes be opposed? Women, he privately admitted to himself, were clearly involved in his life one way or another. Mrs. Bowes continually sought his advice on spiritual matters while at Berwick, too much so, he had to be honest. But it pleased him that she sought his opinion and recognised his authority. He would have been less than a man, if he had not thought so. The words of Calvin came back to him that, as it was contrary to the law of Nature for women to rule, a woman Sovereign was the punishment imposed by God on a nation for their sins, not least Mary Tudor of England. The man of Geneva, who had gained the unstinting admiration of John Knox, had confessed that in exceptional cases a woman ruler like Deborah, might be a great blessing, and the Scot agreed with this. But, when it came to Calvin's opinion that, whether a tyrant or a Deborah, her people must obey her, he could not agree.

Knox pursed his lips and pulled at the reins of his steed, as he reacted to Calvin's words, and the bit cut into the horse's mouth, causing the creature to rear up. Aye, it went against his grain to accept such a passive approach. He had not replied to the great man's words. He had given the impression that he had accepted John Calvin's answer. He had politely cut short the discussion. Who was he to argue with such a great theologian?

This was the reason he had undertaken this tour of the Swiss City States, to find the opinions of the Protestant pastors there. Bullinger at Zurich, Pierre Viret in Lausanne, whom Master Calvin had recommended as a close friend and trustworthy colleague, Farel at Neuchatel, and those at Basel, Berne, and St. Gallen. He would visit Viret on his way back to Geneva, he had decided.

Even now, the outskirts of Zurich loomed up below in the valley, as the group descended from the Alpine pass, where their meadows were already in full bloom with their enchanting carpet of multi-coloured spring flowers. Knox breathed deeply again. It was a far cry from the chafing galley oars. The Lord was good. He still thought that the creation of elaborate private gardens, which some of the nobility of Scotland and England had cultivated, were a waste of time, when there were better things to do. One could appreciate God's creation without going too far. There were much more important actions, like this meeting with Heinrich Bullinger, and theological discussion with the Reformer.

The immediate impression John Knox had of Bullinger was of a man of confrontational and strong character. His very face exhibited it, a broad chin, firm bones, and open, challenging, eyes. His chin showed more than a growth of hair, which he clearly shaved regularly. Here was a man of action, whereas Calvin had been supremely a man of profound thought. Bullinger welcomed him, especially when the Scot passed on the letter of introduction from Calvin.

"You are a very blessed man to have John Calvin for a friend, and so you have myself as a friend also." He glanced once more at the message and its gist. *"This brother, a Scot by nationality, seeks the advice of Zurich's theologians. , and is travelling to meet you, not unwillingly, I hope. They say that under the young King Edward VI, the King of England, he laboured energetically for the Lord. He is now eager to increase his knowledge."* Bullinger was impressed by the very abruptness and simplicity of the message. He thought back to his own conversion from Roman Catholicism and his time as a student at the University of Cologne, where openings had been presented for the advance of Protestantism but not taken, and the Church of Rome had returned in greater power than ever over that great and historic German city. Every new weapon, like this powerful little Scot, must be utilized to advance the Protestant Faith. He looked up at Knox and scrutinized him intently.

"You need encouragement, Herr Knox. You have been away a long time from your homeland, yes? Have you received much news?"

"The occasional message from Scotland, Herr Bullinger, usually when I have been in Dieppe, and visiting the *Rue des Ecossais,* where an Inn frequented by refugee Scots is the source of whatever news finds its way across the Channel." He remembered that this was the German-speaking part of Switzerland." But I confess that I thirst for news from across the Channel. It is a great comfort to me to hear that many Protestant pamphlets are being distributed across Europe from secret printing presses on the Continent of Europe. I have not an inkling where these darts of truth are being sharpened." Bullinger knew at once that John Knox spoke sincerely, for his character was an open book.

"The spies of Rome are on the lookout continually, and one must be careful of the hapless and needless word allowed astray." Bullinger was quite impassive, though Knox was certain that the man before him was at the centre of the intricate web of Protestant propaganda." Sometimes I have heard of the unknown authors of these pamphlets signing themselves, *'From Rome'* or *From the Pope's Castle of San Angelo'*, and even from towns, which everyone knows do not exist!" Bullinger allowed himself an enigmatic little smile, which indicated that he knew more." It is driving the authorities in England mad with frustration, but things are not good there." He frowned severely. "Hundreds of Protestants have left England's shores.

Mary Tudor has brought back Cardinal Pole from his exile in Italy, and he will have her hunt down all Protestant heretics and burn them! She is determined to restore Papal power and to stamp out Protestant belief. She is an idealist and believes sincerely that persecution saves the souls of we heretics! But, thanks be to God, it is to our advantage that King Henry II of France has a bad relationship with Mary Tudor of England, and so grants asylum to English Protestants, and even to give financial help to gentlemen such as Thomas Stafford and Peter Carew." Knox was much too polite to show his amusement at Bullinger's attempt with his German tongue at pronouncing these English surnames." But the King of France cannot stand Protestant clergymen, scholars of any kind, and zealous women. So, be careful, if you return to Dieppe, particularly among the peasantry of the French countryside, for only in the south in the mountains of the Cevennes and in the area of the Languedoc have the common people been influenced by the Reformed Faith. It is to the nobles and merchants of France that you must look for support in part, and to such as La Rochelle. As for Denmark, King Christian III only wants Lutherans, no Zwinglians, Calvinists, or Anabaptists. He is very particular about it. So, that door is shut to you, Herr Knox."

"The Lord has not led me to go to Denmark, Herr Bullinger," replied Knox curtly, the Scot's feathers ruffled by the slightly provocative tone of the Swiss German, whose firm gaze was that of a man with equally-fixed principles and ideas. After all, he had come all the way across Switzerland from south to north to see Bullinger, only stopping briefly for a short conference with the pastor in Neuchatel, William Farel, Calvin's fiery predecessor." I have come to you to ask your advice on serious questions."

"Then I will give you serious answers."

"In both England and Scotland we are ruled by women, who are idolaters, Mary Tudor and Mary of Lorraine. Is it always right to obey a ruler, who condemns the true religion and enforces idolatry, like the Mass and the worship of the Virgin Mary, blessed be the fruit of her womb?"

"Absolutely not!" Bullinger's words were incisive and authoritative in an age when the words of the monarchy were regarded as close to God's." The Godly ought to resist, as in the prophet Daniel's case, to risk of their lives. But remember our Lord's commands in St. Matthew! Do not be afraid of those can kill the body, but cannot kill the soul. Rather be afraid of the One who can destroy both the body and soul in Hell!"

"Be that God or the devil, Master Bullinger?" Knox enquired aggressively. This man provoked him positively, as iron sharpens iron." It seems to me that both can do it." He regretted his words the second he had uttered them. He knew they were wrong.

"Ah, you Scotsmen, ever the controversialists! You must know that only God can do that!" Heinrich Bullinger's own bold jaw jutted out in turn. He was not only similar to Knox in a certain trait, but he was almost also the same age." Do you know that there is a saying circulating on the Continent, *Scotus est piper in naso, He is a Scot, he has a pepper in his nose'*. You Scots are known far and wide for your holiness of temper and pride, swift to avenge any imagined slight on you or your land. As the French put it, *'Fier comme un Ecosse. Fiery as a Scot.'* As if that's not enough, the French also have a saying about your carefulness in trading, *'The Scot brings in a small horse first, and afterwards a big one.'* So, you have a lot to live up to, Scotsman."

Bullinger fixed him with an unwavering stare, but one which contained a distinct twinkle in his eyes. Knox bridled slightly, but he knew he had met his match on this occasion. There was no point in winning an argument and losing a potential ally. He was learning that one could not antagonise and influence a person at the same time.

"May we return to what really concerns me, Herr Bullinger?" Knox responded, regaining his calm." Must we obey a ruler or magistrate, who enforces idolatry and condemns true religion? Are men in high positions, who possess castles and towns, entitled to defend themselves and their followers by armed forces against ungodly violence? By Natural Law and God's Law women should be subject and not rule. What say you?"

"If a woman succeeds to the throne, it would be dangerous for pious men to resist Civil Laws." Knox could perceive the slight guardedness in Bullinger, but much less so than in Calvin." There are cases, you well know, Herr Knox, where men are ruled by women, as in the case of Deborah. The Lord overthrows the unjust and despotic ruler through those to whom he affords the opportunity. Athaliah, the wicked daughter of Jezebel, was righteously killed on the orders of Jehoiada, the High Priest."

The story of the deposing of the tyrannical Queen Athaliah of Israel and her death outside the Temple of the Lord, in the place where the horses entered the Palace grounds, was familiar to the Scots preacher, for he had often dwelt on its cogency for England's situation. She had been intending to destroy the whole royal family, to take the throne again after Jehu, the mighty warrior of God, But Jehosheba, the daughter of King Joram of Judah, took Joash, the son of Ahaziah, from among the Royal Princes, who were about to be murdered. She put him and his nurse in a bedroom in the Temple to be hidden from Queen Athaliah, his grandmother. For six years, while the wicked Queen reigned. , the boy, Joash, and his nurse were kept hidden in the Temple of the Lord. But in the seventh year, God's perfect number, the time had come for revolution, and Jehoiada sent for the commanders of the units of hundreds and the guards to come to the Temple, where he made a Covenant and put them under an oath. The High Priest showed them the King's son, Joash, and commanded them, fully-armed, to guard the young King in the Temple of the Lord. Jehoiada then crowned the boy, presented him with a copy of the Covenant, and proclaimed him King. They anointed him, the people, clapped their hands joyfully, and shouted "*Long live the King!*"

Knox so admired this incredibly dramatic story and his spirit longed to have been there at the glorious crowning of the Lord's anointed so long ago. How good it was to have a Godly ruler, something he had known only for a short time back in Scotland. He admired just as much the resolution of those who had achieved the destruction of the evil Queen Athaliah, and most of all, the courage of Jehoiada, the High Priest.

The dramatic, but terrible, end for the Queen had come, when she appeared at the Temple, and, enraged at the sight of the young King standing by the pillar, as was the custom, shouted out," *Treason! Treason!*" Jehoiada ordered her to be taken out from the Temple between lines of soldiers, for he could not desecrate the sanctuary of the Temple. Athaliah was led to where again the horses entered the Palace grounds, and there she was put to death. Jehoiada then made a Covenant between the Lord and the King and the people, that they would be the Lord's servants. He also made a Covenant between the King and the people.

Something in Knox's spirit responded to the very word Covenant and all that it meant. It echoed with a sense of security, trust, strength, and comfort. He longed with all his heart for a Covenant between the Lord and the people of Scotland. It might lead to the pulling down of some spiritual strongholds, like images and altars, and the cleansing of Scotland's Temple. The children of Israel had gone to the Temple of Baal and torn it down, and smashed the altars and idols, killing Mattah, the priest of Baal, in front of the altars. All the people of the land rejoiced. Joash was only seven when he was proclaimed King of Israel.

"I am pleased with your answer, Master Bullinger, for I have not been encouraged in my personal views in this matter, even by Master Calvin, sir. As the Spirit is set in the times in which we live, so God allows us freedom of conscience. But I feel convinced that the Lord would have us oppose tyranny in whatever form, if it opposes the freedom of worship of God's people."

"I am sure Master Huldreich Zwingli would have agreed wholeheartedly with you, if his militancy had not led to his unfortunate premature death at the Battle of Kappel, fighting bravely for Zurich. He was a fervent patriot, but I doubt if you would have agreed with his theology, my friend, for Zwingli was a friend of the ancient Greek philosophers, Plato, Aristotle, and Plutarch, and even believed that he would meet these sages of antiquity in Heaven. I have taken up the mantle of Zwingli here in Zurich. But," he smiled quietly," I am not saying that I am in accord with all his theology."

"How can he say that he will meet such as Aristotle and Plato in Heaven?" gasped Knox." They knew not Christ!"

"Be not overzealous, Knox, for our minds are limited, and maybe it was those Christ went to preach to, seekers after truth, before he ascended to be with God our Father." It was the start of an animated discussion between the two Reformers, which continued for hours.

But it was with a satisfied mind that days later the Scot finally departed in amicable mood from this plain-speaking man of Zurich. Like Calvin, Knox was not a philosopher and was impatient of speculation, and to consider the question of whether the ancient Greek philosophers were true believers was something that he found distasteful to argue over. Christians were fellow-workers with a transcendent God, not to the Scot in a mystical sense, for neither Knox nor Calvin were mystics, but as brave soldiers in the army of the Lord against the power of evil.

Energy, rather than deep feeling, was the proof of being right with God and having a pure conscience. The consciousness that the Lord was looking down happily on him was a spur to action. Majesty, holiness, dignity, and grace rather than love and mercy were the attributes which John Knox thought of when he thought of God in Heaven.

So it was that Knox trekked back over the mountains to Geneva with his bodyguard, stopping over at Lausanne with brother Pierre Viret, the Protestant Pastor there, but again Viret was too cautious to support Knox's views on rebellion against established rulers. Yet the Scot was strangely satisfied with his tour of the Swiss City States, even if Heinrich Bullinger had been the sole figure to agree with his extreme approach, for within himself he knew that the others were just too wary to commit themselves to rebellion against Kings and Queens. His confidence was further boosted by the happy welcome from his friend, John Calvin, and news to encourage his self-esteem. He had been exhausted; his thighs strained by the long, body-jolting, journey through the high mountain passes, when at last they reached the city on Lac Leman. John Calvin's thin features were lit by an eager light.

"My beloved brother, good news, you have been invited to be the pastor to the English -speaking congregation in the German city of Frankfurt! It is signed by twenty one distinguished men. You must accept it and go immediately is my recommendation before they invite another, for I am sure it is a place of conflicting opinions." Calvin's face was a scene of varying emotions itself, aware of the excellent prospect for his respected colleague, and of its potential dangers." But first, how fared your conference with the Swiss pastors? Happily and blessed, I pray?"

Calvin looked out from the corner of his eye, for he was as yet a little afraid of the fierce Scot's uncompromising opinions, though he had acquired a deep affection for John Knox's bold nature and strong emotions.

"Well enough, Pastor Calvin, well enough!" The Lord is uniting hearts throughout Switzerland, and we shall see yet a united Protestant Church across Europe! Berne, Basel, Neuchatel, Lausanne, St. Gallen, and Zurich, all welcomed me with open arms."

He hesitated and stopped short of revealing details of his discussions. There was a time for discretion." But tell me of this news from Frankfurt." His heart beat faster, uplifted by this new prospect, and he restrained his excitement.

"I have to warn you, brother, that the congregation is a mixture of English refugees and Belgian, Protestant, Walloons. I suspect the Walloons are an awkward sect. They have been afflicted by a wanderlust, it seems, and have been unable to settle anywhere, including Glastonbury in England, and have been refused entry to Denmark, Hamburg, and Lubeck!

There would have been some negotiating over the form of Service with the Walloons, but they are a good mixture of races and are for the same forms of worship as ourselves. They would be an ideal fraternity for you, my brother. The Lord has done great things for you, as I have seen your perfect preaching gifts and the fire of the Spirit in you, which infects your hearers with the same flames. It would also be a challenge to you.

Frankfurt is a great city, and a Protestant one, a free city of the German Holy Roman Empire ruled from Vienna, with full powers of self government over its own affairs. It, like Nuremberg and Strasbourg, has adopted Protestantism, and has stood firm as a bastion of the Reformation in the midst of Catholic South Germany, like these other cities. But I must tell you that, although Frankfurt has two Mayors and a City Council, it is a few powerful merchant families who really control the city. Johannes Von Glauburg is the man you must seek out, a prominent member of the Council and head of one of the three most influential and richest families in Frankfurt. You must win Von Glauburg over to your side."

Calvin, for all his life and study of things of the spirit, was well aware of the vital importance of wisdom in politics. Knox gazed down at the floor of Calvin's study in meditation. He was sure that the Reformer of Geneva was not trying to get rid of him, as some troublesome burr on his flesh. They had enjoyed too close fellowship for that. But John Calvin genuinely desired his best. However, the Scot had been supremely content in this magnificent. Swiss city, permeated with the fresh, invigorating, air of political and religious freedom.

"I am loathe to abandon Geneva and yourself, my beloved brother. I have come to love you and your city above many things. After the violence of St. Andrews, the pain and despair of the French galleys, the strife and strain of bringing the wild townspeople of Berwick under the gracious reign of God, and then the double mindedness and untrustworthiness of the English nobility, at last I have found Geneva the most perfect school of Christ that has existed on Earth from the days of the Apostles." John Knox was torn by opposing emotions.

"It is true that things are much calmer now in Geneva with the expulsion of Ami

Perrin, the leader of the Libertines. We are now imposing mercy and discipline, and this is drawing more and more pious refugees into our city. The very population has trebled to twenty thousand. People are not attracted to chaos and tyranny."

"I shall seriously consider your proposal of accepting the invitation to the pastorate at Frankfurt, but first I must go to Dieppe to hear what news there is of England and the furnace of persecution that is being stoked there. The memory of the horrors of burnings and executions under that tyrant Jezebel, Mary Tudor, is only too real to my mind. The gift of foreknowledge is often a hard burden, but a blessed and encouraging one in the times of darkness." Calvin silently nodded his assent and held his peace. The mystery of God's foreknowledge left little room for human foreknowledge in his theology. All things were pre-ordained of God, even disasters.

Knox was concerned deeply about his dearest Marjorie and her mother, Elizabeth, back in England, as he heard the martyrdoms were increasing and his heart trembled. But a threefold cord cannot easily be broken and he wrote from Dieppe to encourage them. Three times he had visited Dieppe that year now. He almost felt within hearing and touching reach of his persecuted brethren and loved ones there.

At least his sister was safer in Scotland. His words were unequivocal and strong in the missive. Even if they had offended no other earthly creature, the last person they should offend was God, who was everywhere and searches all hearts and wills. God's indignation, once inflamed against the disobedient, can be appeased by no creature on Heaven or Earth. He received sad news that there had been not only compromises, but even defections amongst his former congregations in England, and he was conscious of not just anger and frustration but depression at the situation over there. This Mary Tudor was not only about to undo the Reformation, but to even establish a Spanish-style Inquisition in England.

The position in England was desperate, and he lashed out in his letters. He must be like a rock against the roaring sea. In his *Admonition to the Faithful.* There he told them that Jezebel had never erected half so many gallows in all Israel as the wicked Queen had done within England alone. Let God's vengeance not be delayed. May Death swallow up all the Lord's enemies, and may they go quickly to Hell, especially that hypocrite, William Paulet, Mary's Treasurer, who at one time had sworn that Mary would never reign in England and had called her an incestuous creature born out of wedlock! This turncoat was like Shebna in the Bible, now fawning before his former enemy, as Shebna, the secretary and treasurer of King Hezekiah of Israel, had shilly-shallied between Hezekiah and Rabshakeh, the emissary of the King of Assyria, Sennacherib.

In Dieppe, where he had returned to what had been his first port of call on the Continent as refugee, Knox heard familiar Scots voices in the street, and on enquiry found that it was suitably known as the *Rue des Ecossais,* the Street of the Scots. In conversation, which he easily fell into with one of the colony of Scots, who resided there, he learnt that their main business was the woollen trade. Like most Scots merchants, their acumen was extremely sharp.

"Aye, it's the fine sheep frae the Pentlands, the Lammermuirs, and our guid Border Hills, that we require to produce the excellent cloth for the Low Countries and their weaving and embroidery. Anything less will nae doo! The Flemings have been expert weavers and dyers for centuries. There's plenty o' them aroond Biggar!" One

Scots merchant told him expansively. "Dieppe is the best Port on the Continent for us Scots. A Scot is never a stranger in Dieppe! Why, the taverns all around the harbour resound to Border ballads about the steel bonnets and the Border relvers, aye, and aiblins, a romantic tale or twa! And sometimes even on the more serious things of life, on philosophy and religion."

He changed his tack now, having discovered that his companion was a minister of religion, exiled for his Protestant faith. "We are eager and anxious to learn of all the new ideas on religion that are surging back and forth across the Channel. At times it is better to learn them in private." He lowered his voice and came closer." Let us retire to that tavern over there for a stoup of beer." He looked sharply in all directions until he was satisfied." Did you say that you have but come frae Geneva? We have some Protestant pastors in Dieppe, recently come frae that city, the most outstanding Jean Venables, who carries aroond wi' him a hidden stock of Bibles newly printed, until his stock runs out, and mysteriously they are replenished from some secret source! I'm sure the Roman authorities would give a lot to ken where his printing press is!" He laughed nervously.

For some hours Knox stayed and taught and debated with the intelligent and open-minded merchant, delving into the deep things of the spirit until late in the evening he made his way carefully back to his lodgings to continue penning his words to the faithful in England in the early morning hours.

'My opinion is that those who tyrannise over the people of England and practise idolatry shall suffer a punishment in this world and a perpetual condemnation and torture in Hell, unless they repent. My situation is that since January I have travelled throughout Helvetia visiting the congregations there, and have reasoned with all the pastors and many other, excellent, learned, men, upon such matters, which, as you will understand, I cannot commit to writing just now. I would gladly utter them by tongue or pen to God's glory. If I thought that I could have you with me as well as some other assured men, I would jeopardise my life to show men what could be done with a safe conscience in these sad and dangerous days, but, since it cannot be done without instant danger to others than myself, I will await the time God appoints. We must be patient. Be assured that a statute by Civil Law is lawful and just, nor is everything that ungodly men allege to be treason a sin before God. But this I leave to when I have the opportunity to speak with you.

In great haste from Dieppe, May10th, 1554,

Yours whom you know, John Knox.'

It was a letter written and sent clandestinely, in which he refrained from giving names or specific instructions, in case the missive fell into the wrong hands. For three weeks he remained at Dieppe, trying to control his anxiety before he wrote again offering advice, this time to the afflicted Church in general across England, to comfort them and help them bear Christ's cross with patience. He exhorted them to refrain from any acts of violence against the Queen and Roman Catholics. He felt also compelled to write letters to the faithful in London, Newcastle, and Berwick, his former preaching grounds, advocating the same restraint.

The danger of following the example of men of violence in the Scriptures like

Ehud and Jehu, and even women like Judith, was that attempts might be made to assassinate Mary and other leading Roman Catholics in England. These were violent times. His brows knitted, as he dwelt on the great problem of violence and war, and as Christians of taking up the sword to punish God's enemies. He had always tried to deter not only others among his brethren from individual acts of violence, but was unconvinced too that even Magistrates had the right to kill those who were God's enemies. He had written to Marjorie's mother, Elizabeth, to this effect. It satisfied an inner need he had to secretly admit to himself that Marjorie's mother was so sollicitous of his spiritual advice, even though it was the daughter he had married.

Taking up his quill once more, he now concentrated, however, on his advice to the Church in England under terrible fire, and gnawed at its end in his worry to get the right words. Wifely love and family matters could be a major distraction.

'I hope that one day Jesus Christ, who is crucified in England, shall rise again, despite his enemies. Beloved brethren, two things you must avoid. One is that you do not presume to be revengers of your own cause, but you must leave vengeance to God, who is able to repay evil men in accordance with their malicious thoughts. The second is to avoid hating with a carnal hatred those who are blind, cruel, and evil tyrants. But you must learn to pray for your persecutors and be deeply sorry that the Devil has prevailed in them. He is leading them body and soul to eternal perdition.

Note well that I say that we have not to hate our enemies with a carnal; hatred. For there is a spiritual hatred, which King David calls a perfect hatred, which is worked up by the Holy Ghost in the hearts of God's chosen people against those who are rebels against God's holy Word. It was this pure hatred which inflamed Jeremiah, when he prayed, 'Let me see Thy vengeance, O Lord, upon Thy enemies.' It is with this kind of hatred that we can hate tyrants and pray for their destruction. It doesn't matter if they are Kings or Queens, Princes, or Prelates. In addition, you should take heart that prayers made fervently with this kind of feeling are acceptable of God, and whoever prays gets an answer according to his words. There is power in our words.

David, Jeremiah, and other prophets saw with their own eyes the red-hot vengeance of God poured out upon the merciless tyrants of their time. I am absolutely sure that some of you, who are groaning and weeping under the heel of the power-mad bishops, shall see God's wrath fall on the pestilential papists. For, as God is unchangeable, He will assuredly stir up another Jehu to execute His vengeance upon these bloodthirsty and idolatrous people.'

The Scots preacher fell back, exhausted by the sheer effort, mental, emotional, and spiritual, that the words had cost him. He felt the strain of distinguishing between hatred of false beliefs and hatred of those who possessed them and taught these falsehoods and persecuted others in the process. It was a fine line. He slept the sleep of the righteous that night.

Having got it out of his system like a purgative, John Knox now went back to fair Geneva. He was loathe to relinquish the study of Hebrew, that strange language of signs for vowel sounds, so different from the Classical languages. Even at the age of fifty, he had almost mastered God's ancient people's speech with the energy of a youth. But the call to Frankfurt was insistent and he had to go, even if with a sense of the unknown. It was nothing new to him, but another adventure of the Holy Spirit. Moreover, he could continue the learning of this alien, intriguing, Hebrew, language in Frankfurt.

"Nature is the garment in which we see God by," said Calvin reflectively one day, as they gazed out over the lovely Lake of Geneva and the soaring peaks of the Jura Alps once more from the window off *Rue des Chanoines*. Knox wondered if he would ever see the wonderful scene again, not that the man of Haddington had much time for Nature's garb, far less gardening. There were more important things. Geneva had been the most perfect school of Christ, no swearing, gambling, no usury, and no blasphemy and false doctrine most of all. "Remember, brother, Geneva will always welcome you back with open arms."

CHAPTER NINE

TROUBLE IN FRANKFURT

S o great was John Knox's love for Geneva that it was two months before he could be persuaded to depart for Frankfurt-am-Main, the mighty German city in Hesseland on the River Main. For days he had wrestled in prayer and finally he had felt that the Holy Spirit said go to the city.

Nineteen miles above its confluence with the Rhine at Mainz, Frankfurt had been founded by the Franks about a thousand years before taking its name from the *Ford of the Franks*. It had been an Imperial City for all of two hundred years, and it was an impressive one. When the Scots preacher finally reached Frankfurt, having travelled up the mighty Rhine river by barge from Basel by way of Karlsruhe, Mannheim, and Mainz, he first caught sight of the great Eschen-heimer Tower, standing 155 feet high, then the attractive red sandstone Cathedral of St. Bartholomew came into view, gleaming in the autumn sunshine, and the equally attractive old Town Hall, known as the Romer, with its quaintly-designed arches and many crow-stepped gables.

He was soon to be impressed much more by the distinguished magistrate and member of the powerful Von Glauburg family. Johannes Von Glauburg was a typically thickset and brusque German, who had a kindly face and welcomed John Knox wholeheartedly.

"How good to have a Scot at last! We have had everyone else here in Frankfurt, the English, French, Swiss, and Walloons! Oh, the Walloons have had a real task settling in! There are only twenty four of them here under their Pastor Vallerand Pullain, but we have given them the *Weissfrauenkirche*, how do you call it, the Church of the White Ladies, and they are very happy. You will like them, I'm sure, Herr Knox, for they are for the French form of worship service, set up by Monsieur Calvin, from whom, I know, you have just come. But I must inform you that, though we have the followers of Luther, Calvin, and Zwingli represented here in Frankfurt, it is the Lutherans who have gained most control, mainly through Pastor Hartmahnn Beyer.

So you will have opposition here in Frankfurt, Herr Knox, since we seem to attract every kind of Christian sect who are under persecution in their own country. Thomas Lever has been a difficult leader, and will cause you trouble, but this I prophesy, you will find a true friend in the other Englishman, William Whittingham. He has the same intense but honest spirit as yourself."

Indeed the German's forecast was exactly true, for in the English refugee, William Whittingham, Knox found a kindred spirit. His first words proved so.

"I am truly relieved, Herr Glauburg, for enemies have been easy to find and friends a wheen more difficult, in particular faithful and steadfast ones," John Knox replied equably, thinking that perhaps there would be indeed a rosebud in the east, or rather the south east of Europe.

"I have been trying to rid myself and my companions of this oppressive Prayer Book that Archbishop Cranmer foisted upon us! It restricts our freedom of worship to reach and pray to God as He sovereignly directs. These responses which the Book forces us to make are so artificial, and all that kneeling grates on my conscience! It is as if we are kneeling to a book, not to God himself. We only kneel to God Almighty!"

"I could not agree more," Knox responded airily, liking this man more by the second." I have long opposed kneeling, particularly at the Lord's Table. It might be taken as an act of adoration, and our enemies might take it as a means to bring back the idolatrous use of the Sacraments. I thank God that I was able to persuade the Council of England to instruct Archbishop Cranmer to draw up the Black Rubric, as it was called, and have it pasted into the Second Prayer Book, which had already been published. The Black Rubric you may be conversant with, I hope, Master Whittingham. It explains that kneeling at the Lord's Supper does not signify adoration of either the bread or the wine, nor any real presence of Christ's flesh and blood. It simply reveals reverence while receiving the Sacrament.

I can clearly recall how I demonstrated fervently to my flock at Berwick-on-Tweed how to handle this thorny problem. I taught them well, and I can assure you, Master Whittingham, that if you can teach such as the stubborn, hard-headed, folk of the Border country anything, you can teach all people! Kneeling to the Sacrament is totally wrong, but the State required it. I accepted it only for the sake of unity. To oppose the Church of England at this point would only have weakened the vital unity we need against Romanism. In London John a' Lasco and his congregation adopted the practise of sitting at Communion that I had recommended. I have had to deal with a civil war in my own spirit, for two principles that I wholeheartedly believe in have clashed within me, obedience to the State and purity of worship. But I do not deem the matter serious enough to merit disobedience to the State."

"I am afraid that I see a storm on the horizon for our happy congregation here at Frankfurt, brother John," sighed Whittingham wearily," for the Englishman, Richard Chambers, and his friend, Edmund Grindal, have arrived from Strasbourg to debate about what is acceptable in the English Prayer Book. I can see as clearly as the prophet Isaiah that a collision is coming which will destroy our peaceful Church here where we have been welcomed with such a generous heart by this fine Protestant city. Frankfurt has shown great bravery since its still under the controlled watch of the Catholic Holy Roman Empire. The Emperor himself has been attending a Conference nearby, so that any rumour whatever of intrigue, confusion, or disharmony will reach him in a trice. People come from all over Europe to the two annual Fairs. At the Book Fair students can obtain texts at a fraction of the normal price as well as manuscripts that are rare elsewhere. So we must take good care not to upset the civil peace, but at the same time we must not compromise in worshipping God in spirit and in truth, none of the bowing and scraping. The Lord wants a humble and contrite spirit alone."

"Let the Church Order be the most Godly and the furthest from superstition. Let us not do anything without a widespread acceptance by the congregation and wider afield among the Protestants of Europe," responded Knox slowly and deliberately." Wisdom is called for and even compromise, where necessary, in inessentials.

But compromise there was to be none sadly. Thomas Lever of the English congregation at Zurich, which had earlier refused to consider sending one of their number to be pastor at Frankfurt, arrived a month later in the German city. John Knox, though secretly irritated at his change of mind on the part of Lever and his probable interference with their worship, accepted Whittingham's advice to allow the liturgy of responses and even kneeling at the Lord's Table until Easter time when a vote should be taken. But before that date was reached on a cold and blustery March day with a chilling wind blowing off the Main and the nearby Rhine, as if to presage the chilling news, Whittingham broke into Knox's study. He had been preparing a sermon on the Epistle to the Romans. But he dismissed his thoughts for the other's face told a story.

"The worst news, brother John! The Englishman they call 'the Cancellor', Richard Cox, has come, a sure portent of trouble!" The Scot screwed up his brows in annoyance, for he had heard of this man, nothing good at all.

"Aye, a troublemaker, if ever there was, who would cause trouble in an empty house!"

Richard Cox had been the Chancellor of Oxford University, and even one of the chief architects of Cranmer's Prayer Book. But he was a notorious character, whose true, destructive, nature and persecuting spirit had come out earlier during the tyrant, Henry VIII's, reign, when Cox had bullied the English Churchmen into accepting the evil King's divorce from his Spanish Queen, Katharine of Aragon, as legitimate. Cox's delight at banning and burning all books he considered unsound was well-known and gave him the nickname of 'Cancellor'. He had been enraged too at Knox's introduction of the Black Rubric into the Thirty Nine Articles of the Church of England, safeguarding the Protestant Theology of the Holy Communion. So, even before his arrival in Frankfurt, though they had never met, he was a deadly enemy of the Scot.

"He's a prickly burr, our Richard Cox, and as sure as night follows day, he or I must go! I have come here to Frankfurt with high hopes of a fruitful ministry in a fresh scene of Christian labour. Now I find it a hornet's nest!" Knox heaved a heavy sigh, but in a moment he had lifted his head, squared his jaw, and pushed out his chest. It was not for him the ducking of a challenge." There is no jouking in the cause of Christ! I am sure that we shall face one another soon," he concluded.

It was not long before 'Cancellor' Cox sought a confrontation with the Scot, and it was to be the severest test, a real battle of wills. The battle lines were drawn up, as Whittingham and Knox were summoned on the orders of the Frankfurt authorities to meet with Cox and Lever at the house of the Walloon pastor, Pullain. The die was cast. Knox had his secret apprehensions about coming to Frankfurt confirmed. The seeds of animosity and dissension had already been sown.

The English exiles at Zurich had signified that they would not come to Frankfurt unless they obtained a security that the Church there would use the same order of service last set out in England by the fine young King Edward, before they fled to safety. Again a groan of frustration shook John Knox. Why had Edward died so prematurely, leaving the way open to Bloody Mary's reign? Why were exiled Protestants behaving like this, fighting amongst themselves, when they had all sought refuge for the same reason, for the sake of the Reformed faith? The enemy, Satan, was sowing his lies as usual, misrepresenting the truth, putting things out of proportion and out of focus. The Zurich exiles were even encouraging their brethren in Strasbourg to introduce the same obnoxious English Prayer Book into Frankfurt. What confusion, the work of the enemy of their spirits, existed, but he resolved not to be drawn into his trap, and to avoid anything that would widen the breech. But, when he reached Pastor Pullain's house and met the notorious Richard Cox, he saw that for a certainty bigotry stared out of his face.

"Ah, Master John Knox, you will be pleased to meet a fellow Englishman. You already know Thomas Lever from Zurich of course." Pullain was all affability, but here was no welcoming acknowledgement from the other two.

"I am a Scot; let me remind you, Pastor Pullain." He deliberately refrained from exchanging handshakes with Cox and Lever, or even nodding in their direction.

"Yes, I forgot. Forgive me." Truthfully the Walloon was not particularly zealous for English people, or even Scots. Their theology had made a bad impression on him during the short stay of he and his small flock at Glastonbury. Here he just wanted peace in their new spiritual home and an end to their travelling." This is Richard Cox, one-time Chancellor of England, come to join us." Knox could not hide his instinctive distaste of the man before him. His black, beetling, brow, spoke of a man accustomed to his own way.

"Mr. Knox, the infamous Scotsman! I remember well your troublesome and petty *Black Rubric in the Thirty Nine Articles.* I must tell you that I opposed it totally throughout without much success. I pray that God will favour my words and actions here. ," he added menacingly.

"Our God has given us all complete liberty to follow the truth, Mr. Cox," replied Knox drily." As for my beliefs, I adhere to Scripture, and will not have any papist practices, not least in the Sacrament. Nor will we have responses, like some little birds that chirrup after one another, nor kneeling as if in some form of pagan worship, as worthy Master Calvin, whom all men of Godly natures esteem highly, wrote to me recently from Geneva. Master Chancellor, or is it '*Cancellor* ', since you are infamous for cancelling books and sermons, which are tolerable fooleries, which might be allowed at the beginning of a Reformation, but ought always to be removed afterwards, unless of course they have a fondness for popish dregs!" Richard Cox, and to a lesser extent Thomas Lever, looked as if they would explode in an apoplectic fit. Cox's features were contorted with rage.

"How dare you accuse me of such, when I have come here to Frankfurt, hounded as a refugee for my faith as a Protestant from England's fair shores? You forget, Mr. Knox that I was the Preceptor to King Edward! But, be assured, Scotsman, that we will do here, as we have done in England, and we will have the face of an English Church!" His face had become fixed in hardened lines and challenged the Scotsman's.

"Masters, Masters, I have brought you here to maintain a tolerant atmosphere in our *Wiessfrauenkirche* not to quarrel!" Vallerand Pullain tried to restore harmony. Too graphically the short period the congregation of the Walloons had spent at Glastonbury came back to him, and there in that place steeped in the ancient legends of King Arthur, Avalon, and even of Joseph of Arimathea and the Christ Child, how little they had understood these strange, contradictory English Thinking that they had a natural bias towards religious controversy, he conveniently forgot that the Walloons themselves were no strangers to theological argumentativeness.

"A tolerant atmosphere, you say?" It was Knox's time to explode." You saw the effects the coming of Chancellor Cox has had on our congregation? Chaos was the result!" The Sunday previous at Divine Service Cox and his followers had answered in loud responses to the preacher, and, when the elders reprimanded them, they had cocked a snoop insolently at them, and continued interrupting the worship.

"It is bringing proper order to the Service, Mr. Knox." Cox was bitter-tongued in his challenge." Your French Service, cooked up like some mixture of garlic herbs and mushrooms, strange to the taste and just as poisonous, by that chief cook, Calvin, lacks dignity and grace and would put even an eager celebrant to sleep with its cowed silence! It has not the sweetness of our English ways."

"You must be mistaking the silence of heart –worship for deadness through your carnal insight!" Knox had been outraged by Cox's disruption, as had the majority of the congregation.

"How is God to tell that you are worshipping Him with your heart, if you don't show it with your actions, or more likely how are men to tell?" Cox saw how his wrong thinking had slipped out, and quickly reasserted his argument, but too late. He passed on swiftly, but Knox smiled quietly." You show God a disservice when you merely sit at the Holy Communion." Another disgraceful disruption had taken place on the Sunday, when Cox, Lever, and their supporters had knelt as the bread and wine was being distributed, causing an outcry of blasphemy. But Cox had ignored their objections.

"We merely follow the Commandments, while you sail very close to popery in worshipping the elements, Master Cox!" By now the Scot's Celtic blood was flushed, provoked by this man. He knew that the aim of Cox and Lever was to gain admission to the congregation of the ancient Weissenkirche and use their disruptive influence to have their way.

"But surely, Mr. Knox," intruded Lever, scornfully pronouncing the title," in Biblical times our Lord and his disciples lay on couches at the Table of the Last Supper?"

"That's not the same as kneeling in an idolatrous position, which is one of worship. You have already said, Master Cox, that our outward action reveals our inward heart." Knox was revelling in the cut and thrust of debate now, and knew that he was winning the battle of words and beliefs. It was shortly after that Pastor Pullain called an end to the proceedings when he saw that agreement was impossible.

As for Cox, he had determined to use a more subtle subterfuge to be rid of the Scot. Meanwhile John Knox had been given permission to preach the next Sunday in the White Ladies Kirk to the congregation of the exiles, and felt led to speak on the strange but very human story of Noah when he became drunk on the wine of his own vineyard, and ended up lying naked in his tent. His son Ham had seen the state of his father, embarrassed, and after consultation with his brothers, Shem and Japheth, they had decently covered up their drunk father's nakedness. It was a simple story but could be used more profoundly.

"These are infirmities of the brethren, which ought to be concealed, but there are other things which openly dishonour God and disquiet the Church, and these ought to be disclosed and openly rebuked." For some reason Richard Cox and his supporters were absent, probably because Knox was preaching, but all knew to whom he was referring." We have had a Committee formed to accommodate all our differences. We have agreed to take some things from the English Liturgy and use others suitable to our circumstances. Five of our most celebrated Divines will settle any of our disputes. But, despite this, last Lord's Day one of our recent Incomers boldly entered this pulpit without permission of our Congregation's pastors, and Mr. Cox and his accomplices mimicked his preaching with their man-made responses."

It had been Lever who had audaciously thrust himself into the pulpit, all planned to impose their way." Their offensive behaviour caused the most terrible confusion in our midst!" He gazed out over the motley assembly of Protestant exiles from so many parts of Europe, from France, Germany, the Low Countries, England, and even North Italy, where the Waldensians, *Vaudois*, had fled from southern France. He secretly wondered at the miracle that there was not otherwise confusion and disharmony already." Nothing destitute of a Divine warrant ought to be intruded into a Christian Church!" he thundered, surprised at his own vehemence amongst strangers." "In that Book," they all were aware what he meant, "for which some have an exaggerated fondness, I will undertake to prove publicly that there are things impure, imperfect, and superstitious, and I will oppose the plans of any to burden a free congregation with such things."

Knox's disgust was evident, and he drew his tongue between his teeth to give a rasping sound. "God's displeasure is upon England, where the Protestants have been slack in Reformation, in discipline, and in morality, with one man occupying three, four, or five pulpits!" He carried on in the same radical vein, ignoring a current of disturbance that had arisen in the rear of the audience. At the end a group hurried out, their faces black as thunder. Clearly some of Cox's faction had been present.

The very next day a complaint came from some Englishmen that he had slandered their Mother Church, and insisting that Cox and his friends should be admitted to the vote in the congregation. This was opposed by the majority of the congregation of the Church of the White Ladies, still enraged at their disorderly conduct, but contrarywise John Knox felt within himself that it was time for moderation and magnaminity towards his enemies, which God would bless, and he persuaded a meeting of the elders to admit Richard Cox and his English supporters to the congregational vote. But he was to regret his imprudent big-heartedness. He had forgotten how many there were of Cox's faction. No sooner was their party admitted, than their voices were heard everywhere in the majority, and Cox, although he had no personal authority, made a pronouncement, which justified all John Knox's fears.

"Cox has discharged you from all preaching in Frankfurt, and all interference in Congregational affairs!" His colleague, William Whittingham, had rushed into his Study and gasped out the dismaying news. But it was ameliorated by a heartening postscript. "But the great body of us are indignant and a representative has been sent to the Frankfurt Magistrates. The good news is that an Edict has been issued that the congregation conform exactly to the worship used by the French Church! The authorities are angry at the confusion our Church has caused the city, and have warned us that they will actually shut up our place of worship, if their order is not complied with." Knox heaved a deep sigh of relief after his initial shock.

"Praise be to God! He brings light out of darkness always, and does all things well!"

But his satisfaction was to be premature, for Richard Cox was a man of a nasty and obstinate nature, not easily put off. He schemed to be rid of this troublesome Scot, who was like a prickly nettle to him, a stinging weed, useful only when its poison had been boiled out of it for soup, as far as Cox was concerned. Well, he would soon be in hot water." God has made me, wiser than all my enemies by His commandments, for they are always with me," Knox continued, as if to encourage himself, and to let his good friend, William Whittingham, see that, no matter what happened in Frankfurt, God's sovereign plan would be revealed soon." Why are thou cast down, O my soul? Hope thou in God!"

In fact his enemies were plotting that very day to finally expel John Knox from the city. They had gathered in Cox's lodgings in the area of Frankfurt the Magistrates had designated for the religious refugees. Cox was addressing Lever and the others in the manner of a zealous bigot and secret plotter.

"We have pretended to cheerfully submit to the Magistrates' ruling, while we with are all, my friends, determined to privately seek to have it revoked and our beloved Liturgy brought back, but I tell you," Here his dark features took on that bitter spirit that characterised his true nature," that the influence of that damned Scotsman has on the Congregation is too great, and we will never achieve this, as long as Knox is among us. We must have him expelled first!"

"That is impossible! He is too entrenched and in league with that weak-willed Englishman Whittingham.

They are like David and Jonathan!" replied Lever, conveniently forgetting that most present were Englishmen.

"Ah, but remember that David and Jonathan became undone!" Richard Cox came back viciously." Here is the man to undo them, Dr. Glauburg!"

A figure detached himself from the rear, and moved forward to the front of the room. He had every trapping of wealth, from his high-necked velvet tunic to the ermine cuffs of his bejewelled leather jerkin. But there was something unworthy and dishonest in his bearing and an obvious haughtiness.

"I am the nephew of the Chief Magistrate of Frankfurt, Johannes Von Glauburg, whom I admire for his astuteness in trade, but he has been deceived by that eloquent rogue, John Knox, who has appealed to his Protestantism. But, as to myself, though I am of course a faithful Protestant," he hesitated imperceptibly," I find the Scotsman's views austere and rigid, but I have here in my hand, you will be glad to know, the means of being rid of Herr Knox for good!" He held up a small book, leather- bound, which John Knox would have recognised." It contains words by Master Knox that are high treason against the Emperor, Charles V, of the German Holy Roman Empire, his son, Philip, and Queen Mary of England.

Tonight with a friend I will go privately to the Magistrates, who are enclosed in the Council Chamber, and show it to them. Do you think that after almost two hundred years as an Imperial Free City that, with the Emperor's Council sitting at nearby Augsburg, they will not be very much afraid of the repercussions for the City, if word of the traitorous charge is conveyed to His Majesty's ears! If so, he could remove the free status of Frankfurt as a Protestant city in a Roman Catholic Empire, controlled from

Vienna, and for merchants to lose their tax free rights in merchant trading is like losing their right arm!" He looked round the assemblage with an intense gaze, and they all knew that this Dr. Glauburg offered them the answer.

"We have Knox where we want him. He cannot escape now, except by leaving Frankfurt!" Lever rasped, while Cox's eyes glowed with satisfaction, such can be the hatred of man for man.

"I shall take my leave now, gentlemen, and be assured that I shall achieve your desire!" Glauburg swiftly left with a companion. In fact the booklet was John Knox's *Admonition to the Protestants of England*, which he had written from Dieppe, encouraging them to stand firm in persecution. Few were ever to know how it got into the hands of Dr. Glauburg. But the deadly portion of it had been actually spoken by the Scots preacher at Amersham in Buckinghamshire back in England to the people there concerning the terrible danger of the rumoured marriage of Queen Mary to Philip, the son and heir to Charles V, the Holy Roman Emperor, a dreaded match to all Protestants. He had pleaded with England not to return to idolatry, and the fatal phrase had been inserted, describing *"the Emperor, who is no less an enemy to Christ than Nero was."* All this had been written in a specific context and at a specific time a few years previous, and he had condemned the cruelty of 'Bloody Mary' in addition, but to the German Magistrates the words were fatal, and they immediately sent for William Whittingham, to them a well-respected member of the English congregation, to come to the *Romer*, the impressive, round, red stone, Town Hall, where they held court.

"What do you think of this Knox's character?"

"He is a learned, grave, and a Godly man," replied the Englishman earnestly, seeing his Scots friend's time there visibly slipping away.

"Do you know of the serious accusation that has been lodged against him by some of your countrymen?" The stolid German Merchant-Magistrates gazed unblinkingly at him, and one handed him the booklet opened at the accusatory place.

"We are well aware of the malice of Master Knox's accusers. On the other hand, we are afraid that the information of the charge might be conveyed to the Emperor's ears at Augsburg, and we will be obliged to deliver up Knox, or worse, to Mary of England! For we hear that much suffering has been undergone there with fire and stake through her." It was Johannes Von Glauburg speaking, his voice full of compassion, for he was a good man." I detest what my nephew has done! He has disgraced our family name by taking part in this underhand work, most dishonourably. But we would ask you to advise your friend Knox to retire privately of his own accord from Frankfurt. I am sure that Geneva will once more offer him a safe haven and Master Calvin welcome him home with open arms. You do understand, don't you?" His stolid face appealed embarrassedly!" We have too much to lose, if the religious equilibrium is upset here."

"I do understand," replied Whittingham quietly, and took his leave without further argument. It was God's will. Back in the street he decided to take brother Williams with him to see John Knox. The pain was too much for one man, but he need not have worried, for the Scots preacher had a clear sight of the sovereign will of God.

"It would be the safest course and most prudent policy for you to leave this hotbed of religious controversy, Master John. Even Lever, your former colleague, has turned against you. They have given you until the twenty sixth of March to depart, having put your affairs in order. Many of your friends here are extremely sad and angry, but helpless to do anything. The powers that be are too strong, and have let the twisted Mr. Cox and his friends have their way. But a great number of your colleagues, who have appreciated your fine ministry here, are intent on wishing you God speed, and, if they may, wish to gather here in your lodgings the night before your departure." Whittingham and Williams extended their hands to the Scot, who instead embraced them wholeheartedly. Tears were apparent on both sides.

"A stone that fits in the wall must not be allowed to lie in the ditch," answered Knox calmly." I may not fit in this wall, but assuredly there are others, where I do. In times of testing a man finds his true friends. Be welcome on that night, dear friends."

So it was that on the night before John Knox's sad departure, fifty of his friends crowded into his humble lodgings and listened to a strong and comforting sermon from the man they admired. There were heavy hearts and a quiet weeping. It was with an equally heavy heart that John Knox embarked on a ferry boat up the mighty Rhine early next morning. It was a cold March day and the wind blew severely off the river, so that he shivered as he grasped the shoulders of the few members of the *Weissenkirche*, who had met with many others, packed together, in a private house the previous night, to say farewell and hear him expound God's Word, but had now come the three or four miles to wave a final farewell to the Scots preacher.

"God be with you, brother John," his friend, William Whittingham spoke hoarsely, as he committed him to the Lord." Nero is still powerful in the lands of the Emperor. The foothold that Protestantism has in Germany is still insecure."

"Aye, and outside of Switzerland Germany is the one real foothold Protestantism has in Europe. Scandinavia is too remote to be considered and Denmark was not too hospitable to the last group of Reformers who went there. Do you think that I have been too pernickety, brother William? I cannot abide the Litany with its responses and private baptism. It smacks of superstition and religious formalism. Bringing women into positions of authority over men, I cannot abide either. It's not that I regard these things as supremely important, but it sticks in my craw to have them forced down my throat.

The problem is that Englishmen like Lever, Cox, and Jewel want a common worship which is English, while I, like Master Calvin, have become a European." He had a width of vision for a Protestant Church which embraced all of Europe and had harmony between different groups of believers in Christ." But for Cox and Lever the Prayer Book was their common bond while in exile, since it is forbidden back in England by that tyrant, Mary Tudor. I am a both a European and a Scotsman, which makes my heart proud!" he added." Am I wrong to take this attitude?" He knew that Whittingham, as an Englishman, would not be offended, for he knew him too well.

"No, no, John, you are a man of wit and learning and an earnest zeal, I have discovered in these few short months together in Frankfurt." Whittingham blinked back the tears, as the wind whipped into his face." You are not being driven from Frankfurt for any point of religion. The secular power of the State is the sheet anchor, on which your enemies depend. Any insult, supposed or imagined, to the Emperor, cannot be ignored, and used against you. Ecclesiastical officials, like Chancellor Cox, are the Pharisees of the Church, and like them, they have cried 'Out, he is not Caesar's friend'. Whatever suits them, whatever side the coin falls on, they use."

"The Church must never be subservient to the State," Knox strongly replied, the normal deep colour in his cheeks whipped up already by the weather." The English Prayer Book is English, and must never be transplanted! Scotsmen have always feared the enchantment of the Book of Common Prayer and the magic it weaves. In the Scottish Order of Service we have rejected the external acts of men, and put all the beauty of holiness into the language. In our Scottish Order the reading of God's Word is not a separate and distinct act, but the part of the work of the pulpit." He even surprised himself with his fervour for things Scottish.

"Your Scottish Order of Service has grandeur, I will agree. but sometimes it bears a dangerous cost in its wake," sighed Whittingham." Recitation is not a test of understanding, as every self-respecting schoolmaster knows." Knox silently agreed, as he nostalgically and affectionately thought back to his days as a tutor to the three young scallywag sons of the Lairds of Ormiston and Longniddry.

"Och, well, to return to my present circumstances, William, Scotland I have left years ago now, and England has cast me out, for it has returned to the Romanism of France and Spain, I am homeless. Even the Geneva, to which I am returning, is an almost unknown city, but at least it is a temporary halting place and haven, where a man might find books of great quality to read and try to forget his past failures."

John Knox felt crushed under a deep depression and that he was passing through a dark valley of Achor. They embraced once more, before the boat pulled out into the Rhine's powerful current. Knox again felt the loneliness of a pilgrim, and drew his cloak closer round him, as he waved back to the little knot of friends, who had gathered on the bank. He remembered St. Paul's instruction for his cloak to be brought to him, and felt the common human need of protection from the cold that the great saint had. Little things were important. Scarcely did he know if he would ever see these brethren again.

But his welcome the second time to Geneva was a wonderful comfort, even more than the first time. Calvin was appalled at the treatment the Scot had received at the hands of Cox and Lever.

"Let not your heart be troubled, my Scottish brother. You shall have rest and study here in Geneva, where you are among your own! The Lord has at last crowned my efforts with victory! The Three Councils, who govern our city, have finally made peace with our Church. We have won some major battles. The Councils have recognised the Church's right of Communion, the right of ministers to exclude from the Lord's Table those who are unworthy, and the admission of foreigners to the privilege of citizenship. It means that you can now be truly one of us, a citizen of Geneva!" Calvin showed an unwonted excitement of spirit.

"God be praised! I already feel the elixir of the pure air of Geneva, so far removed from that of Frankfurt, which has been made rank with the stench of man's pride and religious hatred. Geneva will again become for me the perfect school of Christ!"

"Be not too hasty, for that rascal, Perrin, and his friends, the Libertines, are still hanging around, but they are gasping for their last breath, like a stranded fish! The new elections have given me a secure majority in the Council chambers. The growing colony of refugees from England, Scotland, Italy, and not to forget my beloved France, have given me their support!"

But the dying strength of the Libertine party, who hated John Calvin so much, was to make one last attempt to inflict its venom. About a month after Knox's arrival back in the city on the Lake, John was sleeping soundly the sleep of the just and beloved of God, when he was awakened by a tumult in the street below. Rising quickly, his instincts telling him that danger and deceit were near; he heard words clearly from a rioting mob.

"Wolf! Wolf! Citizens, bestir yourselves! Save Geneva! It's about to be sacked by foreigners! The French, the French are taking over the city! Slay them, slay them!"

This was madness, crazy words of no sense. He peered out towards the Lakeside, where he could just make out a confused bunch of figures waving lighted torches. He knew a mob, especially when they were drunk, and the potential danger they presented.

"These foreign scum are trying to take over our city, patriots! Rise and join us!" This was clearly a riot that had been deliberately fomented, and he knew that the false accusation that Calvin had been intentionally bringing in French Huguenot Protestants into Geneva in great numbers in order to take over control of the city from the native Swiss was being used by his enemies. The Scot could do nothing but resort to prayer that God would bring this revolt to nothing and bring confusion to their enemies, the Libertines. With a last gaze down at the flickering torches, Knox retired to seek the Lord in prayer at his bedside. The effectual, fervent, prayer of a righteous man was an extremely powerful weapon. He lost track of time, and fell asleep at prayer. In the morning a calm-faced Calvin came to see him with good news.

"Last night was the last squirm of a dying foe, my brother. A mob of rough fishermen and boatmen were primed by Francois Favre and Ami Perrin with a lot of free wine and bribery, but, praise to our God, our faithful, loyal, citizens not only shut their ears to their evil shouting, but also their windows and doors! Soon the drunken louts gave up their mad cause, and some of them, I believe, fell into the Lake. I pray no one drowned. In the morning our city guard rounded up the remnant. Perrin and Favre have both fled from Geneva." They both gave thanks to the Lord.

At this time Knox was becoming very worried about a wild sect which had arisen in Germany and had spread to Switzerland. What worried him most was that this particular sect had raised its ugly head from among the Protestant ranks. The name they went by was Anabaptist, and, though they had been suppressed in Germany, they had insidiously spread their tentacles to other countries. He brought up his deep concerns to his senior colleague one day.

"They are a dangerous sect, these Anabaptists, Master John, for, though they claim they are the enemies of Rome, the spirit of turbulence and wild fanaticism accompanies them everywhere!"

"Oh, indeed, brother John, you are only too right!" replied the man of God." For sadly outbreaks of mad fanaticism of this kind and not infrequently accompany great revolutions, like our great Protestant Reformation, when the minds of men, dazzled by a sudden burst of light and released from the galling chains of a civil and religious despotism, fly to the opposite extreme of anarchy and wild opinions." Deep wisdom seemed to shine out of John Calvin's eyes." Whatever the reason," broke in Knox quickly, as if almost unconsciously rejecting any justification by his superior minister for the rise of the Anabaptist sect," the defenders of the old system of Rome, seize on this wild group as the ideal argument against all change. It is perfect fodder for the papist cannons to demolish.

Almost as bad, I have heard that some of those who might have joined us have drawn back into the Roman Catholic Church's shelter, when they saw these extremists. These Anabaptists claim some spiritual perfection, and regard the early Jewish church as carnal and worldly. This strange sect confine themselves almost entirely to the New Testament, and this has led them to deny infant baptism, civil magistracy, the right of national Churches, oaths, and defensive wars. How wrong can they be? But, worst of all, they have become infected by the Arian and Pelagian heresies, which are the most subtle and insidious spiritual diseases that the devil can inflict on the Church! To reduce our Omnipotent and Eternal God to a created being, is a doctrine straight from Hell!" A righteous anger filled every particle of John Knox's being.

"No less is the incredible idea propounded by that deceived monk, Pelagius, that original sin does not exist. Some Anabaptists have adopted this mad heresy!" "Calvin's long face was filled with a genuine sadness." They have joined with the Romanists in misportraying the doctrine of predestination and grace as coming from a God of injustice! They refuse to recognise that Divine choice is dependent on Divine love. The Lord chooses us; we do not choose Him, unless His Holy Spirit enlightens us. We can depend upon the solid Rock of our Salvation, Jesus Christ!" The man of Geneva was infused with an inner joy, but Knox turned him back to the problem of the Anabaptists.

"I hear that these dangerous Anabaptist principles are creeping into Scotland even! I am afraid that they may instill their poison into the minds of some of my brethren back in my homeland. I must write back to Scotland and warn them." Calvin agreed totally and quietly recognised a homesickness in John Knox." In their crazed opinion for Communion they require such a purity as was never found in the Bible! If there is anything which God did not predestinate, I do not know of any. If anything was ever done, or shall be done, in Heaven or Earth, which He might not have stopped, if that had been His pleasure, then God is not omnipotent."

The inescapable logic would have been hard to refute by the greatest theologian. A zeal for God's good character had now consumed Knox's dark features, which became even darker, for his blood was up." If the three properties of wisdom, free will, and power, are denied to God, what still remains? Nothing, I say. But, as we know, brother, the wisdom of God is such that it compels the very malice of Satan to serve to His glory and to the profit of His elect!" John Calvin of all people piously nodded his concurrence with a powerful Lord God supreme over all. No speck of doubt was allowed by either man.

"God's power is infinite, so that no creature in Heaven or Earth can resist it. His Divine will is so free that none of His creatures dare call it in question and demand why He has done this or that." It was Calvin's turn to be animated over his favourite doctrine.

By now the magnetism of his homeland was drawing John Knox more and more.

Later he sat down and composed himself for what was a difficult letter to the Protestant Lords in Scotland. He again had the delicate task of communicating his advice on resistance to supreme rulers. He had already sought that of the most learned theologians on the Continent. Surely God had put rulers in place, the Bible said, but what if they were oppressive rulers? He prayed fervently for wisdom, and sought to breathe an ardent spirit of piety into the missive. In reality it was not hard to excite a resistance of the independent and haughty Barons of Scotland. Their obedience to the monarchy was precarious at the best of times.

News had filtered through from Scotland that their nobles had recently refused to co-operate in a war against England, which they saw as just in the French interests. But the presence of French troops enraged their patriotic spirits. But as he penned the words, John sought to purify the minds of the nobility from selfish and worldly principles. Too often, he knew, the nobility were motivated by a desire for wealth, lands, and castles. He must commend them to the conduct of the princes and heroes in the sacred pages, not from profane history.

'My Lords, it is for the glory of God, the advancement of the Kingdom of Christ, and the emancipation of our country from civil and spiritual thraldom, that I write to you.' Knox's pen was not the most delicate and smooth on occasions, and he was aware that his words could often irritate by their outspoken seeming severity. So he took good care not to offend the nobles.' *It must not be for your own honour, private revenge, or aggrandisement, that you should seek. Rumours are abroad here that a Rebellion is intended in Scotland. I would solemnly warn you all, who profess the Protestant Faith, to avoid all links with this, and beware of making friends with those, who for self seeking promotion try to disturb the lawful Government. You are the guardians of our national liberties, and there are limits beyond which obedience is not due. You ought to resist until you are driven to extremes by tyranny. Don't give your loyalty to what is unworthy.'*

With a sigh of satisfaction he laid down his quill. He felt certain that the right time, the *kairos* time, to return to his beloved land was near at last. The news had come that the bloodthirsty Mary Tudor had died. English exiles were preparing to return home. English military help could again become available to assist the Protestants in Scotland. His blood coursed through his veins vigorously. Not least was the wonderful prospect of seeing his darling Marjorie again. His entire being ached for her, It had been too long. He had no fear of her father, for her mother's permission at Norham Castle was enough.

Then one day there came through Geneva a Scots emissary on his way to Rome. Why should he stop off to see Knox? Was he in the pay of the enemy? The messenger requested to see John Knox, who was even more wary when he heard his words.

"I am John Gray, and am journeying to Rome to ask for Papal approval of the appointment of the new Bishop of Ross." Knox was astonished, and glared at the man.

"What do you want with me? Don't you know that I am your deadly enemy? I am entirely opposed to Papal control and beliefs, aye, and its very existence! I am a Protestant Reformer. That is why I am exiled!" The man seemed unperturbed.

"I have a letter from the Lords of the Congregation for you, and I have the feeling that it will change your mind." Knox's amazement was only increased, when he opened it to read a total encouragement from the Lords that the time was now ripe for his return. Their conviction about this was complete. Joy filled his heart.

"There is also a note for Master Calvin," added Gray impassively. Was he aware of its contents, Knox wondered. He seemed a strange carrier. The Lords were economic with their words, and a messenger was a messenger, as long as he could trust him.

Whatever, he now had a very good man as a colleague in preaching to the English-speaking congregation, and felt he could leave the sole charge of his flock to Christopher Goodman. The Protestants in Scotland had now been permitted comparative liberty to profess their faith, and the time was propitious. In a few days he gave a fond farewell to Calvin's fair city and unobtrusively crossed France to Dieppe. Somehow France's air seemed different, lighter, and, when the old seaport was reached, the answer was clear. Dieppe was in a great turmoil.

A Protestant revival had been sweeping France, and a crowd of 10,000 had even marched through Paris down the Rue St. Jacques, singing Protestant songs. But the immediate problem was how to reach Scotland. His temper had become very irritable after a third letter to the English Court, requesting permission to travel through England, had been refused, because of Elizabeth's extreme offence at his outburst against female rule. So on the twenty second of April, 1556, with a brave heart he set sail backed by a strong spring wind direct for the port of Leith.

RETURN TO SCOTLAND

When he returned, Knox was astonished by the progress made by the Reformed cause and the eager reception given to him by all classes in the community. Wherever he directed his footsteps, he met with a great joy and enthusiasm throughout Lowland Scotland, especially in Edinburgh and the fertile land of Fife, where his memories had been so poignant doors were opened everywhere to admit him. The mansion houses of Earls, Lords, Barons, and Burgesses, were at his disposal, and were used by John Knox as centres for preaching the truth to the surrounding districts. Multitudes flocked to hear the Gospel preached in all its simplicity and purity.

The preacher was overwhelmed with a quiet joy, as he saw the dream which he had long entertained in exile being on the threshold of being fulfilled. Whenever he accepted an invitation to a certain mansion or house, he remained there while in that district, so that he might be easily found by all who wished to see, hear, or consult him. That was what Christ, his Master, had enjoined his disciples to do when He sent them on missionary tours. He had said," *Into whatsoever house you enter, there abide.*" But, as he was shuttled from one mansion and castle to another by the Earls of Argyle and Glencairn, the Lord of Lorne, and Erskine of Dun, often under cloak of night, he had to be very careful of betrayal, for the Reformed faith was as yet in the minority in the land.

One very important meeting took place in the house of a close friend, James Sym, a burgess of Edinburgh, with whom he secretly lodged in the hollows of the Cowgate below the famous Canongate. Knox had ridden in after dusk; his cloak happed around his features. Word had been surreptitiously spread abroad to gather at the Burgess's house, and dark figures, including not only a good few nobility, but many countrymen and their wives, flitted down through the Cowgate. They came eagerly thirsting to hear the Gospel from the brave preacher's lips. He held not back in his outspoken encouragement, as he cast his firm gaze around the enraptured audience packed into the living room where a generous supper had first been served.

"Those who have a zeal for Godliness must not be compromised in their faith by even an occasional, or the slightest, conformity. I urge you to withdraw from all rites and ceremonies of the Roman Church and to band together for the defence of Protestantism, in case it should prove necessary. You must gather together for private family worship, and weekly meetings for corporate Bible study and discussions. As you become familiar with the Word of God, out of you shall come the leaders and elders of our Reformed Church!" His words and steely look challenged them to the core, and most were to rise to the challenge. Within himself, however, John Knox was sure it was still early days in the tide which would sweep away the old and sweep in the new. This was only the end of the beginning. The major bulwark of the Mass had to be removed.

At the end of the meeting he was approached by the young Lord Erskine of Dun, a quiet mannered, gentle, noble, who seemed convinced of the need for radical change.

"I would be honoured, Master Knox, if you would attend my House of Dun in the County of Forfarshire, and there explain more fully the way of the Bible."

His appeal could not be turned down, though he had the invitations to Finlayston House of the Earl of Glencairn near Port Glasgow, and the Argyle Castle Campbell at Dollar, sheltering beneath Clackmannanshire's Ochil Hills, to be fulfilled. But the House of Dun was to be a key turning point, as it was there that Lord Erskine made his final break with Rome. For a full month he had hosted John Knox at his mansion, where he preached exhaustingly twice every day. A huge number of the county gentlemen and ordinary folk, from ploughmen to smiths, assembled in the spacious drawing room. It was time to cut one of the main arteries of Rome and free the people to the glorious truth of free access directly to God Himself without priests. The priesthood of all believers was the Lord's desire.

"The Lord's Supper is a gift to man from God, while the mass is a sacrifice by man to God! In the Last Supper those who participate acknowledge that they are redeemed from sin and death, but through the Mass worshippers seek forgiveness in vain. For all sat at our Lord's Supper, dressed alike, and eat and drink together, while in the Mass the priest is distinguished by his position at the altar and his vestments. He alone participates in the elements." The fire of God's truth now ignited the Reformer and this fire would set the heather of Scotland alight.

"The Mass is an idolatry, an invention of man set up to worship God, an abomination that falsely claims to remit sins. There can be no compromise between the immaculate spouse of Jesus and the Synagogue of Satan, led by the pope! The Church of Rome is that Empire, predicted by the Book of the prophet Daniel, that is to devour the saints! Its power in Scotland must be broken and her people set free!" The audience was absolutely astounded by the sheer audacity of the statements, enough to send its propounder to the stake, but somehow a spirit of secret joy seized their hearts and minds that this was God's truth and that He had already forgiven them through Christ. No more indulgences were needed, nor purgatory.

At the end Sir James Sandilands invited him to his mansion at Calder in West Lothian, and with a ready spirit from Dun Knox was given safe passage to the noble's home. Here again multitudes attended his ministrations to his astonishment almost, but here there was a vital aspect for the future of the Reformation in Scotland. At Calder all the chief nobility came together, Lord Lorne, who was to become afterwards the Duke of Argyle, the Earl of Mar, and most of all, Lord James Stuart, the half brother of the child Queen Mary in France, married to the Dauphine, potentially the most powerful man next to the Regent, Mary of Guise. Knox's heart leapt when he met Lord James Stuart, and recognised in the quiet assurance of this man of the Royal line a person who could be a faithful friend of himself and Protestantism. There was a strength and loyalty in James Stuart's soft grey eyes.

"I have longed to meet you, my Lord. I would desire your Royal favour, as well as our Lord God's of course."

"And I have heard so much of the preacher who is setting alight to our dear Scotland, as if a veritable Samson had sent forth three hundred foxes with flaming torches tied to their tails." Lord James Stuart smiled, for he was a man who sought balance with humour in a world of serious religion." My desire is to hear what you have to commend of these new doctrines to myself and these Lords, that we may decide where our religious allegiance lies."

The challenge was before Knox, and so for the next hours he concentrated all his considerable powers on Biblical teaching on salvation by faith alone and all the deep doctrines of the faith that he had learnt from Calvin. At the end was triumph, for all three Lords approved of his doctrines of the Reformation. John Knox knew that he must cement this milestone in faith, and the opportunity must not be lost.

"I would strongly urge, my Lords that we all enter into a Covenant of Faith to maintain and promote the pure Gospel to the utmost of our ability and opportunity. As with the Covenant between Jehovah and Israel, this will bind us together in an unbreakable unity!"

So it was agreed, and after its formulation by Knox, the noblemen and many gentry present signed the document. With a glad heart Knox returned from Calder to Edinburgh, where he spent a few winter months in teaching and promoting the cause. Then he was strongly compelled to fulfil the promise he had made to visit Sir William Cunningham, the fourth Earl of Glencairn, at Finlayston House, near Port Glasgow, on the Firth of Clyde in the County of Renfrew, and from there proceed to a preaching tour of the lands Kyle and Carrick, an area known for their radical thought in religion and politics.

The Lollards had a generation before lit a tiny spark of Reform in faith from the worldly corruption which had set in, and was fertile ground for planting Protestant seed. So it was in early January, 1556 Knox had set out westwards to Glasgow, the small Cathedral town of St. Mungo, nestling above the banks of the shallow, meandering, river Clyde. He knew not for certain, but he had heard that its few thousand inhabitants were not only enterprising in trade but open to the movement for reform. They did not want to be left behind in anything that would benefit the people of Glasgow and cast envious eyes towards the east. Passing through its few neat streets and apple orchards, waiting to blossom in spring, he sensed the promise of its commercial growth.

The bulky outline of the ancient fortress of Dumbarton stood out on the opposite bank of the Firth, as his small entourage rode on that bright January day down to the mansion of Finlayston House at Langbank, standing high above the estuary. Glencairn's welcome was full, as the Earl had already committed his heart to the Protestant faith. Sir William Cunningham did not bear fools gladly, and could not abide half measures.

"At last Finlayston affords you hospitality, Master John, and the chance for its walls to absorb your preaching, let's pray they can stand its power, for they have already withstood the strong winds of the Firth of Clyde for too long!" He laughed gruffly.

"It is the walls of false doctrine and the traditions of men that must be blown down, my Lord," Knox replied equably.

"Let me furnish refreshment for you and your men, and send for my estate workers, tenants, and neighbouring gentry to gather for your sermon. I doubt if my biggest room is sufficient for the numbers!" Glencairn laughed. But John Knox had already caught sight of the great yew tree, which stood in the stately grounds near the house.

"The weather is fine, Earl, and that mighty tree there looks worthy of a great occasion. Why do we not hold the preaching beneath that yew? The Cathedral of Heaven is good enough for us."

Later over a hundred had gathered beneath the branches of the mighty yew tree, which reminded John Knox of the ancient yew in the grounds of Ormiston Castle seen ten years before, with its dark green needles contrasting the rare red berries peeping out from the foliage. The broad twisted limbs of the tree sheltered the congregation, not far from the mansionhouse, and, as he gazed at the scarlet berries, the preacher was reminded of the precious blood of Christ.

Knox was inspired by the scene, overlooking the wide Firth of Clyde, invigorated by the winter sun and the whipping wind. His sermon was touched from above as he presented the free direct access to God for all with forgiveness of their sins. Not one person there but entered the Kingdom by faith. At the end his mind turned to celebrating Holy Communion in the Reformed fashion, which he had already done elsewhere at Calder and Edinburgh, but would be the first known time for many generations in Scotland's south west, maybe for hundreds of years, and not the Mass.

"Let us celebrate the Last Supper in the Holy Communion, my Lord Glencairn. Do you have suitable vessels for the bread and wine?"

Glencairn became flustered and looked around, confused. His normal, bluff, confidence had deserted him. He looked around at his servants in vain, and they looked back at him askance.

"We have silver candlesticks, my Lord," said one servant.

"Candlesticks? What good are these, my man?" Sir William retorted in annoyance.

"Turned upside down, my Lord," replied the servant boldly." It is silver too." He knew the importance of the honour due to the elements, even if they remained bread and wine symbolising the Lord's body and blood. Cunningham glanced sidelong at Knox, embarrassed.

"As long as they have not been used for any unsanctified purposes," John Knox spoke calmly," the candlesticks are hollow and can contain the wine, and the stands can act as the *patens* for the bread. Our Lord used simple elements and leaves the power with the Spirit."

So it was that the bread and wine were passed out to everyone present in commemoration as a memorial service of that sacrificial death of the blessed Lord Jesus Christ on Calvary's hill once for all, no longer by a priest taking their place as an intermediary between them and their God re-enacting the event. The depth of this simple but profound service, which took place that day for the first time likely for hundreds of years in Scotland's south west, abolishing the Mass, was to have a lasting effect on many generations of Scots to come.

But back in Edinburgh Knox was to be met with threatening news. His growing popularity, the impulse the Reformation was receiving from his incessant preaching, and the increasing numbers who were ceasing to attend the Mass, had alarmed the priesthood, who had determined to silence the Reformer and bring an end to his career. One day, where he lodged with James Sym, the burgess suddenly rushed in with dismay on his countenance.

"The Bishops have summoned you to appear before them at the Church of the Blackfriars on the 15th of May! They will certainly condemn you as a heretic, and who knows what end they intend? You must not go, and we will smuggle you out of the city!"

But the preacher knew it was time not to run but to face up to the enemy, and so he resolved to obey the summons and defend the doctrines he taught. His courage was rewarded, for he was amazed when he set out on the date prescribed to find he was surrounded by a concourse of his supporters among the gentry and nobles, and when he arrived at the Blackfriars Church, there was a strange silence. Glencairn, who had come all the way from Finlayston, immediately surmised the reason.

"Ah, they have lost courage and taken cold feet, Master John! The clergy have been overawed by the great influence of your support among the gentry, afraid that, were they to try you, the result would be only to strengthen your cause, and cover themselves with shame! It is a great victory for our cause!" he cried in triumph.

"If what you say is borne out, Sir William, then it is a God-given opportunity to preach the truth!" John replied, and led the way into Blackfriars, where, instead of appearing as a culprit for stirring up false teachings before a tribunal, he preached to a larger audience than he had ever done before, as the news spread like wildfire and the townspeople from all classes of Edinburgh society poured into Blackfriars Kirk to hear this preacher who had bearded the highest clergy of the Roman Church in their own den. The triumph was complete. The fiasco of the Bishops had been in fact been their fault, when in their panic they had made a silly pretext not to hold the tribunal. They were a laughing stock of the people behind their backs.

But in the midst of his small and temporary triumph, there was to come another, unexpected, challenge. A letter came from Geneva from his old, English-speaking congregation there, whom he still thought of longingly. His heart missed a beat and he felt a tearing of his emotions. It was an earnest entreaty begging him to return to his ministry in his favourite Swiss city as a co-pastor with the Englishman, Christopher Goodman. What was he to do? His dilemma was gut wrenching, just as they were on the threshold of something momentous. But if anything, he was a man of decision, and it took only a fraction of time to decide. He must return to his favourite little flock in Geneva. It wasn't yet the Lord's time, 'kairos' time, in Scotland. Meanwhile the seed had been sown. Let it grow without the assistance of man. Enforced growth would never last. God alone would give the increase.

It was with a settled mind and heart, therefore, that he prepared to ride to Castle Campbell at Dollar, a subsidiary fortress to the Earl of Argyle's main residence at Inveraray on the west coast. Nestling under the shadow of the rolling Ochil Hills, it lay in the glen formed by the two streams that poured down from the overhanging heights. For some reason the fortress was known also as Castle Gloume. But there was nothing gloomy about the greeting of the elderly Duke of Argyle and his cousin, Campbell of Breadalbane.

"Beloved pastor, welcome, welcome! I am delighted to tell you that our fair Castle

Campbell has had its name changed by Act of Parliament from Castle Gloume, which fair upset my father! Our God has set the sunshine of his face upon us, has He not?" Argyle sought the preacher's reassurance.

This was to be the last port of call for John Knox preaching the newly rediscovered Biblical truths of salvation by faith alone in Christ without the intermediacy of the Pope and his priesthood, to be replaced by the priesthood of every believer, before departing again for the Continent, but this was not known to the Campbell nobility. Knox had also promised them a celebration of the Holy Communion service in the Reformed fashion, which had been eagerly anticipated by the powerful Argyle family, who had been so instrumental in scaring off the enemies of Knox. Every member, wives, children, and grandchildren, had been laboriously transported from Campbell country in the Highland west.

Their thirst for God was fully satisfied, as the man of God preached in the magnificently manicured grounds of Castle Campbell before a very wealthy family and their many servants, attired in lace, velvet, buckled Italian leather shoes, and finest brocade, but he was no longer unnerved by the face of man. The fear of man brought a snare, whether in Geneva or Scotland. At the end of the dignified Service of Holy Communion, this time in the finest silverware, which followed, it was his difficult task to announce his imminent departure once more from Scotland's shores. The Campbell Lords were astounded and annoyed.

"You say that they are your little flock over there in Geneva? We are your equally precious flock here before you, Pastor. We have been greatly edified by you!" It was Campbell of Breadalbane imploring the minister to remain, using all his Gaelic grace and honest zeal." Abandon your thoughts of abandoning your Scotland, your own land and people, just when you have been miraculously delivered from the menace of the Bishops! We are on the very threshold of a religious revolution in our land! Would you leave us now of all times?"

"My Lord, I have no answer, but that I feel that this invitation is a call from Providence. In these situations one cannot consult with the flesh, I am afraid. I consider it my duty to God to obey the call." There was pain in his soul, as he saw the deep hurt and fear in their eyes. It was a fear that they would lose everything gained.

"If God so blessed your small beginnings, so that you continue in Godliness, whenever you are pleased to command me, you will find me obedient to return."

With these enigmatic words the preacher turned away, and the Argyle Lords accepted the inevitable. Little did they know that John Knox had already sent instructions to Marjorie and her mother in Northumberland to sail from Newcastle for Dieppe and that he would catch them there, in lodgings, in the famous *Rue des Ecossais*.

THE FINAL RETURN

Back in Geneva, time passed for the Scot, three happy years in fact, fully occupied with his theological studies and his busy pen, but, nevertheless, it was comparatively a season of rest and refreshment. In the society of his dear wife and her mother, in the fellowship of Calvin, Beza, Goodman, and other kindred spirits, in the warm affection of his flock and in many other pleasant ways his second Geneva sojourn was the most restful and enjoyable period of his life, an veritable oasis, coming between the trials and strain of his past and the storm and stress that he had soon to face. It was at Geneva that Marjorie presented him with two sturdy sons, Nathaniel and Eleazer.

By consent they had chosen the first child's name as 'a gift of God', the name of the disciple from Cana of Galilee, brought to Jesus by Philip, to whom Jesus promised a greater vision of Christ as the Son of Man and link between Heaven and Earth. Nathaniel was also one of the disciples who saw Christ in his resurrection appearance by the sea of Tiberias. It was a name of honour, as was Eleazer, signifying *God had helped,* the name of one of Aaron's sons, and of whom the famous High Priest, Zadok, was descended. Knox's cup of joy was full.

Yet he still could not resist the temptation to pen a Treatise against the unjust rule of women, and in 1558 he penned his fatal Document, '*The First Blast of the Trumpet Against the Monstrous Regiment of Women',* which was to cause him so much trouble, had he foreseen, but his gifts were limited.

But in1559 an invitation came again from his native land, and he was convinced that the fullness of time had now come to enter on the great work in Scotland, which all the labours of his past life had been leading up to. Wisely he decided to leave Marjorie, the boys, and her mother back in Geneva, since if anything, the danger was greater than before, with the Queen Regent, Mary of Guise, full of spite and antagonism towards the Reformer, and yet he felt led to return. Strange were the ways of God. He felt a little relieved to be away from the constant solicitations of Marjorie's mother, continually asking questions on obscure and personal religious things.

It took him almost four long months, from when he left Geneva at last in early January that year till he arrived in Leith on the second of May. His letters to the new Queen of England apologising in as reasonable terms as he could muster without humiliating himself, had been ignored. William Cecil, Lord Burleigh, Elizabeth's Secretary, had replied in diplomatic terms. He deeply regretted the lack of wisdom he had shown in his First Blast of the Trumpet against Women's rule that it only meant some women. He would not write a second. Elizabeth had been furious and refused him access to journey through England, hence the long, circuitous, way through France, the Low Countries, and even north Germany to reach Scotland.

Young Argyle, the Earls of Glencairn and Morton, Sir James Sandilands, and Erskine of Dun were all eagerly waiting that fine May morning to welcome him back, when John Knox finally returned to Scotland's capital for the last time from his long exile on the Continent. He had been stimulated beyond his imaginings by ministering to the small colony of English refugees, whose bright scholars had kept him sharp-minded and on his toes. In fact, what with his clearness of conscience and contentment of heart, he would have been happy to spend the rest of his days in the wonderful atmosphere of the Swiss city, if it had been God's will, but he was certain it was not His will. After all, the Genevan Bible had been already translated from the Hebrew and Greek with his considerable help.

"Ah, Master John, the longing of my eyes and of my spirit have at last been fulfilled! My prayer is that this will be the end of your journeying." Glencairn, his long and faithful friend. , clasped the preacher to his breast, as the latter alighted from his steed, exhausted but content. The voyage from Dieppe had been cold and bracing, without any rest at an English Port, due to the continual offence taken by the Queen of England towards him but he was nevertheless full of hope, and a quiver of anticipation went through him that the Reformation was near.

On the slope of the Canongate and beneath the familiar sight of Arthur's seat above, Knox embraced these older saints, whom he hoped would be pillars of the coming Revolution in religion, without whose leadership it would not be possible. These were God's instruments. But when he found himself close to the young heir of the Earl of Argyle, Knox refrained from embracing him. He had become too accustomed to this Continental habit, and, anyway, he had a prior enquiry.

"But where is the good Earl, your father?"

"He has departed this life a short time ago, sir," answered the son quietly and sadly, but with a strong conviction of God's Providence." He was constant in the true faith of Jesus Christ, and renounced every impiety, superstition, and idolatry. In his last words, he commended that I should suppress these things with all my power and study to set forth the true preaching of the Evangel." Knox was impressed with the sincerity of the young man, but he was still unstable, he was sure, as he knew that before Argyle had led a rather loose life.

"God be merciful to you, my young friend! He has great plans for us all, brethren." He gazed round them" It is good to see your beloved countenances again, and breathe again the fresh Lothian air!"

"Come up to your lodgings in the Canongate meanwhile, John," exclaimed William Cunningham, Earl of Glencairn," and I shall inform you of the latest thoughts and pronouncements of the Queen Regent and the Provincial Council." He laughed scornfully.

He lost no time as soon as they were esconced in an upper room in the lower Canongate. The capital as yet did not have a majority of Protestants, and they couldn't be too careful. But, as they partook of some claret, Glencairn excoriated the recent printed Act of the Council.

"The common people mock it as '*The Twapenny Faith*' that the Provincial Council have spread throughout the land. It has the most trifling rules, about who does and who does not wear caps, shave their crowns, wear the stippet streamers on their sleeves, hoods, and long gowns, things of no importance in God's eyes and man's! It does not touch the theological rub; it avoids the issue of doctrinal truth, the Mass, the authority of the Papacy, the falsehood of purgatory, prayers to saints and Mary, and the sheer, blatant, immorality of the clergy!

Our good Archbishop Hamilton has slyly granted some little reform of the many corruptions, like a few less infant children inheriting rich benefices to try to persuade the people that they have the Reformation in mind. None is to enjoy a Church office or benefice but a priest. No man of the Kirk should look after his own bairns, but should minister spiritually to those of others. If any priest is found in adultery, for the first fault he should lose the third of his benefice, for the second a half, and for the third fault the whole benefice! That will touch them where it hurts!"

"I think if this law is adhered to, half of Scotland's clergy will be out of their benefices!" quipped the Earl of Morton dryly." It's a fact that, if two out of six hundred Scotsmen are clergy, two out of seven illegitimate bairns are priest's bastards!"

"The Bishop of Moray also decreed the absolute authority of Canon Law, with a true and just execution and interpretation for all," continued Glencairn, ignoring Morton." So far, so good, but no change in doctrine. The rub is that the persecution of Protestants has been decreed by the Queen Regent and her Prelates. Mary of Guise has more faces than the Janus, the two-headed god of the Romans!"

"Do not talk of such pagan blasphemous superstitions, Cunningham!" John Knox reprimanded him savagely. "God will not bless such talk!"

"My apologies, I simply meant that the Queen Regent is able to suit her words to her audience, even if they contradict one another."

"So long as she shows her true face to me, I am not worried about her other faces." Knox's ever-ready wit had not been blunted by his hardships or sojourn abroad.

"Aye, aye, John, but will she? Mary of Guise has made her opinion open that the Scottish Crown Matrimonial of her teenage daughter, Mary, in France, should be granted to her husband, Francis I, and so France and Scotland will be one Kingdom, and, mark this, that the subjects of both realms will have equal liberty, Scotsmen in France and Frenchmen in Scotland! This is designed, you may be sure, to deceive Scotsmen, blinded by the lustre of high positions and any profit they may gain.

The French wish to control all of Scotland! But fortunately the wind of truth has blown away the mist of ignorance from the eyes of most people in a short time when the greatest and highest positions in Scotland, it was found, were to be appointed to Frenchmen. Monsieur de Rabie was to keep the Great Seal, Bartholomew Villemore would be Comptroller, and all the riches of Melrose and Kelso Abbeys have been given '*in commendam*' to the Cardinal of Lorraine!"

"The poor Cardinal of Lorraine!" The natural ruddiness of Knox's cheeks, which had retained their colour, despite his fifty four years, mounted to a fieryness of sarcasm and indignation." What a scandal! Lorraine was Archbishop of Rheims by sixteen and a Cardinal by twenty three! He has two other Archbishoprics, Lyon and Narbonne and even wealthy bishoprics. Kelso is the richest regal monastery in all of Scotland.

What can Lorraine want with more? Corruption and greed have made the Church of Rome sick! It is bad enough when the nobility get the governing of convents." The Lords of the Congregation shifted embarrassedly, for none were exempt from corruption in that age." The wealth of these foundations is set before them like a mark before a poor bowman "

"Their aim is all wrong. They covet these ample revenues, not for the help they can give to their brethren but solely for the high posts, that they may fill their own pockets."

"We are all agreed, otherwise why should we endanger our own livelihoods and our very lives!" retorted the Earl of Morton, staring Knox in the face. Sometimes the thread that united the Reformed party could be wafer thin and severely tested.

"Och, aye," interrupted Glencairn, to ease the tension," to return to the crafty plotting of our Queen Regent, she sails off to every corner of our compass to get our precious Scottish throne secured to France. With one voice she says to the bishops and priests that she cannot do what she wants in the realm, and that we, the Protestant heretics and confederates of England, have banded together to stop all good order.

But then she tries to persuade them that if the Church is favourable to her in obtaining the Crown of Scotland for her daughter's French husband, they will soon see how she handles these heretics and traitors! High-sounding words, but, I am certain, she is not deceiving them in this promise. And then she says to the Protestants that she keeps it in mind how often they have petitioned her to see Reformation in the Church, and that she would gladly consent to it but for the power and craftiness of the Archbishop of St. Andrews and leading men of the Kirk. But if her daughter is allowed to devolve the authority of this realm to the King of France, she will grant whatever changes we Protestants wish for. You see how double-minded she is? She has only France's interests at heart!" Cunningham of Glencairn's violent spirit would not take much to transform it into physical violence.

"Rest quiet, my good Earl. God is with those that are of simple and true hearts," said Erskine of Dun calmingly.

"But the old loyalty to one Lord of this realm, which has done so much to bond our society, has been loosened so much, with men changing sides under pressure by subtle shifts in the politics of our land, and not least the inducement of money. Others collaborate out of fear." The Earl of Morton was a realist, if anything.

"I hope that you are not inferring that I am one of those 'assured Lords', bought by English gold?" Glencairn bristled angrily, thinking back to when fifteen years before King Henry VIII had attempted to bribe him with a pension of £1,000." They are but petty Lairds and Burgesses!" By now he had laid his hand on his sword hilt.

"No, no, Glencairn. I ken your heart is leal. Don't let disharmony enter our ranks! Did not we five sign a Bond as Lords of the Congregation of Christ to establish the most blessed Word of God and to renounce the Congregation of Satan with all its superstitions? No, I only think of the very words of Mary of Guise to Sir Ralph Sadler, the English Ambassador, that the Earl of Arran was the most untrustworthy man in the world. Whatever he determines today, he changes tomorrow. The English Ambassador privately told me that the world is so full of falsehood that he simply knew not whom he could trust."

"Gentlemen, gentlemen, my Lords of the Congregation, in whom I put my trust!" Knox intervened. "To important matters, how goes the cause in Scotland? Has all my work in Scotland gone for nothing in the time that the Lord allowed me to return from exile?"

"Surely not, Pastor," responded Glencairn with vigour." At least eight Burghs have been won over to the Protestant Faith, Ayr, Brechin, Dundee, Montrose, St. John's town of Perth, St. Andrews, and Stirling, and of course Edinburgh to a greater extent, where the leaders of the Council have turned to the truth.

But only in two towns, Dundee and St. John's Town of Perth, is there a sizeable Protestant population and presence. Here in Edinburgh our strength is concentrated in the wealthier merchants and lawyers and their wives, who have been attending house cells in secret to have readings of the Holy Bible, commentary on Scripture, and the administration of our Holy Communion, just as you taught us at Finlayston House, when the Lord forgave us for the use of candlesticks for Communion vessels. ," He laughed embarrassedly." Aye, we have a privy Kirk, but the time is coming when it will be a public Kirk, and it will be soon, John!"

"Aye, it will be very soon, be very sure!" John Knox replied, his eyes alight, "It is the year of the favour of the Lord and the vengeance of our God!"

"But we must beware the craft of the Queen Regent, good Master Knox," interrupted the prudent Laird of Dun quietly." I have just returned from Stirling, and the Regent is in a fury at the way our Protestant preachers have been spreading our Biblical beliefs like wildfire. She is enraged that the Provost of Perth, Lord Ruthven, refuses to suppress the religion there. He told her that he could control their bodies, but not the consciences of the people."

"That is a miracle for Lord Ruthven, who shilly-shallies on vital decisions, as far as I am concerned," growled Glencairn.

"Continue, my Lord Erskine," said Knox impatiently.

"She has also commanded James Haliburton, Provost of Dundee, to apprehend the preacher, Paul Methven, But Haliburton is a good man, and faithful to the cause, secretly passed on word to Master Methven to avoid the town for a time for his own safety." A murmur of thanksgiving for such men as the bold Provost of Dundee went round the group.

"She has also tried to stem the rising tide by sending men to persuade the towns of Montrose, Dundee, and St. John's Town, to restore the Mass, even though they had received the Evangel and turned Protestant. But they achieved nothing, thanks to God, for the hearts of the people have been bent to follow the truth of the Bible revealed, and abhor superstitions like relics and prayers to the saints, and idolatry like the Mass! I have a strong feelings that many religious images have a precarious future," Lord Erskine of Dun gently.

"There is no hope or future in idols," responded Knox drily." The end of idols and idolaters is sure." He was in no mood for the casting down of idols, however, and changed the subject." It is more than three months since I left Geneva, -I loved that great city of God!" - he broke off with a longing groan," and they have been long, weary months, Elizabeth of England has been so much offended at the *First Blast of the Trumpet against the Monstrous Regiment of Women* that she implacably refused to permit me to pass through her lands on my way home and visit old friends, though many have gone to their reward at the hands of that wicked harlot of the House of Tudor."

He thought lovingly of the great Thomas Cranmer, the rather weak-willed Archbishop of Canterbury, who had revealed at his end such amazing courage at his martyrdom on the funeral pyre at Oxford as to thrust heroically into the fire first the hand which had signed his former recantation of the truth." Truly Cranmer had sown the seeds of the Reformation forever in his death, and become the architect of the EnglishReformation. "Three times I begged Sir William Cecil to remonstrate with her, but she stubbornly refused." John Knox sighed with frustration. "England has refused me, and yet I have been Queen Elizabeth's sure, though secret, friend, in situations, which even Cecil, my Lord Burleigh, with all his myriad of spies and intelligence agents could not have remedied. I have written a warning to him of the danger."

He lowered his voice furtively, as if the very walls had ears. His life for the past six years had been one of pursuit, exile, and most of all, vigilance, and so, even among seeming friends, the last had to be retained.

"What do you mean, Master John?" Morton enquired curiously, always alert for any threat to his safety.

"As I passed through France, I learnt details of a subtle conspiracy hatched by that she-wolf, Catherine de Medici, to dethrone Elizabeth and place our Scottish Princess on the English throne. She has the lass, Mary, in her claws over in France to influence her in whatever direction her scheming mind desires. As a faithful friend of England, my desire is to expose what I know of the plot to Cecil." His face was grim." On the very ship, in which I crossed there was an agent carrying the Seal engraved with the arms of England to be given to that other imposter from France, the Queen Regent of Scotland!"

"No? Their arrogance knows no limit!" Glencairn's face was black as thunder." But were you safe on board such a vessel, brother?" Above all the other Lords of the Congregation even, the good-hearted Sir William loved Knox, to him the supreme hope under God of the Reformation.

"They did not ken who I was. I went by the name of William Sinclair, my mother's unmarried name, and was merely for them a solitary traveller from Europe returning homewards to Scotland. Even my accent, I have to confess, as you will have noticed, which has been changed by my exile, didn't give me away. The Lord uses all things for his purposes." Just then excited voices outside in the Canongate below were heard, and they were rejoicing.

"John Knox has come! John Knox has returned! The Protestant cause has been saved! He will lift our banner high again. *Jehovah Jireh!* The Reformation gangs merrily ahead!" A small crowd had gathered, who had been told of Knox's presence within by one who had caught sight of his unmistakable features near the window of his lodgings above. Annoyance creased the Reformer's brow, as he gazed down upon the knot of citizens.

"Have them keep quiet, my Lord Morton, for the time is not yet to stir the land. The enemy is still triumphant. I am an outlaw, and can be arrested at any time." Lord Morton moved to obey his command, but Knox grasped his arm for a moment." But tell them to take their courage in both their hands, for our time will be soon."

Quickly the little group dispersed quietly up the Canongate, but obviously renewed in spirit. The man of God had returned. John Knox spent two nights secretly lodged in his beloved Edinburgh, nursing his nostalgic memories. Then on the third the party of nobles returned to his lodgings. Concern showed on their faces.

"Word has got to Mary of Guise that you have come back, and she has summoned you and other Reformed preachers to Stirling to abjure the doctrines of the Protestant Faith. What will you do?" It was Morton, who spoke with a deep anxiety.

"I am uncertain as yet what God would have me to do, for Satan is still raging across Scotland to the utmost of his power; I defy her challenge, and I have decided to hasten to Perth to be present with my brethren. We must be as wise as serpents. We would all be helpless in the hands of the Regent at Stirling, where the town and the castle are one, whereas at Perth, in which the majority are for the Reformed cause, there are city walls, unlike many of Scotland's towns. It can be defended against our enemies, my Lords of Arran and Chatelherault and Monsieur D'Oysel's French!" John Knox's grey eyes gleamed with fervour, and his jaw fixed, rock-like." By my life, or by my death, or else by both, I want to glorify God's Holy Name! I ask your prayers, my friends, that I might not faint in the brunt of battle even. There is an old Jewish proverb.' *When the tale of bricks is doubled, then Moses is sent for.*' " He allowed himself a little, self-confident, smile, to go with that raw humour which was an indispensable and inseparable part of the Reformer. He had the trust in God of a Heaven-sent prophet.

"Aye, may it be so!" breathed Erskine of Dun deeply.

The Lords of the Congregation, faithful to their commission and sollicitous for the preacher, refused to leave Knox, and together they rode towards St. John's Town of Perth. As they came through the Lothians and Fife, heading for the wooded hills of Perthshire, hundreds thronged to support them on the roads and bye- ways. By the time they reached Lindores Abbey, perched on the edge of the Firth of Tay, a dozen miles from St. Andrews, a large force accompanied them, and a fire had kindled in John Knox's belly. He felt the spirit of Christ in the Temple.

It was time to cleanse the Commonwealth of Israel from idolatry. It was *kairos* time, the Lord's time, and no man, or devil, would stop the Holy Spirit from flooding the land of Scotland. As he looked down on Lindores Abbey, he experienced a strange fire burning in his bones and his spirit. The ancient Benedictine Abbey, overlooking the silver Tay on its rugged promontory, had been founded four hundred years before, and the monks there were proud of its history as a centre of pilgrimage and a place honoured by monarchs. Sited near the village of Newburgh, Lindores Abbey's days were numbered, for no help was to come to the community of monks that day, when they faced the unbridled wrath of a nation inflamed by the widespread corruption of a rotten Church. Its splendid isolation was part of its undoing, as the forces of the Lords of the Congregation and the Reformation swept down upon Lindores Abbey like an avenging angel.

"Yonder is the home of a nest of vipers, who have lived off the fat of the land, and pretend to represent God! Shall we not rightly be God's instrument to rid the Kingdom of Fife of such?" It was an unknown member of the force, who voiced these fierce sentiments. His features were filled with a religious ferocity, and he pulled at the reins of his snorting, sweating, steed. He had dared almost to challenge the preacher, who led them. In anger Knox outstared the aggressive soldier, who sheepishly cast his head down.

"The Lord will show us what we should do, without interference from ignorant men!" The man shrank back, but in fact the fire of destruction had taken hold of Knox's spirit too, and with a hoarse cry he shouted to Glencairn, Sandilands, Morton, and the others," "Let us remove the instruments of the false and deceitful Mass and the idolatrous images from this Abbey!" The word spread like wildfire through the company, and with a destroying zeal they poured down upon Lindores' unsuspecting community of monks.

Despite the widespread luxury and indolence that had afflicted many of the Abbeys, monasteries, and convents of Scotland, a number still retained something of their original discipline and pristine holiness in their solemnly-taken vows to God, and ironically among these latter were the Benedictine monks of Lindores Abbey. In accordance with the rules of their founder, St. Benedict of Nursia, they led a simple life of prayer and contemplation, and fulfilled the Divine Office of praise and adoration in psalms, hymns, and spiritual songs in Latin, and Scripture readings at set hours of the day. So it was that the frightened monks paled in consternation, when the concourse of fierce Protestants pulled up their exhausted steeds at the doors of the Abbey, and hammered on them till they were opened. Soon the Abbot was summoned to a window above, his face full of indignant surprise and a little fear.

"What in God's Name do you wish here? Why are you so full of a behaviour that threatens our Abbey of Lindores?"

"We are on our way to St. John's Town of Perth, but as the Reformers of Christ's holy Kirk in Scotland, we wish to see the removal of all idols that are contrary to the Word of God and a hindrance to worship in spirit and in truth," Knox replied with a certain calm control of the fervent tide within his breast, as he prayed that his actions were right, for many are the actions of man that he can only justify for his own reasons without the imprimature of God.

"The curse of God and our Holy Father, the Pope, be on you, you wicked heretics! I am the Abbot of Lindores Abbey, which has been the sacred destination for hundreds of years of countless pilgrims. Even the last three Kings of Scotland have bowed their proud heads here! Do you know this? Will you desecrate such a house of God, you ignorant men? Have you no hearts? The Queen Regent shall hear of this, and her vengeance shall be swift and strong. Now, depart from this holy place at once!"

For a moment even John Knox was rebuffed and hesitated, but immediately regathered his determination. The spirit of Elijah and Paul seized him once more.

"We shall not depart, until, as the hand of the Lord, we have cleansed this Abbey of all its unscriptural practises! We call no man Father but that which is in Heaven, as the

Bible teaches." Knox spoke with an authority in his voice, equal to that of the Abbot, and their eyes met and clashed with a fervent, religious, zeal." It is God's work to purify His Kirk in Scotland of all false worship. Rid yourself of all these vestments and content yourself with a simple gown. Leave the Kirk of Rome and turn to Christ's Kirk founded on His infallible Word!" Neither of them waited for a response, for one of Knox's men shouted aggressively.

"Make a bonfire of all Popish vestments!" At that many rushed off to the Chapter House, the Sacristry, the Refectory, Dormitory, and other parts of the Abbey. The Benedictines had many activities in their community, study, meditation, reading, and copying of the manuscripts, lecturing, discussion, cooking, and translating of the Latin and Greek Scriptures. As a Benedictine Abbey, it had an intake of young boys, chosen for their aptitude.

They were taught in the ways of the Order, to laboriously copy the Scriptures, the Service Books, and the writings of the Early Church Fathers such as Augustine, Tertullian, Chrysostom, and Origen, in the most beautiful and elaborate variety of colours and styles. In many Monasteries laziness and a life-style of self indulgence had taken over the monastic communities and the disciplined teaching of the young had lapsed, but the irony was that the Abbey, on which the Reformers had chosen to exercise a just anger, Lindores, was one that had not fallen from grace. Such are the ironies of human life.

"You ignorant men, how can one give up what does not belong to one? None of our holy brothers are permitted to own the smallest possession! We have perpetual vows of compassion for the weak and poor, and to live a cloistered life of prayer and meditation on the inner self!" The rage of the Abbot towards Knox and his fellows had abated a little, but it made not a whit of difference, as the men in a frenzy of destruction ran hither and thither across the cloisters and garth, and not only were windows smashed indiscriminately, but vestments from the monks' closets and costly manuscripts were piled onto the bonfire, which by this time had reached giant proportions. In all revolutions of men, even the best intentioned, sometimes the good is swept away with the bad. In a small way this happened now in the holocaust that was sweeping across Scotland by the Spirit.

And so the tide of zealous Reformers, who accompanied John Knox, rode into St. John'sTown of Perth, where they were met by cheering crowds, who in this walled City felt safe from the Regent Mary's French forces to express openly their stand for the fledgling Protestant Faith. He was immediately invited to preach from the pulpit of St. John's Kirk in the Mercat Cross. He took full advantage, feeling in his heart that it was for such a time as this that he had come to the Kingdom of Scotland to preach the Kingdom of God in its purity. Would he ever have this chance again?

That day on the eleventh day of March John Knox excelled himself, and, if ever there was a venue other than the famous Kirk of St. Giles, which suited such a fiery sermon, it was St. John's Kirk of Perth. It was not particularly striking from the outside, except for the tower and graceful spire, but once inside one was immediately struck by the Church's size, which inspired a feeling of awe. The skillful window lighting brought out the vaulting of the central tower and all together gave the impression of a Cathedral. Its carillon of mighty bells rang out its musical summons to the townsfolk to attend, and they packed in to listen avidly to the new-found faith, rediscovered from its roots.

The tutor of Haddington did not disappoint them. He preached powerfully, his whole heart, soul, and body animated, imbued with a surging strength. His message touched mainly on the dangers, deadly to the soul, of false Gods, whether in the vain imaginations of people, or in the images of stone and wood, which men were fatally inclined by their sinful, fallen, nature, to make as substitutes for the one true God. By the end a wave of excited conversation swept across the crowded Congregation, but, nevertheless, there was still no warning of the cataclysm to come. As yet the atmosphere was of a friendly enthusiasm, and Knox bade them go in peace with a benediction.

Most of the Congregation had filed out, when suddenly a Roman Catholic priest, in a spirit of spite at the open condemnation of his Church and in a temerity that made him oblivious of the danger that his action was about to provoke, entered the Kirk. In a mood of hurt pride the priest carried the vessels and accoutrements of the Mass, and, when he reached the altar, which, unlike Lindores Abbey's, still stood inviolate, he dressed in the green, ornate, robes of his office, and draped the altar in a white cloth, stood ready to celebrate the Mass, round which the Roman Church had built her structure of worship, where in its eyes, if not God's, a re-sacrifice of Christ's unique act on the Cross took place. But all at once a youthful strident voice interrupted his intended action.

"Master Knox says that these are just poor bits o' bread and wine, and you're no' a magician!" An outspoken, maybe impudent, laddie, who was standing nearby, quipped impertinently.

"How dare you, you insolent ragamuffin!" retorted the enraged priest, and cuffed the boy severely around the ear." Take that for your cheek!"

But the local lad was fired up, and he picked up a stone, which had probably found its way into St. John's Kirk on the sole of a citizen's brogue. With force he threw it at the priest, but, whizzing randomly and narrowly past his ear, it struck and shattered one of the many saints' images nearby. The crash echoed round the spacious Church, in which a small part of the congregation still hung around. The act aroused them, already enthused by Knox's fierce sermon, and they rushed to take the laddie's part. The commotion attracted many outside, who also rushed back in. The preacher from Haddington had aroused passions that even he could not control now.

"Thou shalt not make unto thee any graven images, nor bow down before them, or worship them!" cried out one Protestant.

"Christ was once sacrificed forever, and cannot be repeated! We are all a Royal Priesthood, a Holy Nation! How dare you concoct a ceremony that God does not teach?" cried another. But, for the most part it was an emotional anger, which suffused them like volcanic fire, that found its outlet in a sympathy with the boy knocked over by the priest.

In a few minutes an eruption of fury had seized the people of Perth, and in what they felt was a righteous rage they tore down the images, altars, and all ornaments in St. John's, and trampled them underfoot. The priest fled in terror, but soon the noise collected a mob of the lower classes. In Perth it chanced that there had been a long-standing feud between the ordinary citizens, many of them very poor, and the clergy,

132

who had lived a life of self-indulgence and even luxury. This was just the tiny flame needed to spark off their pent-up fury at the corruption of the Church. Some crowded into St. John's, their hot faces breathing fire, but, finding out that their help was not required, they poured out again into the streets with cries to their fellow citizens.

"Let us pull down the Monastic Houses of the Grey and Black Friars and the Carthusians! They have lived in the lap of luxury and lorded it over us for too long! We are the true citizens of St. John's Town of Perth, and this is the Lord's work! Nothing will stop us!" They never stopped to ask themselves if this was truly so.

"Aye, now is our chance. We are the hands and vengeance of God!"

Rapidly their fervour rose, and shortly mob rule reigned throughout the streets of Perth. Even John Knox could do nothing, as he tried in vain to raise his voice above the clamour. The seeds of Protestant teaching had already been sown in Perth and Dundee by preachers such as Paul Methven, and taken root. So the gentlemen and more sober part of the inhabitants stood aghast at the unpremeditated tumult happening before their startled eyes, as the mob charged through the lanes, wynds, vennels, and causeways of Perth, seething like human lava, and just as dangerous. They had armed themselves with hammers, axes, and metal bars, which they grabbed hold of from any sources.

"There will be the Devil to pay for this!" quoted a scared merchant, not daring to interfere.

"Let's pray that it is the Devil who pays, and not God's people!" replied another pointedly, as they sheltered together in the refuge of the *Cross Keys* Tavern.

Through the window they could make out the ferocity outlined on the faces streaming by. Sure enough, the rioters, an irresistible force, reached the Grey and Black Friars Houses and that of the Carthusians close by, where the monks, friars, and nuns cowered in a conscience-stricken, fear, slain by the memories of the lives of indulgence they had led, caring little for the souls of men.

The Carthusian Order had been founded 500 years before by St. Bruno of Cologne, had begun its work in the quiet isolation of the French Alps at Chartreuse, dedicated to the contemplative life of meditation, prayer, study and manual labour in their orchards and gardens, each living in a hermitage situation. It had, however, departed far from its original disciplines. No longer did the lay brothers and sisters provide the material needs from their farm harvest. The whole city was in a ferment. When finally the dust had settled and the monasteries had been destroyed, John Knox remarked to his friend, Glencairn, summing up his feelings, in a resigned manner.

"It was a foolish action of the priest, but there is no excuse for what has been the work of the rascal multitude, who often care nothing for true religion." He determined to have words with the Earl of Moray for measures to be taken for the protection from future threats to religious buildings in the floodtide of Reformation, which he prayed would cleanse his beloved land. But the French under Mary of Guise, the late King's widow, were still in control. Monsieur de Rubie was in possession of the Great Seal, Bartholomew Villemore was Comptroller of the country's finances, and the Cardinal of Lorraine would get his greedy clutches on the Abbeys of Melrose and Kelso.

The hypocrisy of giving the revenues of Abbeys to men, who discharged no duties in these rich establishments almost made him apoplectic with righteous anger. Even the freedom of Scots merchants was severely curtailed in French towns like Rouen, and in addition they were forced to pay exorbitant tolls. It was time to break the old French connection, he was sure, and to seek vital military and financial help from England. Ancient animosities had to be banished from the souls of the Scots and English, whose spirits were open to the voice of the Lord. He had not forgotten that his very father, William Knox, had died on Flodden's tragic field along with ten thousand other brave Scots souls but a generation before. Yet, as he prayed in his spirit, he became convinced that the future of Scotland and England would be one.

"The Queen Regent's cause will only be served through this will full destruction by the ignorant mob. Her cunning will utilise it to the profit of the Roman Catholic Church, and the Protestant preachers will be represented as causing all this violence. We must be wise, and ask our God who gives wisdom liberally."

"Amen to that," echoed Erskine of Dun.

If truth be told, Knox and the others were very afraid of the reaction of the Queen Regent towards the rioting and destruction in Perth, for Mary of Guise exercised her rule on her daughter's behalf over in France from Stirling, only thirty miles away, where her French and Italian troops also were based. Why, the very volcanic eruption that was Stirling Castle could be seen from Kinnoul Hill, overlooking Perth. She was not likely to ignore such happenings. It had been two days before the furore in Perth had died down.

If John Knox could have been supernaturally transported to the Great Hall of Stirling he would have seen Mary of Guise. The well-built and tall Frenchwoman, of sharp intelligence and administrative ability even to the point of austerity at times, received the news of the destruction of the Perth monasteries with a rage that was incandescent. Her face convulsed, she turned to James Hamilton, second Earl of Arran and First Duke of Chatelherault, a man of great personal pride, who had humiliatingly turned back from an initial, superficial, decision to become a Protestant to do penance for his supposed apostasy and to receive the Catholic sacraments in the Church of the Franciscans in Stirling. In fact it had been the very day before the tiny Mary Stuart had been crowned Queen at nine months sixteen years ago.

If the inner thoughts of James Hamilton had been revealed, his ambition was that in due course his son would be the bridegroom of Mary, Queen of Scots, and this aim had controlled all his actions thereafter, with the purpose that this marriage would keep the Crown in Scotland under the control of her own Scots people, especially the Hamiltons. Though deeply disappointed that Hamilton ambitions for supreme control of Scotland had been thwarted by the young Queen's marriage to the young Dauphine of France, Arran had hung around like a dark moth in the not unlikely hope that the pale, sickly, heir to the French throne, Francis, who suffered from a chronic respiratory sickness resulting from a difficult birth, would die young, and this would revive Hamilton hopes. Arran prayed for that early death daily.

This then was the unprincipled nobleman, who still recalled with an unhealthy clarity how on that day, the ninth of September, those sixteen years before, at the Coronation of a helpless infant in the Chapel of Stirling Castle, he had borne the Crown. The Earl of Lennox had carried the sceptre, and the Earl of Argyle, who was of royal descent, had borne the sword, but, he, a famous Hamilton, had borne the most important thing, the crown. The pro-English nobles had stayed away then, the Earls of Angus, Glencairn, Cassillis, and Maxwell, and Arran was not likely to forget that. This man was, therefore, fertile soil for the invective of the Regent against the insurgent Protestants, as was the other man present, the Abbot of Kilwinning, a cruel person with an inveterate hatred of the new religionists.

"I shall utterly destroy this town of Perth, man, woman, and child, consume it with fire, raze it to the ground, and sow it with salt as a monument to perpetual desolation! They are set on rebellion, nothing else!"

"Majesty, it is high time to nip this bunch of heretics in the bud before they gather strength," replied Arran." Have D'Oysel gather his troops at once and march on Perth. The English will never dare to intervene, and, even if they did, they could not relieve Perth in time. But remember that Perth is one of the few towns outside Edinburgh to be strengthened by solid walls."

"In addition the Monastery of Chartreuse was the birthplace of James, the First of the Stuart Kings! This was the desecration of a Royal tomb, iniquitous in the sight of God and men!" The messenger had not told her, if he had known that John Knox and his noble supporters had permitted Adam Forman, the Prior of Chartreuse, to take away with him as much gold and silver as he was able to carry, but in fact it would have made no difference to the fierce anger of Mary of Guise. Little was heard of Adam Forman afterwards.

It might just have touched the heart of the Frenchwoman, if she had been aware that the sheets, general clothing, blankets, and covers, as good as any an Earl in Scotland could have afforded, which had been found in the House of the Grey Friars, had been given to the poor, along with the eight large puncheon casks of salt beef, wine, beer, and ale, much more in fact than men professing poverty ought to have. After all, she knew what it was to survive, one of twelve children. But the amassing of wealth was the last desire of the man of God, who had returned to his beloved Scotland to lead her Reformation.

"No honest man shall be enriched by the value of a groat in our Reformation. Make sure it is so," Knox had instructed the Lords of the Congregation in the aftermath of Perth." I am determined, by life, or by death, or else both, to glorify God's Holy Name. Pray for me, my friends, that I shall not faint, even in the brunt of the battle." The words came from his heart.

"We shall, Master John," responded Erskine of Dun and Sir James Sandilands of Calder almost simultaneously with sincerity.

"Let us strengthen the town's fortifications. Unless I am much mistaken, a storm is coming upon us. But first, my Lords, let us pen a joint letter to the Regent, disclaiming all rebellious intentions. We will assure her that we would gladly have suppressed the riots. All we ask for his liberty of conscience and the Reformation of religion." Though unafraid, Knox did not invite trouble.

"But we shall not crawl to her," growled Glencairn defensively. No Frenchwoman would humiliate a proud Scotsman." We'd better write to the French commander, D'Oysel, Captain Serra La Burse, and the other French Captains that we know too, and appeal to their good sense as men, that they are not called by their Master, the King of France, to fight against Scotsmen. If they start a bloody war with us, it will last far beyond our lives, we must tell them, John," insisted Cunningham." "Perhaps they will intervene with that woman?"

"Be at rest, my dear friend, for God is with us, and things shall come to pass, as He wills, and His will is best. ," Knox soothed the Laird of Finlayston, and withdrew to his lodgings to draw up the open letter to the Regent. He must be discreet in his language, and ask the Lord for wisdom, which He was ready to grant liberally. He would pray too that the young Earl of Argyle and Lord James Stuart, both committed to the Protestant Faith, who were with the Queen's Regent, would change to join the Lords of the Congregation's side. Argyle had not wished to be disloyal to the Crown, a mistaken loyalty. He would need such powerful men, especially the Earl of Moray, Lord James, whom Knox knew was a man of deep wisdom. But if he had known it, only the language of military force would move the Regent.

The Regent, though passionately devoted to the House of Guise and the interests of France, had lived long enough in Scotland to know that it was easy to rouse the spirit of the Scots nobility, and not so easy to calm it. She knew that the Lords of the Congregation and the Protestant faction numbered now in its ranks some of the highest and best in the land. Was it not a dangerous thing to exasperate such men?

When the letter from Perth was laid upon the cushion beside her in the Chapel Royal of Stirling, where she was accustomed to sit at Mass, she looked at it cursorily, and put it in her pocket of her gown. The French commander, D'Oysel, and his Captains received their letters from the Protestant faction, delivered by some of their own French soldiers, who were Huguenot Protestants, and they were hesitant to move against Perth. But the anger raised in Mary and the instigation of the priests to rid the realm of these heretics was too powerful for the hesitant D'Oysel and his officers. As he gathered his troops in the esplanade and upper slopes of Stirling Castle, he whispered under his breath.

"I pray that we are not sowing to the wind to reap a whirlwind." Commander D'Oysel well knew that xenophobia against the French was not yet widespread, but that it did not take much for these warlike Scots to be roused. He was aware that Lord James Stuart, half brother of the young Queen, was the one Scot with sufficient political sagacity to negotiate terms to satisfy the Reformers and the Queen's party, but that his sympathies could be lost easily. As a Protestant, he could cross into the other camp, if the Regent became too aggressive, as would Argyle. The balance was very fine. He gazed from the battlements of Stirling northwards towards the walls of Perth, only too aware of the key position of this Castle, the gateway to the Highlands. He disregarded the northwest, which for all he knew was another world, For Monsieur D'Oysel had never set foot there, and moreover the Highland chiefs there played little part in the political scene in the Kingdom of Scotland, but were set on their petty feuds.

He would never understand these Scots, who were prickly as the burrs, which D'Oysel often found stuck to his clothing when he walked abroad in the Scottish countryside. They were as ready for an argument as the small contingent of Italian mercenaries, whom Catherine de Medici, the mother of his young King, had attached to his command. Yes, Stirling was in a strategic place, bounded by the gently rolling Lammermuirs and the Ochils to the east and the rugged mountains to the west. He pursed his lips and his sallow skin was stretched in a frown. Once out of Stirling, his forces would be exposed.

It was all too easy for Mary's intolerant brothers in France, who controlled her actions so much from over there. They did not have to fight. He gave the order to prepare to move out, and the Captains marshalled the men and horses.

That night a silent figure with a small retinue slipped out of a side postern gate in Perth's wall, and galloped away on horses that had been waiting, pre-arranged in a nearby copse of wood. Early the next morning the Earl of Morton with a long face awoke their preacher. But the strain lifted when he saw the authority and sense of assurance depicted on that broad brow and grey eyes.

"Lord Ruthven, the Lord Provost, has defected and left our cause! He has joined the Queen in Stirling. How could this happen with a man, who was a stout supporter of the Protestant cause? Ruthven's defection will bring great discouragement to many hearts!"

"Don't be depressed, Lord Morton, for I foresee that Lord Ruthven shall come back to our cause before very long." Knox's eyes had misted over in the manner of a prophet with a distant look. He had never sought to publicise his gift, aware that God granted spiritual insight and supernatural power only to those who would use them not for their own glory." My Lord James Stuart, Earl of Moray, and the young Earl of Argyle will also return to our side, I prophesy." A glint of mystery was in his een, and the Earl of Morton, who was normally in awe of the man of God, stood back, his mouth wide-open. He was a man rather of pragmatic approach, and was out of his depth.

Although within half a day the populace of Perth had been encouraged, the tension still existed that they were too weak to oppose the professional French soldiers of D'Oysel. The citizens exercised as trained bands in the streets of the town. It was time to buckle on their armour. One day in late May a cry of triumph sounded out from the walls.

"Look, our brethren are coming to our aid!" Sure enough, steel bonnets could be seen streaming down from the surrounding hills by all paths, from the north, south, east, and west, into the natural bowl in which Perth lay. It soon became apparent that they were supporters of the Reformation from Fife, Angus, the Mearns, and Dundee. They were well armed, and these arms were waved excitedly, as they advanced into Perth, and embraced the citizens.

Their hearts would have been even more uplifted, if they had known that further south in the Kirk of Craigie in the town of Ayr, the Protestants of Cunningham and Kyle were gathered to decide what they should do to help their brethren in deadly danger. For some time it was debated whether there was wisdom in marching north, or if it was entering into the lion's den. They would leave Ayrshire, Kyle, and Carrick exposed, if they marched on Perth, some said. Others doubted they could make a difference. Suddenly, Alexander, the young heir to the Earl of Glencairn, barely able to contain his zeal, burst out.

"Let every man act according to his own conscience. Others may do as they will; I will join my brethren in St. John's Town of Perth, yea, although I should go alone with a pike on my shoulder. I would rather die in that company than live after them!" With these words of stinging rebuke and powerful resolve, Alexander Cunningham of Glencairn glared at the other leading men of the Reformed faith in Ayrshire, and marched out of the Kirk. He was not his father's son for nothing, and longed to be at the front of the battle with his fiery parent. In a moment the spirit of the rest was ignited, and one and all of them shouted for young Finlayston to return.

"Aye, ye are richt, my Lord! Our hearts are convicted. We ken your father, the Earl, is with Master Knox now in Perth, and in deadly danger. We must also the restore the times of preaching from Master Knox in Kyle and Carrick these three years and more past when he gave his all for us!" A local Laird spoke out." We cannot, and must not, let him down in his time of need!" A loud shout of agreement rang throughout the Church.

"Aye, let us spread the news to Glasgow, and have the Lyon Herald announce it through the streets by the sound of the public trumpet that all men of courage and conviction are required at this hour to march on the French, and relieve Perth from their threat. No foreigner will take our land or our faith!" Glasgow was to wholeheartedly answer the call.

The stage was set, as Monsieur D'Oysel and his army of 3, 000 advanced north to within ten miles of Perth. He was uneasy, as some of his army had not been paid, including the small number of French Protestants, called Huguenots, in his forces. In addition he was nervous that only 500 Scotsmen at most had marched with him, and that they would be regarded as a foreign army of occupation, not as a protector of the Regent from an English invasion. He was in no mood to be taken by surprise by a Scots force in the rear. He approached to within ten miles of Perth to find the gentlemen of Fife, Angus, the Mearns, and Dundee with their followers drawn up a mile from the town, ready and willing to face him, rather than sitting behind their walls but taking the initiative. John Knox's prayer that the first major confrontation with the French would be won, was about to be answered.

A May morning shortly before he had climbed Kinnoull Hill overlooking Perth's fair city, and in its bright sunshine he had been quietly thrilled by the astonishing view from near eight hundred feet over the Tay estuary through Fife to the Lomond Hills, and to the north it took in the mighty Ben More on the west and the dark Lochnagar to the east. The waters of the Tay sparkled as it wound its way through the lovely Perthshire fields. It was one of those joyful mornings when everything in nature, even the early rowan berries, shone brightly in the spring sunshine. It was a good time to be alive, but it was also a fateful time and place. Perth, he knew well, was a vital city both in its location and its history. Its eminence derived from its proximity to Scone, but two miles distant, where from antiquity the Kings of Scotland had been crowned since seven hundred years before Kenneth McAlpine had united the warlike Picts and Scots into one Kingdom.

Now was the time to unite Scotland again as one spiritual Kingdom in one true faith under the one true God. No matter that Edward of England had stolen away the talisman of the so-called Stone of Destiny, for it was but a bit of a superstitious bauble to him. More relevant was that God would deliver them from the French, for his cheeks tightened as he stared out towards Stirling, and from the heights of Kinnoull he made out a mass of men and cloud of dust from their horses within about ten miles distant. Aye, it was the French, and, furthermore, unless God intervened, Mary of Guise would take her revenge for the destruction of the monasteries, and not only them, but the Abbey of Scone, which he had not been able to prevent the mob from ransacking. The Lord would intervene, he was absolutely certain, but he prayed in case.

"The enemy is in sight, Master." His reverie was interrupted by one of the tough Fifeshire soldiers.

"Aye, I ken well, my man," answered Knox shortly, slightly irritated that his meditation had been disturbed.

"But do you ken that they have sent an Embassy to treat with you and the Lords?" replied the soldier with typical Fifeshire bluntness. He was slightly blowing, having hurried up the hill to pass on the information, and was a little chagrined at his reception. Fife folks had little time for airs and graces.

"I'm sorry, my friend. You are one of those who have ridden to our aid, are you not, and I thank you in God's Name. Let us go down and meet them outside the walls. God guide our words!" The soldier grunted, quietly pleased at the preacher's words.

It was the familiar figures of Lord James Stuart and the young Earl of Argyle, accompanied by the Prior of St. Andrews, and Lord Semple, who met the Protestant leaders. The wise, brown, eyes of the Earl of Moray were filled with embarrassment, clearly uncomfortable that he had to negotiate against his conscience.

"It deeply saddens me to meet you again in this situation, as well as my Lord Argyle, Lord James," said Sir William Cunningham aggressively." Why is your Protestantism so deceived by your misplaced loyalty to the Regent? Loyalty needs a guiding spirit."

Moray bridled slightly and winced visibly, but bit his lip, while Argyle shifted uneasily on his horse. Uncertainty ruled in Scotland, and divided allegiances were common. No one knew what the future held, unless the Almighty granted secret words of encouragement to some men. The preacher from Haddington was one of these, and his strong gaze held that of Moray. There was a powerful bond between the two, which would be severely tested more than once.

"You will know that we have written to the Regent, disclaiming all rebellious intentions, my Lord. Rebellion is worse than witchcraft, God tells us. The preachers and magistrates of Perth would gladly have suppressed the riots, if we had been able." Knox spoke in a matter of fact manner, and there was no hint of pleading in his voice." All we ask is freedom of conscience and worship, and, as you know, the Reformation of religion in Scotland." His tone had risen somewhat now, and there was a demand in it, even though he was only too aware that Mary of Guise held a superior force of French at a distance of only ten miles.

"The Queen Regent is enraged at the destruction of the Carthusian monastery, where the remains of the first of the Stuart Kings lie. She would have Perth completely destroyed, if she had her way at this moment. But the French Commander is a moderating influence, and I shall use all my advice to ensure that yourself and all the other preachers are not outlawed, Master Knox." The Earl of Moray was a man of deep sincerity." As for my loyalty, Glencairn, God has always been my guide, and, until He shows me otherwise, I shall remain to advise the mother of my Queen, but, if she should prove false, I promise that I shall leave her side." Here he fiercely returned the glare of Glencairn.

"Aye, and I too," broke in young Argyle equally firmly.

"We shall hold you to it," retorted Glencairn. Further negotiations did not achieve any progress, and finally my Lord James and his party rode off to the waiting Mary of Guise and her French troops. Knox had not liked Lord Semple, who had said little. But he knew in his spirit that the man was a deadly enemy. He would misrepresent him to the Queen Regent.

But the turning point came when the ambassadorial party returned to the French Camp, and was met by a serious-faced D'Oysel.

"Gentlemen, while you were negotiating, a fresh support for the Reformers has come into sight from the south, and it's a large force. We are in a quandary, for our reinforcements from France have not arrived. We have no choice but to propose terms of accommodation with those in Perth. The Queen Regent is still in a total rage, so that all your persuasive powers are needed, my dear Scotsmen, to change her mind." D'Oysel was seriously worried that French control in Scotland was beginning to slip away. Argyle took him at his word, however, and used all his wisdom in his interview with the Regent.

"The Protestants in Perth are united in their resolve to fight for Christ and the Gospel, they say, sword in hand. I have to tell your Grace that I will continue to support you, if you grant them concessions, not otherwise." The Earl was youthful and inexperienced, and glanced nervously at Mary of Guise, whose emotions were unpredictable. She glared at him, her Latin blood on fire, but she had already been cautioned against rash action by D'Oysel.

"Go on, my Lord, but be careful that you do not overstep yourself." She bit her lip, and drew in her breath to contain her impatience.

"I propose that both armies be disbanded, and the gates of Perth shall be thrown open to your Grace, but nobody is to be punished for the removal of images or any changes in religion. The Reformation must be allowed to go forward. No Frenchman must approach within three miles of Perth, and, most importantly, Perth must not have a French garrison." The Regent's eyes were sparking with fury, but the Earl of Argyle carried on.

"Finally, all controversial matters are to be reserved for the meeting of Parliament."

Much of these terms had been compiled in fact by Lord James, but he felt too closely related to Mary of Guise as half –brother to her daughter, the young Princess Mary. Emotional ties could betray a person.

"Are you finished, my Lord of Argyle? It seems to me that you are not entirely unbiased. Did not your father give refuge to the heretic, Knox, once in his Castle of Campbell at Dollar?"

The pique in her voice was not hidden by her French accent, but in fact increased. However, after many tantrums, she finally conceded to the terms, but Lord James Stuart for one felt a distrust of her word, as he perceived the hooded look in the Regent's eyes.

John Knox was equally filled with distrust, when the favourable terms were brought through. Reading the missive to Glencairn, however, there was some satisfaction in his tone.

"I still do not have any confidence in that Frenchwoman." He had to search his soul that his deep-seated animosity against all things French did not influence his opinion.

"But Argyle and Lord James have gone security for her good faith. If she proves false in her word, they call God to witness that they will desert her and join the western leaders. At least that is something to be glad about."

"Och, aye," grunted Glencairn non-committedly.

"I shall preach in St. John's Kirk's pulpit and exhort everyone of our brethren to be faithful and thankful. God has prevented bloodshed, but I'm sure that the Regent will break her promise. I'll exhort no one to weaken in their will for our cause, since the Treaty will be kept by our treacherous foes only until the Regent and her Frenchmen feel strong enough to break it." Knox hesitated, "We must depart from Perth soon, and God's Spirit tells me that I should preach the Kingdom of God in the Kingdom of Fife."

In his mind he visualised Crail, Anstruther, and St. Andrews, the string of pearls that made up the coastal towns, as his next ports of call. A vision arose of that mist-shrouded day off the Fife shores in a French galley, when from the deepest despair God had granted him the promise that he would again preach in St. Andrews Parish Church. The will of God, if delayed, would always be fulfilled. The wheel had turned full circle, and he rejoiced within, not just for himself, but for all of Scotland.

THE SPREADING FLAME

On the second day of May the Protestants of Perth marched proudly out of its gate heads held high. The valley, in which St. John'sTown of Perth lay, rang to shouts of triumph. John Knox rode with them as far as necessary, before leaving the main body, accompanied by his usual guard and his servant, Patrick, to head for Crail, arranging with the Lords of the Congregation to meet them within the fortnight at St. Andrews. Now was the time of high tide in the nation's affairs, and his spirits rose as he was met not only by the fresh May winds, but also by the wildly enthusiastic welcome of the common people of Fife, as they rode first through Angus and the Mearns, which were already on fire for the Reformation, and then through the ancient capital of Dunfermline.

The people were like tinder, just ready to be set on fire by his tempestuous eloquence. When at last the party reached Fife's most picturesque Royal Burgh of Crail, their horses' hooves clattered to a standstill on the cobbles of the Marketgate. Word had gone ahead of his coming, and the Town Provost was tumbling over himself to meet the preacher.

"Welcome to the Royal Burgh of Crail, Master Knox! Long have we been yearning for your return to Scotland to lead us to freedom from the shackles of Rome, and the cleansing of our Kirk from all that has polluted it! We are proud to boast that Crail has had the biggest fish-market in Europe, and our ships frequently come back from the Low Countries and Scandinavia with full cargoes, but we are just as proud to have you preach in our Collegiate Church of St. Mary's." He pointed over towards the far end of the Marketgate. Knox nodded in a pleased manner and gazed eagerly at the crow-stepped Kirk. These gables were a common feature among the sparkling, white-washed, cottages, with their attractive, bright red, pantile roofs, which surrounded the quaint harbour. These were common to all the Fife coastal villages, influenced as they were by the Dutch connection. By now Knox was like a thoroughbred stallion in his spirit, panting at the start of the race, so eager was he to preach and spread the flame of the word of faith in God alone. His thoughts were broken by the loquacious Town Provost again, who was desperate to please.

"During the building of the Church, the Devil is said to have hurled a great boulder at it from the Isle of May." He gestured out to sea, where the low, misty, outline of the small island could be made out." The boulder split as it flew through the air and one part landed only a wee bittie away from the Kirkyard gate, ye see yonder? It still sits there, bearing the Devil's thumbprint!" He tried to laugh, but stopped short, when he saw the grim look on the minister's face.

"None o' yer superstitious scrapings out o' the Devil's scrapbook, my man! The accuser of the brethren will send many a missile in your direction, a muckle more dangerous than any rocks from our earth, and, unless you wear the armour of the Lord, you will indeed bear hard the Devil's thumbprint on your person till your very end, and it will cause you great pain, and maybe take you to Hell!" Knox's cutting words and penetrating stare silenced the loquacity of the Provost of Crail.

But secretly Knox was pleased at the moderate prosperity of the fishing village as a result of its trade with the Continent. As an exile in Europe for almost nine years, he highly appreciated the importance of the Continental connection, and equally that a Scotland which was one of the poorest and most backward in all Europe, needed such trade in fish, furs, iron, and wood. Scots Kings had been weak-willed for many years, some often just children controlled by unscrupulous nobles. He desperately wished to see a prosperous Scotland with a harmony of spirit, educated in mind, and adequately clothed and shod, in fact the establishment of God's Kingdom on earth, as the Lord's Prayer proclaimed.

He turned towards the Collegiate Kirk of St. Mary's, with a glance towards the other end of the Marketgate, where the grim Tolbooth stood with its striking Dutch tower, and at that minute its Dutch-cast bell tolled out. Would it sound out the death knell for the infant Reformation, or was this but the igniting of the spreading flame, which would sweep across the villages and towns of Scotland with the fire of the Gospel? What better place to start than the Kingdom of Fife? He must win over the common people, as well as the nobles. The death of the old man, Walter Milne of Dysart, in the terrifying flames of martyrdom at St. Andrews the year before had infuriated Fifeshire, and he knew only too well from Perth the dangers of mob rule. From the time that he had first raised the standard of truth in his native land, he would never shrink from danger, never seek after his own advantage or ease, never compromise with the enemy, and never be bribed into the silence of a coward.

By his eloquence he would arouse the spirits and minds of a fierce and unpolished people. A Church, which had grown fat on the material wealth of a poor nation, almost one third of its entirety, must be torn out by its roots, so that no longer could the crows alight in its branches. Its idolatry, whether in the sacred images and holy wells, false portrayal of the Lord's Supper, or the just plain arrogance of its human authority, must be continually thundered against in the pulpit, and this was the root and branch of his preaching in the Collegiate Kirk of Crail. The fisher folk of the East Neuk drank in the strong cordial, hanging on his every word. If there was more of the Old Testament judgement in them than New Testament love, it was occasioned by the fierce words of the prophet Jeremiah, that one has to pull down and root out before one can build up.

"Like a scarecrow in a kail patch, their idols cannot speak. They must be carried because they cannot walk. Do not fear them. They can do no harm nor can they do any good. The living God alone is worthy of our worship in spirit and in truth! God's Temple must be cleansed of all false trappings and fripperies not found in Scripture, and our heart's Temple too! Examine your hearts, good people, for only a people pure in heart can oppose our enemies, and our enemies are near.

The Regent, the Frenchwoman, has reached the Palace of Falkland, and has already, I have heard, sent that empty turncoat, Archbishop Hamilton, back to St. Andrews. Shall we let them threaten the work of Christ in Fife?" His voice rang out through the rafters of Crail Kirk, and the people responded with a powerful roar that must have frightened the thousands of seabirds that roosted on the nearby Isle of May. In fact the razorbills, gannets, guillemots, shags, gulls and puffins rose in an indiscriminate cloud that squawked their annoyance for many minutes. As God took care of these birds, He would take care of his servant, when he entered the lion's den of St. Andrews.

That night an equal indiscriminate smashing of images, whether public or private, took place. It was the beginning of a wave of religious zeal that swept the coast of Fife, along the crescent of small fishing villages with their neat, horseshoe-shaped, harbours. Anstruther, but a handful of miles from the all-important centre of St. Andrews, where he knew his destiny lay, was his next port of call. The early June sunshine shone on his fiery preaching, as everywhere the country folk were flocking in to support the Reformation from all parts of Fife.

"Reinforcements seem to be raining in from the clouds," remarked John to a companion, trying to keep his excitement under control." It is a sign of the Lord's blessing."

"Aye, guid Master Knox, and, unless I'm mistaken, there is important assistance to oor cause arrivin now." The worthy pointed to a party of horsemen riding fast through the east coast haar that was hinting to arise.

As Knox strained his eyes, he recognised the unmistakable figures of Lord James Stuart and young Argyle. He could not make out who the others were. He grunted lowly with the satisfaction that comes with the fulfillment of a prophetic gift. They had discovered the Queen Regent's treachery. He met the party, as the horses, breath steaming in the early morning air, pulled up with a flourish. John Knox did his utmost to ease their embarrassment with a friendly greeting. No one likes to be proved wrong, or of suspect allegiance.

"You are a welcome sight, my Lords. I perceive that God has opened your eyes to the Regent's true character, that her word cannot be trusted."

The diplomacy, grace, and charm of Lord James made it easy to accept the preacher's rebuke as he swung from the saddle, but young Argyle was clearly ashamed and subdued.

"Aye, minister, you were right. The Regent has broken every article of the Treaty. The French have entered Perth, fined many of the inhabitants, banished others, and French troops have taken over the garrison. Mary of Guise has ordered Romish worship alone to be permitted within the walls of the city. In accordance with our sacred promise, my Lord Argyle and I have abandoned the Regent's side and come in full support of the Lords of the Congregation, I think you know my Lord Ruthven." Lord James identified the third prominent figure in the group. "My Lord has also revised his convictions."

Ruthven shiftily avoided Knox's angry gaze and shuffled uneasily. This was the former Lord Provost of Perth, who shortly before had deserted his charge for the Regent's side in a hasty decision.

"Are you sure that you have chosen the right side and cause this time, Lord Ruthven?" Knox's voice rasped unmercifully to make the other squirm. "Take thought lest you have made another mistake."

"My conscience has brought home to me how mistaken I have been, and that the Lords of the Congregation have the true cause of Scotland at heart!" Lord Ruthven tried to put a brave face on it without losing too much of that face." I can only ask your forgiveness, Mr. Knox, and that of the Lords for my error."

"Our Lord's forgiveness is aye available on request, but men's forgiveness is another matter. Our Lord requires a constancy of heart and spirit, Lord Ruthven, like that of my faithful friend, Lord Erskine of Dun." The last was a sharp barb; for Knox knew well the hearts of men and that the most effective rebuke is when a man is unfavourably compared with another man. He now turned from the chastened Ruthven, as if dismissing him, and addressed Lord James, who of all Scots he respected, whose genuine humility made him seek no personal aggrandisement, a rare quality in that self-promoting age, Knox had to admit.

"I aye warned you agin' the Queen Regent, and that to promote a woman to dominion over any realm or nation is a thing not only repugnant to nature, but contrary to the revealed will of God. It is subversive to good order and to justice itself." Knox tried to steel himself against any personal animosity, and to keep his mind fixed on his belief about God's divine will and function for his creation. He did not find this easy, since he was personally drawn to women, he found.

"I well remember, brother John, but you must also be aware that in Holy Writ St. Peter commends that we honour the King, and, therefore, the Queen. St. Paul too says that we are to be subject to the authorities in power, for they are instituted by God. But let us not dispute," he changed his tack, and smiled affectionately, "when a united front is vital in all that our Saviour is doing in this land. We have come to you before joining the Lords of the Congregation at St. Andrews. Shall we expect you there within the week?"

Knox saw the wisdom of his words, as they had to remain united, and surely St. Andrews was the scene of his destiny and God's. His sojourn in Europe had taught him patience and insight. With renewed faith he waved them farewell from the steps of Anstruther's Kirk. His personal life was lonely, for Marjorie and his beloved sons, Nathaniel and Eleazer were still absent, back in Geneva. He remembered vividly how the children of his brother Antoine had been to John Calvin not a distraction but a distinct inspiration to the great Reformer by their happy laughter in the house in the *Rue des Chanoines*. The danger was too prevalent to have them with him yet, but his heart yearned for them, and he prayed for God's fatherly comfort. Underneath the man of iron was a man of flesh. He still experienced a deep frustration that through the perceived insult he had given to Queen Elizabeth of England they were not allowed to return through England. In vain he had written to Secretary Cecil to intercede.

As he wandered the shore near Anstruther and listened to the plaintive cries of the gulls, he besought the Lord to restore his family to him at this time of crisis, and to permit them to return through England, which was so much easier. Throgmorton, the new English ambassador in Paris, could just be the right person to mediate with the proud Elizabeth, for he had heard that Throgmorton was a man of compassion and political understanding of what was expedient.

It was certainly expedient that he be reconciled to the English Queen. He had to admit that, from being a fragile figure in the early years of her reign, Elizabeth had assumed the authority of the strongest of men, bravely surviving threats to her life, and supported by the most powerful intelligence network under Francis Walsingham, her Secretary of State, and William Cecil, Lord Burleigh, her chief adviser in domestic and foreign affairs, as clever a man as he had ever known. Beside Cecil, William Maitland of Lethington, the Scots Adviser to the throne, whom he recalled from his intermittent visits to his native land as a fence-sitting Protestant, too clever for his own good, held no comparison. If only through his correspondence with William Cecil, he felt that the Englishman was a cut far above Maitland.

In fact by his rather sly ingenuity and general cleverness William Maitland had come to be nicknamed 'Michael Wylie', or the 'Scots Machiavelli', by the Lords of the Congregation, but it was more of a jest. No, he must win Cecil over to the Protestant cause in Scotland, especially in the matter of sending soldiers and money. He determined to preach at Anstruther Kirk the following Saturday and in the pulpit of St. Andrews Holy Trinity Parish Church the following day. It was time to seize the day. As he said a silent farewell to the seabirds, he vowed to himself that the next time he saw them, the Reformation would be complete, and his beloved family would be around him.

"The Archbishop of St. Andrews has made a public threat against you, Master, that if you dare to preach there, you will be shot!" Back at his lodgings in Anstruther a breathless messenger had blurted out." His exact words were that a dozen bullets would hit you on the nose." If the situation had not been so serious, the words would have sounded ridiculous.

"Take a message back to that coward of an Archbishop, and tell him that it is a very different man from the timid tutor of times past, who will preach tomorrow in the pulpit of Holy Trinity Church, though all the powers of Hell oppose him!"

But when the day of decision came and he proudly rode up the breadth of Market Street of the Cathedral town, remembering as yesterday the momentous events of the Castle siege, his reluctant chaplaincy to the garrison, and the cold treachery of the French and Strozzi, he was met by some of the Lords of the Congregation. Erskine of Dun had his usual serene look, the Earl of Morton with his pragmatic gaze, but the Earl of Glencairn possessed an anxious look.

"We have consulted together, Master John, and we have decided that you ought to keep silent for now. You ought not to run the risk of endangering your own life, and of those who would shed the last drop of their blood in your defence'. Your enemies are deadly serious."

"I will not be moved, Glencairn, from boldly preaching in the place where God first called me to preach the Gospel. Would you have me be unfaithful to God, man? What ails ye? Where is the famous Cunningham courage, taken away from ye by pestilential priests? Ten years ago, faint and fever-ridden in the bowels of a French galley-ship, I vowed that I would preach again within the walls of St. Andrews Parish Kirk!" The Reformer's face was suffused with high colour, as a Godly anger rose in him, and even the bold temperament of William Cunningham drew back" As for the fear of mortal danger to myself from mortal men, let none of you be anxious. My life is in the hands of Him, whose glory I seek. I neither desire, nor need, the hand or weapon of any man to defend me. I only crave a hearing and, if it is denied me here, I must seek where I may have an audience!"

At this point, Knox had raised his voice to address the crowd massed in Market Street by now, and the people of St. Andrews cheered him to the echo. It warmed his heart that the common folk were for him, despite the Bishops' threats.

"There are occasions when it is a proof of superior wisdom to disregard the ordinary dictates of prudence, occasions when to face danger is to avoid it, and to flee from it is to incur danger." Knox continued with a deep conviction, as deep as his wisdom." If you, the Lords of the Congregation, and the chief support under God of the Protestant Reformation, suffer yourselves to be intimidated by the bravado attitude and threats of Archbishop Hamilton, our cause at the very outset will have received a blow, from which it will not be easy to recover."

"But our retinue is as yet still small. We still don't know the disposition of the town, despite the crowd before you. You ken how fickle crowds are. . Their Queen Regent lies a short distance away at Falkland Palace with her army, ready to come to the Archbishop's aid. It is not prudent just now." Glencairn was unusually cautious.

"Your fears have made you deaf, Sir William. What did I say about prudence?" John Knox silently rebuked the powerful nobleman with a steely look." Now, when Christ's providence has brought me to this place totally beyond all human expectation, I beg of you not to hinder me." The group of Lords was silent, and by it acquiesced.

The next day the atmosphere in St. Andrews was tense with anticipation that a high point in Scotland's history was about to be reached. Not only the ordinary inhabitants packed into the parish church, but the Provost and Baillies, forby the country folk, who poured in from the rural surroundings. There was no sign of the Archbishop's men, and, when John Knox gazed out over the sea of faces, gripping the rim of the high pulpit, he experienced nary a quiver of fear. In quietness and confidence shall be your strength, was the promise of the Lord. Do not fear the face of man, was His command.

"My Father's House shall be called a House of Prayer, but you have made it a den of thieves!" he thundered out the condemnatory words, and the bold timbre of his broad, Lothian, accent, now returning in full force after his years of Continental exile, came forth clear as a bell. Once a Scot, always a Scot. What was it that Heinrich Bullinger had said to him at Zurich? *Fier comme un Ecosse, Fiery as a Scotsman.*

"When our Saviour came across the money-changers and sellers of sheep, cattle, and doves in the Temple, He was enraged and filled with the fire of God. Our God is a consuming fire, and cannot abide the hypocrisy of men! The whip of cords He made was the scourge of the Lord, which lashes the consciences of men! Did our Saviour treat these profane traffickers in the things of this world with velvet gloves? No, our Lord ejected them from the Temple of Jerusalem! They had sold a wheen of sheep, kine, and cushie-doos for profit, things which the Auld Covenant required for sacrifices.

They had polluted God's holy, sacred, House, and made Mammon their God. Our Lord overturned their money tables, scattered their hardheid coins, and drove the owners, their sheep, and kine, headlong from the Temple. They had turned His Father's House into a market, and zeal for his House had consumed him. So has a wealth o' bawbees and power consumed the Church in our land under the Papacy! It is time to cleanse the Temple in our beloved Scotland. It is time to sound the trumpet across Scotland, for God is watching, and God is with us! No more indulgences, no more masses, no more selling of benefices, no more immorality amongst the clergy, no more stripling weans appointed as Archbishops, and no more idolatrous images of saints and

John Knox preaching at St Andrew's

apostles to be worshipped, but the pure and unadulterated worship of the true and living God in spirit and in truth!"

His words had risen to a crescendo of power, to be greeted at its climax by a resounding, rumbling, assent from the assembled concourse. As the fire had gathered in his eyes and his beard had visibly bristled, Knox's whole body seemed verily to launch itself almost from the pulpit, which looked frail compared to the human and divine power contained in it. His right arm projected far beyond its confines and beyond his Geneva gown, which flew in many directions, as if with a life of its own. It was even a deliberate ploy by Knox to mention the familiar Scots coin, the *hardheid*, with the lion head symbol, which like the Temple coin, was becoming debased in its metal.

"What does God require of Man, demands the prophet Amos, but to do justly, love mercy, and walk humbly with your God." His eyes flashed and some of the nobles gathered near the pulpit, and some of the mitre-clad Bishops, enclosed in a box slightly further away, who had dared to come, shied away from Knox's penetrating gaze. It was all too close to home, and the storm clouds were rising. There were to be no interruptions, and no threats certainly to the life of the man from Haddington.

For the following three days John Knox preached and with such eloquence and overpowering force that every single religious image and picture that could be found in St. Andrews was smashed. But the forces of the Queen Regent were not far off and her rage was incandescent, and even the hesitant Lieutenant of the King of France, D'Oysel, was confident that he could easily defeat the forces of the Protestants, which his scouts said had scattered, and so he had advanced from Falkland to Couper Moor, a mere six miles from St, Andrews. But no panic ensued in the ranks of the Lords. Knox did not attempt to interfere in the sphere of military matters, recognising that his remit lay within that of things of religion and the spirit. A lookout amazed to see the great numbers of the opposing forces, reported back in haste to D'Oysel. His advice was immediate to the terrified Mary of Guise.

"You must make a truce, Majesty, and offer a pardon to them; if the Lords of the Congregation will disband their men, and give their word that they will burn no more Abbeys, your Grace."

"Their word? What do these heretics know about sacred oaths?" She expostulated." Their promises are as flimsy as spiders' webs! Do you forget so easily what they did to Perth and its holy monasteries and statues?" Her own memory was that of the bigot, conveniently forgetting her own deliberate betrayal of her word regarding that town.

"Madam," D'Oysel had reverted to a more form of address to show his frustration," we have no option. They easily outnumber us. We must give our pledge to remove all Frenchmen from Fife. I am certain, they will be satisfied with nothing less."

"Very well, D'Oysel, bring back the soldiers to Falkland!" Her high-pitched tone was filled with nervousness "It will be warmer for them in town rather than out on these freezing Scottish moors." She glanced away out of a window towards the Royal Tennis Court of Falkland Palace. It was the pride and joy of the Stuarts, built for her deceased husband, King James V, twenty years before, and much longer than that before another Royal Tennis Court was to be set up in Hampton Court by the tyrannical but highly intelligent Henry VIII. It took her mind off her troubles to dwell on the beauty of this Palace, the Hunting Lodge and favourite home of the Stuarts for over two hundred years, and much the work of French artisans. She turned back to her French lieutenant, and put on another face.

"Send Commissioners to settle matters with these Lords of the Congregation." But again it was a deceitful ruse to gain time. She would retreat but only to regain Stirling, which had been lost to Protestant forces from the south, and thus to cut off those in Fife.

Lord Lindsay and the Laird of Waughton were the chosen representatives of the Lords, and they came to the French camp with full powers to negotiate, but from a position of strength, yet at the same time to show that their intentions were not of rebellion against Mary of Guise and only for freedom for their religious beliefs as Protestants.

"We have offended no man, nor seek the position of any man," Lord Lindsay addressed his opposite number." But if anyone threatens our lives, they will find fierce resistance! We have been sent to sue for concord and harmony, lest innocent blood is shed, for we have no quarrel with any man, nor seek their blood." Lindsay's words were conciliatory, but his demeanour was unflinching.

It was promised to the representatives that all Frenchmen would be withdrawn from Fife and that within two or three days Commissioners would be dispatched to St. Andrews to confer on a final agreement. Meanwhile, Lindsay and Waughton received a document, signed by James Hamilton, the Earl of Arran and Duke of Chatelherault and Monsieur D'Oysel, to the effect that an eight days respite would be granted, in which to settle affairs. But John Knox, who had accompanied the army out to Couper Moor, was suspicious and did not trust their word. He had now been unanimously appointed secretary and plenipotentiary of the Lords of the Congregation, some of whom had sheepishly admitted their inability to write clearly and well. Knox had groaned within at the ignorance and semi-literacy of many of the rough-cast nobility and one day had confessed privately to his servant, Patrick.

"Some of the peasantry of auld Scotland are better educated than her nobility, Patrick," he declared indignantly, but his man discreetly kept his own opinion. Wisely too Knox did not allow any of the Lords to hear these sentiments, but he longed fervently for the day when schooling was widespread across Scotland, with an Elementary School in every parish and a Grammar School in every Burgh. One day his vision from the Lord, though it tarry, would be fulfilled.

Meanwhile, John Knox's suspicions were proved well founded, for the days came and went with no sign of the Commissioners. They had been deceived again. Just then their actions were decided for them, when news came through that Mary of Guise intended to seize Stirling. The anger of the Lords was widespread, but none more than that of Knox.

"Shall we lose Stirling again, my Lords? Do you forget that great occasion there when the Lord encouraged us all from the pulpit that He alone would give victory to His children in the end? How downhearted you were then and how your drooping spirits were revived! Your faith in God was strengthened, and you turned your faces steadfastly to the future!" These tough, warlike, but Godly men cheered and shouted with fierce determination in response.

"We shall not only save Stirling, Master John, but we shall turn out the French garrison of Perth, seize the town, and then on to Edinburgh!"

Glencairn was hugely animated, even for him, and was supported to the echo. "Nothing shall stop us!"

That night John Knox knelt in prayer, as was his custom, but with a greater fervency that the Lord would grant victory to their arms. But he knew that the real battle was in the Heavenly realms, to be wrestled and won in prayer. Sure enough, like a tide the army of the Congregation swept back to Perth, and the 400 strong garrison of dejected French troops finally trudged wearily out of the fair city's gates, after they had not been relieved within the agreed twelve hours. The tide continued on to historic Scone, the scene of the past coronations of the Kings of Scotland. The helpless Prior Patrick Hepburn begged the avenging force in vain not to harm the ancient stones of Scone, only too aware that he had played a leading part in the horrific martyrdom of the eighty year old former priest, Walter Myln, in St. Andrews.

"I promise that I will vote with the Lords of the Congregation, sires, if you take pity and spare the ancient Abbey, Scotland's most sacred. I beg you in the name and love of Christ!" Prior Hepburn pleaded in the face of the implacable eyes of Haliburton, the fearless Provost of Dundee, and the zealous Glencairn. He saw no responding expression of mercy. To the Reformers this was the year of the favour of the Lord. This was the year of the vengeance of their God.

"We will have none of it, Prior! Where was your mercy at the burning of auld Walter Myln, eighty years of age? He was a living stone. If we have our way there will not be a remnant left of Romish superstition throughout Scotland! We will harm no one, but remove all false religion and gaudily painted images." Provost Haliburton vociferously addressed Prior Hepburn. He was barely able to restrain the zeal of the crowd pressing in behind now within the spacious grounds of the Abbey. The smell of incense and numerous images of Christ, the Virgin, and saints, brightly glistening, only served to further provoke their righteous ire against a Church, which had lived in luxury while its people lived in poverty, and whose departure from the purity of the Faith had been high-lighted by the true teaching of Knox, and Myln, Wishart, and Patrick Hamilton before him. The occasion was ripe for pulling down and plucking up.

"We must stop and ponder before we destroy what cannot be replaced, Provost Haliburton and my loyal Lords! We must consider first Prior Hepburn's vow to join our cause." It was the powerful voice of Knox, cutting sharply through the din of the violent mob. Molten anger can do great damage to any cause. Within Knox knew that if the Reformation was to have a chance of success, men like Prior Hepburn would be needed to build a solid foundation for the Reformed Kirk.

"Our zeal must be tempered by wisdom, Provost." The militant Dundee man glowered at him to begin with, but then accepted the rebuke submissively." We must recognise our enemies, and our friends as well. They who are not against us are for us." In a short while Provost Haliburton was won over to the new movement of God.

Since his return to Scotland it had been the deepest hope of John Knox to obtain help from England, In June, just a month after that momentous event, he persuaded his trusty friend, William Kirkcaldy of Grange, to write to Sir Henry Percy, Governor of Berwick, Duke of Alnwick, and Warden of the Marches, who in turn wrote to William Cecil, Lord Burleigh, Elizabeth's powerful Secretary.

"Don't forget that England has been our friend in time of need, ever since the days of our imprisonment, William." There was a brief silence between Knox and Grange, as their minds went back ten years to hear again the hated beat of the drum and the pull of the painful oar for one, and the other the inside of a monastic prison. Though they were back safe in Edinburgh by now, the French threat was still great, even if their troops were confined to the region of Dunbar on the east coast.

"Aye, Cecil has sent encouraging sounds, Master John, but," Grange hesitated, "he thinks that you have to make more humble overtures and apologies to the Queen of England for your rudeness, his word not mine, "He hastened to add." William Kirkcaldy had always been blunt, and their friendship could stand the test. Knox bridled, but the after effects of his blast against female government a year before still had to be regretted.

"I shall pen an apology to Her Majesty," he promised determinedly, though his secret anger threatened to boil over. His missive was sent off urgently by way of Percy, expressing his warmest attachment to Queen Elizabeth and his deep distress at having offended her. How often must he apologise to her? He declared that he had long desired a perpetual concord between England and Scotland. This was the best prospect for both realms. If the Queen would embrace it, this was the golden opportunity. In an act of bold faith he even begged for an interview with Her Majesty. He had not met her, but heard that the Virgin Queen was of a formidable mind. But he got no reply, and his frustration grew.

In the coming weeks confused and conflicting letters and rumours abounded. Code names were adopted with cryptic signs, and parchments held over flames in closed apartments, upon which writing suddenly appeared, penned in copperose solution. Lords Glencairn, Argyle, Ruthven, Boyd, and Ochiltree signed an address to the Queen with an accompanying letter to Cecil. Its words were terse.

"The wisest and best men in Scotland have longed for the union of the realms. Such a golden opportunity should not be cast away. We have fought against those beasts who have been friends to France and enemies to England.
We implore your Majesty to stand by us. We promise to accept any conditions, which your Majesty might reasonably require."

Knox was much displeased at the last clause, and was with much difficulty persuaded. He never knew the mind of Elizabeth, and was still frustrated at her ignoring of his last request for an interview. But he was mightily heartened that the Lords had emphasised their desire to advance the Gospel, put down the tyranny of the clergy, and defend the liberties of Scotland.

But a new possible chapter in the unfolding drama that was encircling Scotland was now opening up. The Scots leaders for a while had entertained the secret ambition that the Earl of Arran, son of the Duke of Hamilton and Chatelherault, was an ideal marriage partner for the young English Queen. At twenty four years old, he was only two years younger than Elizabeth, an earnest Protestant, and the next heir to the Scottish throne after the princess Mary. Who could be more suitable, they conjectured, taking no account of human taste. But, unfortunately for immediate plans, young Arran had been forcibly detained on his Chatelherault estates in France as security that his father remain loyal to the French Regent in Scotland. But news came one morning to change all this.

"The Earl of Arran has fled from France, hiding in the woods of Poitou, and from there he has escaped to Geneva!"

"God be praised!" breathed Knox." Brother Calvin will be a faithful friend and adviser to him, and keep him on the right road. He could not want a better teacher for a young man of royal blood." The preacher refrained from saying that the man of Geneva would discipline the young Scot from falling into the sins all too common to Princes in sex, gambling, and bad language.

"How to get him to London and bring him before the Queen of England is the difficulty!" broke in the Earl of Moray." The French, the Austrians, and the Spanish are all on the lookout to catch him. Cecil is the only man who has the political expertise to bring Arran to the English Court from Geneva! He has the shrewdness that knows the politics of the European intimately."

They would have been comforted by Cecil's response, when he cryptically sounded out his Queen in the most highly courtly language about her feelings, but rather presumptuously assumed her interest in the Scots nobleman. Without receiving any positive signs from the taciturn Elizabeth, after much thought he summoned the astute courtier, Henry Killigrew, a colourful, piratical figure, with much European experience.

"You are the ideal man, Killigrew, for my mission! I wish you to bring back this awkward Scotsman, Arran, from Geneva. It is a stronghold of the Protestant faith, so you should have no problems. It is just possible that he is the ideal husband for our Virgin Queen that we long for to secure our royal future, and just as important, unite Scotland, that tumultuous nation, with our nation." Cecil's normally self possessed look changed for a moment to an eager spirit." You are the fittest person to be entrusted with so difficult an enterprise. But be careful, for Arran is wanted by almost every Catholic Court in Europe. So you must not go by Antwerp, too dangerous, for they will be watching it, but by Embden in Friesland. The Protestant cause is strong there!" The plan was set in motion.

But Knox and the Scots Lords would not have been so overjoyed, if they had read the letter of Cecil to Sir Henry Percy, the Warden of the Marches on Scotland's borders.

"The Scots should be given promises, money, and men, in that order. At present I have no money to spare for our Scots allies, but give them no hint of that. But don't let the Scots be cast down in despair, for England will not allow their ruin. In whatever way you can, kindle their fire. For, if it is quenched, the opportunity will not arrive again in our lifetime. Whatever the Protestants mean to do should be done with all speed, for it will be too late when the French come." Cecil, if anything was a pragmatist, but not without deep human concern.

Balnaves, the Fifeshire lawyer, and his old friend, Knox was so glad to say, had joined them to assist them in the correspondence with England. Not only his tongue but his pen was that of a ready writer. His literary expertise made up for the lack of formal learning among the nobility. The hearts of Knox and Balnaves were close-knit.

"Percy has been replaced by Sir James Croft, I hear and this Croft is a slippery one, he accuses you of being double-faced, Master John," Balnaves guardedly informed Knox one day.

"They accuse me, these double minded hypocritical politicians!" John expostulated indignantly.

"Don't worry, brother John, the English are aware of our desperate needs."

The French had shocked the forces of the Reformation by a lightning march from Dunbar to seize the port of Leith, and threaten Edinburgh. Things had changed rapidly in the speeding drama that was engulfing Scotland. The Protestant leaders watched from the safety of Calton Hill." They will send men, but the only question is when," said the astute lawyer." Meanwhile, the important thing is for your Reverence to stay out of danger. Without you we are without a natural leader, with no spiritual head. You know the heart of the Regent, for the Papists have publicly offered a reward to anyone who should seize or kill you? Be sure that there are those, actuated by hatred and avarice, which would lie in wait for you in an unguarded moment. You are the soul of the Congregation! Again, I repeat, be careful!" Balnaves pleaded anxiously. Continual vigilance was the price of freedom.

Knox did admit that in his preaching travels throughout the Lowland's countryside, although most drank in his words thirstily, he saw also spite-filled eyes occasionally.

That summer matters did not improve among the Protestants. Word came that their hope for a Royal link with England, the young Earl of Arran, had secretly arrived at Greenwich and Cecil had gone to meet him. But their expectations of a love affair had been smashed, when Queen Elizabeth, who knew her own mind if ever any woman did, saw the not unpleasing Scotsman at Hampton Court, and rejected him at first sight. At home impatience had seized Knox at the continuing delay in English help and the seeming lethargy of the Lords of the Congregation that had allowed the French to occupy Leith. They now could only gaze down in helpless frustration from the height of the Canongate, as the French, like so many worker bees, fortified Leith and its harbour. John raged to John Willock, his colleague, who had been appointed pastor and minister of St. Giles, and together they prayed within against the paralysis that had seized their cause.

"I ken the fickleness of our people, of all people. They are like a weather cock, blown whatever way the wind directs! Cecil must be told that I will not answer for what the Scots people will do, if England continues to delay sending soldiers to support the Protestant cause! That subtle French woman has secretly infiltrated our ranks with her lies. Our numbers are decreasing daily. We are disunited and dispirited!"

"It is the time for strength and faith, for the initial success that often comes in such great movements has passed, and the hard challenges are before us. Some of our troops are on the point of mutiny for want of pay.

God's curse on that cowardly thief, Bothwell, for stealing the money sent from England! Edinburgh has not yet been totally won to the Reformation.

She is neither fish nor fowl, John. Our very own lives are in deadly danger of assassination." Willock and Knox, the brothers John, grasped one another in a close embrace of fellowship, and they prayed together fervently for their land.

John Knox ended it with a momentous prayer and plea.

"Give me Scotland, or I die!" God would hear that prayer.

But things got worse, and surreptitiously the Regent's forces, mostly French, slipped into Edinburgh by night. The city was then like one cut into two in a geographical and structural sense, the upper end of the Royal Mile reaching to the Castle, and the lower end, reaching from the Canongate to Holyrood Palace, so that control and watch over the Castle area was very lax and careless. Lord Erskine, an unfaithful relative of Erskine of Dun, who was of a different quality, had seized Edinburgh's powerful Castle for Mary of Guise without the slightest Protestant intervention or a shot being fired. Its few guards were quickly overpowered.

In addition, when Lord James Stuart and the young Earl of Arran, now secretly returned from France under a pseudonym, rode out with all speed to try to retrieve the £10,000 in English gold, stolen by the adventurer and robber, the Earl of Bothwell, in a surprise, sudden, attack on his Castle of Crichton, they found that the arrogant, unscrupulous, opportunist had escaped before them. They returned to discover that a daring attack by the French forces in Leith had captured the only two good guns the Protestants had in Edinburgh. Their position was becoming precarious. A grave Lord James came to see John Knox one day.

"We must abandon Edinburgh for the present, John, but only until we can gather our forces together once more. We have been too lethargic and lacking in wisdom."

"Abandon Edinburgh? No, no, Lord James! If we surrender Edinburgh, we are undone, and the whole cause may be lost!" Knox was half in anger and half in despair.

"Never, John! Where are your eyes? Edinburgh is neither one, nor the other, and has still to be wholly won over to the cause. This is the opportunity to secure the faith and win over other parts of Scotland, just as important as the capital and probably more faithful, like Dundee and the Mearns, which have been one of your mainstays till now, Stirling, the gateway to the north, Perth, where the Reformation was sparked off, loyal Ayrshire, and not to forget the Border towns of Kelso, Jedburgh, and Dumfries in Galloway. In the words of the Scripture you so dearly love to quote, is it not time to loosen the tent pegs and extend your ropes?"

The Earl of Moray was eloquence itself in his plea, and Knox was touched

"Forby, your life is likely to be sacrificed, if you remain in the capital. John Willock can take charge of the Tolbooth Kirk. St. Giles is too close to the Castle." He refrained from saying that Willock was more moderate, less fiery and likely to be controversial.

So it was that the Protestants retreated from Edinburgh rather dejected, but not without hope, though the jeers of the French soldiers in the Castle and even distant Leith stung their ears and their spirits, as they left. But Knox had no option except to acquiesce, and, as things turned out, the next two months were to be ones of glorious triumph, as he toured, preaching the good news of Christ's Kingdom round Scotland. Hope was to spring forth again.

ENGLAND TO THE RESCUE

I t was the last week in July when a small group of riders detached themselves from the main body of a few hundred, disconsolate looking, soldiers, encamped again on Calton Hill, overlooking Edinburgh. To the south they had a panoramic view of the Pentlands and Moorfoot Hills, to the east the Lammermuirs and the prominent lumps of North Berwick Law and the Bass Rock, that island Patmos, and to the north over the blue waters of the Firth of Forth the fertile Kingdom of Fife. The Castle on its crag a mile away stood as if it had been there for eternity. This was a city that had lived hand in hand with its history. But it was a matter of deep frustration to the particular member of the group who was venting his anger just then at the situation, in which the Reformers now found themselves, that the strategic citadel of Edinburgh was in the hands of their enemies.

"It is a great shame to me, gentlemen, ," said the normally sedate, Erskine of Dun in deep ire," that a relation of mine, Lord Erskine, as Governor of Edinburgh Castle, has declared for the Queen Regent, and is, therefore, commanding the streets of Edinburgh with his cannon. That Castle has aye been the despair of its enemies! We are caught between Lord Erskine's cannon and the deep waters of Leith, where the French fleet is expected any day! How stupid!" Even then he and the other Lords of the Congregation and Captains of the depleted Protestant forces turned their attention to the old port of Leith, where the distant figures of French soldiers could be seen building a siege wall.

"How short-sighted we have been," continued Dun, throwing his arms wide in the direction of the French," to allow D'Oysel and his handful of half-starved Frenchies, whom we had all but locked up in Dunbar for three weeks, completely at our mercy, to then escape from our clutches, even when we outnumbered them ten to one! Not only that but to capture Leith as well! How can we expect the English to come to our aid, when we do not even help ourselves, but simply fold our arms, and expect others to work for us?"

"I agree that we have had several reversals of fortune," intervened Lord James," but now is the time to negotiate a Treaty, and gain vital time, my Lord of Dun. The initiative we gained has been thrown away!" It was the turn of Lord James Stuart, normally even tempered, to express his irritation. Tempers were becoming brittle.

"A lack of energy and self reliance will let us down, my Lord," replied Dun dryly." The Regent has a devious spirit and has been trying her utmost to flatter, bribe, and threaten some of our Lords to win back their allegiances. She would spend the very crown of France rather than give up Scotland. ! We must be careful, James, for some of our fellow Scotsmen are fickle creatures." Erskine was observant of human nature, and like the God, whom he worshipped; he knew what was in man." How fares Master Knox?"

"The last I heard he was engaged in an arduous preaching journey. He never seems to rest, and tests his body to the utmost. He has covered the Border towns of Kelso, Jedburgh, gone on to Dumfries and Ayr, from where he has set Stirling, Perth, and Brechin alight once again. I understand Montrose and Dundee are eagerly awaiting the fiery Gospel words of our beloved pastor. I pray he is safe, my Lord Erskine." Lord James's eyes were moist, as he dwelt on the disaster to the Reformed cause, should something happen to Knox. The French had put a price on his head, and traitors abounded, when the hearts of men were deceitful and susceptible to greed. Attempts had already been made to assassinate him, and he could not forget the struggle he had in persuading John Knox to leave Edinburgh with them. The danger to him had been too great, but Knox had been obstinate.

"It would be easier to move Edinburgh Castle Rock than change Master Knox's mind, once he is set on a course of action." They both laughed." All classes are affected by his sermons. The careless are aroused and the faithful are strengthened." Suddenly Lord James's mood changed, and he wrapped his cloak around himself, as the cold winds blew over Calton Hill. Turning to the Earl of Glencairn, he enquired anxiously. "What is the news of the Earl of Arran?" They all knew that the exiled Earl, once the most powerful man in Scotland, had returned to England from France at the end of July. The news had spread like wildfire, raising some hopes, crushing others. Would he be the ideal husband at last for the English Queen?

But it was not to be, for when Elizabeth met the Scots noble first at Cecil's house, for she wanted to keep it undercover and then at Hampton Court, Arran came nowhere near her desire in a man. For about a month the Earl of Arran, now in the Protestant camp, had been kept hidden in London, then Elizabeth had decided that it was too dangerous, with Noailles, the French ambassador, always sniping at her ear and ever alert for signs that she was helping these pestilential Scots and giving harbour to this powerful man. So he was secretly sent north under a feigned name.

"Sadler and Sir James Crofts have informed me that *Monsieur de Beaufort* has just come over the Border." Glencairn's broad Ayrshire accent put a cutting edge to the assumed French name, and showed his dislike and distrust of any Scot, who had changed sides." He is being entertained in a safe house. He will be kept secure there until a time is ripe to bring him back, and God will show us when that is."

"I doubt if *Monsieur de Beaufort's* coming will have any influence on the situation. Things are at a low ebb, but the tide will turn again. I have an assurance." Lord James Stuart's faith in a sovereign God, who controlled all things after His perfect will, was very deep." But these French locusts down there are a plague we can do without. The ones at Leith are bad enough, but the arrogance of those who inhabit the Castle and upper reaches of the city is unbearable! They strut up and down our High Street and mock us openly, imitating our landed titles! I swear we will be avenged on these French lice, foreigners in our land, and they will be driven out of Scotland very soon, b'God!" He swung savagely at his mount's bit, and the whole company followed him, as they cantered down Calton Hill; and away from Edinburgh in the direction of Stirling. There they had made their headquarters since the French threat to the capital. Lord James was determined that, as soon as John Knox returned from his preaching tour, exhausted or not, he should be sent to Berwick immediately to negotiate with Sir Henry Percy of Alnwick for English soldiers and money to be sent. They were in desperate need.

Meanwhile, in the famous Cathedral of St. Giles, a disgraceful scene was being enacted, which was an affront to the Protestant people. During a service a number of Captains of the French forces marched in disdainfully with soldiers and began to kick at the creepy stools to send them flying. At the same time they swore and abused the

158

preacher, John Willock, who fortunately was a man of great self control and wise in how he handled opposition. But he was severely tested, as the soldiery with ribald jokes pointed at his Geneva gown.

"Where are your vestments, priest? You are but a false heretic, appointed by a bastard Church, whom the Holy Father in Rome has condemned to Hell! Where are the articles of the Holy Mass? You have conjured up your God out of your own barbaric Scottish imaginations, inspired by the Devil!" With their French tongue they attempted to imitate the Scots accent of the Scots, which only increased the anger of the Scots, who had come to worship and be inspired by Pastor Willock. Blows were nearly struck in the Kirk of St. Giles. Barely did John Willock come between the soldiers and the Congregation.

"We wrestle not against flesh and blood, my people, but against spiritual wickedness in high places! Don't let yourselves be aroused and give way to anger. These ignorant men know no better!" John Willock pleaded for calm in the uproar of sound, which seemed to scrape across the Cathedral's hallowed atmosphere like a knife across metal. An alien spirit had invaded the precincts of God." Blessed are you when men persecute you and say all manner of evil against you. These men will get their reward, perhaps sooner than they expect." Willock uttered the last sentiment with powerful presentiment that sent the French soldiery hurrying out of the Cathedral, still cursing, and mocking, but with a slightly chastened look.

Had he but been aware of these scenes, John Knox would have been incensed, maybe beyond control, for he was of a different calibre to his fellow minister, though both God's men. But it was a triumphant Knox, on the crest of a wave of spiritual power and success, who came in reply to the request of Lord James. In a chamber of Stirling Castle he was freshly enthused from his expensive tour. Despite the military setbacks, God had singularly blessed his sermons. The nobility, merchants, and the common people had heard him gladly. As the Earl of Morton had once advocated to him, John Knox had set fire to their tails. The Earl of Moray now grasped him warmly by the shoulders. After a full exchange of news on the different fronts the real purpose of Lord James came to the fore.

"It is imperative we have English help. There is no option, Reverence, and you are surely our Ambassador to Sir Henry Percy at Berwick? You alone know England well and how its people think!" Knox did not respond to the request, but they talked and prayed long into the evening, until it was decided, what was a fateful step.

Shortly after Robert Hamilton and Knox, ministers of the incipient Reformation, strode firmly down to the harbour of Pittenweem with purpose in every step. Theirs was a mission of vital importance, and on it could be dependant the whole Protestant Reformation.

"Our rebellion is on the side of the angels, brother Hamilton, and we must not forget that!" he reassured his colleague, as they passed down by the Mercat Cross, symbolic that the Royal Burgh of Pittenweem possessed the right to hold markets in perpetuity, and then past the attractive white new cottages, known as the Gyles. Pittenweem, the centre of the fishing industry in the East Neuk of Fife, was expanding slowly but surely." There is an old saying, Robert. God save us from our friends, and we'll manage our enemies ourselves well enough. We must find out now just who our true friends are."

"Aye, the English by all this secrecy show that they are not committed yet to our Reformation! Berwick is maybe on the English side of the Border for now, but on what side are the English?" Master Hamilton was irritated, but Knox, deeper in faith, soothed his spirit. The narrow wynds of the fishing village converged onto the harbour, often a mass of vitality, sound, and salty smells, and soon they were bucking south down the Lothian coast. Gazing towards that coast, they saw St. Fillan's cave, the home of the seventh century Celtic saint, who had given the town its title.

The two preachers did not voice their thoughts, their hostility to the idea of making the cave into a shrine to the saint by the Augustinian monks of the Priory of Pittenweem, but they had real admiration for the brave Celtic saint, Fillan, in his heroic work for the eternal Gospel in a dangerous, pagan, land. But such indwelling thoughts were soon swept away as the vessel was rocked and buffeted by the ever-present east coast breezes, and they were blown by Coldingham and its Priory and, then past the fishing town of Eyemouth. Knox was now a man hardened somewhat to the rigours of the sea after numerous Channel crossings and, not least, his nineteen months in the French galley. Robert Hamilton, however, did not have a stomache impervious to the wild tossings of their boat like a cork in a storm, and he suffered accordingly.

While Hamilton groaned below, Knox faced unflinchingly into the wind and prayed for him, but more urgently for their reception by Sir Henry Percy, Governor of Berwick, and Earl of Alnwick, who was an unknown quantity to him.

When none too soon the ship alighted at the harbour of Holy Island or Lindisfarne, as it was called, a messenger from the English Government greeted them guardedly and asked for proof of their identity. This cloak of secrecy which entailed them landing at this little known anchorage, had already annoyed Knox, but this was too much.

"I am well enough known in Berwick, my man, when I turned its Godless garrison towards the salvation of Christ!" Knox snapped back, but, nevertheless, showed the man the document of credit from the Lords of the Congregation. The messenger stammered, discomforted by Knox's glare and equally by that of Master Robert Hamilton.

"I-I-I am sorry, Reverence. Also, I have to say that my Lord, Sir Henry Percy, is absent from the north, and that Sir James Croft, the Captain of Berwick and Warden of the Eastern Marches of England will receive you. I am sure that is acceptable." He assumed a pose now of a slight pomposity towards the Scots." But we must hasten at once across the causeway, while the tide is out."

"Well, let us go, man!" Knox brooked no assumed command from an English lackey.

Cloaks flying in the wind, the party rode hard over the two miles of the watery causeway, hooves sinking in the sand and gravelly stones. The ship's captain had timed his arrival well. Knox glanced up at the small, fortress, castle, perched precariously on a rock on the seaward side of Holy Isle. It was clearly garrisoned, with armed guards looking down menacingly from the ramparts, but his inner thoughts were chiefly occupied with the historic associations of Holy Isle, where the Church of St. Cuthbert and Aidan had given it a special holiness.

He cast his memory back ten years to when during his Berwick ministry he had visited the sacred site and heard again the epic story of how Aidan had established a Church and monastic community there to convert the pagans of Northumberland in 635. He recalled that a beautiful, wonderfully-illustrated, manuscript, called the Lindisfarne Gospels, had been written for Eadfrith, Bishop of Lindisfarne, at the beginning of the eighth century, a magnificent fusion of Irish, Roman, and Byzantine artistic elements in the Hiberno-Saxon style. Secretly he longed to have seen it. They passed the tiny village of Lindisfarne in the fertile south west of the islet, and crossed the causeway to the mainland.

The threat of Danish raids had caused the monastery to be abandoned, and the monks had fled inland with the body of St. Cuthbert to be buried in the famous Cathedral city of Durham. But the monastery had been restored on Holy Island two hundred years later, when the threat was ended. Knox longed for the purity and missionary zeal of the ancient Celtic Church. Yet he scorned the legend that St. Cuthbert's body remained in a perfect state of preservation in his tomb in the mighty Durham Cathedral. This was false superstition, and his broad features screwed up in a spiritual antagonism, as the riders turned into the north-east wind and towards Berwick. It was bracing, even in the summer months. He shivered, but it was not with cold. He was no longer in the first flush of youth, but he was now fifty four years of age, and his body creaked a little. The Lord would doubtless, in the fullness of time, raise his physical frame again, renewed and transformed, soon enough at the Resurrection. He looked forward eagerly to seeing the walled town of Berwick once more, and recalled his love for this broad land of England. England had been good for Knox, and good to him. He had once written words from deep in his heart, before he had fled to Dieppe from bloody Mary's cruel hands.

'Sometimes I have thought it impossible to remove my affection from the realm of Scotland, and that any nation or realm could have been equally dear to me. But I take God to witness that in my conscience the troubles in England's realm are twice as painful to my heart as the troubles of Scotland.' Could such a thing be possible, he had wondered.

He wondered, however, if he could now say that. After all, it was because of the overwhelming threat of being crushed by the French force, thus meaning that the fledgeling Scottish Reformation would die at its birth, that he was now in England. They had given promises, but no money or men. As if that was not enough to deeply anger him, the English authorities had insisted that Knox come to them under a cloak of secrecy, hence the condition that he and Hamilton land on the unobtrusive Holy Island, rather than the populous Berwick, where he was known. He had fired off letter after letter to Lord Burleigh, Elizabeth's ingenious Secretary of State almost begging for assistance. Once more anxiety gnawed at his vitals, as he dwelt on Lord Cecil's reply, which quoted the Queen's very words. *She would look before she leaped.* Why did she hold back and preserve a cowardly caution? Now was the perfect time to seize the God-given opportunity to interview with a powerful army on behalf of the beleaguered Protestants of Scotland? He had apologised enough to that Queen for the rude words in his book.

They had passed the ramparts of the mighty Bamburgh Castle and the village of Belford. It seemed ironical that he was heading back towards Scotland by land. Soon the familiar outline of his beloved Berwick hove in sight, and, as they passed beneath the arch of the South Gate, a local was seen to open his mouth as wide as a North Sea haddock, as he gaped at one of the strangers. Sir James Croft welcomed them at the Castlegate with a disarming gentleness.

"I apologise for the absence of Sir Henry Percy, who has been called to London by Her Majesty. But I keep in touch with Scottish affairs through my Lord Burleigh and Sir Ralph Sadler, our Ambassador in Edinburgh."

When they were safely esconced in his study, Croft assumed a serious, but no less friendly, manner.

"You have no further to go after our subterfuge. Yet I would advise that neither of you Scots should be seen in public in the streets of Berwick, for the Queen Regent has her spies, even in England, and lest you two preachers should be absent for too long from being advisers to your Lords of the Congregation. They are zealous patriots, of that I have no doubt, my Lords Glencairn, Argyle, Ruthven, Boyd, Ochiltree, and of course, Lord James Stuart, but they really need your wisdom badly. They have written to the Queen that for a while now the wisest and best men in Scotland have desired the union of our two realms and that this golden opportunity should not be lost of accomplishing it. For the sake of all they hold dear in this life and the next, they have implored our Queen to stand by them, and promised not to deny any conditions she might require in return." Croft glanced archly at them, seeking their reaction." I also understand that my Lord Cecil has received another letter at the same time?" He looked quizzically at Knox, as if not wishing to monopolise the dialogue in this cat and mouse game.

"Aye!" Knox took up his challenge." It stated our desire to advance the Gospel, put down the tyranny of the clergy, and defend the liberties of Scotland! And I maun add that we would never cease to pray for the junction of our realms under the Protestant faith!" Knox reserved to himself the provision that he did not include a common monarch." But we need troops and bawbees desperately, Sir James Croft! In the name of God we need them now!" Knox's voice rose in an aggressive appeal, but the Englishman remained the essence of calm.

"Neither can be promised, I am afraid, Master Knox, until you appoint someone of real authority to command you." Knox and Hamilton looked in puzzled anxiety at one another.

"Who?" asked Hamilton. "We have many distinguished men of real authority, some of whom you have mentioned already."

"Lord James Stuart. What better man, of an honesty, piety, and patriotic fervour, could you want?" interjected Knox.

"No! I have to say that none mentioned, including Lord James, are sufficient for Her Majesty's requirements. But a man like the Duke of Chatelherault, Lord James Hamilton, would be ideal." Croft watched their expressions like a hawk.

"A Hamilton!" Knox spat out the name in exasperated disgust." Can they be trusted to advance anything other than Hamilton power?" He refused to erase from his memory the fact that Chatelherault had been with the enemy, when they besieged St. Andrews Castle. He must have known of the treachery of Strozzi and the French, which led to the galleys. It was not enough that Arran had since declared himself a Protestant.

"How can Elizabeth trust men without a leader?"

"Then elect one!" replied Knox peremptorily, and, mentally accepting the grave situation for the sake of the greater good, he added a sting in the tail." We will elect any man Her Majesty thinks fit." He breathed deeply, throwing in his final card in a bid for English aid." But if the Protestants of Scotland cannot have support at once, we will not trifle. We will seek the next best remedy to preserve our safety, not that we will go over to the French side, but we will give up the struggle and leave Scotland to the enemy. Then England can take the consequences of what will ensue for themselves!" The idea that England should have a neighbour north of the Border controlled by France appalled Croft. Knox knew that Scottish heads and hearts, no matter how dedicated to their native country, were not equal to the task against the superior French. Croft knew it too, and sighed sympathetically.

"Let us hope and pray, Master Knox, that it does not come to that. I believe your wife and two sons are still in Geneva. You must miss them very much. We shall assist them to return through France to Scotland. Our envoy in Paris, Sir Nicholas Throckmorton, thinks highly of you, Master Knox, and has commended your zeal, faith, and integrity!" He barely avoided saying usefulness to England, which would have given the two Scots real umbrage." Be assured he has intervened with Her Majesty on your behalf. Your reputation, my dear Scotsman, goes before you on the Continent of Europe."

Knox said nothing, only too aware of the false side of flattery, but content to think of the happiness he had felt in his beloved Geneva with his dearest Marjorie and the boys, the lively lads the Lord had given them, Nathanael and Eleazar. What greater names could he have assigned to his rapscallion laddies, little sinners though they were? His heart ached for their presence. He could not be a leader and a Barnabas, encouraging others, without encouragement to himself. Within the man of iron was a man of flesh.

"Now, gentlemen, take your needed rest and repast, and remain here, for I am waiting for Alexander Whitelaw, who is returning with Lord Cecil's answer to the Scots Lords."

Two days before Knox had departed from Pittenweem, Alexander Whitelaw, a man with a deep faith in the God of the Protestant Reformation, a great admiration for John Knox, and a genuine affection for the English, had travelled down to London with two letters from the Scots preacher to the Secretary of State and to the Queen's Majesty herself. Knox himself trusted Whitelaw implicity, and knew that Whitelaw had been recommended by Sir Nicholas Throckmorton to Cecil from Paris even.

"But I beseech you once more, gentlemen, to remain secretly here in Berwick Castle! It should be about two days." Knox swallowed his pride and bit back a sharp retort, for he liked Croft.

So it proved, that in two days Whitelaw returned in a spirit of real excitement. There was a personal missive for Knox, who opened it eagerly. It was from William Cecil, written from Oxford. But it left him morose and unsatisfied, even if the English politician admitted more or less in the letter that his answer was obscure in its meaning, but assured him that it would soon become plain. He wished John Knox God's prudence, and made a veiled allusion to Knox's view on the unfitness of women to rule. Knox could not abide all this cryptic language. He looked up and grunted non-committedly to Hamilton, but said nothing in reply to the other's enquiring look. Whitelaw retained the other letter significantly.

However, Knox noticed that his faithful friend appeared anything but well, and that it could well be a fever. His insight was proven right, for on the voyage back to Edinburgh a bout of shivering overtook Alexander Whitelaw, and he was left to convalesce there, while Knox and Hamilton rode on eagerly to Stirling, where the Lords of the Congregation had set up their headquarters, since the French at the time in Dunbar had been too dangerously close to Edinburgh. His friends awaited his arrival nervously, and Knox too waited in impatient suspense while Glencairn opened the letter from England. The Lord of Finlayston snorted in anger.

"That master contriver, Cecil, is so vague! He assures us of nothing! I fear there's no comfort in England!" He threw his arms up in desperation.

"I despair of the English! Let us make no more requests of them!" shouted Lord Ochiltree. In a trice Knox had leapt to his feet to urgently intervene.

"We must not give up hope, my Lords! That is the way of the devil, the Valley of Achor, the Valley of trouble! We must exchange the valley of trouble for a door of hope. The English Council has resolved to support us Protestants in Scotland, I tell you, against the Queen Regent, but only in secret for now, as they cannot infringe the Treaty of peace with France." Knox pleaded. After much grumbling, finally Glencairn and the others acquiesced with Knox.

"Och, Master John, you may have the license and liberty to write back to the English Council, as you think best!"

John Knox travelled to St. Andrews, his favourite residence, and there he composed his reply to Cecil, as he gazed out over the North Sea breakers, whose frothing power helped to inspire him as he sought God in prayer for the appropriate words. He knew that the Lord of Hosts was certainly with him. The battle was not his, but the Lord's, yet it still had to be fought with the Lord's weapons. Cecil appreciated plain language from others, despite his own equivocation.

'I was prevented from coming to meet you personally for a number of reasons. I had no clear indication of what your mind was. When Sir Henry Percy first requested to speak with me, the French were furiously pursuing us, which dispersed our forces. So I daren't leave Scotland exposed. Through Master Whitelaw, Kirkcaldy of Grange, and Sir James Croft, I know of your great goodwill towards us, but with all our heart we desire your favour with the Council. Unless money is supplied without delay, the money to pay our five hundred soldiers for past services, and to gather another thousand foot soldiers and three hundred horsemen, every man will be compelled to seek their own safety. I can assure you, as flesh is of flesh, some Scots will face the hardest of lives before they will compromise with the Queen and her French.

It may appear dangerous for you to support us and break a promise to the

French, but I hope that you may consider that our destruction in Scotland will really be your greatest loss, and, when France are our complete masters, which God forbid, they will be poor friends to you. I have heard that Seigneur de Bethencourt has been braying, after delivering threatening letters to Lord James Stuart that the King of France and his Council would spend all the Crown of France to obtain our complete obedience. They still try to corrupt some of our great men with money, unsuccessfully I must say, but some of our side are so poor and cannot serve the Reformation without support. If England stands by as a neutral, you know what will happen. Some of our Council have already departed, disappointed in our hopes. You know how dangerous it is to let time drift in this manner. I commit you to the protection of the Omnipotent,

Yours to command in Godliness,

J. Knox.

From deep despondency then it was with the greatest joy that in a short time word arrived that, if men of trust were sent to Berwick, they would receive a great amount of money for the cause and later more than sufficient men and gold for their needs. The sun now shone on their prospects. Henry Balnaves, the faithful lawyer, who had suffered much for the faith, was a wise choice, and on his return in triumph it was found there was enough gelt for their immediate needs.

"This will last until the end of next year!" exclaimed Balnaves excitedly, as the golden bawbees poured out of his saddlebags." Sir James Croft has requested that we send another deputation shortly for more English guineas. Praise to God, the Lord is our Supplier! But I would recommend that a strong extra guard be appointed for its wild country round the Border lands, where they have been reiving for generations! I made it safely but my guard kept close as we crept over the Tweeddale and Lammermuir Hills. The glint of helmets gave away enemies, but they weren't strong enough perhaps?" He laughed nervously.

Sir John Cockburn of Ormiston, the father of the laddie John Knox had once tutored with the greatest love and earnestness, and now grown to a fine young man of twenty five, was sent off to collect the second gift. Unhappy news was to come back with him, when a weary and dispirited Cockburn rode in with his troop. He slumped from the saddle, blood congealed on his forehead. His face told it all, as the Lords and their attendants crowded round their messenger in the esplanade of Stirling Castle.

"It was that renegade, Bothwell, who ambushed us not far from his bandit fortress of Hermitage in Liddesdale. There are deep folds in the hills there, which can hide an army. There was three thousand pounds in English gold in our pouches, if there was a bawbee!" In total chagrin Ormiston complained bitterly of his fortune." He is a knave and a cutthroat, James Hepburn, and has learnt it from an early age! They came out of the woods suddenly without warning and we were outnumbered. He was no doubt in the employ of the Queen Regent, though I doubt if she will see anything like that amount of money! Bothwell is too canny for that, and not just an unscrupulous adventurer, but an educated rogue.

The Bothwells suffer from a continual penniless poverty that makes them try to marry into wealth. Remember how his peacock of a father, Patrick Hepburn, courted

Mary of Guise in a vain competition for her hand? Like father, like son, James Hepburn is a vain, ambitious, creature, who will one day come to a bad end. His attack, as I have told you, came too unexpectedly for my guard, and I have lost some valuable, loyal, companions to his vicious rabble!" Cockburn stared earnestly at them, as to confirm that he was telling the truth, as if any would doubt his story.

None did, and he was taken away to have his wounds attended to, and for a moment silence reigned amongst the Confederate Lords. Was this a fatal wound to their hopes? In the continuing state of tension that prevailed in the land, it was decided that the Earl of Glencairn, Lord Boyd, Lord Ochiltree, and their supporters should continue to be based in Fife. They arranged to keep in touch regularly with the others, particularly regarding the movements of the French troops.

The French forces, which had been half starved, while hemmed in at Dunbar, had now broken out, and, reinforced by fresh soldiers under the new commander, Count de Martiques, had marched on Edinburgh, which had been left relatively unguarded and exposed. The new Commander was not of the same high quality as D'Oysel, who was a man of wise moderation. The Count de Martiques was of an irascible character, like Mary of Guise, and, when news filtered through that powerful English forces were massing on the Border, it brought out the cruel streak in the French nobleman. The whole countryside of Lothian was ravaged on his orders. The soldiery destroyed everything that they couldn't use, while the cowed population looked on. All available food was carried off to Leith, Edinburgh's ancient Port, where the French had made their headquarters, sheep, oxen, cattle, and even the nags of poverty-stricken labourers.

Anything that might fall into English hands was burnt. But to safeguard their interests, in case the whole countryside turned against them, Count de Martiques issued orders that neither gentlemens' houses, nor any part of Edinburgh itself were to be burned, as they retreated to Leith. However, a foray was made west to the area around Glasgow, and the cruelty of the French made a scar that was not to be forgotten for a long time.

By now Glencairn and his friends had wisely taken refuge in their strongholds of Ayrshire to wait. All this time too John Knox lay at St. Andrews, like a prophet in his prayer cell, beseeching God to intervene in a mighty way. The tide must be turned. Surely this was the year of the favour of the Lord, and He would bless their work? As he walked on the sands with his servant, Patrick, he turned in one of his sudden frenzies of violent emotion that his loyal servant had come to expect.

"Thanks be to the Lord, Patrick, that Fife has seen these bloody worms driven out!" Those of a gentle and more passive disposition would not have an idea of how deep a contempt the preacher now felt for the French." We must persuade those who are still deceived in our land that the French connection has brought us nothing but sugared poison! Our whole future lies in friendship with England! France is but the fleshpots of Egypt!"

Had he but known it, he would have been encouraged by the scene taking place at the English Court, where Maitland of Lethington, the Secretary of the Lords, was present, when Lord Burleigh gave an ultimatum to the great Queen.

"Your Majesty, I cannot emphasise more seriously the situation. The Emperor

Charles V is aiming at the sovereignty of Europe, which he cannot obtain without the suppression of the Reformed religion "The headstrong Elizabeth's eyes flared, as her patriotic pride was roused." My Queen, we must see the Protestant Reformation running on the same lines in both England and Scotland. Secretary Maitland of Lethington here has come to plead the cause of the Revolution under Knox. Lethington has told me that, while others snip at the branches of Popery, Master Knox cuts away its roots to destroy the whole!" In fact Burleigh was dissembling, as he knew that the subtle politician, William Maitland, though a Protestant in name, had no particular love for Knox, and that the last words he had quoted were from another source than himself. But Lethington, ever the diplomatist, gave out no indication of his annoyance, and remained silent.

"Has not money been sent already to stem the French advance?" The Queen enquired irritably. She did not like to be forced before she was prepared.

"Bullion to pay for 1,500 arquebusiers and 300 horsemen has been passed to the Scots through Sir James Croft, but now is the moment to send troops by land and sea in their thousands."

"Perhaps it is just a distraction to leave our southern shores exposed?" She lifted a suspicious eyebrow.

"Never, Majesty!"

"And what of that man Knox and his audacity in attacking our female prerogative? Are we to forgive and forget that?"

"But, Madam, he has given note on that account of his sorrow times without number, and it is well known that Master Knox's integrity and influence is vital with the Lords of the Congregation. In fact his life is constantly threatened by assassination." Burleigh held her eyes in his, and the deep-set orbs of the English master of intelligence refused to look away.

"He is the soul of the Congregation. He preaches by day and writes letters by night. By his presence, his public discourses, and private advice he animates the whole body and defeats all schemes to corrupt and disunite the Lords of the Congregation and the people. Your Majesty is well aware of how easily one can be deceived by those enemies, whom one thinks our friends, and death can be but a stab of the poiniard or a poisoned chalice away." Again he held the Queen's gaze. Elizabeth, who had risen from the position of a helpless girl at the mercy of ruthless courtiers and Lords to be her own Royal Mistress and mother of the nation, was only too frighteningly familiar with the political intrigue that surrounded her throne and of the undercurrent of threat to her life and position, not least from Jesuit plots. William Cecil could see that his words had found a target with unerring accuracy, and that the sympathy of the Queen was at last engaged, and her assistance won. Knox was no longer the dark moth and dreadful figure she had imagined, and his cause must be helped.

Back in Scotland a scene of great drama and seething with excitement was being convoked in Edinburgh in the last week of that month of October. A nationwide assembly of nobles, lairds, barons, and Burgh representatives had been summoned together for the first time without the Regent's assent. John Knox and John Willock, a man whom Knox had much in common with, were both present. Willock, who had shared the hard experience of exile with the other in the Dutch port of Embden in Freisland, was the perfect foil for John Knox. He had been a Franciscan monk, but when his heart was touched by the fire of the Reformation, Willock had fled for his life to England.

There his outstanding learning and courage had impressed the English leaders, he had become the chaplain to the Duke of Suffolk, and been given the living of the ministry of Loughborough in Leicestershire by the Duke. John Willock had the unique distinction of being a clergyman of the Church of England and a minister of the Presbyterian Church of Scotland, and, as they walked together up to St. Giles Cathedral, Knox was aware strongly how important Willock was to him, how versatile and talented he was, that he even became a physician in Embden. As John Willock was a native of Ayrshire, it had been right to appoint him as Superintendant of the West in the new Protestant Kirk still being precariously formed. He laughed slightly, as he cast his arm around the other's shoulders.

"Aye, be sure and remember, Master Willock, that you are in a Presbyterian Kirk, when you ascend this pulpit! Not all of us have taken the clerical coinage of both the Episcopal and Presbyterian Kirks, so take care you are not confused!"

"Dinna be feart, John! A double-minded man is unstable in all his ways." Willock returned banter for banter in good measure.

"You ken that you have been chosen for the St. Giles ministry because you are considered more affable and prudent than me by the Lords, and less likely to be assassinated! You are less fiery, they say, but just as pious and learned." It rankled with Knox slightly, even as he joked, but he accepted it with a patience and equanimity that was often tested." Such are the ways of men," he sighed.

"Naw, naw, Master John!" responded Willock in his broad Ayrshire accent.

"Ye ken surely that your life is more precious than any position of precedence?"

They had arrived at the great Kirk, and it was easy to tell that the spirit of patriotic fervour and religious zeal had taken over the representatives. The atmosphere was like a boiling cauldron, wonderfully useful at a feast, but deadly dangerous when tipped over. The whole authority of rulers and Regents was being brought into question.

Gathered as they were, more than three thousand crammed into St. Giles Kirk, it was not unsuitable that the two Protestant clergymen's opinions should be sought. Both the veteran preachers stood firm and resolutely before their fierce audience.

"What think ye, preacher Willock, have we, the representatives of the people, the right to deprive the Regent of power?" A rugged Scots voice shouted out powerfully from amongst the throng below.

"In my judgement, founded upon reason and Scripture, the power of rulers is limited." Willock, the calmer man temperamentally, answered in measured words and tone." Rulers might be deprived of their authority on valid grounds. By her fortification of Leith and her introduction of foreign troops, the Queen Regent has shown a fixed determination to oppress our Kingdom, and so can be justly deposed from her position by the nobles and barons of this realm of Scotland, not least since she has continually rejected their petitions for reform of the Kirk." His last words were almost drowned in the thunderous acclaim by the congregation. When it had died down, Knox was asked what his opinion was. He slowly ascended the pulpit stairs to stand beside Willock.

"I assent fully to the opinion of my fellow minister and brother in Christ, and the Assembly in my judgement can act on that opinion with a safe conscience on three conditions." The congregation was suddenly silent, and, as Knox paused, they almost suspended their breath. Though his once coal-black hair had now become flecked with grey, John Knox was still an impressive figure, and his aura of power held his hearers spellbound.

"You must not allow the misconduct of the Queen Mother to alienate your affections from the allegiance due to your rightful Sovereigns, Francis and Mary." There was a low gasp. For all his devotion to the Lord his God as the supreme sovereign of his life, Knox was yet a deeply loyal Scots citizen. It amazed some present in the Assembly. Surely this was a man of huge contradictions?" Secondly, be sure that you are not motivated by a private hatred and envy of the Queen Dowager, but only by looking to the safety of the Commonwealth, and, thirdly, any decision that you come to must allow our Regent to be re-admitted to office, if she is sorrowful for her conduct and submits to the advice of her counsellors of this realm." When he ended, the applause was even more thunderous.

CHAPTER FOURTEEN

A TOUGH TRIUMPH

I t was January, 1560, a vital year in the social and religious revolution that was sweeping this tough land of Scotland. Out in the Firth of Forth eight vessels lay at anchor within sight of the Port of Leith. They showed no colours, but everyone knew who they were, including the group of Lords of the Congregation, who had returned once again to the vantage point on Calton Hill. They were aware that the ships were on their side, but it was a total exasperation to the Earl of Glencairn, not a patient man at the best of times, that he could see the fleur de lis still flying from the Fort of Leith.

"Why has Sir William Winter taken no action? They are like so many ducks feeding out there! Is he waiting to be attacked by D' Oysel's French. Does he no 'ken that a French squadron is on its way, unless our agent at the English Court has deceived us? There are more double agents around than fleas on a dead rat, I'm thinking! I was under the impression that the English were coming to our assistance?"

"But, my dear Glencairn, Lord Cecil has informed us that all the preparations were for war and that Elizabeth had rejected the Council's cautious approach and accepted his advice. Queen Elizabeth has resisted the French and Spanish influence at her Court. We must be grateful and thank her for that!" Young Erskine of Dun ignored the slight snort from Sir William Cunningham, which he was used to." We know that Lord Norfolk is waiting on the Borders at Berwick with thousands of troops. Just tak 'tent, have trust and patience, my brother, and don't make any move." It was the wisest advice for forethought, and Sir James Sandilands of West Calder, at whose house Knox had preached to an eager assembly of local lairds, nodded quietly in agreement at this good sense.

"Don't tell me to have patience, Erskine! Now is the time to strike, when the iron is hot. Elizabeth of England has kindled the fire in Scotland, but she will not fling the first stone! What good is that to us?" Sir William's fury was unabated.

But it would have been somewhat softened, if he had known that the French fleet had been destroyed by fierce storms, smashed upon the shores of Flanders. What a deliverance by God that day, for the fleet was carrying 4, 500 troops, well-armed, under the command of another of the hated Guises, the Marquis d'Elboeuf. But God's goodness had allowed the English fleet under Admiral Winter, after it had left Gillingham at the end of December under specific orders from their Queen, to weather the very same storm. God's overarching grace was revealed. After a weary month eight out of the thirteen vessels had limped into the Firth of Forth. There Sir William Winter remembered his instructions only too clearly. He read again the document and the relevant words.

'Remember that your principal part is to impede any more help coming to Scotland from France, and make it easier for the French to leave, you understand. You may provoke a quarrel, if you do not obtain a reason. Sink and destroy any vessels that attack you. Seize powder and guns for yourself. But, if you are challenged, say that you are acting on your own responsibility, and do not admit that you bear the Queen's

Commission. No excuses must be given to France." He was also informed what reason to present to the Queen Regent for their presence in Scotland, if challenged. In fact Mary of Guise, suffering an illness which her physician could not cure, was to send an angry enquiry to the English Commander.

Patiently Winter had waited in the bay, playing this cat and mouse game, and finally one day provoked the French into firing a stray shot at one ship. The Englishman needed no second invitation to order an immediate broadside against the French Fort. It was completely blown up and some vessels seized. Winter was triumphant. The patience game had paid off.

"We have them where we want them! They cannot get out of it or in! D'Oysel cannot escape Leith to get to Stirling. The Queen Regent has her answer." He turned to an officer.

"Send to Norfolk in Berwick to march at once, and with the help of his troops the work will be done!"

The decisive action taken by the English squadron did in fact bring a response from the Regent in beleaguered Leith. A small vessel under a white flag approached Winter's ship, and the Regent's emissary demanded peremptorily by whose orders they were there. Winter had a ready answer.

"I have been sent to sea to search for pirates, and have entered the Forth to watch for them. Barbary corsairs are frequent raiders of our coasts, God's curse on them, you must know. They have kidnapped even women and children as slaves, and are completely ruthless." It was certainly true that cruel Arab corsairs from the North African coast and ports like Tripoli and Tangier had often without warning raided the coasts of not only Britain, but Italy, France, the Low Countries, and even Ireland to return with all kinds of booty to their lairs, but mainly slaves.

They had continued their raiding with impunity, for their harbours of refuge were too shallow for normal European vessels to enter, but sufficient for low Arab ships. But the French messenger stared angrily at Winter, both clearly aware of the deception going on and the emptiness of the words. The falsehood had easily slipped off the tongue of the Englishman. After all, had he not the Royal authority for the deception? The French emissary departed in a high dudgeon. Unfortunately word came back from Berwick that the Duke of Norfolk had no orders to move and was staying put meanwhile.

"It is enough," said Admiral Winter to his subordinates after initial disappointment." D'Oysel's lines of communication with the Queen Regent have been cut. We shall starve them into surrender!"

Mary of Guise, now deeply sick, had in fact been taken to the Castle of Edinburgh, which in this divided city was still in the hands of her supporters. The English seaman's hatred of the French was no less than the Scots. The winter had been a severe one, and had he but known it, the French garrison would soon be reduced to eating rats, and even a handful of grain to them would be a precious possession. A climax was coming in this almighty battle for the soul of Scotland that was taking place. Admiral Winter grew impatient, however, to see the mission complete, and Leith seized from the French. He chafed at the delay, especially when he saw how helpless D'Oysel seemed, trapped in the Port. The reply from Norfolk at Berwick was exasperating.

"No orders to move! Common military sense and policy commands our orders! Are not the French our enemies, and would they not make Scotland the back door to England? Why else are we here?" He omitted to add that otherwise no normal Englishman would involve himself with this barbaric, troublesome, northern, Kingdom.

He had a foreboding that a key opportunity had been lost and so it was to prove. One day by surprise D'Oysel showed tremendous resolve and ingenuity to lead his troops out of Leith, starving and desperate, to the haven of Stirling. Not only that, but, having fully refreshed themselves, the French had the audacity to return secretly, well supplied, to occupy Leith again. They had done all this, despite the English fleet remaining in the harbour, watching night and day to keep the French waking. But the weather was severe, with thick mists falling frequently, and under one of these D'Oysel had taken advantage to march in. In addition, the captains and crews were fully occupied tacking their sails to the battering winds and battening down anything loose. Winter continued to be angry at the Scots, for the Lords of the Congregation had been indecisive and careless.

"If these Scots had been as diligent on land, as we have been at sea, D'Oysel would not have escaped to Stirling!" he complained in a letter to Lord Cecil," The Protestant Army has left Edinburgh, and they have left all the cruel work to us. Only Lord James Stuart seems true to their cause. As for the preacher Knox, he has gone on his preaching travels and so is not much use to rally these idle Scots to defend their own capital!"

But it was to all turn out to the advantage of the Protestant cause. The laxity of the Scots obliged the English at Elizabeth's Court and the Queen herself to abandon their line of a cautious policy they had hitherto pursued. Things moved quickly, express riders raced north and south, and soon the Treaty of Berwick was signed between the nations early in the new year. It guaranteed the Scots the needed help in their desire to be loyal to their absent young Queen in France, and yet to be free of French domination. Politics were an intriguing mixture, a double-edged affair often, with the Courts of England and France treading precarious tightropes, and words exchanged of equivocal and subtle meanings, dependent upon the hidden agenda of each side. The plain speaking of John Knox would have been ill at ease in it all, but he was most happy preaching his beloved Gospel in Scotland's countryside, and when he heard the news his joy was unbounded. At last the end was near. The two nations had come together, bound in a common purpose.

"We cannot antagonise and influence others at the same time," he observed poignantly to one of the party who had accompanied him on his tour of the south-west and Borders as a guard.

But it was a triumph that had still to be implemented militarily. Though in spiritual things the power, he realised, had been left in the hands of the Protestants. Already the Roman Catholic Church in Scotland was waning everywhere. Every place of worship was almost universally deserted, except in places which had been occupied by the ailing Regent and her foreign auxiliaries. Ah, he had heard, now that he returned to Edinburgh, that she was near death's gaping door, and he wondered how that irascible nature was facing the final judgement. The hold of the Roman system on the opinions and affections of the Scottish people was supported only now by force. John Knox prayed fervently for the expulsion of the French finally from his land. The feeble priests of Rome had lost all enthusiasm for their ceremonies and rites. God was ringing down the curtain on Rome. A new dawn was arising of joy and liberty of worship in the Holy Spirit, to satisfy every heart.

"Now is the time to set up our Reformed Services peacefully and wisely, wherever ministers can be found," Knox expostulated to his friend, Willock. "It is the year of the favour of the Lord. The nation and the people have already made their decision. Praise God for His Sovereign power, for He has overruled in the affairs of nations!" The breech of Henry VIII, that strange mixture of genius, tyranny, and dissolution, had awakened the attention of the Scots to a desire for Reformation.

Then, as Knox mused on God's overarching plan for his children, on the premature death of the young Protestant King Edward VI, which had been regarded as a disaster, he realised that the political alliances of England with Spain, and France with Scotland had paradoxically prevented any great plans between the two great Continental powers against the Protestant faith in Britain. Truly God worked in mysterious ways His wonders to perform. He was the Divine tapestry weaver in a work, where its rear side appeared a meaningless cross stitching. Now, when the vicious House of Lorraine was to come to power in France with the sudden death of young Francis I, it would be too late.

But the Protestant victory was only possible through military might, even though when he heard that storms had smashed the fleet of the Marquis D'Elboeuf off Flanders, and only nine hundred troops had been able to land at Leith, John Knox had rejoiced in the miraculous deliverance.

"God has fought for the defence of Scotland! He is the God of battles!

Ye ken the prophet Isaiah believed this, and so do I." He had in fact written urgently to Croft, the English mediator, to have an English fleet sent to the Forth to intercept D'Elboeuf's fleet, in case the French should capture Stirling and St, Andrews. But God had done the work for him.

Yet things were still not good. During January and February the French and Congregation troops had fought a guerrilla war in the snows of Fife. The daring raids of the Earl of Arran, the resourceful Lord James, and the brave Kirkcaldy of Grange on the French line of march as they slogged wearily through the sodden fields of Fifeshire had seen them destroy bridges and houses the French might use. Cruelty was shown on both sides. Knox kept closely in touch with the latest news of the campaign, and, though he and Willock had gained access to St. Giles again, he was in a spiritual ferment and very depressed that only 500 horsemen and 100 foot soldiers had joined the Scots partisans. The mass of the people of Fife had shown no patriotic enthusiasm, and seemed cowed. Knox burned with ire, especially when the contemptuous words of the Regent, now esconsed safely in Edinburgh Castle nearby, were reported to him.

"Where is John Knox's God now? My God is stronger than him, yes, even in Fife!" He could imagine her sarcastic French voice and curling lip, and he ground his teeth in rage. His God had not failed. It was these fellow Scots, neither hot nor cold, full of indecision. He wrote at once to Arran and the other Lords, reproaching them for not going to the assistance of the English fleet off Leith.

"*Your English allies have lain in the Forth for the last fifteen days inactive. Except for Lord James, Earl of Moray, they have received no more help than if they were off the coast of their mortal enemy!*" His irony was at his sharpest and most intense. Surely united they must stand? Internal weakness was their worst enemy. Many days and nights he and John Willock, and at times Christopher Goodman, the English pastor, who had now returned from Geneva, spent in prayer in the side chapel of St. Giles, the cold seeping through his bones. He was getting older, and the strain of his years in exile and at the galley bench was beginning to tell.

But on the twenty ninth of March the sharp winds blew in the good news that a mighty force of 9, 000 English troops, under Lord Grey, the biggest they could muster, had marched over the border and made contact with the forces of the Congregation at Prestonpans. All the French forces of 3, 500 and 500 Scots fellow travellers withdrew to Leith, knowing full well that the English, augmented by Scots mercenaries hired by English money, far outnumbered them. Knox had instinctively distrusted the idea of hiring mercenaries, when he heard it.

"Men's hearts are not for rent! Freedom is not bought, nor is God for sale! How will the Lord bless our work through hired swords? The English Army has been sent as allies, and for that we are grateful." He expressed his fears and frustrations to Willock, who agreed. His fears were to be well founded.

For Admiral Winter, patient and experienced as he was, at last saw the opportunity for action, and early in April, with the weather improving, he gave orders to open fire on Leith.

"It's time to blast these Frenchies to Hell and Kingdom come!" he shouted to his Captains." You know fine where their guns are!" Sure enough the English cannon concentrated on St. Anthony's Church steeple, and from eight powerful men o' war vessels a fusillade poured forth, so that soon both the French guns and St. Anthony's bells were silent. The English sailors roared their victory, but it was to be a premature triumph. In a surprise attack of incredible audacity in the spring gloaming the French broke out of Leith and attacked the fresh trenches, which the English had dug. They leapt agilely over the deep trenches, entered the English camp, spiked their cannon, and after the hottest of skirmishes, retreated to Leith, leaving two hundred and forty dead. The Anglo-Scots alliance were devastated and filled with bitter disappointment.

When word came to Elizabeth, she was enraged that her proud soldiers should be so disgraced and humiliated. She sent orders to continue the siege with increased vigour. The gloves and mask were now off with France. She sent an additional 3, 000 troops from Berwick. Again things looked fair, as the English with renewed confidence advanced upon the French lines, with Lord Grey certain of success. Their guns blasted continuously at the high walls of Leith and the town within. The flames rose high in the evening sky. In his tent, almost deafened by the roaring guns and the shouts of triumph by his men. Grey dispatched a letter to Norfolk, waiting in Berwick.

"Leith is in ashes, and is still burning yet, even yet!" He let his feelings of victory filter into his pen, scratching excitedly. But once more it was to be another false dawn.

In the morning an amazing sight greeted the attackers. Bright mayflowers adorned the ramparts, which were partly-demolished, a clear sign of defiance. The French were not subdued after all. Lord Grey with narrowed eyes stared at these stubborn walls. They were still very high to scale, and he would not be the first to climb a ladder up such ramparts and risk death at the hands of its defenders.

If they attempted and failed, it would mean disastrous defeat. He much preferred the safer option of tunnelling under with mattock and spade. He had a sense of indecision. As a military man, he despised such politicians as Croft, just a useless, weak, go-between from Elizabeth's Court, and their letters were filled with thinly-veiled acrimony. He was convinced too that some of the Scots mercenaries were not pulling their weight, and he was scornful at their apparent cowardice.

An atmosphere of depression began to affect the English camp, and some soldiers even deserted. Most grumbled at their lack of pay. All this pressure was too much for Lord Grey. Early in May he gave orders for an all-out assault on Leith by land and sea. But a total disaster followed, as the French cannon and muskets cut the English and their Scots mercenaries down, when they charged over the exposed ground carrying scaling ladders. Few reached the walls of Leith. Even Admiral Winter's cannonade seemed to have little effect. At the end of a dark day eight hundred officers and men lay dead. Back in St. Giles, where Knox and the other ministers were seeking the face of God in prayer, bombarding the gates of Heaven, Sir William Kirkcaldy of Grange interrupted their intercessions and his report brought fresh fuel to their supplications.

"These English soldiers have little quality and toughness! I would that those who carried out King Henry VIII's Rough Wooing had been like that, for we would not have suffered such devastation, but driven them pell mell! As for the mercenaries, they are full of cowardice, not true Scotsmen. I beg of you, Master John, request Sir Ralph Sadler, England's ambassador, to send further reinforcements from the Duke of Norfolk, and to send men this time! If they don't come, the whole thing will fail, I tell you. ! If the French knew how weak we are, it might be extremely dangerous for us."

"But what is the condition of the French, Grange? God will not abandon us now, I promise you. The secret of the Lord is with those that fear Him. They shall keep His Covenant." Knox respected the boldness and courage of William Kirkcaldy and his own words cheered the latter.

"Blessed are those who trust in the arm of the Lord, but," John Knox paused," we shall, nevertheless, request Sir Ralph Sadler for more soldiers."

The preacher was astute enough to know that the spiritual and the physical went hand in hand. He knew well and liked that strange parable which was mentioned only once in Holy Writ, that of the unjust steward who was clever enough to safeguard his future when about to lose his position with his master, by winning friends throughout dishonest means Christ had commended his shrewdness, though not his dishonesty of course.

"Aye, I judge that the Frenchies must be near to starvation, but D'Oysel will not surrender easily."

In fact the French had scarcely a loaf of bread in their camp. Even the Queen Regent, becoming more sick every day in Edinburgh Castle, knew that matters were becoming desperate. But she was keen to know just how long Sieur D'Oysel could hold out, and tried an ingenious method of communicating with the besieged City. She sent a French soldier, dressed as a Scots mercenary, carrying a cipher written on a pocket handkerchief, to try to get through the enemy lines, but he failed.

Another secret message was inscribed in invisible ink of copperose solution upon the back of a seemingly innocent letter sent asking medical advice from a doctor in Leith for her condition. It almost succeeded, for it was well known that the Regent was very ill. Her messenger was about to be allowed through the besieging lines, when a suspicion arose. The letter was seized and immediately taken over by one of Lord Grey's staff and examined over a fire. Suddenly the unseen writing appeared. Eagerly Lord Grey with great satisfaction informed the terrified messenger, who expected to be hung any moment, of his reply to his Mistress.

"Go back to the Castle, lackey, and tell your Mistress that I will keep her counsel on the war, but that such wares as hers will not sell until a new market is found!" The irony in his words was enjoyed by him, for he had found out from her message just how bad were conditions within the walls of Leith. Mary of Guise had counselled Sieur D'Oysel to hold out to the last. The much relieved messenger, his neck still whole, fled back to the Castle.

The end was near. Secretary Cecil himself, worried about the outcome, came north and arranged for a week's armistice, which resulted in a remarkable event. The English and French officers shared their provisions on the sands of Leith in a picnic, as the French called it. The contrast in what they brought could not have been more illustrative of the situation. From Lord Grey's camp were brought hams, capons, chickens, wine, and beer, while the French produced a solitary fowl, some mouldy bread, a piece of baked horse flesh, which was a delicacy in France, and six delicately roasted pieces of meat, which the English did not dare guess the identity of, but suspected were from the rat population.

Behind the scenes murky goings on were taking place in the political-religious sphere, an attempt by the French Protestants in a conspiracy at Amboise had been made to overthrow the Guises. The rising was suppressed but it meant that the French were wary of over-committing themselves in Scotland, since it would bring them into direct confrontation with England. So in a surprise move they invited their former enemy, but new ally, Spain, to assist them in suppressing heresy in Scotland. But here the snag came in to this ambitious move in the chessboard of European politics. King Philip II of Spain saw that, Roman Catholic fanatic though he was, if he helped France annexe Scotland, they could then invade England more easily. The French rivals, whom he secretly despised and hated, could then control the vital English Channel and prevent the Spanish from having access to the Low Countries. Even then it was touch and go, for a force of 4, 500 mercenaries were gathered in the Spanish Netherlands, ready to leave for an invasion of Scotland, but the astute Duke of Alva advised against it, preferring to let the French stew in their own juice. The disastrous destruction of a Spanish fleet by the Barbary corsairs in the Mediterranean was the final decider. Other things were more vital. God was working out his perfect plan for Scotland's Protestant Reformation through the affairs of men, Knox saw. He was the great Divine tapestry weaver, he often thought. Thus by sheer desperation and necessity the proud French were brought to the negotiating table, and on the 6th July, a crowning of the hopes of John Knox and his brethren took place when the Treaty of Edinburgh was announced. But a month before this an event happened, which precipitated it. Word came to the Duke of Chatelherault and Lord James Stuart at Leith in a missive to attend the Queen Regent.

"I am sorry for Scotland and my own share in her suffering; I ask forgiveness of those towards whom my Government has been prejudiced." Lord James was amazed secretly at the spirit of repentance that suffused her features and was evident in her whole manner. Pain was also equally evident.

"Your Grace, true forgiveness is always available for true penitents. Surely the Lords of the Congregation and the people of Scotland will readily forgive you?" He just refrained from adding that forgiveness was needed for the great sin of dividing the nation and causing civil war.

"Madam, God is doing a new thing, restoring the former purity of the Church, and we must sing a new song, as the Holy Scriptures tell us." Again he refrained from bringing up how the old Church had brought scorn upon itself by attempting to support its sinking cause and to recover her lost reputation amongst the common people by the pretence of miracles wrought at the so-called holy wells and springs of their saints. The exposure of their false superstitions and impostures, when the boasted miracles failed to appear, laid it open to the public's derision.

"Your Grace, I beg of you to see Master John Willock, our Godly chaplain of St. Giles, before you face eternity." His eyes appealed with great sincerity to the Frenchwoman.

The dying Regent's dark eyes for a moment blinked back tears, and then a shutter seemed to go down over her lids. She continued to hear all that Chatelherault and Moray had to say with attention, but in fact afterwards, when they had departed, she sent for a Roman priest, from whom she received the sacraments of that Church in a spirit of religious fear. Sadly, at the end Mary of Guise had refused the lifeline of hope offered by the Protestant, Biblical, faith, and went out into the unknown.

Things had now come to an impasse, with the French depressed at the situation and their lack of guidance, and the English only too ready to end the siege. Their troops were exhausted, as the summer wore on and the heat of the August sun set in. Some were even in rebellion and secretly deserted. The ten thousand men threatened to become drastically reduced, and so wise diplomacy on both sides at last saw an agreement reached. Both the French and English forces would be withdrawn and Scotland left to sort out her own political and religious future. But both knew that the foundation for the Protestant Reformation had been well and truly laid, and after a deep and agonising struggle, which had almost torn her apart, Scotland had become at last one of the most secure Protestant nations in Europe.

A milestone had been reached in the turbulent times of the Reformation and the very air seemed different. There was the end of the French influence in Scotland and that of the Roman Catholic religion. But now the whole responsibility of establishing the Protestant Faith throughout the land fell upon John Knox, John Willock, Christopher Goodman, and the other ministers. The Lords of the Privy Council had appointed them to draw up a plan for the new Church, based upon Scripture. It would be centred on the *Book of Common Order*, which had so impressed its stamp upon the Reformer, when he had spent these so happy years in Geneva. He had now cast off this nostalgic longing for that City State upon Lac Leman. Scotland and its future was the reality. But the *Book of Common Order*, nevertheless, agreed upon in that Swiss City, was agreed upon in Scotland.

"There will be four kinds of permanent office-bearers in the Church, first the minister or pastor, who will preach the Gospel and administer the Sacraments. Then there will be the doctor of teacher, whose province it will be to interpret Scripture and confute errors, even amongst those who teach Theology in Schools and Universities." Here John Willock gazed pointedly over at the academics gathered amongst the nobility of the Privy Council, as if distrusting of secular educationists, who might be more influenced by worldly wisdom than spiritual insights." There will be a ruling elder, who will assist the minister in exercising ecclesiastical discipline and Government." Pastor Willock pursed his lips determinedly.

"Accountability will be the theme of our Protestant faith, after the tyranny of Rome and the control of the Papacy. Lastly, the deacon will have the special oversight of the revenues of the Kirk and over the poor. In addition, as there are not a sufficient number of ministers to supply the whole country, it has been found necessary to appoint serious-minded people to read Scriptures and common prayers. They will be called lay readers, and, if they advance in knowledge, the readers can become exhorters from the Bible. But they must be examined before they can be admitted." There would be no half measures in this revolution of religion, and no laxity in carrying it out. One monopoly would be replaced with another, and Willock and the other ministers saw nothing wrong in that.

The Counter Reformation on the Continent, in attempting to purify the Church, had merely widened the gap. But there were to be more than a few teething troubles in Scotland's Reformation. Pastor Willock took a deep breath." In our *Book of Discipline* a great emphasis will be laid on a national education system. An Elementary School will be provided in every parish, and a Grammar School in every Burgh, in which there shall be a teacher qualified to instruct in Religion, Grammar, and the Latin tongue. No child shall be prevented by poverty from attending school, and bursaries shall enable them to go to University." Though these were Willock's words, they were Knox's vision.

"Where is the money going to come from for this vast expense?" broke in the Earl of Morton, a sly look in his eyes." The poor are everywhere. Beggars, vagrants, and vagabonds of every description swarm in bands up and down Scotland! The entire population of gypsies, sorners, and idle fellows, who threaten others on the King's highway, are past counting! Who will pay to educate them?"

"We will educate only those who show talent, my Lord." John Willock refused to react to what was a foolish question." We are not patrons for stubborn and idle persons, who run from place to place and make a craft of their begging. The Civil Magistrate ought to punish them. But we must care for the widow and the fatherless, the aged, impotent, or lamed who cannot work for their sustenance. For these and those people, who honestly have fallen into decay and penury from no fault of their own, provision shall be made from our abundance. God will show the wisdom and means how this can be done in every part of our realm." Willock could not avoid seeing the cynicism, scepticism, and plain unbelief writ large on the features of the nobles, and in some clear hostility. Their self-interest was being touched at the quick.

"Are we not talking of education, not groats, bawbees, and shekels, Master Willock?" Knox interjected, annoyed at the turn of the emphasis." I propose that a portion of the Estate of the Old Church should be allocated to the poor and the education expense." Knox spoke out vigorously with conviction, daring the Barons to their faces, only too aware that opposition would come from those, whose God was their belly and love of money their purpose." The idle should be set to work under disciplinary conditions."

"Now this I like! It speaks sense to my mind!" agreed a selfish Lord," and it speaks to the situation!" What he really meant of course, Knox knew fine, was that the proposal provided the landowning nobles with a ready supply of cheap labour, forcibly acquired. The stout and sturdy beggars, who swarmed along the highways, were a constant source of worry and trouble to the authorities." Any legislation to remove vagrancy is welcome." The aristocrat was already thinking ahead of abjectly paid workers in the mines and salt pans in a form not much better than that of medieval serfdom. Salters, colliers, and coal bearers would not be leaving their employment without their masters' permission.

No employer would be able to take a collier or salter without a testimonial, or he would be liable to a fine of £1, 000 Scots. All this was to come into effect in post Reformation Scotland, and, if his prophetic gift had included such visions, John Knox might have been concerned. But in fact the dim glimmerings of democracy were arising in Scotland, he would have been happy to know. Now men of lowly birth, buoyed and inspired by great spiritual ideas could, and would, offer stern resistance to oppression and threaten Kings on their thrones. A sense of spiritual equality was coming to the people of Scotland.

"Kings and Barons may still oppress and bully, my Lords," Knox was full of fire by now, sparked off by the worldly greed and human pride before him," but let it now be known that there is a King of Kings and a Lord of Lords! Men can now hear of One who is greater than Caesar, to whom the meanest cottar can have direct appeal!" The self seekers amongst the nobles, lairds, merchants, and clergy gathered before the Committee quailed before this human volcano, this latter day Amos, the Prophet of Israel, whom God had taken from being a simple shepherd of Tekoa to become the instrument to flay the consciences of ancient Israel's rulers for their injustices against the poor, whom they would have sold into slavery for the price of a pair of shoes. A sense of individual worth was to arise in Scotland and a conviction of spiritual independence that was to shake the land to its roots, and snap the shackles of the old feudalism. A notion of equality before God was to grow and develop, so that fear of the Lords and Barons was gradually destroyed.

"Let us send the schoolmaster out to all corners of the land, and let the people be taught! The Universities too shall be liberally endowed. As for the Kirk, each minister will have an honest provision, which will secure him against anxiety and poverty. This will consist of forty bolls of meal, twenty six bolls of malt, and a moderate sum of money to supply other necessities for his family as a stipend. Superintendants will receive more in travelling expenses."

A few of the Protestant Lords, whose faith in the Lord was tainted by regarding the Reformation partly as a stepping stone to obtain the rich benefices of the Roman Church, kept tight-lipped at these terms in *The First Book of Discipline*. They could hardly object to the proper support for the new Kirk, and even Lord Erskine, later to be the Earl of Mar, had to bite his tongue, for he had a spendthrift Jezebel of a wife, and he also knew that his kitchen would be a lot less well-stocked, if these expenses were made.

"A knowledge of Hebrew will be made a necessary branch of education," John Willock recommenced the exposition of the details of the Book of Discipline, which was to form the backbone of the Protestant life and faith in Scotland." Pastor John Row will form the first Hebrew Class in Scotland."

Here he indicated in an openly admiring way the brilliant academic, Row, who waved away any praise in a self-effacing manner in accord with his humble nature. In fact in Row's school the boys spoke only in Latin in their classes. John Row instructed his own son, when just eight years old, to read the Hebrew Scriptures to the rest of the boys at dinner.

"We propose that a College should be erected in every notable town, in which Logic and Rhetoric shall be taught along with the learned languages." Everyone knew that by the aforementioned he referred to the ancient Greek and Latin speech, but a few quizzical looks seemed to ask which would be regarded as notable towns.

"Like the Republics of Greece and Rome, let us regard our youth as no longer the private property of their parents, but as publicly belonging to the nation. Despite the confusion in which our country now finds itself, let us make sure that learning continues to progress! Our three national Universities will have an enlightened approach to literature." His eyes were full of an unalloyed enthusiasm, and made a heartfelt appeal to the assembled audience. Gradually a sustained applause, if less than full-throated, broke out. The greater part of the Privy Council went on to subscribe to the First Book of Discipline.

The stage was set for the General Assembly of the Reformed Church of Scotland then to meet in Edinburgh on the twentieth of December, the year of grace, 1560, when a cataclysm took place in the Heavenlies over Scotland and she broke from the spiritual control of Rome. Knox's heart was burning with exultation and a spiritual pride in his nation took him over, when on that cold winter's day they gathered in the first General Assembly, forty members, of whom only six were ministers, to guide the religious future of a nation. But gradually the numbers appointed increased, and a Moderator to maintain order was fixed at every meeting, but in fact the harmony of spirit present was so great that the Moderator was almost redundant, as if God invisibly was in charge. But, it was like, all human life, to have the good mixed with the tragic, for a terrible personal loss was to rob John Knox just then. Man is born to trouble, as the sparks fly upward, as Job said.

He returned one night to their Canongate home, weary from the heavy weight of Scotland's religious responsibility. He was disillusioned deeply by the enforced abandonment for the moment of his dream for education, poor relief, and a healthy provision for the Reformed Kirk. A sadness seemed also to reign over his house, when he arrived. Marjorie had been ill for some time, a fever brought on by the strain of the great responsibility which she voluntarily shared with her husband, and a sense of fear seized him. It was borne out when he heard within the sobbing of his two lads, Nathaniel and Eleazar, but the blow was not lessened. Then the hysterical weeping of Mrs. Elizabeth Bowes, his mother-in-law, brought home to him the horror. It could only be one thing. His beloved, dearest, affectionate, spouse, Marjorie, had passed away.

The loneliness was like a cold blanket, which enveloped John Knox's soul. His deep appreciation of women was summed up in his love for the English maiden from Norham Castle, who had been one of his mainstays in the storms of his tempestuous life. He entered the house, and, controlling his sorrow, held his two sons close in an embrace of fatherly love and comfort, as they clung to him. He had already decided that the lads should be sent south to be educated at Oxford, which was safer. Their mother would have been pleased, despite her love for her great Scotsman and all things Scottish. He muttered prayerfully, audibly or not was unimportant, the words of Job.

"The Lord gives, the Lord takes, blessed be the Name of the Lord!" His acute grief was to come later, when Marjorie's lightsome spirit was missing during the onerous duties that lay ahead of him. As for Elizabeth Bowes, he groaned inwardly, for her almost continual dejection of mind was becoming a burden to him. He never seemed able to cure her of her spiritual depression, no matter how often he encouraged her.

Within a week of the funeral of Marjorie Knox a letter arrived of deep and highest regard for his deceased love from John Calvin in Geneva. It was a mighty uplift to his heart. The mighty man of Geneva had said how Marjorie had been the ideal partner for the Scot, a humble helpmate and carer for her family. His honour of Calvin made the words like a sweet medicine to him. He had been in regular touch with his former colleague and still close friend, and sent many letters seeking his expert advice during the birthpangs of the Reformation in Scotland.

He certainly needed great wisdom, for he now realised that the Book of Discipline was too radical and visionary for those who were now effectively running his beloved Scotland. He did not want an influx of former priests, now unemployed, and other time-servers into the Church. He needed truly converted Protestant ministers, grounded in their faith, not ones who did not share the beliefs they had fought so hard to secure. The Roman Catholic nobility, under the notorious Gordons of Huntly up in the north-east, were still a potent, if unpredictable, threat, seeking to overthrow the Protestant faith. The problem of obtaining the hundred and twenty pounds salary for each of the ministers of the thousand Churches the Protestant Kirk aimed to set up throughout the land was immense.

He knew there were plans afoot over in France to raise a new army to invade Scotland in the spring, and that there had been sent secret emissaries to seek to encourage the depressed Catholics, who were still loyal to their religion. So speed was of the essence to establish the Reformed Kirk firmly, for he was doubtful if the Queen of England would put herself to the expense and unpopularity with France, as to protect them against a second invasion. Things must be hammered out immediately with Willock, Goodman, and others.

"Calvin has laid out for us the true theory of Church Government," he urged them," when he described the Church as a community, in which Christ only is its head and all its members are equal under Him. The ministry is given to the entire Church and is distributed amongst many officers. All who hold office do so by the election of the people. The pastor will ordain the elders and deacons for life. The Presbytery will alone have the power to dismiss a pastor. We must avoid men who assume power to themselves. For too long that has been the corruption of the Church!" His face blazed in that powerful anger. So it was that, as they prayed and discussed together for long hours, the final form of the Government of the Reformed Kirk was thrashed out.

Yet the crunch was to come, for the right to raise revenue, the old thorny question, was not transferred to the new Protestant Church. Knox saw again the greed of the worldly staring him in the face, and he and the ministers were enraged.

"Where will the money come from to establish the new Kirk?" Knox shouted." We rightly claim the revenue of the old Church. Even in England the resources of the clergy was given to the Reformed Church!"

After much humming and hawing, excuses, tight-lipped moans and protests, a compromise was arrived at, and a deal struck. But it was a close-run thing.

"My Lord Erskine has two reasons for refusing his consent," remarked Knox scathingly, when afterwards closeted with the other clergy in a side chapel of St. Giles. "First, he has a very Jezebel for a wife, and, second, if the poor, the schools, and the Kirk had what belongs to them, his kitchen would want two parts or more of what it now unjustly possesses!" The others laughed easily.

"His God is his belly," Goodman returned." I hear Erskine lives high on the hog! We could suggest fasting as a way of removing sin!"

"It's not hard to understand, for some of these grasping nobles have seized Church lands already." Glencairn and his close coterie were needless to say above that. But finally agreement was reached. The old Church would keep two thirds of the wealth, until its members died out, and the remaining third would be divided between the Church and the Crown. But Knox was far from satisfied.

"Two parts freely given to the devil and a third has been divided between God and the devil! And I predict that it will be not long before the devil has the two thirds!" He looked fixedly round his audience." Guess what the Church's share will be then?"

They all knew only too well that the likelihood of his prediction being fulfilled was great and prayed that God who had begun a good work, a wonderful spiritual revolution with effects for all time, a special cleansing of the Church, would bring it to a prosperous conclusion. The spurious authority of the Pope had been banished from Scotland forever, and the day had dawned for a vibrant Protestant Church throughout the land, which would bring untold blessings to countless generations.

CHAPTER FIFTEEN

ROYAL CONFRONTATIONS

As John Knox strode purposely down Edinburgh's ancient Kings Street, the *Via Regia*, as Latin put it, his feet sounding smartly on the square paving stones, he steeled his heart for the coming confrontation with the young Queen Mary. It was now exactly one week since the new Queen had arrived at the port of Leith with two French galleys. Well did he remember that dismal day, at about four o' clock in the morning, when, although it was a summer's day in mid August, the very face of Heaven seemed to weep. It had been wet, and the mist so thick that one man could scarcely make out another at a few yards distance. The sun had not shone for two days before, nor for two days after her arrival, though it was high summer, but most of the people seemed blind to this portentous sign of foreboding.

The multitudes of the common people had rejoiced, taken by her beauty, as they vied even at that early hour for a sight of the young Queen, but a girl of nineteen. Numerous bonfires had been set up all that night of the nineteenth of August, and a whole choir and orchestra had sung and played psalm tunes on the fiddle, and on the rebec, that other popular stringed instrument. Knox snorted, when the memory rose of how almost five hundred, sincere-hearted, subjects had serenaded this unknown Queen on the first night of her arrival back in the land of her birth after thirteen years. But only two days before this summons to the royal presence, what had she done but celebrate the Mass he detested so much in her Chapel Royal of Holyrood Palace?

His informants had also told him that a Frenchman, named Brantome, a writer, who had accompanied the widowed Queen from France at her request, had said that the singing of these psalms by her simple, enthusiastic, subjects outside the royal chamber was a terrible discord played on wretched fiddles, which grated on the Queen's ears and kept her awake, and that she only pretended for appearance sake to like their singing and playing. She had requested that they perform a few more evenings as a sop only. There was something John Knox instinctively did not like about this young Queen, even before their interview. He grated his teeth.

Aye, he felt that would be typical of this Queen, an outward charm and acquiescence to the will of her subjects, but an inward determination to go her own way. His old antagonism to dictatorial Queens came back to haunt him, Mary of Guise, this lass's mother, and Mary Tudor, the persecutor of the English Protestants. Was this Queen any different? Hadn't her father, King James V, it was well known, said before he turned his face to the wall and died prematurely at Falkland Palace said *It cam' wi' a lass, and it will gang wi' a lass?* ' Knox had been introduced momentarily to her shortly after the two French galleys had slipped quietly through the mist into Leith harbour at last.

He had gained an immediate impression of a tall, auburn-haired, young woman, swan-necked, of a fairly lovely appearance and sophisticated manner, but he knew sufficient of feminine charms not to be taken in. The worth of a good woman was far beyond rubies, Proverbs had taken pains to inform all true Christians, and he was only too conscious of the blessings to the heart and soul, not to forget the body, of female encouragement and companionship. His dearest wife, Marjorie, had borne him two fine boys, now four and two, and her mother had faithfully followed him to the Continent. Her husband, Sir Ralph Bowes, the Captain of Norham Castle, who had, despite the preacher's solicitous preaching and evangelising, remained with the Roman Church, had died some years before, and disinherited his wife. But with him had died the hostility of that family, which seemed a lifetime away now. That was a relief to his spirit. The vindictiveness of Marjorie's uncle, Sir Robert Bowes, too had been particularly trying to his soul.

In fact there had been times when Mrs. Bowes continual questions on religion had wearied him, but her genuine sincerity of spirit had always touched him, and many times his prayers, and even tears, had been shared with Elizabeth Bowes. They had also been shared with Mrs. Anne Locke, the wife of the London merchant, who had with her husband's permission, joined him in Geneva, along with Mrs. Hickman. Aye, he had enjoyed the company and confidence of many women, so different from the three Royal Marys, who had impinged on his life in a major way. He had been especially attached to Mrs. Anne Locke.

He glanced up at the solid merchant houses on the Royal Street, which, along with Holyrood's Palace and Abbey, had been restored after the English "*Rough Wooing*" some seventeen years before, when the Earl of Hertford had burnt both. But only the wooden frontage had been destroyed, and the stone structure behind had survived. Edinburgh was a city not easily wiped out, situated as it was on a hill, a Roman mile in length, and half a mile in breadth. At the Western extremity raised a hill on a steep rock, and on the rock a fortress on an extinct volcano, with a deep valley on all sides, except towards the city on the east. Except from that side then, the Castle was impregnable. It could not be scaled, even with ladders, so steep and hard was the rock face, on which hawks were in the habit of building their nests, though enterprising youths were known to be let down from the Castle in baskets to rob their nests. The fortress which was Edinburgh Castle was known as *The Maiden's Castle*, after *Edina*, a Celtic princess.

At the far end of the *Via Regia* lay John Knox's destination, the Palace and Abbey of Holyrood, surrounded by delightful gardens and enclosed by a Lake at the bottom of a hill to the east, known as Arthur's Seat. Another hill nearby, facing north, was known as *The Hill of the Wild Boar*. The countryside round about was certainly extremely fertile, with pleasant meadows, little woods, lakes, streamlets, and more than a hundred castles of varying size within a proximity. Deer, hares, and conies, hunted often by Edinburgh's gentry, abounded in the Park of Holyrood.

John Knox's gaze was inevitably drawn towards Arthur's Seat from the direction he was heading. It seemed to glitter in the sunlight, and he was reminded that precious stones, especially diamonds, had been found in the mountain. But the Gospel was the pearl of greatest price, no matter how men disdained it and manipulated for their own gain. But the magnificent, turreted, Palace of Holyrood now loomed up, with its three fair towers, which had been built in the case of two by the young queen's father, James V, in the manner of the Scottish Renaissance, but which owed a debt to the French masons, who had been employed in its construction. It must have commended Holyrood Palace to present, critical French eyes, he thought. But, as he noticed, safety was not neglected, as the elegant Palace was approached by an iron drawbridge, and the windows of the staterooms had iron gratings, not easily removed. The gardens on all sides were laid out beautifully in parterre fashion. He had still not overcome his bias against gardening, his annoyance that precious time, especially in vital times, should be wasted in flower and herb gardens. It came back starkly how he had very nearly offended Earl of Argyle during his stay at Dollar's Castle Campbell, when he spoke scornfully of the practise of gardening, when the Campbell leader had devoted himself to an attractive, hanging, terrace in the Castle grounds, though cramped as they were.

As he approached the iron drawbridge, he scorned to dwell on the superstitions and folk tradition attached to the name of Holyrood Abbey and Palace. The cross, on which the Saviour had died, was an ugly thing of agony, which caused excruciating pain to the Son of God, before he willingly surrendered his spirit to the Father in Heaven who gave it. The Abbey had been raised for devotional reasons, which had been planted by God in the heart of King David some four hundred years before. But the fanciful story, which filled the minds of the credulous, concerned a hunting expedition undertaken by King David and his nobles in the forests surrounding Scotland's capital. When hunting in the forest of Drumselch, the King's horse had bolted and thrown him. They had been chasing a great stag. He was protected from harm from the creature by a cross, which had magically appeared between its antlers. King David had then founded the Abbey as an Augustinian monastery in memory of his deliverance. In it he placed the Black Rood, a relic supposedly from the true cross brought north by Queen Margaret, Malcolm Canmore's English wife, when she fled to Scotland from the invading Normans. When King David's subjects arrived to comfort their alarmed King they fell on their knees and adored the holy cross. Tradition said they held as a Heavenly Providence that the cross appeared, and that it was strange that no man could tell what material it was, wood, or metal. The deer itself had fled away and vanished in the same place where the Holy Rood Well had arisen. When King David returned to his castle, he was admonished in a dream to build up an Abbey in the exact spot where he obtained the cross.

Knox was filled with conflicting emotion, as he dwelt on the legend. Man was a born story-teller, and loved to use his imagination in a dream world. But he was only too aware that there were dreams from man and dreams from God, who would provide the interpretation. God's servant, Joseph, had been the Lord's instrument in Egypt to help the Children of Israel in a time of starvation. But the legend of the Holy Rood seemed to him of no practical use to man except to tickle his fancy.

Crossing the drawbridge, the man of God felt a rising nervousness at the coming confrontation. What the young Queen would be like, he had no real measure. Their contact had been so brief. Guards ushered him fairly deferentially into the Palace, and a courtier, whose manner was a little less respectful, took him along a long corridor to the Queen's chamber room. Her tongue possessed a mixture of a French intonation with an adequate grasp of the Scots dialect as he was to find. But there was something in the way she held her head and in the look of her eye. But all hidden thoughts were banished, just as he noticed out of the corner of his eye that Lord James Stuart, the Queen's half brother and a good friend of the Reformation, was present slightly behind the Queen. Two Royal maids hung shyly in the far background. The new Queen of Scots, so tall and graceful, advanced with her white hand held out for his acknowledgement. He took it and bowed for a moment, but did not kiss it. If he was embarrassed and out of his depth, he hid it well.

"I hear, Master Knox, from the short time that I have been here in my dear country of Scotland, that you have a blunt way with words."

"Life at the oar of a French galley ship does not produce carpet knights,

Madame," he replied evenly, but he would not enlarge on the point. He saw the blood rise in her pale complexion.

"Life has not been easy for any of us, sir," she retorted firmly, no doubt thinking of the premature death of her husband, the Dauphine and King of France." Do you have the Latin sir?" Mary asked, changing the subject.

"So much do I have, and think so highly of the ancient languages that I recommended in the recent Book of Discipline, which received the sanction of Parliament at the beginning of this year of grace, your Majesty, that, wherever there is a church, a school, in which Grammar and the Latin tongue be taught, should be attached to it." She nodded her approval, recalling with pride her own Latin compositions at the French Court." I also believe that besides the Universities, every town of note should have a College in which a knowledge of the Arts, at least Rhetoric and Logic, together with the learned languages, should be acquired." He judiciously did not add that through the avarice of the nobility the Council and Parliament had as yet not given any pecuniary aid to his dream of nationwide education. However, John Knox, in his indefatigable faith in the sovereign power of God was certain that one day it would be implemented, despite the sinful nature of man.

"I approve, Master Knox. Methinks that our ways are more similar than I have been told. But why have you really come to this Royal interview?" She arched her young brows disapprovingly." Is it not to tell me what to do? I am not of your Church, remember, but of the Holy Roman Church."

"Yes, Madame, but I have the right to warn you no less of any thing that may hurt Scotland than any of the nobility, for both my vocation and my conscience demand plain speaking from me." Knox could see the ire rising by the moment, but would not change his approach.

"You have raised a part of my subjects against my mother and myself! You have written an abominable book against my authority. I will have the most learned men in Europe write against it. You are the cause, sir, of great sedition and slaughter in England! I have even been told that all you do is by necromancy or witchcraft!" The faithful preacher could not believe the shocking words issuing from her. Where had she learned such lies? The dam of Mary's false calm had at last broken, but even then John Knox was shocked by how vituperative were the Queen's words. Mary's eyes were darkened with a mixture of anger and fear. The Reformer drew in a deep breath.

"Madame, may it please your Majesty patiently to hear simple answers, and first, if to teach the truth of God in sincerity, if to rebuke idolatry, and to will a people to worship God in truth, to raise subjects against their Prince, then I cannot be excused. For it has pleased God of His mercy to make me one of many to disclose to this nation the vanity of the papist religion and the deceit of the Roman Anti Christ. As for the Book which seems so highly to offend your Majesty, I am happy if all the most learned men of the whole world shall judge it." He spoke these words with great dignity, powerful and contentious though they were, zeal for Biblical truth had been uppermost in his mind three years before when he had written it. His boldness of spirit had been at its ascendancy then, when still in distant Europe, but he had moderated a little.

"Do you think then that I have no authority?" The Queen's eyes sparked and that unusually smooth skin reddened slightly.

"Your Majesty, learned men in all ages have had the freedom of judgement. Plato, the philosopher, wrote *The Commonwealth*, in which he damned many things in the world, and requested many things be reformed. Yet he did not upset things. If the realm finds no inconvenience in the Government of a woman, I shall be content to live under grace, as Paul was to live under Nero." Her eyes narrowed, as she misconstrued his meaning." My hope is that, so long as you do not shed the blood of the saints of God, neither will my writings hurt you or your authority. The book was written specifically against Mary Tudor." He tried not to make it an apology.

"But did you speak of women in general?"

"That is true, Madame, but things which were stable are now called in doubt. The anchors have been cast loose in this land. I was resident in England for five years, preaching in Berwick, Newcastle, and London. If in any of these places, any one could prove that there was fighting, plotting, sedition, or mutiny through my words, I will confess to it. But no one can." He stared her straight in the eye unflinchingly, until she quailed." Also when my enemies slanderously accuse me of the Black Arts and necromancy, which are expressly forbidden by God, I have many witnesses and my own clear conscience that I have preached against them and those who practise them." By now the Queen clearly was regretting her wild accusations, and Knox took the opportunity to apply the Bible's teaching to her untutored mind in Scriptural things." My prophetic gifts are not the marvels of Merlin, or the dark prophecies from the powers of darkness. But they are from the pure Word of God, the Bible, secondly, they reveal the invincible justice of God, and thirdly, they concern the normal way that God sends punishments and plagues on the wicked!"

"Do not speak to me, as if I am a pupil in school and you are my teacher!" Again her annoyance had arisen." But you have taught my people to receive another religion than that which their Princes allow. How can that doctrine be of God, since our God commands subjects to obey their Princes?" Her pert chin pointed at the Reformer, as Mary looked down at Knox from her superior inches, awaiting his answer. Mary was little off six feet. Knox knew now there was much more to this woman than he had thought. He had to be very careful in this game of cat and mouse that they were playing.

"Madame, subjects are not bound to shape their religious beliefs in accordance with the mere wishes of their Sovereigns." He took a deep breath." Princes are often the most ignorant of all in the matter of true religion, as we read in histories, both before and after the death of Jesus Christ. If all the descendants of Abraham had followed the religion of the Pharaoh of Egypt, what religion would we have in the world today? Or if all men in the days of the Apostles had been of the religion of the Roman Emperors, what kind of terrible religion would there have been on the face of the earth? The prophet Daniel and his fellow Israelites were the subjects of Nebuchadnezzar and Darius, but they refused to be of their religion.

Shadrach, Meshach, and Abednego all would have been burnt alive rather than worship the pagan gods of these Emperors. Daniel prayed publicly against the expressed commandment of the King. And so, Madame, subjects are not bound to the religion of their Princes, although commanded to give them civil obedience." Again Mary strove to retain control of her obvious anger only with a supreme effort, as the

Reformer's words bit home with irksome power and the authority of inescapable logic.

"Yes, but none of these men raised swords against their Princes."

"Aye, yet you cannot deny they resisted."

"But not by using the sword." Their dialogue was cut and thrust, as if to put actions to their words.

"God did not give them the power." Knox's rejoinder was short.

"Do you think, Master Knox, that subjects with the power may resist their Princes?"

The one-time tutor of Haddington knew that this was a vital question in their confrontation, and he braced himself.

"If Princes exceed their bounds, they may resist. For the obedience to Kings and Queens is not greater than to one's father and mother. But a father can be taken by a frenzy and kill his children. If the children band together, take the sword away from their father, bind up his hands, and put him in prison until his madness is past, do you think, Majesty, that his children are doing wrong?" He stopped for a moment to fix his gaze on the young Queen, who was becoming increasingly upset by the second, a mixture of sheer amazement, anger, and unbelief at this bold and indomitable, man, the like of whom she had never met before, least of all among the fawning courtiers of the French Court." It is even so with Princes, who try to murder the children of God, who are their subjects. Their blind zeal is nothing but a mad frenzy, and, therefore, to take away their sword, until they are brought to a more sober mind, is quite right."

When he had finished, Knox sensed that the Queen was almost paralysed with total astonishment. Her face had altered to an unnatural paleness. Silence then reigned for about quarter of an hour, during which time the Reformer remained calm in the tense atmosphere, which was now almost tangible. In the rear the Queen's half brother, Lord James Stuart, was clearly nervous about Mary's reaction, and the two Maries, her handmaidens, huddled together in the far corner of the Royal chamber, were terrified. Knox knew without the slightest doubt that it was not possible to be polite to this Queen without being untrue to his nation and Scotland's cause. She might be an unfortunate Queen, but it would be a still more unfortunate Scotland, if she was made happy. He was sure that before him was a Queen, who, for all her outward charm, cared most for her own will and passions, cared somewhat for her creed, but at heart cared not very much for Scotland. France had been her home for thirteen years. He did not quite know how he knew, but he was just certain.

"What has offended you, Majesty?" It was the anxious voice of Lord James Stuart, which at last broke the silence. Mary did not answer, but gave him a slightly scornful glance. Ignoring his presence, she once more spoke to Knox, icily cool.

"Well then, I see that my subjects must obey you and not me. They'll do what they want, and not what I command, and so I must be subject to them, and not they to me." Her irony was lost on Knox, who at once rejected the ridiculous accusation she inferred of disloyalty.

"God forbid that I would ever command any to obey me or give Scottish subjects the liberty to do what pleases them. I long for Princes and subjects to obey God. It is not a slight to you, Madame, to be subject to God. God craves for Kings to be foster-fathers to His Church, and Queens to be nurses to His people!" John Knox's features glowed with a love for God.

"Yes, but you do not belong to the Kirk that I will nourish. I will defend the Kirk of Rome, for I believe it is the true Kirk of God!"

"Your will is no reason for believing that, Madame. Neither does your opinion make the Roman harlot to be the true and immaculate spouse of Jesus Christ. Do not wonder that I call Rome a harlot, for it is polluted both in doctrine and way of life. Indeed, Majesty, I am ready to prove that the Church of the Jews which crucified Jesus was not so far degenerate from the ordinances that God gave by Moses and Aaron to his people, when they denied the Son of God, as the Church of Rome has declined. For more than five hundred years it has declined from the purity of religion that the Apostles taught!" A prophetic fire blazed from Knox in his incredible boldness.

"My conscience does not tell me so," responded Mary, paradoxically calm.

"Conscience, Madame, requires knowledge, and I fear that right knowledge you have none," Knox replied coolly.

"But I have both listened and read much!" Mary had indeed been a child of considerable academic brilliance in France, and had even recited a poem in Latin of her own composition before the King of France and his entire Court, when not even twelve years old." Why, I have penned letters in Latin to many great people, even my cousin, the English Queen, and the Cardinal of Lorraine, my uncle!" She resisted saying that in a moment of youthful zeal she had even penned a note to the great Protestant Reformer of Geneva, John Calvin, but had not posted it. In it she had prayed" May Christ, the Son of God, bring you back to the faith." It would of course have been in vain. Mary Stuart was also a child of the Renaissance, encouraged by Catherine de Medici, who was a patron of the Arts. Who, then, was this wild, unlettered, and fanatical man, to insult her, accusing her of ignorance?"

"Let me ask you then, did the Jews who crucified Christ Jesus, who read both the Law and the prophets, hear them interpreted the way they wanted? Have you heard anyone teach anything except what the Pope and the cardinals allow?"

"You interpret the Scriptures one way and they another. Whom shall I believe? Who shall be the judge?" Mary held her arms out in a gesture of frustration.

"You ought to believe God who speaks plainly through his word. The Holy Ghost is never obscure. What is obscure in one part of the Bible is explained by another. Your Church but affirms that the mass is God's institution and a sacrifice for the quick and the dead. We deny both points. The Protestant Church affirms that the mass is nothing but the invention of man! Christ died once for all."

"You are too hard for me to argue with, but if my teachers were here, they would answer you." Mary's hostility was now open.

"Madame, I wish to God that the most learned Papist in Europe was here to sustain your argument, and you could wait patiently to hear the matter reasoned out to the end. I don't doubt then that you would see the vanity of your religion."

"Well, then you may perhaps get that sooner than you believe," Mary answered enigmatically.

"So you say, but I refuse to believe it. How often the papists in this country and others have been invited to come to a Conference, and they refused, unless they were to be the judges!" Knox laughed, and this time it was his turn to be ironical." If you can ever prove to the contrary, I will confess that I have been deceived." His assured tone was unmistakable.

The Queen had the words in her mouth dashed away and with them her passionate anger, which had brought her near to tears, by a servant interrupting to say that dinner was served. Mary, whose frown sat ill on her graceful features, was like that of a child, who cannot get her own way. She was uncertain what to think, and signed to Knox that he was dismissed. Again she looked down from her imperious height on the Protestant minister, several inches shorter, in an attempt to lower the self confidence of this brazen clergyman, but in vain, for already John Knox's demeanour had changed to that of a humble subject no longer defending the truth of God.

"I pray to God that we may be blessed in God's Commonwealth, as much as Deborah was in Israel's." he spoke with a sincere, gentle, voice, but the Queen gave a scornful laugh, as if she doubted that sincerity, and swept out of the chamber, as Knox and the others bowed. The Reformer's exhortations had been in vain on the woman, indoctrinated in Rome's ways, who despised him as a heretic. Lord James followed her but gave Knox a pleading glance for he foresaw further tears and stormy scenes.

But John Knox prayed for strength to stand firm. A man of iron was needed by Scotland. Shortly after, his close friend, Glencairn, enquired anxiously of him in the ante chamber.

"Well, master, what is your conviction now of our youthful Queen?" Knox paused in meditation before replying.

"If she has not a proud mind and a crafty wit, as well as a hard heart against God and his truth, then my judgement fails me." But inwardly he had to confess there was a strange chemistry between this Queen and himself. She brought out negative feelings of personal rancour and pessimism in him that she might endanger all the great work he and the others had fought so hard to establish. He prayed fervently for wisdom.

In his lodgings in the Canongate, Randolph, the English Ambassador, sat writing to the chief minister of Elizabeth, William Cecil, Lord Burleigh, on vital information on the situation in Scotland.

"Master Knox spoke up on Tuesday last to the Queen, our Majesty's cousin. He knocked so hard upon her heart, I have heard he made her weep, but, as you know, my Lord, some women will cry in anger as much as grief. As your Honour has exhorted us to boldness, I can assure you that the voice of one man, this man John Knox, can in one hour put more life in us than five hundred trumpets blustering in our ears. As for Mary, Queen of Scots, I am convinced that whatever the policy of the best brains of France's leading men, and the deceit of all the subtle brains in Scotland, are all "fresh in this woman's mind, or she can bring it back with a wet finger." Randolph had been long enough in Scotland to grasp some of her witticisms. The Scots dialect rubbed off on all who came in contact with it, couthy, direct, and expressive, and Randolph enjoyed it. "This man Knox has no reserve or hidden nature. I am not always in agreement with his opinions, yet he is a man to be respected. Things have settled down in the Borders, where there has been so much reiving, theft, and raiding on both sides, with the appointment of James Stuart as Lord Lieutenant. I personally suspect it was an attempt to get rid of him by the Queen, since, though he is of the Queen's very blood as her half brother, he is firmly of the Protestant faith. Remember King Saul appointed David as Captain against the Philistines that he might be killed in battle. But, just as David was a hero, so has Lord James been in the Borders warfare, and men fear and obey him. Twenty eight members of one clan were executed at Jedburgh. Its wild country, but Lord James is a man of integrity, whom we can trust and count on in a crisis with France, your Honour. He has refused to be bribed to save the guilty. I understand from him that he has met our Lord Grey at Kelso, and agreement has been come to for good control on both sides of the Border. The Debatable Land will be debated no longer!" He hoped the inscrutable Lord Burleigh would not think him smart. He could easily be withdrawn from the ambassadorship.

"In closing," he continued writing," let me add that Mary, Queen of Scots, has had a dream. It was of horsemen surrounding the Palace of Holyrood, which made her very afraid. It may have been her female fantasy, but the result was that the Town Guard of Edinburgh has been put on the City Watch under the command of Lords, Robert Stuart of Holyrood House and John Stuart of Coldingham. Sentinels have been posted on pain of death to keep to their stations. I think it displays the extreme nervousness of our gracious Majesty's royal cousin, that despite her popular tour of Linlithgow, Stirling, St. John's Town of Perth, Dundee, and St. Andrews. These Scots go from one extreme to another, Lord Cecil, welcoming her with open arms, loading her with gifts in each town, despite their new Protestant allegiance. You should have seen the fawning pageantry here in Edinburgh, with the keys of the capital being delivered to the Queen by a pretty boy descending as if from a cloud. London and our great Queen would not have tolerated such buffoonery! Lord Bothwell is a dangerous man with a powerful retinue. Lord James Stuart is consumed with love for the Earl of Cassillis's sister. Who knows when these things might be of profit, my Lord?" The astute politician was shown in the Ambassador Randolph's last words to an infinitely more astute minister at the English Court in London.

Randolph sat back with a sigh of satisfaction. It was night time, and he gazed down on the Canongate from his wide oriel window to see late-night revellers wending their way home under the flickering lights cast by the occasional flambeaux fixed to the wall. Some of Edinburgh's citizens, he observed, rolled in their gait, some shambled, and still others slouched. Easily distinguishable were the quaint figures of the caddies, the artful, knowledgeable, barefooted, youths, who acted as guides to visiting merchants and travellers to find their Tavern or Inn, such as the famous Blue Blanket. Often they would carry the traveller's heavy baggage. The Ancient Order of Caddies of old Edinburgh was a unique order of street urchins, presided over by the Chief Caddie, whose knowledge of the labyrinth of lanes, vennels, closes, passes, and wynds was so detailed that they provided an indispensable source of information to visitors to the capital. Their payment was regulated by the Chief Caddie, and, if broken, the individual miscreant was held to strict account. The English Ambassador had heard numerous stories of these smart street urchins with amused admiration, and it occurred to him that if necessary, the letter he had just penned to Elizabeth's Court could have been entrusted faithfully to an Edinburgh caddie. Yes, she was an old and fascinating city, this Edinburgh, he thought. *The Blue Blanket*, he had learned, traditionally went back to Crusader times, when one of the banners of these soldiers of Christ was known as *The Blue Blanket*. Randolph would have been even more amused and intrigued if he had known that one day a game known as golf, already played on the Leith links, would employ people to cart their clubs round the course, who would be known as caddies.

No doubt the customers in the Inn would be playing at the cards at this hour, the backgammon and the dice, as well as in countless private homes. Randolph had always enjoyed backgammon, and felt like the relaxation after the concentration of the letter to Burleigh, who was a hard man to please, he thought. He would call on one of his English retinue. Things were not really that different in Scotland's capital from London and the south in general, though definitely colder. The wind fairly whistled off the North Sea and down the high Street. But, yes, they played at catch pully or tennis, football, golf, shooting at the butts with crossbow, longbow, and culverin, and, just like the English, annual horse races, with a silver ball or cup to the victor. Betting was just as prevalent. Dress among the well-to-do was much the same as south of the border, and in the Low Countries over the Channel. Randolph honestly considered that the ruffs round the neck were often overdone and gave the impression of what John the Baptist's head must have looked like on a platter. His job made his humour a tinge rough. Then of course the enormous farthingale frame, which the women used round their skirts, often seemed to him ridiculous.

Then, as he looked down on a drunken reveller staggering up the Canongate's slope, the Englishman was reminded of how for some peculiar reason every May Day these Scots celebrated the annual frolic known as Robin Hood and Little John. This was a medieval legend of at least four hundred years old, and yet strangely it was so ingrained in the Scots tradition and folk lore that hostile legislation could not even wipe it out. He laughed to himself, when he recalled how a few years before the Regent of Scotland had passed a statute forbidding the celebration, maybe because it was so English in its origins, he thought. But her efforts were in vain.

How ironic that what was a legend of an English folk hero should become a drunken orgy that the Scots populace clung to with such tenacity. All, who chose to, could take part, and the result was horseplay of the coarsest kind, which ended in pandemonium and riot and not a little inebriation. What a strange people these Scots were. Randolph had long ago concluded that the Robin Hood and Little John festivities were the equivalent of ancient Rome's Saturnalia to keep the people happy, bread and circuses. Ah, well, he knew human nature and its weaknesses and inconsistencies. He rang the bell for his servant, time for backgammon.

By December the young Queen, still in the first year of her reign and the honeymoon period, had returned from Fife and her favourite Castle of Lochleven. The sound of late night festivities emanating from Holyrood Palace reached up one night to the Canongate. Poisonous rumours spread that the dancing and merry-making was directly connected to the triumph of the French Catholic Court over the persecuted

French Protestant Huguenots and a terrible massacre of the town of Vassy. The gossip said that the Queen had received mails saying that her uncles, full of devilish hatred had again begun to stir their tails and victimise the poor Protestants of France. This had culminated in the massacre. Could it be that the loud ""hoochs" long after midnight were related to that wicked deed somehow? Fury seized John Knox, and the very next day he preached in St. Giles against Kings, the learned, and judges, who show ignorance, vanity, and a hatred of virtue.

Within a day a discreet knock came on his door, and when his man, Richard Bannatyne, answered, he brought news that a former student wished to pass on a message. It was to be pleasant and yet not so welcome surprise, when a young man of about thirty years old, fine bearing and demeanour, entered. It was his one-time scholar, Master Alexander Cockburn, eldest son of Alexander Cockburn, Laird of Ormiston

"Ah, young Cockburn, I scarce believe it! How long since I tutored you in the intricacies of Virgil?"

"Fifteen years, maybe more, good Master Knox." The diffident young man hesitantly replied.

"How fare you, though to my ageing eyes you are grown considerably and handsomely, but one must never judge externally?"

"I am at the Queen's Court to learn how to conduct myself in political administration and courtly politics. My Lord Moray has taken me under his wing". He looked down as he spoke, conscious of the negative response in the other, his former mentor.

"There is good and bad here, Master Ormiston, poison in the pot." Knox could not hide his frown or his disappointment. Had he tutored the youth for this?

"What kind of message do you bear?"

"Her Majesty wishes to have a conversation with you, Master?" Ormiston's embarrassment was obvious. As for Knox, he had never, and would never, seek an interview with this irascible young Queen, but always remained calm, though on the defensive. This would be his second confrontation with Mary, and no doubt it was to answer the outspoken sermon. It was not that she had heard his words, as she had refused to turn to the new thing that God was doing, in which He was cleansing the Church, and, therefore, she never came to hear him to preach in St. Giles.

"False rumours have been circulated that you spoke badly of the Queen. I ken the lying sources that have been spread them abroad."

"No matter, Alexander, be not concerned. They have deliberately chosen you because I am familiar and friendly to you. My enemies are clever." Would she be insolent or hysterical this time?" I shall attend Her Majesty shortly. God go with you, young Ormiston, Do not forget your roots."

"Never, Master Knox!" He never would.

When the preacher reached Holyrood this time, he was much less apprehensive than on the first occasion. Steel had moulded his character, and all that had been gained for the Reformation through pain was not going to be lost to the face of a beautiful woman. He found the Queen in her bedchamber this time, accompanied by Lord James Stuart, the Earl of Morton, Secretary Lethington, and some of her Guard. Lethington he suspected, in fact had been the means of distorting his sermon to the Queen. The Court Ladies, including the four Maries, and even the common servants, hung around in the background. There was a distinct lack of courtliness in the air, however, about her approach to her adversary, as she fixed her almond eyes on him coldly.

"I hear that you have spoken irreverently of me, John Knox, and have worked to bring the contempt and hatred of the common people upon me. It is reported to me that you have preached well beyond your text." Mary continued to harangue the Protestant preacher for a while, as he waited patiently for her to finish.

"Madame, this is often the just recompense which the Lord gives to the stubborn of this world. They are often compelled to hear the false reports of others. I do not doubt that it came to the ears of the proud Herod that our master Jesus Christ called him a fox, but they did not tell him how odious it was to murder an innocent when he beheaded John the Baptist to reward the dancing of a harlot's daughter. So those who have reported my words, because they want credit at Court, they have found a way to please your Majesty by flattery and lies." He fixed his gaze on her steadfastly, so that she would have no doubt of his sincerity." I ask your Majesty to hear me rehearse my message, as near as my memory will serve me." At an almost imperceptible nod of her head, he continued.

"After I had described the dignity which befits Kings and Queens, the honour God has placed in them, and the obedience that is owed to Kings as God's lieutenants. I asked what account shall most Princes make before the supreme judge, when murderers, and oppressors are praised by them, and the poor people of God in France are driven into exile and banishment. The throne ought to be a refuge for the oppressed innocent." While remaining as controlled as possible, there was fire now in Knox's voice and his broad cheeks were flushed. The Queen's own pale face became reddened also. The massacre in Vassy should be a matter of national repentance by any Christian nation.

Princes, it seems, are more exercised in fiddling and dancing than reading God's word. Fiddlers and flatterers are more precious in their eyes than men of wisdom and gravity." His eyes dwelt on the sly Maitland of Lethington, well named "*Michael Wylie*", for his thin, saturnine features displayed all the deviousness of the infamous Italian politician, Machiavelli. Maitland avoided his look and turned away guiltily. John Knox was in full flow and the North Sea would not have turned him back, but surprisingly was to be brought to a halt prematurely." As for dancing, though I find no praise of it in the Bible unless it's to the Lord, yet I do not completely condemn it, as long as two sins are avoided, first…that you do not neglect your principle vocation and, that you do not dance for the displeasure it gives to God's people." Astonishingly, the Queen seemed to drain of all her hostility, and appeared meek.

"Though your words are sharp enough, they are not as bad as I have been told. Stronger words were reported. If in future there is anything you take issue with me on, you should come to me personally and tell me, and I will hear you."

A few more words were uttered, before reasonably happy on both sides, she lightly dismissed him. He was unsure of this other side of a woman who would continue to challenge his opinion of her before their course was finally over. He must have given the impression of a confidence, for as he passed, a courtier loudly remarked to another.

"He's not afraid."

John Knox turned sharply but without rudeness in response.

"Why should the pleasant face of a gentlewoman make me afraid, when I have looked into the faces of many angry men, and not been?"

Perhaps it was as well that Mary had retired beyond earshot, or the preacher may have had to revise his opinion again. Mary, Queen of Scots, had many faces. If he was honest to himself, John Knox was both attracted and repelled by this young Queen. It was as if she was an exact shadow of his more turbulent self. A further experience of that conflicting emotion was to come soon, for he was summoned to Holyrood Palace again the following Tuesday. This time a lasting example of her turbulent character was provided, as the Queen refused to accommodate the Protestant Reformer and his new, revolutionary, beliefs. The young Lord Erskine of Dun was present in the chamber, a moderate and respectful nobleman.

"I am not master of myself, Madam, but must obey Him who commands me to speak plain and to flatter no flesh upon the face of the earth."

This bluntness was too much this time for Mary, who suddenly burst out into a howl of angry frustration and a great gush of tears which poured out like a pent up dam that had been broken. The mild natured Erskine tried to intervene with diplomatic words.

"Your Majesty, you have to mitigate your anger. For you have no need to be angry, for you have so much beauty, excellent manner of speech, great learning and skills in knitting and tapestry, I hear. Everything is in your favour, and I assure you, Majesty, that all the Princes of Europe would be glad to seek your favour, and your hand after the sad death of the Dauphine," Erskine stumblingly brought his eulogy to a close, for he saw from the thunder on Mary's countenance that he was merely casting oil on already flaming fire. Her colour mounted to almost the redness of her hair. In contrast Knox stood still, without any alteration in his countenance for a good while. At last he broke the silence.

"Madame, in God's presence I speak to you, I never delighted in the weeping of any of God's creatures. Indeed I can scarcely endure the tears of my own boys, whom I correct with my own hand." His thoughts drifted for a moment to the few occasions he had chastised Nathaniel and Eleazar with a stiff willow rod for wilfullness," Much less can I rejoice in your Majesty's weeping. But since I have offered you no just occasion to be offended, but have spoken the truth, as my calling requires of me, I must sustain, even if unwillingly, your Majesty's tears rather than dare to hurt my conscience, or betray the Commonwealth through my silence." But, despite his calming words, the Queen was even more offended.

"I command you to leave my chamber, and await my pleasure in the anteroom!"

Her tone was peremptory, irate, and condescending. The royal control had gone and Knox humbly withdrew.

The Lord of Dun remained with the Queen to be joined by John Stewart, Prior of Coldingham, the Queen's brother. John Knox remained outside patiently with the gorgeously apparelled ladies in waiting. He tried to engage them in spiritual conversation in vain. At last the Lord of Dun came out and asked Knox to depart to his own house until called for again. He never was summoned again to Holyrood Palace in her seven year reign.

The only other royal interview of significance with the prevaricating Queen was when Mary summoned him to her Castle on Loch Leven in Fife's bonnie corner. Here in the fifteenth century keep on the picturesque Loch belonging to the Douglases she had tried with a gentler persuasion to request his help in the troubled marriage of the Earl Argyle with one of her ladies in waiting, but really it was to get Knox to change his mind towards the tolerance of the Roman Catholic mass. When it was not successful in the latter in the dining room of Loch Leven Castle, though the man of Haddington agreed to lend his assistance in healing the marriage of the Earl and Duchess, the Queen the next day asked him attend her while hunting on the moor nearby with her favourite pet merlin. But Mary, Queen of Scots was no more successful in slackening his iron stand for doctrinal truth. To the end he would be a man of iron. But as he turned to ride back to Edinburgh, he never looked back and feared for the Queen's end.

A GREAT DEBATE IN KYLE

"The Abbot of Crossraguel, this Quinten Kennedy, has been a sore thorn in my flesh, just like that Ninian Winzet of Linlithgow! But I believe Kennedy is a real danger to the work of the Reformation in Scotland. His publication in defence of the Mass is a powerful and persuasive word to tickle men's ears and entice them back into falsehood. He is a man of smooth eloquence and determination, I have heard." John Knox revealed his thoughts and worries to his confidante, Lord James Stuart, whom he trusted implicitly." He has even issued a challenge that he is ready to defend his beliefs against all who would attack them. I cannot avoid this debate, my Lord, or I would not sleep easy."

"You do not need to answer him, brother John! You run the risk of ridicule, for Quinten Kennedy is an eloquent rogue indeed. The Reformation has already triumphed by the power of God, praise His name!" James Stuart was always one to avoid confrontation, if possible, to advocate discretion, and to remain in the half shadows of the back-ground, influencing the political scene from behind and using his position as half-brother to the Queen to moderate the relationship between her and the more fiery Knox.

"No, no, my Earl of Moray! I am already due to visit Kyle and Galloway, as well as Cunningham and Carrick this autumn. I have promised my Lord, the Earl of Glencairn, that I would see him again at Finlaystone, and preach for him, perhaps under the great yew tree, if the weather is suitable. Gilbert Kennedy of Dunure also desires my presence, though he's a dissembling rogue, but, if you ken his temper, he's a man better not to disappoint, though not to trust! Since Maybole is the rendezvous for our debate, what better too than to break our journey through Ayrshire at Dunure? Yes, I shall write to this Abbot Kennedy to make good his promise and dispute with me publicly. What an opportunity to make propaganda for our Protestant Faith. ! I would prefer St. John's Kirk of Ayr as our debating chamber, but needs be as needs be. I shall commend that we have forty supporters present on each side, that it may be known at the end throughout the country who is on the Lord's side! I am confident of success, for the Lord is faithful to those who are faithful to His Word." Moray was not so sure, as strange were the ways of men with men and their devising of truth." But I am concerned for the payment of our faithful ministers, who struggle to get by with the hundred and twenty pounds stipend. I am blessed with two hundred pounds Scots forby some of the favours from my merchant friends in the congregation, a barrel of Burgundy wine and freshly baked bread on occasions. They who preach the Gospel should live off the Gospel."

"I promise I shall speak to the Lords of the Congregation, Master John," The word of Moray was his bond, though Knox knew it would take more than that." But I advise you that you take a strong bodyguard with you to Maybole. The countryside around is still in a troubled state and rife with beggars and gypsy-types. You have already had attempts on your life."

"I have said that the Lord is with me, and He is a strong tower. What need I more?" Knox looked sharply at the Lord, irritated. He was ever the cautious one, while the Reformer never doubted his destiny. He was immortal till his task was done.

"Nevertheless, I shall arrange for a hundred spearmen and swordsmen to accompany you at least. You are no good to the cause dead, John." he soothed any ruffles in Knox's temper. The preacher knew better than to argue with this wise statesman, who had done so much to keep the Reformation ship on an even keel.

So it was that John Knox set out towards the end of September of fifteen sixty two from Edinburgh with almost one hundred and twenty men on a preaching tour of Kyle and Carrick, a land noted for its vigour and openness to change and radical thought. St. Conval, the Celtic saint, almost a thousand years before had brought the Good News to Cumnock and Ochiltree, and the Lollards of Kyle had stood for an early dawning of the Protestant truth. Abbot Quinten Kennedy, the Benedictine Commendator of Crossraguel Abbey at Maybole had by this time sent a message to Knox refusing to accept the town of Ayr as the rendezvous for the debate. Maybe, Knox surmised, he was wishing to avoid a disturbance as much as possible and feared too public a scene. Instead he had suggested the house of the Lord Provost of Maybole. John had no option but to accept. Now, moody and meditative as the weather, he rode through the rolling countryside with the trees brown with the autumnal sear, determined to deal with this audacious Roman prelate, who dared to challenge what the Lord was doing across Scotland. The man must be humbled in his pride. Never did Knox for a moment fear the humbling might be his own.

As his large party rode into the valley where the pretty town of Maybole nestled, he was conscious of the great concourse that had gathered on the outskirts, and on into town. Most were waving and cheering, but some were grinning, clearly looking forward to the entertainment of a theological debate, which would be great fun. This less than pleased the Reformer, for he came on a serious mission, but the coarse humour of the crowd was inevitable.

However, as he thought back, it had been a huge encouragement to stop off at Finlaystone House, overlooking the fine Clyde estuary and the mass of Dumbarton Castle on its volcanic plug. There again he had enjoyed great fellowship with the Laird of Finlaystone, whose militant Protestant spirit always invoked a kindred spirit in Knox. Well did he remember how Glencairn had roused the people and raised a strong force in the west country to face Sieur D'Oysel, the Governor, and his French forces threatening Perth with destruction and death.

The Earl had shown great tactical intelligence by avoiding crossing the Forth, where the French would have been prepared for him, and instead gone by way of Stirling and caught D'Oysel in the rear, which caused the Frenchman to seek terms, and thus saved Perth. Aye, Glencairn had been like a right arm, and Knox was grateful. But even more clearly he recalled the unorthodox means used by them of celebrating Communion at Finlaystone by their use of upturned candle-sticks, but of course he had taken the precaution they had not been used for any unsanctified purposes. It had appealed to Knox's grim sense of humour, and, he was sure, God's also. Aye, he needed such a Barnabas, for it was a lonely task to be in the forefront of such a spiritual revolution, overthrowing an authority established for hundreds of years. Like the point goose at the front of the v shaped skein, honking across the sky in autumn, it was a hard job, bearing the roughest of the winds and cold, and rain.

Although the authority of the Pope had been abolished by the Scots Parliament two years before and he had preached that memorable sermon in St. Giles to implement it, even yet the Reformation wasn't safe. Yes, it had been a good sermon, he admitted to himself. But, though the magistrates and baillies of Edinburgh were in a Protestant majority, the population of the city was not as yet Protestant. Also the Protestant leaders and nobility were not all of the same quality of metal, a lesson he was gradually finding out, he thought grimly. He complained of it bitterly to the Laird at Finlaystone.

"Our leaders are a motley collection of conservatives, trimmers, fellow-passengers, and self seekers too often! Many are of an unholy alloy mixed with the gold!"

"Aye, there are those in it for their own selfish motives, for possessions and position! It were ever so." If anything, Glencairn was a realist.

"Their greed for the Old Church's wealth has stifled my dream of an elementary schooling in every parish for even the children of the meanest peasant. When I described my vision, some of our gracious gentry told me I had a dream of my own fond imagination." Knox tried to remain without bitterness, but it was so hard.

"Aye, some of the nobility are no' worthy o' the peasantry," admitted Glencairn with honest candour," and certainly no' worthy of the Lord! As the Lord says, ill-gotten wealth brings no profit. Like gold rings in pig's snouts, so is a beautiful woman without good sense, and I fear that our Queen is such a woman. She has education aplenty, reads and writes in Latin like a Roman citizen, speaks Italian, Spanish, and apparently some Greek, and of course that womanish language, French, a' wi' a glib tongue! She can dance brawly tae, it is said," he added the last quickly in case his friend assumed for the slightest moment that he had attended her gay Court Balls, "sing her French ditties by Marot, play the lute, and is gracious and athletic. Is there any end to her talents? She is keen on the golf too. But beware of it, Master, for the Queen lacks common sense, and is the prisoner of her outward senses and desires." Cunningham was quite fierce in his warning, but Knox needed no admonition.

"Having been rescued from puddle of papistry, do you think that I am going to permit Mary Stuart to put all that we have gained in jeopardy, my Lord? I have told the Queen face to face that the Mass is more fearful to me than ten thousand armed enemies being landed in any part of the realm! I may not be of born of noble stock, only from the humble Sinclairs and Knoxes of Giffordsgate, but God has given me a forehead of brass and a pillar of iron to face up like a Jeremiah to Kings and Queens!" Knox's chin jutted out determinedly." Her Majesty accused me of rebellion. Rebellion is worse than witchcraft, and what is 'much waur than witchcraft? I am content to live under Her Grace as was Paul was to live under Nero. But your advice is timely, for our young Queen listens all too easily to the wrong advisers, like that master trimmer, Maitland of Lethington, whom the common people justly nick- named *Michael Wylie*. To think that it was I who responsible for his conversion to the Protestant Faith. God forbid that I was responsible for what he has become!"

"Some say she has deceived many by a her pretty face, that she is without wisdom, but she has combined the practised cunning of France with the subtlest brains of Scotland, At least that is the opinion of the Sassenach Ambassador, Randolph, he confided to me. As for that snake Lethington, Master George Buchanan, who is no fool but perhaps the greatest Latin scholar in all our land and perhaps all Europe, regards him as a creature who will change his coat at the slightest sign of danger. Maitland is never a man to be caught in a fixed position He has won the Queen's ear. But the true spirit of religion is lacking in Maitland. I heard it on excellent authority that he said in private blasphemously that God was a boggle of the nursery to scare simple children. Lethington is concerned only about expediency, and that is why the Queen had trusted him to use him as her Ambassador to her cousin, Elizabeth. She is playing a game close to her chest."

"Kings and Queens, in my view, have no fidelity further than what's to their advantage." Finlaystone was frankly much more in awe of the Reforming preacher.

"Ah, I'm happy to see that great yew tree there out in the lawns grounds, under whose wide canopy I preached in power!" The dark needles seemed to flicker in recognition, as they hung from their strangely dark, unnaturally-shaped, branches

"Aye, but the blessed tree is growing so muckle that it's causing so much shadow outside the drawing room, and my good wife has complained that she has problems in stitching and tapestry! She'll have me move it next!" He laughed half only in unbelief.

"The weakened Roman clergy have begun to come back in confidence and strength, and say they are willing to debate gladly with the main Protestant ministers. We must fight them blow for blow. This Quinten Kennedy has stepped forward as the champion of their tenets. If the Earl of Cassillis is his uncle, then he must be a right rascal!" He commented scornfully and almost spat in disgust." But he is a dangerous rogue, all the more as he has been roused to condemn the corruption of the Roman clergy and take up his theological weapons after some neglect. Aye, the Abbot of Crossraguel is a skillful opponent!"

"Not least when he says that the Scriptures are only a witness but the Church is the judge in every controversy. What arrogance and an affront to God's Word!"

Knox thought back to the many twistings and turnings which had at last brought about the famous debate. His colleague, John Willock in fact, had been preaching in the area of south Ayrshire near Maybole. Kennedy had challenged him to a debate on the substance of the Mass. The challenge was accepted, the venue fixed, but the Abbot refused to appear unless his opponent would agree to submit to the interpretation of the Bible given by the ancient doctors of the Church. It was clear to Knox, Willock, George Hay, and other ministers of the young Protestant church that this Quinten Kennedy was a shrewd tactician, who had made the Mass a great subject of his study as the keystone of the Popish arch. Knox was determined to down this enemy who had show such arrogance and discourtesy to his respected colleague, Willock. But much fencing continued to take place, how many witnesses and recorders there should be. There would be much jouking to do in this battle royal. George Hay had been sent from Edinburgh to preach in Carrick and Cunningham that autumn. Kennedy had offered to debate with him, but no meeting had taken place. In the middle of that summer the Abbot had read out in the chapel of Kirkoswald a number of articles in connection with the Mass,

Purgatory, praying to saints, and the use of images, and said that he would defend these teachings against any attackers. This to everyone was an open challenge, and would spread like wildfire in a tinder-dry forest through Ayrshire, Abbot Kennedy had promised to give a more full presentation of his views the following Sunday. By what some might say was a coincidence of the Holy Spirit, John Knox was on a preaching tour in that part of Ayrshire to strengthen the new-born faith. He had immediately determined to attend Kirkoswald Kirk on that day, and hear the Abbot and grant the disputation he had desired. When strangely enough, the Abbot had not appeared, it had been a deep disappointment to Knox. He had prepared prayerfully and studiously for what was a key to their triumph. But, instead he had marched boldly up to the empty pulpit and preached himself in Kirkoswald chapel.

What sort of man was this Kennedy of Crossraguel? He had proved to be an elusive and difficult opponent and had refused to be pinned down. Knox's frustration had increased, when, as he descended the pulpit stairs, having preached a vibrant message on one God and one mediator, a nervous messenger came up with a letter in his sweaty palm. It was of course from Kennedy to the effect that he had heard that the Protestant leader had come to that country especially to seek a disputation, and offered to meet him the following Sunday in any house in Maybole with no more than twenty persons allowed on each side as supporters. This man was deliberately provoking him, trying to upset his confidence. Knox asked God for a quiet and calm spirit, and returned a message that he had come not to dispute but to preach the Gospel. He was fully willing to meet Kennedy, but on the date given he had a previous engagement in Dumfries. He would fix a date as soon as was convenient.

By now Knox was becoming wearied of this fencing, and longed to come to grips with this man, who was as slippery as an eel. When he returned to the capital, after correspondence at last it was arranged for the twenty eighth of September in the house of the Provost of Maybole at eight o clock in the morning.

John Knox's thoughts returned at last to the dining room of Finlaystone House, and he ended the conversation with the fiery Glencairn, before they both said anything they regretted, and retired to bed early. It was a fair journey to Dunure. Forby, he knew the Bible's injunction to be angry and sin not, and let not the sun go down on one's wrath.

From Renfrewshire Knox and his retinue moved down the Ayrshire coast to stop off at the ancestral seat of the Kennedys of Cassillis, Dunure Castle, overlooking the fishing village grouped at the foot of the rocky outcrop. Lime was also mined and produced in a local kiln. Gilbert Kennedy, the 4th Earl of Cassillis, was an irascible character and dubious host, who bore neither fools nor rivals gladly. Essentially a self seeker and worldly man, Gilbert Kennedy was in the throes of a bitter quarrel over the very lands of Crossraguel.

He squinted from under his beetling brows at Knox, but avoiding his gaze, his already ruddy face redder from the roaring fire that blazed in the main hall of Dunure Castle. He greeted the large party from the other side of his drawbridge with a certain amount of caution.

"A' didnae ken that ye wid hae so mony men wi' ye, Maister Knox. Dunure'll be hard pressed tae pit up so muckle a group. The mair part o'ye maun bide doon in the village." Knox was not put out to hear again the broad, harsh, vowels of the Ayrshire dialect. He had honestly been relieved that when he returned for good from his years of Continental exile. , he had been easily able to regain his beloved Scots accent and dialect, which he had feared he had been in danger of losing. The over delicate French pronunciation and too guttural German had not suited him.

"It is nae trouble, my Lord Earl, for we shall not bide long. As ye ken, we have business in Maybole." The main body of horsemen was sent back to the tiny fishing village clustered below for what little accommodation it afforded. The remainder followed the surly Earl of Cassillis into Dunure Castle. It made them dizzy just to look down. As for Knox, such things did not affect him. As the wise man of Proverbs advocated, he kept his gaze always straight on the road ahead.

"Aye, I ken ye hae business wi' a relative o' mine, Abbot Kennedy, Commendator of St. Mary's Abbey of Crossraguel, a smooth rogue if ever there was, a Romish cleric too clever by far! There is nae love lost atween us, I tell ye! He is aye criticising me because I care for my own. Does the Guid Book no' say that, if ye dinna care for your rain, ye are worse than a pagan? I wish ye all success in your war o' words wi' Abbot Kennedy." Knox was not taken aback that Gilbert Kennedy already knew all the details of the coming debate, for news in the spiritual powder keg that was still Scotland, travelled faster than the swiftest corbie. Despite the abolition of the Papal authority in Scotland by the Reformation Parliament two years before, much had still to be done. John Knox was only too aware that many snipers were ready to expose him and the Reformation doctrines to ridicule, whether by Roman clerics, like Quinten Kennedy or Ninian Winzet, or some worldly courtiers, who despised his moral purity. He was wary of this man before him, for he suspected that the Earl of Cassillis was secretly a supporter of the Queen.

"We are but breaking our journey, for the Lord has need of a fresh vessel the morn, when we will arrange our debate at Provost Grey's house in Maybole town. I had argued strongly for St. John's Kirk in Ayr as being more suitable for refreshment for men and horses, but my Lord Abbot refused to be moved. If his stubbornness is to be a common characteristic of him, then the Lord alone knows how long the engagement will be."

"Ye maun be canny wi' my cousin, for he wisnae elected the Commendator of St. Mary's because of his stubbornness alone. Ye will hae to tickle him oot like the brawest fisherman, for Quinten Kennedy will dive doon tae the bottom like a sulking salmon. Mark my words!" One of Knox's bodyguards took note of this description, and found it so apt, when later on the real occasion it fitted the action of Knox 's opponent exactly." But a curse on that damned Stuart, who challenges my right to the lands of Crossraguel! If I had him in my power, I'd roast him alive on a spit, by God!"

Knox's eyes flashed, as he raged inwardly at the spite-filled nobleman's blasphemous tongue. He believed that in spite was such that, given the chance, Gilbert Kennedy would put his terrible threat into operation. By now he had been on the receiving end of hospitality, and dined on roast capon and pork, washed down by the abundance of claret and port available. Knox and his escort, who had been chosen for their sobriety, partook only of the wine what was sufficient for their bodily needs. The Earl's liberal reception did not give him immunity from a stern rebuke from the preacher.

"Do not blaspheme the Lord's Name, nor take it in vain, my Lord Cassillis! You use the weapons of this world! They have a habit of returning upon your head. Whatever dispute you have with this man Stuart must be taken before the law of the land, as spiritual disputes must before the Kirk! Do not have the pride, which takes the law into your own hands!" But, somehow, Knox had a prophetic vision that this man Gilbert

Kennedy would end up at the harsh end of the law.

"A thousand pardons, Master Knox. May I put my Castle Tower at your disposal in Maybole? The Black Vennel, where Provost Andra Gray dwells, is an awfu' hole, no' fit for a man of God such as yourself!" The man was at his cringing worst, and Knox could not abide him, but had to thole his ways.

"No need, my Lord, for all has been arranged to hold it in the house of Andrew Gray, Provost of the Collegiate Church in the Black Vennel. The subject will be our Lord's teaching on the Last Supper, and my heart's contention that the Mass is a blasphemous twisting of our Holy Communion."

"Be careful, Quinten Kennedy is, as I have told you, as slippery as an ell as well as secretive as a sulking salmon!" Knox was sick of this man trotting out the same things and of his very presence.

"Don't worry. I will insist, my Lord, that a record be kept of all of our words. I wish the nation to know publicly how false Romish doctrine is. The burning, pure, Word will smoke out all falsehood and give it that death blow! Crossraguel has won for the papists, where the debate should be. I shall insist on my right for the clerk to make a record." Gilbert Kennedy glanced across at his words, slit-eyed with the look of a worldly cynic.

"I'd rather be that one's dog than his friend, Master," commented one of his guard to Knox, as they retired.
"'Tis true," responded the preacher.

Next morning they left early, and none too soon for the Reformer, ill at ease with the Earl's spirit, and eager for the battle of words. Even now, in the crowded Mercat Square they were met by the elderly provost, Andrew Gray, and with him was a distinguished nobleman, clearly keen to meet the great preacher.

"Welcome to the capital of Carrick, Maister Knox!" Andrew Gray's accent was as broad as that of Cassillis." Maybole and the whole of Kyle and Carrick have about turned out to hear your words of wisdom. Like a fledgeling bairn, the Protestant faith has been weaned on the pure milk o' the Word, and we are langing tae lippen tae the man wha abune a' has gien it birth." Like all men descended from Adam, John Knox was subject to the weaknesses of the flesh, and for a moment his pride covered him with confusion, before his better nature reasserted itself.

"I thank you on behalf of the General Assembly and the whole Church of Scotland. I can but ask for wisdom from God, who gives liberally."

"May I present my Lord of Carrick, who is in winter residence in Maybole?"

John Knox dismounted and doffed his clerical cap as a mark of respect and courtesy. It was always in his nature to accord to men the respect due to their position, but without the slightest hint of servility. He alone feared God above, but like his Master must grown in favour with God and men.

"Let me assure you, Master Knox, that I have heard you preach in St. Giles and that my residence here coincides by a happy chance with your coming to Maybole, but if

I had been at the very Court of London itself, I would have brooked no delay in coming here for this momentous occasion." The Earl's voice was cultured and educated, clearly instilled at a seat of great learning. Knox liked him.

"My Lord has resided within England's borders?" Knox enquired respectfully, conscious of the Earl's authority within the region and the need to win all legitimate support for the coming confrontation.

"Indeed, good preacher, I studied at Oxford's hallowed halls, and wandered her cloisters, when the Lord sent Martin Bucer, Tremellius, Fagel, and other great Protestant theologians to us from Europe's shores, that we might have the benefit of their deep learning. I was later given to understand that you were there at the time?"

"Aye, my Lord, I had that rare privilege. For myself, I have a vision that one day Scotland will have a Grammar School in every parish and burgh, and will provide a race of scholars to confound even Europe's men of letters. This will be the work of God, who makes the faces of men to sharpen one another, as iron sharpens iron."

"May God strengthen your arm in this, for surely the gentry of this land will not." The tone of the Earl of Carrick was that of the realist rather than the cynic.

"I have found it even so already, my Lord. Shall we repair to our place of debate in the Provost's abode here?" Knox was eager for the fray.

"Certes, to the Black Vennel, Gray! The Abbot of Crossraguel may be there before us, which would not be fit." Knox preferred to ignore the touch of humour from the Earl.

But in fact Quinten Kennedy had already arrived with his followers and what seemed a whole cartload of books in tow. Knox was immediately struck by the calmness of his opponent, as he waited patiently amid the crowds who surged excitedly around. In a religious age this was a great event to break the humdrum of their existence. As he came close, he observed that the Abbot was about the same age as himself, but that his health was very frail. Lines of worry furrowed his brow and grey liberally streaked his hair, in contrast to that of Knox, which was still jet black in the main. However, it was obvious that Abbot Kennedy was a formidable opponent, for sagacity and learning gleamed from his mien. They both nodded to the other, each wary, like two wild creatures of nature circling one another.

"I wish, Abbot Kennedy, that all my company be present at our disputation and that a public record be made by my clerk of the proceedings." Knox tried to keep from sounding peremptory, but without success.

"Why do you bring so many people with you, if you are confident of truth? I agreed to only forty men present on each side." The Abbot was curt, and just barely hostile.

"None ever feared that truth be heard but those whom truth would accuse. I shall agree to that number, if you will agree that my clerk here makes a detailed report of our debate, and that I open with prayer." The Abbot blinked quickly, but as quickly he regained his steady poise.

"I object to your individual right to open in prayer. The Lord Almighty is transcendent, and only on the side of truth, and, therefore, his favour cannot be gained, even by prayer. As for the proceedings, I will accept that your scribe takes notes."

"If God's favour cannot be gained by us, you will not object then that I pray?" Knox knew that he had caught the Abbot in a trap, and Kennedy acquiesced.

"At eight o'clock of the morning each day then until we have resolved who speaks the truth? I observe that my Lord Abbot of the House of Cassillis has as many books with him as I have men."

"These are the works of the Early Church Fathers, Tertullian, Augustine, Chrysostom, Cyprian, and Origen, and bear the stamp of their authority." Knox felt the weight of his words, but would not let him off the hook. He knew intimately of the history of the North African Church of the fourth and fifth centuries.

"But did not Cyprian dispute against Stephen, the Bishop of Rome, supporting Bishop Cornelius against his rival, Novatian?"

"Bishop Cyprian's theology was centred on the unity and uniqueness of the universal Catholic Church, and told us that he no longer has God for his father, who does not have the Church for his mother." There was something of the cockerel in this Abbot in his crowing, and Knox was vexed, but he was sharp in his reply.

"Cyprian also said, Abbot, that there was no Bishop of Bishops, and that they equally possessed the Holy Spirit and are sovereign in their own Sees. Where does Ithat leave the Pope of Rome and his false and arrogant claims? But I am more concerned with the authority of God's Word." He felt they were getting off the main track. Knox, while being desirous of remaining courteous at all times, was determined to be as ruthless as possible in taking advantage of every opening." When the Church of Rome has become so corrupt since then, what chance has it of interpreting the Early Fathers correctly?" He saw the rage rise in Crossraguel.

"What chance has the Church," retorted Abbot Kennedy, glancing meaningly towards the Earl of Carrick," of remaining untainted, if the grasping nobility, as soon as they gain a benefice, if they have a brother or son, who can neither sing or speak properly, is immediately mounted on a mule with a side gown and round bonnet. It is a question then of whether he or the mule knows best how to perform the office!" Quinten Kennedy's tone was scathingly ironic, but John Knox could not but admire his boldness and honesty. Meanwhile, the Earl of Carrick hung his head in shame, for, while a man of integrity himself, he knew well the moral turpitude of many of his peers among the gentry, Gilbert Kennedy of Dunure notably. At times a child, whom one would not hardly trust with an apple, is given the responsibility of guiding five thousand souls to the gates of Heaven."

But before a full-blown argument could be begun, they all wisely retired to their quarters in Maybole, whose houses seemed to creak at the seams that night to accommodate the increased numbers. The Dark Vennel was darker than its narrow confines normally brought about at eight o'clock next morning of an autumn day, as folk crowded up its restricted way to the venue, which was soon filled with animated supporters. A nervous tension had made them chatter unnaturally and made the atmosphere fraught. Knox waited till the uproar of the excited audience had died down from slanging each other. It was like the sound of a hive of angry bees.

It had been a momentous year. At its beginning he had gone to Angus and the Mearns to preside in the vital election and admission of the excellent young Erskine of Dun as Superintendent of the region. With good reason the General Assembly had declared Erskine as apt and able to minister. For he had done much to advance the Reformation cause. Well did he remember the packed, eager, gatherings in the Forfarshire House of Dun to hang on his every word. At the start of the year he had also presided at the installment of John Spottiswoode as Superintendent of Lothian, good, trusted men. Aye, things had been going well, but then there was that dangerous Catholic uprising in Gordon country in the far north east by the arrogant Earl of Huntly, but, praise to God, it had been nipped smartly in the bud, and its leader received his deserts on the execution scaffold at Aberdeen. Yet no sooner was that ended than the equally dangerous Archbishop of St. Andrews was trying to rouse the Roman Catholics of the south, and the strong rumour had been passed on to him that the new Queen's avowed aim was to have the Catholic profession restored throughout the kingdom. The Popish clergy had gained renewed encouragement and come out of their burrows to begin to boast that they were ready to dispute openly with the Protestant ministers. The man who had stepped forward as their champion was right in front of him.

He started to pray aloud for the presence and supernatural wisdom of God into the situation. He had already prayed for these things in the spirit. When he had finished, there was a momentary silence.

"By my faith, that was well said!" admitted Quinten Kennedy, and Knox was impressed. Here was a worthy opponent.

"I am not here to defend points already determined by the lawful General Councils but I am ready to defend the sacrifice of the Mass." Kennedy went straight to the point, but Knox set to demolish its whole structure at once.

"We have to state clearly the subject in question, its name, form, and action, the opinion generally entertained of it, and the actor with the authority to do what he pretends to do. All these I am prepared to show in the Mass are destitute of any foundation in Scripture, and that the Mass is not a resacrifice of our beloved Lord Jesus Christ, who was once only sacrificed on the Cross." The Abbot looked perplexed by the barrage of legal language, the result of the expertise Knox had gained from his early days as a notary. Kennedy was aware of disputing on his opponent's ground, and not on his own. He must confuse the issue.

"I will dispute the truth of any man's Mass, yes, even if it was the pope's own Mass. I will maintain nothing but Jesus Christ's own Mass, according as I have set forth in my book." Kennedy spoke with a confident arrogance. But Knox saw the chance to pin him down. The Mass was no sacrifice, but a human concoction.

"I am delighted to hear you say that you will defend nothing but the Mass of Christ, for, if we adhere to nothing else, we are on the very point of Christian agreement, as I am ready to allow whatever can be shown to have been instituted by Christ. As to your Lordship's Book, I confess I have not read it, and I request that a definition be read to me from it." A murmur of approval buzzed round the hall from Knox's supporters. Whether any of them knew the subtler points entailed, Knox was doubtful, but they would be educated in true theology in the future.

"Let me qualify my assertion, and say that I mean to defend no other Mass except that in which its substance, institution, and effect is appointed by Christ at the Last Supper; the Mass is the sacrifice and oblation of the Lord's very body and blood offered by Him at the cross." Knox drew in his breath. This was his chance.

"For the very first confirmation of this in the Holy Scriptures, I rest upon the oblation of bread and wine by Melchisedek, the High priest of Salem. Christ is, as you know a priest after the Order of Melchisedek. Melchisedek offered bread and wine to God, as Christ offered his body and blood in the Last Supper, which is the only instance in which the priesthood of Christ and Melchisedek can agree."

John Knox was taken aback, for his opponent had dragged up a most obscure reference in the Old Testament in Genesis, as well as in the New Testament in the book of Hebrews which were the only references to the highly mysterious figure of Melchisedek in the whole of the Bible. For a moment he was caught off guard, and he saw triumph in the face of the other. Quickly he gathered his thoughts and replied. "The ceremonies of the Mass, the opinion that it procures the remission of sins of the quick and the dead, the belief that these ceremonies have a stronghold on the consciences of men, all these ought to be taken into the argument. No ceremony brings us the ear of God and the forgiveness of God!" Knox almost shouted, as he ended his vital point with a powerful rejoinder. Things were hotting up.

"Do you deny that the bread and wine, which Melchisedek, the King of Salem and Priest of the Most high God, offered to Abraham, were precursors of the elements of the Last Supper?" The crowd was swaying to and fro, shouting their approval or disapproval, and Kennedy of Crossraguel's supporters vociferously approved his point.

"But who was Melchisedek, King of Salem? Who knows? He was a figure of mystery, without father or mother, without descent, with no beginning of days or end of life. What human figure have you ever heard of like that?" Knox's men were loud in their backing.

"We are dealing, Master Knox, with what the bread and wine were, not who Melchisedek was!" Kennedy answered angrily." My definition of the Mass in its substance and effect is nothing else, but the real sacrifice of the blessed Lord's blood and body as offered in the Last Supper!"

"That is absolute lies! We cannot separate who Melchisedek was from what he did!" But he switched his attack." However, I propose to fix the sense in which the word sacrifice is used in the argument." The Reformer had the bit between his teeth and carried on with a vengeance." There are sacrifices for expiation, propitiation, and of thanksgiving, the *eucharistiae*. The discipline of the body, prayer, and almsgiving are called sacrifices in Scripture. I wish to know, therefore, whether Abbot, you understand the word in the first or second of these senses?" The Abbot was clearly trying to control his frustration, and raised his voice in reply.

"I will not dispute at present what you mean by a *sacrificium propriatorium!*"

Kennedy showed his competence in Latin was the equal in measure to that of Knox, though a neutral observer would have detected in both an equal academic pride rather unbecoming of God. But in that hall in Maybole neutrality was nowhere to be detected." But I hold the sacrifice on the cross to be the only sacrifice of redemption. The "so called sacrifice "of the Mass is the sacrifice of commemoration of the passion of Christ!" It was highly heated by now, and there were frequent "Oos" and" Aas" of triumph and scorn from the gallery.

"How can it be a sacrifice and a commemoration at the same time? Impossible! You have exposed your very contradictions! You have yielded the very point. I readily grant that there is a commemoration of Christ's death in the celebration of the Last Supper." Despite their noisy reception of the different arguments, there was a distinct restlessness among the audience, and both sets of supporters were frankly confused by all the terminology.

"I insist that you bring out the warrant you say you have from Scripture!"

"I deny that the Mass is a sacrifice for the sins of the quick and the dead!"

"You may deny what you please, but where I began, there will I end, to defend the Mass according to the article in my book." It was Knox's turn to be frustrated by this man, who indeed ducked and dived like a sulking salmon slipping beneath a riverbank. For a few minutes there was an irate altercation in which words were wildly thrown like jagged missiles, arms thrown out aggressively, fingers pointed critically, faces became red with self righteous indignation, and all Christ's love was forgotten. Finally peace was restored, when the Earl of Carrick came to the rescue with words of wisdom which moderated the two feuding clerics.

"Reverend gentlemen, we are assembled here to find the truth of God's Word, not to exchange verbal blows," he enjoined them. John Knox was ashamed of himself, that he had allowed unholy wrath to get the upper hand of him, and returned to the subject of the debate.

"Your Lordship's ground is that Melchisedek is a figure of Christ in that he offered to God bread and wine, that it behoved then our Lord Jesus Christ to offer his body and blood in these forms. I answer in reply to your ground that Melchisedek neither offered bread nor wine unto God, and therefore, you have no assurance for your point."

"Prove that!" retorted the Abbot.

"According to the rules of just reasoning, I cannot be bound to prove a negative. It is incumbent on you to bring forward some proof of your affirmation, concerning which the text is silent. Until you do this. , my Lord Abbot, it is sufficient for me simply to deny it."
"I am sticking to my text," Kennedy continued obstinately." I insist that you show for what purpose Melchisedek brought out the bread and wine then, if it was not to be offered unto God?"

Knox was losing his calm once more and becoming annoyed at this slippery theologian. Why should he have to explain such an obscure text and mysterious interpretation?

"I do know this, that today through our mighty Reformation our Protestant Church has made the elements available to all men and women, from nobleman to peasant, and in accordance with revealed Scripture the elements remain bread and wine, a commemoration feast."

"You are avoiding the question!" The Abbot was triumphant, resembling a dog with a rat, determined to hold on, strangling it to death.

"Och, if I have to state my opinion, I say they were intended by Melchisedek to refresh Abraham and his company."

The Abbot's face now positively gloated, for he had gained the point he sought, and he had a number of objections to this natural explanation, but, before he could enunciate them, Provost Grey brought an end to the day's proceedings. Much to the relief of all concerned, who were exhausted, especially the audience, who were looking forward to retiring to the Inns and Taverns for refreshments and to argue who was in the ascendant Knox knew he had been in a spiritual battle himself, and he prayed fervently that night for victory.

When the company convened the following morning, the Abbot immediately went for the exposed part of his argument that Knox had left.

"Master Knox, surely you will admit that Abraham and his company had a sufficiency of provisions in the spoil they had taken from the enemy in their recent victory against the pagan Kings, and did not need Melchisedek's bread and wine? Secondly it is highly improbable that one man, and he a King, should carry as much as would refresh three hundred and eighteen men!

"Surely a King would carry more than a hundred fold of that amount of food and clothes in his retinue. It was given as appreciation of his victory over the Kings of Elam, Goyim, Shinar, and Ellasar." He had refamiliarised himself overnight with the details of the story of how these Kings had defeated those of Sodom, Gomorrah, Admah, Zeboyim, and Bela, capturing Abraham's nephew, Lot, and all their flocks, herds, and provisions, Abraham had at once mustered his retainers, men born in his household, three hundred and eighteen of them, and pursued them as far as Dan, where they surrounded the enemy by night, attacked them, and chased them as far as Hobah, north of Damascus. Abraham was returning from his defeat of the confederacy, when the King of Sodom went out to meet him at the Vale of Shaven. Abraham had with him all the flocks and herds stolen, and his kinsman, Lot, and his animals. It was there that Melchisedek, priest of the most High God, and King of Salem, this shadowy figure, had brought forth bread and wine and blessed Abraham in the name of the God of Heaven and earth.

This God had delivered his enemies into Abraham's hands. In return Abraham had given him a tithe of all his booty. Then Abraham had shown his honest heart by giving back to the King of Sodom all the valuable possessions stolen by the four Kings, even to the last thread or latch, or shoe. It was all about the magnaminity of the father of faith, Knox thought frustratedly, not about this mysterious person, Melchisedek, and his bread and wine. He was chagrined that this fox of an Abbot had pulled this blindfold over his eyes, when he had really intended to pull down the mass and all its false teaching.

But he replied that it was not unusual that the physical needs of Abraham and his three hundred and eighteen men would be supplied after an exhausting hunt in pursuit of the enemy. Somehow the debate had begun to go stale. So the second day passed uneventfully. When they met on the third day, the Abbot presented a paper in which he stated another objection to Knox's view of the Genesis text. Again a fiery confrontation took place, and, if they had been young bulls in the arena, hot air would have been issuing from their nostrils, with loud snorting and a stamping of hooves. Knox asked again for the promised proof of his argument, so suddenly the Abbot arose and, crossing the hall with a dignified tread, handed him a small book.

"The proof is in that!" There was a concerted sigh of boredom from the audience. The whole disputation had become tedious and uninteresting. A big disappointment was felt on both sides that the excitement they had eagerly anticipated had not transpired, though initially it had everyone on their toes.

"If anyone were to bring bread and wine in to us, it is presumable that we will not hang around to debate long why they have been brought! I think we would go ahead and eat it!" "The Earl of Carrick whispered caustically to his neighbour.

"My retinue is complaining about the lack of entertainment here in Maybole also! Its time this debate was ended or we'll starve to death!

As if to fulfill his wish Knox proposed that they should adjourn to Ayr, and finish the debate. But the Abbot refused and said he would come to Edinburgh for it, provided the Queen gave her permission. Upon this unsatisfactory agreement, the whole company dismissed with much girning and greeting all around. John Knox returned to Edinburgh, an exhausted but a wiser man, better prepared to take on future opponents. Word had come that Ninian Winzet, a teacher at Linlithgow, had begun sniping at him. He sighed with much relief that when Abbot Quintin Kennedy circulated the report that he had won the dispute, the record of the proceedings had been kept faithfully by the notaries. If truth be told, neither man had won, but neither had God's Reformation been hindered, Knox was sure. But God's displeasure at the wickedness still abroad in Scotland was to be evident in the last week of January of the new year when a vast rainfall deluged the land, and a terrible cold which then froze the sodden earth, , so that it became one sheet of ice. Birds and fowls of all kinds, large and small, froze so much they could not fly. Many died, though some were taken pity on by people, who unfroze their feathers by the fire. It seemed as if the very sea stood still, and neither ebbed nor flowed for twenty four hours. Men observed in the heavens what they thought were two armies in battle, with spears and many weapons, riding on horseback. Truly the battle was in Heavenly places.

During this time Mary Queen of Scots had arranged banquet after banquet, trying to entice many of the nobles onto her side against John Knox, but, thanks to God, they had been impervious to her persuasions by food, drink, and merry making. The honeymoon period of the Queen was wearing thin.

THE BATTLE OF LANGSIDE

The next six years saw the slow demise of the young, Mary Queen of Scots, who had come that misty morning to Leith harbour from France with such high hopes, and the final setting of her sun. A combination of obstinacy not to hear God's voice through his servant, John Knox, and marriage to the wrong men had dragged her down. Henry Stuart, Lord Darnley, the Earl of Lennox, had been an incredibly foolish choice, a foppish, childish, jealous, man, who, when she showed merely a human affection for her Italian Secretary, David Rizzio, had become incensed. Some of the Lords of the Congregation had seen an ideal opportunity to recover a strong position before the Parliament of March, I565, when their lands might be confiscated to pay for the new Kirk's expenses and ministers.

In truth the new Protestant Church was identifying with the poor and common people of the land than the nobility and this was angering them. So these less than godly nobles made an ungodly pact with the insanely jealous Darnley to murder the favourite of Mary, Rizzio. Their wicked deed was enacted on an early March night in Holyrood Palace, while the Queen was giving a dinner for friends in a small room leading off from her suite. Darnley burst into the room together with Ruthven and other young bloods. They dragged the screaming Rizzio out of the room and stabbed him to death. Darnley had become full of hate for Mary, and perhaps hoped that she would miscarry at the shock of Rizzio's death, and even die, so that he could succeed to the throne alone of Scotland and claim the English throne. Things became so clouded with intrigue, jealousy, and unease in Scotland that John Knox. , aware that he had never liked the Italian incomer and upstart, took refuge in the north of England, since he could have been suspected as involved in the assassination. He saw all the great work unravelling, if God was not Sovereign, and brought a solution to the nationwide confusion. He stayed away for six months during this time of great strain for him, when his close relationship even with the equable James, Earl of Moray, had also become estranged. It was truly a time of great testing for Knox, but then he had found that nothing worth having ever came without testing.

Fortunately God causes even his enemies to follow His foreordained plan, and Mary showed great wiliness to bring the weak - willed Darnley back into her good graces. Rumour and counter rumour abounded about the relationship between Mary and Henry Stewart, Lord Darnley, but in July, 1566, Darnley's child was born to her. The latter began to behave in a psychotic way, perhaps fearful that the child would supercede his claim to the throne. A rumour even blew on the wind that he was plotting to take his wife's life. Scotland was now a cauldron of intrigue, far from John Knox's vision for a Reformation Scotland. Could things yet be saved?

In fact the immoral adventurer, Bothwell, the untrustworthy Maitland of Lethington, and the not much less trustworthy Lord Morton hatched a plot to assassinate the dangerous and now paranoid Darnley, who had actually been ill for some time with the pox. Mary had nursed him when they stayed in Glasgow, though she had lodged in the Provands Lordship, while he lay on a sickbed in a house also nearby the Cathedral of St. Mungo. Gossip said that Mary had already become fascinated by the dashing Bothwell, and written secret letters to him as her lover, kept in a silver casket, but they were never found.

Whatever her reason, whether to have him near her to care for him, or inveigle him into a deadly trap, Mary persuaded Darnley to leave his ancestral lands of Lennox and Crookston Castle, and come to Edinburgh with her. A plot had more chance of succeeding in Edinburgh, where his enemies resided. So it was that Lord Darnley was convalescing in the Balfour mansion at Kirk o'Field, just outside the walls of Edinburgh, less than a mile from Holyrood. Coincidentally, the house faced across the quadrangle to the town house of his rivals for power in the land, the ambitious Hamiltons who could have been involved, public opinion said. Mary stayed not in the same room, but in the one beneath Darnley.

She was conveniently away at the celebration of the marriage of her page, Bastian, at Holyrood Palace the night when a gunpowder explosion rocked the Kirk o' Field. The house was blown up but Darnley, given prior warning when he saw the soldiers out to do the deed, fled into the garden, but there was no escape, and he was strangled along with his servant there as he fled in his nightgown. The foolish young King's life had come to an end at twenty one years old. The public word was that the rascal Bothwell was guilty, though Mary's name was tainted, and her increasingly erratic behaviour played into the hands of her accusers, though there was no evidence.

The swashbuckling Bothwell in the centre of Edinburgh faced off his enemy, the Earl of Lennox, full of hatred at the murder of his son, and began to pay his court to the widowed Queen, who seemed defenceless against Bothwell's charms and bravado. At last a ceremony took place with the absent John Knox's colleague in charge, the minister of St. Giles, John Craig under threat of death from the dastardly James Hepburn, the fourth Earl of Bothwell, in which the latter married under a Protestant ceremony Mary, Queen of Scots, now a travesty of the young, confident, woman, who had arrived in Scotland six years before, Scotland was now in upheaval, for many of the nobles began to band against the ambitious Bothwell, and at Carberry Hill near Musselburgh the two forces came face to face. Mary refused to surrender but the battle was quick and decisive, and Bothwell fled like the opportunist he was to Orkney, and later exile and death in a Danish castle prison.

As for the once proud Queen, she was led in humiliation through the jeering streets of Edinburgh before a population, which once had cheered in admiration of her poise and beauty. Threats of even death were not far away. But she had been reprieved of that sentence and sent to imprisonment in her once favourite castle of Loch Leven.

To this turbulent scene then did the hero of this tale return from temporary exile south of the Border. It was time to come back to his land, even if it was to finish the work he had begun, and say his farewells. John Knox never did things by half. The period was violent, and unstable, and in the quicksand of changing loyalties, John Knox prayed for consistency and deeper trust in the God who did not change. Too many of the nobility seemed to change their opinion with the weather, drawn by power, possessions, or lucre. His one hope now, with the Queen discredited, was the tiny child at Stirling, destined to be King, a Protestant King.

It was at this point that news came that the Queen had escaped from the Castle of Loch Leven, and he groaned inwardly, and prayed for God's guidance and strength. When would this woman see the path of God?

Standing on the tiny island in the beautiful Loch, the Castle had at one time occupied most of the island, but the level of the Loch had been lowered. It had been a Royal castle since the days of Independence, when Wallace stormed it after capture by the English. In turn the English besieged the keep but was relieved by Sir John Comyn. It was visited by Robert the Bruce and held against the traitor, John Balliol. But two centuries before the castle had passed to the Douglases. But the atmosphere in the Castle was tense, for the mother of Sir William Douglas, Margaret Erskine, had been the mistress of Mary's father, King James V, to whom she had many illegitimate children. So Sir William's mother had always resented the presence of Mary on the throne of Scotland, when her own son, the Earl of Moray, could have been there instead. But one of the sons of Sir William present on the island, the young, handsome, George Douglas, fell in love with the still charming Queen, now a figure of tragedy, who was forced, it was said, to sign abdication papers presented to her by the Lords Ruthven, Melville, and Lindsay, who had been sent by Moray, in favour of her baby son, now under the Regency of Moray, her half brother. But few felt that a peaceful settlement had been reached, and so it proved.

Mary 's health improved, despite all the rumours filtering out of her island prison that she given birth to a daughter, who was smuggled over to France. Mary, previously bereft of hope it had seemed to her, began to think of escape, even though her conditions of incarceration had been made more comfortable by the arrival of some of her ladies in waiting, in particular her favourite, Mary Seton, and Lord Melville had taken pity on her by having velvets and wigs sent for from Edinburgh. She wrote secret letters which were smuggled ashore by George Douglas and another Douglas youth of about fifteen, wee Willie, who was also bewitched by Mary's charm. These letters were to her supporters, and they brought back encouraging news.

"The Hamiltons, Huntly, Eglinton, Cassillis, Rothes, and even the Earl of Argyle are on your side, Majesty!" burst out young Willie.

"And I have plans for your escape, which must succeed!" George Douglas added. It was difficult to know which of them was the more naive. Whatever, the winter, with all its risks not least in the crossing in bad weather, set in, and more depressing months in the island's cold isolation had to be endured.

During this time George Douglas left the island once too often on a trumped up excuse, and the Regent Moray's mother, Margaret Erskine, who had never ceased to watch Mary like a hawk, finally suspected the young man's sympathies, and sent word to her son in Edinburgh. Shortly a detachment of soldiers arrived at Lochleven with orders from the Regent to banish George Douglas from the island.

"The Regent, on the recommendation of Lady Douglas that you are in cahoots with that woman, at one time our Queen, has ordered you to be banished from Loch Leven," said the captain roughly. The handsome features of Douglas were a mixture of anger and disappointment.

"She is not that woman, but your rightful Queen, captain!" But the soldier dismissed him to collect his possessions. However, before he took the ferry, the former

Queen having heard the news, sent for the young man.

"I have deeply valued your loyalty to me, young man, and this I give to you as a token between us, so that as a sign that all is finally ready for my escape, you send it back to me." With that Mary brought out a glittering pearl from a pouch and gave it to George Douglas.

But young Willie continued to take messages back and forth unnoticed to gather support on the mainland for an uprising. As too young he was never suspected. However, the indefatigable George from afar came up with an ingenious plan for the Queen to dress as one of the laundry maids who crossed occasionally to the island, and escape on their boat. It almost succeeded. But just as it was nearing the shore of Fife, one of the boatmen noticed the long, white, fingers of the finger holding her muffler tight against the stiff, cold, breeze. Curious, he reached over and removed the muffler.

"Hold! It is the Queen! She is trying to escape by a subterfuge! Turn the boat back at once, otherwise we will be punished severely!" he ordered the other two.

Security was immediately tightened on Loch Leven Castle islet. But if ever Mary, the now deposed Queen of Scots, had two loyal friends, it was the young Douglas brothers. The day before the Queen's final escape, in keeping with the promise, a boatman arrived with Mary's pearl earring. His story was that before he left for France George Douglas had asked him to deliver the earring to one of Mary's maids. Mary of course knew that it was the long-awaited signal. Early in May young Willie, now back in his gullible father's good books, persuaded Sir William to allow May Day celebrations, at which much imbibing was common. Young Willie, now much more canny, appointed himself the Abbot of Unreason, who could make a slave of anyone for a day. So he got most people drunk. He then cleverly pegged down every boat but one.

Mary feigned sickness and secretly dressed as a servant girl. After Willie had picked up the castle keys from the dining table by dropping a napkin over them, they escaped together with Lady Jane Kennedy across the courtyard. He then locked the gate, threw the keys into the mouth of a nearby cannon, and they rowed ashore on the one loosed boat. There Mary was welcomed by Lord Seton, and of course her faithful George Douglas. With a party of horseman Mary rode to Niddry Castle in West Lothian, where she spent the night. Next stop would be Hamilton Palace, and its power base. So on the 2nd May, 1568, the stage was set for Mary's final fling and demise.

"Let us head for Dumbarton Castle, which is held by my faithful Lord Fleming for me! There we will be secure! It's impregnable!" Mary exclaimed to the Duke of Hamilton in Hamilton Palace, where she had marched from Fife, gathering men, until they possessed a powerful force of 6, 000 men.

"Let us avoid a confrontation with my half brother, the Earl of Moray. I have had too many confrontations in my life!" She thought back to innumerable occasions with Scottish nobility and individuals like John Knox. They had been disastrous for Mary, totally unable to handle them.

"You may have to face Moray, unless you keep to the south side of the Clyde, and Moray remains on the north bank. Keep clear of Glasgow, which has never been for your Majesty. We must march by way of Rutherglen, Crookston, and Paisley." The Duke of Hamilton advised her.

"These rascal MacFarlanes have opted to support your enemies and betrayed their past loyalty to the throne," complained the Duke of Argyle, conveniently forgetting that Knox would have said the same of a man, who earlier along with his father had so welcomed the Reformation at Castle Campbell. The fact that Argyle didn't look well, in no way excused his switch of allegiance. At least acknowledgement of who he considered his rightful monarch rather the raw pursuit of personal advantage motivated the sickly Argyle.

Meanwhile the Regent was holding a Court of Justice in Glasgow, eight miles away, when the news broke of the Queen's escape. Moray could scarcely believe it.

"I cannot believe it! The Queen was safely secured until we decided what to do with her," Moray was uncertain whether to believe the unwelcome news but two hours later it was confirmed. In truth Moray's heart was sad that it had come to this, as Mary was a blood relation after all. He would have been further disheartened, if he had carefully observed the effect of the news on some present. They fidgetted shiftily, looked around uncertainly, and refused to meet other's eyes, not least Lord Boyd, who had been in Moray's secret counsels. That night some slipped away silently, including Lord Boyd, and rode to join Mary at Hamilton.

Glasgow in the mid sixteenth century was a modest town of only around three or four thousand, clustered round the High Street leading down from the 12th century Cathedral of St. Mungo past the Cross by the Saltmarket to the slow, meandering river Clyde, only nineteen inches deep in most places, but the rich haunt of salmon. Fishing and weaving were the common occupation, but as a Cathedral town it had seen on the instigation of Bishop Turnbull the establishment of Britain's fourth oldest University, begun in 1451. It had started in the Chapterhouse of St. Mungo's Cathedral and moved to the Rotten Row and a building known as *The Auld Pedagogy*.

In fact just five years before in 1563 the Queen had given 13 acres of land belonging to the Black Friars on the High Street to the University in an act of generosity and foresight. But now things were different and generally the people of Glasgow had turned against her. Now the region then between Glasgow Cross, stretching from Glasgow Green, and the Barrowfield was known as the Burgh Muir or the Gallowmuir, so called from the common gallows which stood on the Glasgow Butts, the road which all criminals took to the place of execution. Here it was that the Regent Moray drew up his forces to oppose Mary. He had gained breathing space by pretending to listen to overtures of accommodation from Mary's party.

"We need time for me to gather assistance from my Earls of Glencairn, Montrose, Mar. and Monteith, Lords Semple, Hume, and Lindsay, and not least, William Kirkcaldy of Grange, whose military experience is vital! I shall put on a show of treating with Mary, to delay our confrontation, but truthfully there is no treating with her now! We must win or be subject to her rebellion!" For the Regent there was no drawing back." We will be hard pushed to match the numbers of her forces."

On the Burgh Muir he must have intercepted the Queens forces, had they marched by the north bank of the Clyde towards Dumbarton Castle. But Mary moved her army along the southside towards Renfrew. 'Meanwhile Moray gathered a force of about

4, 000 on the Gallowmuir, including 600 inhabitants of Glasgow, and about 300 MacFarlanes of Arrochar and Luss, who had become alienated from the former Queen of land favour. Their rough tartan plaids and Gaelic war cries of *Loch Sloy* mingled with the more sedate but no less warlike cavalry and dragoon infantry.

"There, Langside Hill!" said Moray, to Kirkcaldy of Grange, fingering his map eagerly." That is ideal for where we can intercept her men! There is a small weaving hamlet of Langside on the hill. We must arrive there first and take up positions." Kirkcaldy readily agreed, and immediately the Regent's cavalry was ordered to pass over the Clyde by a ford, of which there were many, as the river, which was to be Glasgow's future, twisted and turned in her wanderings from its source high in the Lanarkshire hills at Elvanfoot.

The whole army made a brave sight crossing, especially the infantry, many mounted behind dragoons, as they crossed the wooden bridge at the bottom of Stockwell Street. It was only a mile and a half south to Langside Hill and the infant King's troops must seize the advantageous position of the hill first. The vanguard of 200 infantry troops, each with a hagbutter, or musketeer, mounted behind him, got there first. They did this easily by way of Pathhead Farm on the hill above the tiny weavers village straggling down the slope of the *Lang Loan* to the marshy valley below, where it led onto the *Bush An' Aik Loan,* bordered by the free flowing River Cart. As expected by its name the rural road was bounded by thick bushes and oak trees. Kirkcaldy at once installed his musketeers in the gardens of the weaver's cottages on the Lang Loan, hidden from sight.

But they needn't have worried, for Mary's forces were delayed by the illness of the Earl of Argyle, one of her chief supporters. She finally arrived, with superior numbers at Clincart Hill. Mary herself withdrew to Court Knowe, a hillock, near to the 15th century Castle of the Cathcarts, which had passed to Lord Semple, who was conveniently absent, for he was of the Regent's party. This was the critical moment in Mary's life. Court Knowe held an excellent prospect of the battlefield about a mile distant, and the blue Kilpatrick Hills beyond. Her forces were drawn up on Clincart Hill, which was a much smaller eminence than the Lang Loan.

The sixteen light cannon which she had positioned on the hill made little impression on the Regent's forces and so with greater bravery than prudence they resolved to risk an engagement and, impatient of delay, the inexperienced infantry of the Queen rushed up the hill to the attack, commanded by Lord Hamilton. Hamilton attempted to force a passage through Langside by sheer force of numbers, but he was met by a fusillade of close fire, completely unexpected, from Grange's hagbutters, hidden in the gardens. Many of the front ranks were killed, throwing the remainder back on those following and adding to the general confusion. Hamilton pushed on, finally reaching the top of the hill, only to find the main enemy army drawn up in good order. Morton with his Border pikemen advanced to intercept Mary's vanguard.

Both sides now met, pike on pike, so that the forest of interlocked spears was so thick that if those behind threw their discharged pistols at the enemy the weapons simply rested on the shafts, as if on a carpet, rather than falling to the ground. Each soldier was encased in a suit of almost impregnable armour, which had led to this stale-mate. The spears stuck in the joints of the armour of the opposite ranks and they all became locked together. At this point they were not fighting but had become just a human barrier. Those behind threw rocks and other missiles over the heads of the front ranks but again just added to the barrier. The Queen's forces became unsteady, and threatened to retreat in panic.

But this was when Kirkcaldy of Grange came into his own. Moray had entrusted him with authority, and he acted with courage. He rode to every wing to encourage and help where the heat was greatest. The battle was now at its height and the outcome still in doubt, until Grange saw that the right wing of the Regent's army, consisting of the barons of Renfrewshire and their followers, was beginning to lose ground. He immediately galloped to the main battalion and brought reinforcements. This was done in such effectiveness and the counter attack pressed with such force, that it broke the enemy ranks. Moray, who had hitherto stood on the defensive, repulsing Mary's cavalry, now charged at the enemy's main battalion. The fight now joined all along the line.

The Queen's men crumbled, and at this point, the fierce three hundred MacFarlane Highlanders came charging in, uttering their Gaelic war cries and oaths, swinging their two handed swords to reinforce the victory, as panic set in amongst Mary's forces, who fled headlong. The fighting had begun at ten o clock and now barely three quarters of an hour later, it was all over. The Regent had given orders for mercy to be shown in the moment of victory and commanded a halt to the pursuit. Nearly 300 of the Royalists fell on the field, while 400 were made prisoners. Only one was known to have died on Moray's side.

"The blood of brothers taken by brothers has stained the soil! I will have no more of it!" exclaimed James Stuart, when prisoners were brought before him, most prominently the Duke of Hamilton, and other Hamiltons, including one James Hamilton of Bothwellhaugh.

"You are all to be pardoned, conditional on an oath of allegiance to King James VI. Master Knox has sent his plea for pardon also from Edinburgh. As the Psalmist said of Christ, mercy and truth have met together and kissed one another. We wish no enemies, but a united Scotland!" If the Regent could have seen the spite-filled eyes of Bothwellhaugh, he might have had second thoughts.

The Regent returned to Glasgow to publicly give thanks to God in Glasgow Cathedral for their victory, faithful to that God who had carried the country this far in tempestuous times. He gave a surprising grant to the Corporation of Bakers in Glasgow, who had particularly distinguished themselves when he bestowed the lands of Partick on them and the sole right of producing bread for Glasgow. This monopoly was to be held for hundreds of years by the mill on the banks of the Kelvin. As for the Clan MacFarlane, accused by some of murder, robbery, and pillage, but respected and feared by many across the Highlands, they were to receive their reward for their key influence at the vital point of the charge which turned Hamilton's men.

It was worthy of MacFarlane history, for this Gaelic Clan had already played its part in the Wars of Independence on Bruce's side, when they earned a fiercesome reputation for daring night time raids on the English, so that the full moon became known as" MacFarlane's Lantern." . Unfortunately Duncan, Laird of MacFarlane, had been killed at the Battle of Pinkie Cleuch against Henry VIII of England 20 years before. However, Andrew, his son, was more than up to the mark, and for their action at Langside he was given the three standards of the Queen's army which they had captured as trophies, and awarded with a heraldic clan crest of a figure upright holding a sheaf of arrows in his right hand and with the left pointing towards an imperial crown and the words of the motto," I'll Defend." For Mary was to be seen as rebelling against the Crown. It was another proud chapter in the history of the Clan MacFarlane.

As for that ill-fated Queen, she fled, panic stricken, with a small group, headed by Lord Herries, towards the Scots border, covering sixty miles, resting only briefly in the village of Terregles near Dumfries, until finally, exhausted, they reached Dundrennan Abbey. There at the Commendator's House of the 12 century Cistercian Abbey amongst its grey hard sandstone Gothic structure, she spent her last night in her Scotland, a country with which she had truly had a love-hate relationship. What could have been surely chased itself round her mind, as she contemplated her sad predicament. She would throw herself on the mercy of her cousin, Elisabeth, whom she had never met but almost felt she had. She knew there was rivalry, but that was only natural with sisterly Queens. As the next morning early in the tranquil setting of the tiny Port Mary beside the Abbey saw the small ferry set to take her across to Workington in Cumbria, Mary lamented to Lord Herries.

"How bitter is the cup that the chastening hand of God has brought me." Her voice was full of sadness." My name is the butt of calumny, my babe estranged. Every hope has gone here. I must throw myself on the mercy of my cousin, Elizabeth. Perhaps she will help me regain my rightful throne?" Her words seemed to disappear like empty echoes into the quiet air." If only my Francis had not died after only two years of our union!"

Herries hung his head in helpless misery, unable to answer, and even if he had, aware it made little difference. Mary stepped lightly into the skiff with her faithful Mary Seton, Joan Kennedy, and a few others, and in a moment was born the short distance across the Solway Firth to Workington, never to see Scotland again. There she stayed at Workington Hall before Elizabeth's soldiers quickly imprisoned Mary in Carlisle Castle. For the next nineteen years she was to be moved from Castle to Castle, a continual embarrassment and problem to the English Queen, as to what to do with her. At one point she seriously considered restoring her to the Scots throne with English help, but thought better of it.

A recalcitrant Roman Catholic on the throne of a now Protestant nation would set up more problems than it solved. But all the time Elizabeth was aware of the Roman Catholic threat and plottings in her own land against her life, not least through her intelligence service, headed by the deeply intelligent and highly informed Francis Walsingham, appointed by Secretary William Cecil, Lord Burleigh, who had been such a close correspondent with John Knox in the establishment of the Reformation settlement in Scotland. But for long Elizabeth was fearful of the consequences of convicting Mary of treason and sentencing her to death, especially, if, in revenge, Mary's son, James of Scotland, formed an alliance with France and Spain and invaded England. Also, how would Mary's execution affect the Divine Right of Kings and Queens in the eyes of the ordinary people? The question was massive.

But finally her hand was forced for her when after evidence was clear that the Scots Queen had foolishly allowed herself to be persuaded to be involved in at least three plots to overthrow her cousin, the last the Babbington Plot, no less than to assassinate Elizabeth. The old fatal weakness of Mary to listen to ill, false, and even evil council was once more her undoing. Elizabeth had indeed signed her death warrant, but entrusted it to her Privy Councillor, William Davison. But he was summoned by Lord

Burleigh without Elizabeth's knowledge to the Privy Council, which decided to carry out the sentence at once before Queen Elizabeth could change her mind. Mary had become a liability in truth that Elizabeth could no longer tolerate after the treacherous Babbington Plot. Mary was put on trial by forty noblemen. She denied the accusation.

"Look to your own conscience and remember that the theatre of the whole world is wider than the Kingdom of England. I have never been an English subject and thus cannot be convicted of treason."

But in fact she was convicted of treason and sentenced to beheading. When news of the execution reached Queen Elizabeth, she was extremely angry and her wrath directed against Davison, the secretary, who, she asserted, had disobeyed her instructions not to part with the warrant for Mary's death. Davison was arrested and thrown into the Tower, and, though later released after paying a heavy fine, his career was ruined.

At Fotheringay Castle in Northamptonshire on the 8thFebruary, 1587, the tragic scenario was enacted out and Mary was beheaded. As she disrobed before her execution she smiled faintly to her executioner.

"Never have I had such assistants to disrobe me, and never have I put off my clothes before such a company!" Blindfolded, Mary knelt before the block on the three foot high scaffold, which was draped in black. By tradition the executioner himself knelt before her and asked forgiveness.

"I forgive you with all my heart," Mary replied.

As she slowly made her way to the scaffold, it is said that her little dog was hiding among her skirts, unseen by the spectators since the layers of her dress were immense. The greying of her hair after nineteen harrowing years imprisoned was concealed by an auburn wig. It took the executioner three strikes to decapitate Mary and her wig came off as the executioner grasped it to complete the grisly task. The little dog refused to be parted from its dead owner and became covered n blood. It was finally taken away by her ladies in waiting and washed.

So died bravely, a Queen bereft of good fortune, it might seem, but who denied herself that good fortune by her mistaken choices on vital times of her turbulent life. But she went to her deserved reward. However, her death took place when she was no longer a major player in the stage of Scotland's theatre, and the major event, the Protestant Reformation had already been secured in its blessing from Almighty God, and its chief player, the man of rock and iron spirit, John Knox, had long gone to his deserved reward too. He was to be remembered by generations to come as the victor in the spiritual battle for Scotland's soul.

TREACHERY AND MURDER

A solitary rider picked his way carefully and surreptitiously through the outskirts of the town of Linlithgow, astride a powerful-looking steed. There was a fell purpose in every movement of his eyes and body, and even of his thoroughbred horse, a neutral observer would say. The horseman's intention was indeed one of death, and as he passed the magnificence of Linlithgow Palace, James Hamilton of Bothwellhaugh thought of how his namesake Sir James Hamilton of Finnart, the Royal Architect and Master of Works, had supervised the renovation of the Royal Palace as well as other Royal prides of King James V at Holyrood, Falkland, and Stirling.

The late King had been the greatest patron of Architecture of all the Stewarts and drew his ideas from the Renaissance opulence of the French Court. Finnart had added a magnificent and dramatic courtyard bounded by four ranges at each corner and in the middle had erected an elaborate Gothic fountain, which had ever after been known as the King's Fountain. As he glanced at it coldly as he rode past, Hamilton of Bothwellhaugh disdainfully recalled that the fountain had been a wedding gift from the King to his second wife, Mary of Guise.

What benefits had Royalty ever brought to the Hamiltons, who had done so much for them and sacrificed so many precious Hamilton lives? James Hamilton, Laird of Bothwellhaugh was a man of fierce and vindictive character. He thought back over two painful years to the scene following the disastrous defeat at the Battle of Langside, when the Hamiltons had given so much for the Stewart cause. Six of the prominent Hamiltons had been sentenced to die, he Bothwellhaugh amongst them, accused of treason. He almost spat as he recalled it in disgust, but feared it might draw unwanted attention to himself. Secrecy was the prime watchword in his present mission. He avoided the eyes of others as he approached Linlithgow.

A new entrance had been created by his namesake on the southside facing the town and on it the armorial carvings which beautifully decorated it. They were of the four Orders of Knighthood that the late King James V had belonged to, the Order of the Garter of England, the Thistle of Scotland, the Fleece of the Holy Roman Empire, and St. Michael of France. Ah, yes, the royalty of Scotland to which the Hamiltons had long attained, in the person of the Earl of Arran, but a curse would seem to have prevented them, and the power hunger of the Stewarts.

Bothwellhaugh cursed the Stewarts within himself as he quietly entered the town, intent on carrying out his ingeniously laid plan. His hatred for Knox, the fiery preacher who had inflamed the opposition to Mary, Queen of Scots and led the Protestant cause, was powerful, yet after all it had been Knox who had intervened with Moray to pardon himself and the five other Hamiltons from execution at Langside. But like others in his position, he was punished by the forfeiture of his property, although his life was spared. Now his wife had brought him as part of her dowry, the lands of Woodhouselee near Roslin, and these precious possessions had been taken and bestowed on one of the favourites.

This rascal had mercilessly take over Woodhouselee, when he was away, turning out Hamilton's wife from her own home, undressed and exposed to the fury of the winter elements. John Hamilton's face set in its own fury even now as he recalled how his beloved through this brutal treatment had become insane and died in his arms. He had vowed revenge, swift and deadly, not on the actual perpetrator of the deed, but on the Regent Moray whom he considered the original cause of it. To further stoke his bitterness, his family prejudice induced him to regard Moray as the usurper of the Sovereign power in Scotland and as the one most guilty of oppressing the House of Hamilton. Even a man of the Church had encouraged him in this desperate resolution. Bothwellhaugh would not go back now.

The Archbishop of St. Andrews could not be wrong. It must be the vengeance of the Lord. The fact that a jealous spirit was also at the back of his mind which he did not allow to impinge too much on his consciousness was deliberately subdued, but for too long had the Hamiltons been prevented from achieving their just deserts. For over thirty years the Earl of Arran, the family head, had been within grasping reach of the Crown again and again, but Arran's head had never had the ability.

He ignored the greeting of a local, as he headed for the house he was seeking. Before reaching the town proper he passed along the Linlithgow Loch and the Palace jutting out into it, and as he did so, James Hamilton could not but see the ideal opportunity to match his noble birth. The outstanding characteristic of the Hamilton family was irresolution. When the contradictory influences were placed on the inconsistent Earl of Arran, it was a well known saying that "whatever the English Lords decided he should do one day, the Abbot of Paisley, John Hamilton, Bothwellhaugh's namesake, the Governor's half brother and brains of the House, changes the next day." Hamilton of Bothwellhaugh would not be irresolute, he vowed, as he rode into Linlithgow town.

"Dae ye ken whither ye are ganging man?" A local enquired of the stranger, slouched low in the saddle of his impressive steed.

"Och aye, I ken well whaur I'm headin', an' it's any o' yer business! I can dae withoot yer speirin'!" The stranger growled and the townsman backed away with an annoyed frown.

The assassin with great deliberation headed for the back garden of a specially prearranged house in the centre of the town. It was not for nothing that it belonged to the Archbishop of St. Andrews. It was the last week of January, and the plant life was bare and in hibernation. He entered as if it was his own property, but taking great care that no one saw him. He even removed the lintel of the gateway entrance and led his thoroughbred into the garden where he tied it up securely, patting the animal to quieten it, all the time measuring the distance towards the gateway.

Only then did Bothwellhaugh take a key and enter the rear door of the house, which looked out onto the main street of Linlithgow. The house, which was empty, possessed in the front a wooden balcony overlooking the street from its second floor. Bothwellhaugh peeped out to ascertain the advantage of his position. He had to be well prepared. He then tiptoed back across the room, and, taking a black cloth from the saddlebag, he had carried he hung it on the wall of the apartment. His shadow would not now be seen from without. A mattress from the bedroom made an ideal cushion on the floor, so that the sound of his feet might not be heard from beneath. Things were not quite complete, and he took clothing from a cupboard, which he seemed to know would be there, and hung them on a line across the window as if washing. A last thing was to be done, and he crept surreptitiously down the stairs and went to the front door, where in a corner all prepared lay a pile of strong wooden boards, a bag of large nails, and a metal mallet.

Hamilton seized them and hammered the boards into place across the door, utilising all of the oakwood. He stood back and surveyed his work for a moment before, satisfied with its reinforcement, he slipped back upstairs. He had used the very minimum of noise in barricading the front door. Having prepared everything for the deadly deed and for his escape, he lay down on the mattress with a loaded carbine, shut up in his lonely chamber to await the arrival of his victim

Meanwhile the Earl of Moray was approaching the ancient Royal Burgh of Linlithgow, surrounded by his considerable retinue and armed guard, but, nevertheless, in some slight trepidation, for a friend had passed on a strong hint that he might incur danger in passing through Linlithgow, where he was known to have enemies. He had been advised even by his friend John Knox, to avoid it by going round on the outside of the town. But he was sure that the step recommended would give the appearance of timidity and decided to hold on his way through the crowded street.

Even now he was encouraged as he came closer and heard the shouting. Moray was widely honoured as a man of integrity in a fairly corrupt society of the nobility, who held out justice for all and so was popular among the common people. He wondered if he would still be as popular, if he succeeded in his designs to have the exiled Queen returned to Scotland to live out the rest of her natural life without any sinister attempts against her. She was still so young and he heaved a sigh, as he rode into Linlithgow town. If only his half- sister had listened to the right advisers, like Master Knox, and married the right men. But the reality was that Mary had made her own decisions; like all human beings, and that his own life had already been threatened by two assassins in the year of Langside, yet discovered in time. He breathed a prayer of gratitude. With a new confidence bolstered by the cheering crowd the Regent Moray rode through the packed main street of Linlithgow. It was as he passed, drawing level with the balcony where the would-be assassin was positioned in wait, that his steed was somewhat retarded by the number of spectators, Bothwellhaugh had time to take deliberate aim and fired his carabine.

The bullet's trajectory took it through the Regent's body and into that of the horse of a gentleman who rode on his right hand, killing it. Moray's attendants rushed furiously towards the door of the house, from which the shot had clearly issued. Had Bothwellhaugh's precautions not been taken so securely, they would have been able to easily force an entrance. But they battered on the reinforced door in vain with the butts of their muskets.

Meanwhile the assassin had slipped out through the backdoor, unencumbered by his weapon, and vaulted onto his patiently waiting steed. He escaped through the garden gate, bereft of its heavy lintel, at speed. But the Regent's guard had poured up a side wynd, though their mounts' hooves slipped on the steep cobbles, and with wild shouts went after the murderer of their beloved Regent. But Bothwellhaugh had not followed carefully from Glasgow to Stirling to Linlithgow and planned the operation so meticulously, only to be caught by a platoon of stupid troopers. Notwithstanding, they pursued so closely that he was almost taken. Then after spur and whip had both failed, Hamilton pricked his dagger into the sweating and wearied flank of his tiring thoroughbred, which inspired it to take a desperate leap over a dangerously wide chasm, which his pursuers' less courageous steeds refused.

"Take your good Regent to Hell with you!" he cried in victory and shouted in mocking scorn, turning to wave his clenched fist at his frustrated enemies. Vindictive to the end, Hamilton of Bothwellhaugh's triumph was complete. Though his future home was to be in exile in France, he cared not a whit. By now the life blood of James Stewart, Earl of Moray, was ebbing away fast. He had been carried to a nearby house, and laid on a bed. As his heart-broken friends stood around, the Regent's complexion could be seen to pale by the second.

"This is all the Hamilton's doing! This comes of over-lenient mercy towards our enemies!" One of them complained bitterly. Even as his body was dying, Moray was able to hear him. "Especially mercy towards murderers!"

"Nothing will ever make me repent of an act of clemency." His voice trembled like a frail leaf in the north wind's blast and then falteringly continued." I commend our young King Jamie to the care of the nobility of Scotland." Slowly he turned his neck and gazed silently, and almost accusingly at each of the high- born, all of the Reformed faith and of the highest repute, each with his own thoughts. Not a few vowed vengeance on the Archbishop of St. Andrews. Knox was heart-broken when he heard of the murder of his dear friend, who had always been like a brother to him, apart from their brief alienation.

Three years had passed, and the Protestant people still grieved over the premature death of their beloved Regent, though the Earl of Lennox had become Regent. Lennox, however, had showed no excessive thirst for vengeance. He had. He had endeavoured to procure a union of parties to produce domestic peace. But men's minds had become on both sides too much exasperated against each other. The Queen's party clung to the dream that Mary would someday return home and take her throne again.

Their flimsy hopes had been bolstered by the switch in allegiance of the great victor of Langside, William Kirkcaldy of Grange, so long the boast of the King's party. Allied to the man, whom John Knox, now failing in his once robust, health, feared most, the shrewd statesman, Maitland of Lethington, this gave renewed hope to them. As Governor of Edinburgh Castle, Kirkcaldy invigorated the absent Queen's adherents. It was another fortress that was to be the key to their future, a fortress that was one of the strongest places in the world, a rock rising almost perpendicular from the water to several hundred feet in craggy height. One night this vital key was unlocked.

The lonely cry of a redshank echoed eerily across the Firth of Clyde to be answered by the broken call of a solitary curlew standing in the mudflats opposite bordering the sand-bank that was to give its name to the tiny hamlet near its shore. It was a dark, windy, night and the lights of the log and turf fires glinted faintly from the small town of Dumbarton, little more than half a mile distant up the nearby river Leven. Only someone close up could have made out the rugged mass of Dumbarton Castle, as it loomed above to two hundred and forty three feet. If the armed men, who had gathered nervously beneath its steep cliffs, had been aware fully how high it was, some might have turned away in panic.

After all, this had been the historic capital of the Kingdom of Strathclyde and the Castle on the twin-peaked summit had been the abode of the Kings of Strathclyde and his British subjects, Dun Breatann, the Fortress of the Britons. Standing at the upper navigable reaches of the river Clyde, it was a key fortress controlling the River and sea traffic into the central Clyde valley and to Loch Lomond and the lands of the Lennox further north. If the ghosts of ancient Rome had been alive that night they would have told how, as the capital of the Roman Province of Valentia, the great Rock had its name changed from the old Brythonic title of Alcluith to Theodosia, named after the powerful, Roman soldier who had formed the Province, and then back again after the fall of the mighty Empire. But preparations were being made to capture this massive, near impregnable, Castle on the Rock, planned in Glasgow.

On an April afternoon just a year after the treacherous murder of Moray. John Cunningham, the Laird of Drumwhistle, a relative of John Knox's great ally in the Reformation fight, the Earl of Glencairn, and a Captain David Hume left Glasgow with an advance force of horsemen to intercept any who might be travelling in the direction of Dumbarton fourteen miles distant up the Clyde. They arrived before it was dark at Dumbuck. a hill about a mile away from the Castle, and were Joined by Captain Thomas Crawford of Jordanhill, a man of great determination and experience who had been appointed by the Earl of Lennox to be in command of the proposed attempt on Dumbarton Castle. He and Cunningham of Drumwhistle both held lands in the Lennox territory and both were hardened soldiers.

Crawford of Jordanhill, who was himself the son of the Laird of Kilbirnie in Ayrshire, that region so strong for the Protestant faith, had with him a Captain David Ramsay and a hundred men carrying rope ladders as well as their weapons. The commander had served as a soldier of the Scots Guard in France, but was later the servant of Lord Darnley and had given evidence after his master's murder in Edinburgh at Kirk o'Field, even accusing the clever Secretary of State, Maitland of Lethington, of complicity. He was therefore a bold Scotsman, who had already shown his mettle and was totally committed to avenging his master, and would imbue his men with that same determination. This was the only stronghold, apart from Edinburgh Castle, which still held out for the Queen, and it had to be taken.

Earlier that day as the mists were yet stealing into the hills, Captain Crawford had stood gazing northwards from Dumbuck towards Ben Lomond, the Beacon Hill of the Romans, and far beyond it, Ben Nevis, the Mountain of Heaven. He harangued his men with enthusiasm and urgency.

"All the signs are that tonight will be sic a one as the brave Earl of Lennox had o'er fifty years ago, a real, mirky, night, aye and moonless but starry, when he captured that muckle lump o' rock o'er there by burrowing under the North entry Gate, Noo is the time to seize the day!" He just stopped short of quoting Latin to his men, for he was an educated man. '. 'Have all the rope ladders been made ready?"

"Aye, Captain, a'thing is ready!" A rough soldier's voice answered." Let us gang forward an ' climb this great hump!" The others assented with a low growl.
"Not yet, my men! This is the man who will guide us. He is a former soldier of Dumbarton Castle." He indicated a man beside him, who had a distinctly surly look and that of a man with a grouse." His name is Robertson, and he knows the way across the

boggy ground between here and the Castle Rock." The reason he had defected was that Robertson's wife had been ignominiously whipped for an alleged theft by order of the Governor, Lord Fleming. This had inflamed the soldier, who had secretly slipped out of a postern gate in the Castle, and informed a kinsman of the Earl of Lennox that he was prepared to lead a party of soldiers up the rocks of the Castle by a route known only to him. John Cunningham of Drumwhistle had been wary of treachery. He did not wholly trust this man Robertson.

"We will offer you a reward, if the mission is successful. But in case you are decoying us into a trap," He had outfaced the man fiercely," we will take custody of your daughter and son-in-law as hostages."

"Why should I betray you?" Robertson had retorted." That arrogant Lord Fleming had my beloved wife flogged for something she didn't do! He has scavenged the countryside around here and despoiled the locals. He boasts that in his hands he holds the fetters of Scotland. Well, I shall break his fetters for him!" Robertson's demeanour was full of hate for Lord Fleming clearly, and could be trusted to that extent.

"We must wait till the darkness has fallen completely," Captain Crawford was speaking again, "and remember the place chosen is the Beak, the smaller of the two summits which ye see, but the steepest, for, think ye, it will be where less care is taken to have a regular guard. Ye ken that means a gey, dangerous, slippery, climb, but a rare chance o' success, in taking them unawares. If any o' ye are feart, ye may withdraw."

There was a silence and not a movement among the ranks for a moment. Then an aggressive rumbling was emitted, which brooked no doubt of their feelings.
"Never! Not when that Papist cleric and assassin, the Archbishop of St. Andrews is harboured within its walls!" It was an officer who waved his fist in anger. "He was responsible for the murder of our good Regent, a true and faithful Protestant!" The Archbishop of St. Andrews, who was involved in the assassination, had indeed sought refuge in Dumbarton Castle from the public's vengeance after Linlithgow.

"Aye, too true, Lieutenant Shields, for that accursed Rock has long been associated with traitors! Was it not Sir John Menteith, its Governor, who betrayed our great Scots patriot, Sir William Wallace, to the English, and held him in Dumbarton Castle there prisoner before the brave hero was carried south by stealth to Carlisle under cloak of darkness and a gruesome death?" Crawford omitted to admit to himself that they were using that same cloak to their own advantage.

"For too long his mighty sword has been kept in its custody! So the time is due for Dumbarton Castle Rock to be returned to loyal hands!" All eyes were fixed on the massive volcanic extrusion, with its twin tops, now dim in the falling darkness, and a grim determination was writ large on every countenance.

At last, when it was dead of night, the small force crept towards the Castle Rock, their swords and daggers bound tightly to their bodies, long rope ladders slung over shoulders. A few seabirds cried to their friends across the mudflats, but that was quite usual, for it was early spring and the weather had begun to get warmer. Lights could be seen on the side of the Rock, but it was a strange other kind of light that threatened to be their undoing. Their route lay across boggy ground with many ditches, but Robertson acted as guide, leading the way and the others following in single file, each coupled with a rope to the man in front. Suddenly some mysterious light sparking and dancing, sprang up as if from the marshland itself ahead of them, and for a moment the raiders became greatly alarmed, fearing they would be discovered, and wondered, their superstitious minds aroused at the phenomenon. The lights seemed to dance before them, as if enticing the soldiers deeper into the marsh. Then as suddenly as they had appeared, they vanished, only to spring up a moment later. Captain Thomas Crawford again took command of the situation.

"Don't be alarmed," he called out in as low a voice as necessary." It's only a will o' the wisp, or jack o' lantern, and is caused by the natural gas around here, nothing to worry about". Again he resisted mentioning the Latin phrase *ignis fatuus*, 'foolish fire', as it was called, brought about by the ignition of the methane gas or phosphorescence found in marshy terrain. The troopers ' fears were allayed for the present, but they became anxious when they reached a burn called Gruggie's Burn, which had been bridged by a tree trunk which had fallen down, or maybe been displaced from the bank. Their suspicions were aroused naturally.

"Dae the garrison ken we are comin' and have removed the tree, Captain?" asked Lieutenant Shields.

"Na, na, Lieutenant, see how the ground of the bank has fallen away and caused it, nae danger!" The Captain replied.

The tree-bridge was replaced and the advance to the Castle Rock continued cautiously. At its steep face all was quiet, and the guards seemed nonexistent. It was a precipitous face, broken up by numerous ledges. It was a difficult operation in the dark and called for a high degree of leadership. Robertson and an expert climber began to ascend the cliff by toe and handholds in the ledges filled with earth and grass. Round his neck the soldier held a rope ladder. At a high point they stopped at a ledge on which an ash tree had fixed its roots, and fastened the rope round its trunk. Then they let down the ladder, which spiralled down to the eager hands of those below. The grappling irons found a secure perch in the crevices of the rock.

At one point the ladders, however, had lost their hold on the sheer face, while soldiers were upon them. Panic set in for a second. A vigilant watch would have heard the noise below and the attempt been discovered and repelled. The attackers paused, their hearts in their mouths, but all was still. The other crisis which seemed insurmountable, occurred when suddenly one soldier took a seizure, which caused him to have a fit of shaking, and the whole rope ladder swung back and forth violently. A greater panic passed down the line. Captain Crawford showed himself worthy of command. With silent gestures he ordered the man to be forcibly controlled, tied to the ladder, and for the ladder itself to be reversed. This was done during which by good fortune the epileptic calmed down and was passive. A joint sigh of relief was released. , and the climb was carefully continued. .

The rampart at the top of the rock was reached about dawn, when a damp mist which had gathered, gave them an added advantage. It was all or nothing now. The rampart was easily climbed with the aid of a ladder by Captain Alexander Ramsay and two of his soldiers, Harry Wetherbourne and George Dundas, though the footing at the bottom of the wall was narrow, slippery, and dangerous. The lone sentry on duty vainly tried to fend them off by throwing large stones at them, before they silenced him, but ere he died his cries alerted the garrison. In fact many of them had been in Dumbarton town the night previous, whoring and carousing, so careless had they been. But as the alarm was raised, Captain Ramsay leapt from the rampart, shouting," A Darnley! A Darnley! God and the King!"

He was set upon by three soldiers but defended himself vigorously until the other two came to his aid. They disposed of the sentinels and by now more of the assault party was arriving over the wall, which soon collapsed because of its ruinous condition, and made it easy for the remainder. Ramsay and a group captured some of the Castle guns and turned them on the garrison stationed in the buildings known as the Wallace Tower, the White Tower, the Windy Hall, and the chamber between the crags.

"Fire! Fire! No mercy!" shouted Crawford, remembering Darnley's murder. But there was no resistance, and some of the garrison showed no heart for the fight, and along with Lord Fleming himself, helped by the misty conditions, escaped down a cleft in the cliff. Fleming, panic-stricken, slipped out of a postern gate of the nether bailey on the water side, and fortunately the river Clyde was at high tide, and a small fishing boat nearby was commandeered. The man who had boasted that he held in his hands the fetters of Scotland, made his cowardly way to refuge in Argyll and finally in France. Captain Crawford, who had deliberately taken up the rear as a precaution in case any had cold feet, though most were cold all over, if truth be told, gathered his men around him.
"My Lord Fleming has trusted too much in the security of his Castle to keep a good watch. Remember, don't harm Archbishop Hamilton! He must be untouched to face a higher justice!" Little did Crawford know that there was a deadly certainty in his words.

It was a simple and easy victory in overcoming the garrison, as the startled men rubbed the sleep from their eyes in the barracks. Only a few fought back and died before surrender was complete. The Archbishop of St. Andrews, John Hamilton, was an abject figure, but still with the spark of defiance, and along with him were captured Lady Fleming, John Fleming of Boghall, Verac, the French agent, who had the look of a pirate, and an unknown Englishman.

"Lady Fleming, your star has set and that of the rest of the Marians," 'Captain Crawford was gentle enough as he addressed her." I have to put you in custody, I'm afraid, but as for you, my Lord Archbishop, I have orders to conduct you to Stirling by the King's Parliament, where justice awaits you, and you will be put on trial for justice!" His eyes bored into those of the cleric, and the message was clear. His end was nigh, and it would not be pleasant. In fact within a few days Archbishop Hamilton was hung high on a tree outside Stirling in his full vestments. Blood lust was abroad and high again in Scotland, and grim humour was not far away. As the body hung swaying in the wind that swept the former Flanders Moss, it looked like unnatural fruit, and one of the bystanders composed some cruel lines of Latin Poetry. It was indeed gallows humour.

Vive diu, felix arbor
(Live long, fruitful tree)
Semperque vireto frondibus
(And always flourish in your foliage)
Ut nobis talia poma feras
(So that you may bear such fruit for us.)

All this time John Knox was in deep distress over the miserable condition into which Scotland had fallen. Moray's death had been as terrible a blow to him as any loss could be, apart from that of Marjorie. He had loved him dearly as a friend, and had more confidence in the Earl's piety than any of the Scottish nobility. One day he shared his heart concern with his faithful servant, Richard Bannatyne, whom he had taken on a few years before to be his helper in annotating his sermons, as his eyes were growing dim, and his hands less steady.

"What a loss we have had in the wicked murder of our blessed Regent, Richard! He found this realm in misery and confusion, and by his marvellous efforts, dispensing justice to all, peasant and Lord alike, he brought peace and quietness to this nation! God's image shone so clearly in the Earl of Moray that the devil and all the wicked, of whom he is the Prince, could not abide it! And so to punish us for our sins and ingratitude for not honouring this precious leader God has permitted Scotland to slide into this anarchy!" John was almost inconsolable for a moment, and his servant's mind went back to a few days previous when his master had preached Moray's funeral sermon to a packed congregation in the High Kirk of St. Giles just three weeks after the infamous deed in Linlithgow. Before the magistrates and ordinary citizens of Edinburgh, the gentlemen of the county, and the nobility of the nation, such as the Earls of Morton, Mar, Glencairn, and Cassillis, and Lords Glamis, Lindsay, and Ochiltree, Knox had thundered his ferocious anger from the pulpit. Tears, sighs, and sadness had filled the air of the great Presbyterian Cathedral, as they all remembered the great qualities, unselfishness, and sincere patriotism of a true Christian, who had put them in the shade. Death had killed their envy of the great man, and now they lamented him when he was gone. Before Moray was buried in grand solemnity in St. Anthony's Aisle of St. Giles John had preached the sermon.

"Blessed are they which die in the Lord, for their deeds shall follow them." The words still echoed in the ears and heart of Richard Bannatyne." God has allowed him to fall at the hands of cruel and traitorous murderers because of our sins!" His servant was brought back to the present speech, as his master was speaking again.

"Surely, master, the Regent was fully loved by yourself and many other worthy people?" He gazed in concern at this remarkable preacher of St. Giles, and was very anxious, for he saw how over the last year Knox's face had aged, with deep lines, his once long black locks had greyed considerably, his shoulders had stooped, and the former vigour in his steps had on occasions become a shuffle.

"Ah, Richard, you are too good for this world!" John glanced absently down from his upper room window of what was the former house of James Mossman, the goldsmith, into the capital's busy High Street below." For every one of these there are two of the former kind. When I think of the wicked note left in my pulpit by a villainous rascal for me to find, accusing the great Regent of trying to place the Crown upon his own head!" Knox's former fieriness had returned and Bannatyne was glad." He said that the dear Earl's ambition brought this end, what falsehood! I traced the lying missive to that rogue Thomas Maitland, brother of that other fox, Lethington. Judgement shall come swiftly from God on that man, and he then shall be without a friend in this world, ye ken." Knox spoke prophetically to himself, as if oblivious of his servant. The aura of the Spirit had come upon him.

"Och aye, I ken all right, Master John," replied Richard Bannatyne, thinking back in his mind's eye once more to that dramatic scene in St. Giles in front of 3, 000, when Knox had first entered the pulpit and been seen by the sharp-eyed to pick up a strange piece of paper left there. His face had changed, as if thunder and lightning had flitted momentarily over it, but he had made no reference to it in his sermon, until at the end he had stopped and gazed round the packed audience. , which held their breath. "There are people who rejoice in the murder even here." An intake of collective breath was clearly heard." Aye, one such person is even in this Church but that unknown wicked man, whoever he be, shall not go unpunished, and shall die where there shall be none to lament him!" The power of a Nathan the prophet was clearly upon him, and Thomas Maitland, the guilty party, shivered as he sheltered in the crowded rear aisle. He had taken the coward's way to leave the coward's message in an empty Cathedral.

Though he told his sister, when he returned home, that Knox was mad, the prophecy was fulfilled in faraway Italy, where Maitland died, lonely and bereft of friends. The spirit of the prophet is subject to the prophet. Bannatyne gazed in wonder at the man of God, in whom the gift was supernaturally manifested.

"Ah, you ken, Richard, I am no longer a young man; toil and anxiety have told heavily upon my strength, and now that Papal superstitions and tyranny have been legally abolished, and the Protestant religion established in this land, and our former sad Queen is no longer a threat to our hopes, I have thought of leaving Edinburgh and even Scotland, and retiring to Geneva, where I would meet my dear congregation again there." His grey eyes filled with longing." How at times I yearn for that time when I was their pastor. What contentment of heart was there in Geneva among my little flock! I would be happy to end my days there, a world away from this troubled and turbulent Scotland of mine!" He sighed, and added quickly in a worried tone," Dinna tell young Margaret any of this. She has enough tae worry her with our three bonnie bairns!"

The young girl bride, Margaret Stewart, daughter of Lord Ochiltree had, despite all the opposition, been a faithful and loving wife, and warmed his old bones, he had to admit gladly. He had indeed astonished both the Papists and the Protestants by his second marriage to so young a girl. He smiled grimly to himself, when he recalled how even the exiled Mary had stormed at the proposed marriage, when she heard that his choice was of the name and bloodline of the Royal Stewarts, and that as a relative her permission had not been asked, as the law of the land said. But, as usual, when he had decided upon a thing, John Knox went ahead and did it. The Lord had given him a wonderful wife in place of his beloved Marjorie. The Lord was good, always. Just then, as if to confirm this Scotland was still a riotous, uneasy, land, where fights might break out at any moment, a commotion was heard below in the High Street, coming up from the Canongait. A strange sight met their eyes at the window.

A group of people were carrying what was a black banner up the street, followed by a fiercely excited mob. But what was on the banner was extraordinary and awoke conflicting emotions in John Knox and his man, Bannatyne, disgust and fear, even if his darker side was drawn to what was depicted. Painted on the cloth was a depiction of the murdered Regent lying dead on his bed and beside it the late King, Henry Stewart, Lord Darnley, lying under a tree in the garden of Kirk o'Field, where he had been found strangled in his nightclothes after the house had been exploded, and finally in this grotesque display at Moray's feet was the little Prince, King James in waiting, kneeling, praying to God to avenge the murders of both. John tried to pull his eyes away from the caricature, but couldn't. The eye affects the heart. His spiritual being revolted. The Edinburgh mob was certainly making great propaganda of it, and was yelling wildly. Revenge and bloodlust was in the air, but for what, he was at a loss. Archbishop Hamilton had already been cruelly hung for the Regent's murder, Bothwell had been driven into exile, and Mary imprisoned in England. What villain had composed this evil banner?

"Vengeance! Vengeance!" The chanting grew great.

"Is this what the Reformation from God was for, Bannatyne? Be sure that black banner will widen the breach between the factions." His voice was filled with horror. "Aye, Master, nae doot it will."

They were both relieved when the unpleasant exhibition had moved further up the High Street. John Knox sank into a chair wearied from strain. For sure the wild procession would receive short shrift from Kirkcaldy of Grange, if it went too near the Castle of Edinburgh, and a cannonball or two would be sent in their direction for their trouble. The defection of Kirkcaldy was a deep sorrow to him, for he had loved him for his past services to the Reformation, and, although he now held Edinburgh Castle against the King, John Knox did not lose confidence in him as one to whom the cause of Christ was dear. Why had the victor at Langside's brave battle changed his allegiance to support the Marian cause? There was no accounting for human nature to support its variations in beliefs and changes in opinions. His mind's eyes went back to the time in the French galley, The Notre Dame, and his companion in pain, James Balfour, then a faithful servant of the Reformation cause, but now an exile wanted for the murder of the same Lord Darnley. Some said that Balfour was in Sweden. Truly the Scripture was right, the heart of man was deceitful above all things and desperately wicked, who could know it?

He and Kirkcaldy of Grange had quarrelled openly, and a wicked rumour had been spread abroad that he was Knox's sworn enemy and had vowed to kill him. Kirkcaldy had vehemently denied it in messages from the Castle, where he governed in contempt of all attempts to capture it and regularly threatened the City with cannonades, but Knox had continued to preach in St. Giles. His friends had insisted on a guard round his home at night, and even to accompany him abroad, though John had protested to them that it was not necessary, not that he went out much now, so broken-down he felt, and almost only to the Sunday Service, not even to the Kirk Sessions.

"My life is in the hands of Him, who has up to now preserved it, and in Him I still place my trust. Isaiah and Jeremiah have taught me to call wickedness by its own terms, a fig a fig and a spade a spade. As for not praying for the deposed Queen, she is not my Sovereign, neither am I bound to pray for her here." These bold feelings he expressed to Lord Glencairn, his faithful friend who had gone through so much for the Protestant cause to see the faith established throughout the land, and always been a bulwark to rely on, when things were tough.

"Aye, aye, nevertheless, John, you ken the treacherous spite of your enemies, and the Queen's party sees you as their chief obstacle to their returning to power. It's amazing that their threat has not gone; they are like a Hydra that needs to have another of its heads cut off!" Glencairn snorted in frustrated annoyance. Knox accepted his advice.

"Let us go out for a wee breath of the caller air, Richard," John said to his servant suddenly." Let me lean on your shoulder once again, my man, and I shall need my sturdy stick, for I feel like a broken-doon horse. Later I wish tae write in my study below for the rest of the evening. Is the oil lamp wick freshly cut and a goodly supply of oil provided?"

"All is ready with a plentiful supply of good oil, master John."

"Guid, as long as the folk o' Edinburgh don't call me the Olivetan like dear brother Calvin's cousin, for using too muckle midnight oil in his studies," he laughed dryly.

"Pit your warmer overcoat on, master. It may be April, but the winds are still brisk doon the High Street." The preacher grunted in reply, not admitting really to himself that his bones felt a little decrepit. Taking his stick and pushing his flat felt cap over his grizzled locks, he allowed Bannatyne to support one arm. He hoped that not many citizens would trouble them, enquiring after his health, or asking some thorny theological question. Why were folk aye speirin', and not minding their own business? They should ask God's opinion.

Fortunately, it was quieter with the departure of the evil procession, and their walk was uninterrupted. They trudged back up the Canongait, for the preacher was wary of trusting himself to the steep vennels. Back home he partook of a light repaste and settled down in his ground floor study to pen some important thoughts. For some inexplicable reason he felt led not to sit in his usual corner, but moved his writing desk to another corner. He thought it might have been because it was a warmer neuk. Ail was silent and the soft lamp light was soothing as his quill scratched away. He must vindicate himself against false accusations.

"My accusers have said that I said that their Sovereign Mary, though she is not mine, is a reprobate and cannot ever repent. This I deny wholeheartedly. I am not within God's secret counsel, I will confess. But one thing I will not omit to deny, that is that I have ever sought support against my native land of Scotland. What I have been to my country, albeit this unthankful age will not know, yet the ages to come will be compelled to bear witness to the truth." So he continued, his quill pen's scratching alone breaking the silence.

"And at the end I will require that all men who have anything to say against me, that they say it plainly, in the same way as I make myself and all that I do open to the world, for I am an open book. It seems a most unreasonable thing that I should be compelled in my decrepit old age, to fight against shadows and howlets that dare not bear the light."

He had just finished, and sat back with a sigh when a slight sound disturbed him from a window. In a flash literally a musket ball flew across his chamber and smashed into the roof of the corner where he normally sat, lodging there. It had come from a street level window. Smoke filled the room, and a scuttling like frightened rats was heard outside. Unafraid and filled with gratitude, John Knox lowered his head and raised his hands in praise to his Lord and Protector.

God's omnipotence and omniscience had indirectly warned his servant of the imminent danger. By now Bannatyne had rushed down from his bedroom in great trepidation, and some of the guard from without had entered in shame-faced alarm. How had it been possible for a potential assassin to escape their notice? None would admit that they had been sleeping. Knox refused to blame anyone. The guilty party had escaped down one of the many closes and vennels that cross-crossed old Edinburgh. The preacher insisted on retiring early, for he wished to spend time alone with his God.

But next morning sharp a deputation came to Knox's house, led by Lords Glencairn, Ivlar, Morton, and Cassillis, clearly troubled.

"We are concerned for your life, good preacher Knox and feel strongly that you should vacate Edinburgh for a period and take up safe residence in St. Andrews, at least until things have settled down or the Castle is captured." It was the Earl of Mar, who spoke hesitantly, a man of fair and moderate views. He knew that the man of Haddington could be intractable and obstinate at times. He searched the preacher's eyes for signs of agreement, and searched in vain.

"Aye, when we heard of the cowardly attempt on your life, we were all incensed!" It was the fiery Earl of Glencairn breaking in.

"Whatever they plot against the Lord, He will bring to an end; trouble will not come a second time, the prophet Nahum promises us. I refuse to leave my Edinburgh house!" retorted Knox." My enemies wish to intimidate me into flight! They can then carry on their traitorous designs to restore the Queen, and to accuse me of cowardice! They will have to carry me bound or a corpse from my beloved Edinburgh!" His old eyes sparked again.

"Never, master John!" replied Mar." Who could ever with a grain of honesty accuse you of that?"

"I tell you again, I will not surrender to them and leave Edinburgh!"

So it continued while they pleaded unsuccessfully with him. At length they departed but returned after consultation with an air of determination about them.

"We are determined to defend you, if attacked, at the peril of our lives, and if blood is shed in the quarrel, which is highly probable, we will leave it on your head alone." Morton spoke, the great leader of the English party in Scotland, who secretly cared nothing for friends, religion, and even his country itself, as long as he acquired power. Though he put on an outward show, selfish considerations had moulded the Earl of Morton, and he was not a true Protestant. He knew exactly how to play on people's weaknesses, and used it now on John Knox, who hated to be the means of anyone's death.

"It's true, my dearest friend and brother. and if you are dead, where is our leadership under God?" broke in Glencairn quickly, for he did not like Morton." And Scotland is on the verge of civil war once more, only this time it's Scot against Scot, with the French gone. Even children are fighting one another, bairns stoning other bairns! Kirkcaldy has sent a force in a daring lightning raid to capture the garrison of Stirling! The rascal is getting above his boots. We must not lose all we have gained, and if you die, we shall lose it!"

John Knox's defences were down, and he knew that he was beaten, and that he would have to leave for a while. Anyway, it was to the Kingdom of Fife where Malcolm Canmore and other Kings once ruled, and his own spiritual home, that he went.
"I will go to St. Andrews, but sorely against my will, gentlemen," He said shortly, and quickly turned away from them to go to prayer. The Lords knew the interview was ended.

SCOTLAND SET FAIR...AND FAREWELL

A s he walked down South Street, in a spiritual reverie, John thought of how the full import of what he had done with the power of the living God and the indispensable help of faithful friends. A fundamental choice had been made to reject the old Church, which had become not the Church, and was, therefore, a false Church. How much they had added to the simple Gospel of salvation by faith alone in Christ, the false intermediaries of the pope, priests, prayers to saints, whether dead or alive, purgatory, the imagined transubstantiation, private confession to man rather than God alone, the sad misrepresentation of Mary, the chosen vessel of God to bear the blessed Saviour. All of it obscured the simple truth of direct access to the loving Father in Heaven, who had sent the son to complete the work of the redemption of a sinful, fallen creation

He silently admitted that brother Calvin had made things easier, for he had in dear Geneva evolved the idea of an elect. God knew His own, and he needed not to make an official break from falsehood, for it never had the allegiance of true believers in the blessed Saviour. The pope of Rome was an imposter who opposed the truth of one mediator, and was, therefore, in place of Christ, anti-Christ. Where had Peter ever made such claims, and where was the evidence that the fisherman and apostle had ever been in Rome, whereas he in fact had been the apostle to the Jews, and Paul to the Gentiles? Anyone surely who had nothing to gain and unbiased understanding of Scripture must recognise so? God had made him a preacher, prophet, and pastor with a theological bent for a purpose, no man who had a tendency to lightheartedness, chitter chatter, about domestic affairs. He had depended on others, wealthy patrons, who afforded him hospitality, and he cared little what he ate and what he wore, as long as it was sufficient, but political affairs, where they impinged on the religious situation, now that was different.

News was coming in from Lord Burleigh, William Cecil, his trustworthy link to Queen Elizabeth about the condition of the exiled, Mary, imprisoned in Fotheringay Castle. Knox was convinced Mary was still a great danger, and recent news had proved it to the hilt. The Ridolfi Plot was as treacherous and insidious as a hidden snake in your bosom. Roberto Ridolfi, an Italian banker from Florence, and fanatical Romanist, had for long been plotting to raise a rebellion of the Roman Catholic nobles in northern England to throw Elizabeth off the throne. But when it failed from lack of popular support, Ridolfi realised that only foreign intervention could restore Catholicism and put the deposed Scots Queen Mary on the throne. The Italian began to clandestinely contact potential conspirators with the nerve and ruthless intention to carry it out.

The Bible had truly said that rebellion was worse than witchcraft. These evil plotters included Mary's adviser and confessor, as she was still following the Roman religion, which had done her no good but much evil, though the obstinate Queen refused to see it. This adviser was a Scot, Bishop of Ross, John Lesley, who saw it as the only resort to free Mary, and so gave his assent to the deadly plan, which included a plan for the Spanish Duke of Alba to invade England from the Netherlands with 10, 000 men. But by God's grace, Knox communed within himself, it had all become unstuck. Through his correspondence with Burleigh, he was told that Elizabeth's skilled and alert intelligence agency under the intrepid Francis Walsingham had discovered the whole plot. By gaining the confidence of Spain's ambassador to England, John Hawkins, an English agent, had learnt the whole conspiracy and exposed it to the Government, and an order for all the plotters to be arrested. Charles Baillie, Ridolfi's messenger, was seized at Dover, with compromising letters in his possession.

After torture, Baillie revealed all. Thomas Howard, the Duke of Norfolk, whom, it was planned, would marry Mary, was thrown in the Tower of London. Ridolfi too, it seemed, had not done his research accurately, for he over- estimated greatly that the northern nobles would raise over 39,000 men, and had conveniently forgotten the deadly rivalry of Spain with France. The Duke of Alba, a Spaniard, feared that, if the plot was successful, a protege of France, the Scots Queen Mary, would ascend the throne of England, and give France, and not Spain, a preeminent position and power in Europe. So the invasion never transpired, and the cowardly Ridolfi, unsuccessful, remained on the Continent, out of harm's way. Not all Italians were like Ridolfi or Rizzio, the little Italian secretary to Mary, who had inveigled himself into the close confidences of the Queen, and paid for it dearly. He remembered with affection the Italian Protestants in Geneva, the Waldensians, who had fled there for freedom of worship. Back in England, Guerau de Spes, the Spanish Ambassador, was expelled from the country. Mary survived just, for fear of Elizabeth to execute a fellow monarch, but from now on she was no longer an honoured guest but a treacherous outcast. Poor Norfolk, the scapegoat, was executed for treason that summer. Such, mused Knox, are the ways of men.

The nations rage, but God will always have His way. As for that tragic, foolish, Queen, who had been so obdurate to the truth which had been held out to her so often, not least by himself in his memorable interviews, what would be her end? Could she be saved as by fire? The preacher of Haddington could not see the future, but feared for her. If only she had listened to God and married the right husband, her life could have been so different, even triumphant and glorious.

As Proverbs had informed its readers, even twice, there was a way which seemed right to a man, but the end of it was death. His heart was troubled still, for his great friend and ally in the Cause, the Earl of Moray, had died before his time two years before at the hands of a murdering Hamilton, and when he had preached in the parish church of St. Andrews, he had denounced the Hamilton faction as murderers. As a result a student called Archibald Hamilton had taken umbrage and refused to attend Knox's services. Such is the pettiness of the world when convicted of sin, the Reformer concluded. He himself was still in a quandary about the place of Archbishops and bishops. Personally, he could do without them and he could live with them, as he had in England. It was not vital.

Just then he hunched his cloak around him against the cold wind, for he was approaching what was left of what had once been the greatest Cathedral in all Scotland. The keen north wind blew through what was now the barebones and emptiness of St, Andrews Cathedral, which in medieval times had taken almost one hundred and fifty years to construct with its vast nave. It had survived winter storms, fire, and the plundering English stripping the lead from the roof during the Wars of Independence. But it did not survive the Reformation and its collective fury. With the coming of the Norsemen and their fury, the monks had fled from Iona and the power base of the Church in Scotland had moved from the west coast to the east coast, and so again it was God's time to move on.

The wind of change wrought by the Reformation brought about the end of the Cathedral. *Reformans et Reformanda*, Reforming and requiring to be Reformed. The Church, like the individual soul, had to be continually transformed by the renewing of the Spirit. Almost exactly thirteen years before he had preached his famous St. Andrews sermon on the very cusp of the cataclysmic change to Scotland's religion, and the congregation were so aroused that they immediately rushed to the ancient Cathedral and destroyed the fittings and furnishings they associated with popery. The end quickly followed. Within three days the Cathedral and friary ceased to function, and within a week all the friars had been expelled from St. Andrews. The cutting hand of the Lord had by necessity to be ruthless, and have no place for sentiment. There had been some debate in the last ten years about restoring this, the greatest of Scotland's medieval Cathedrals, but John Knox had steadfastly opposed it. The break had to be complete.

Just then his eye was drawn towards the hundred foot tall St. Rule Tower nearby, and again the tradition that the Greek monk, St. Rule, or some called him Regulus, had brought five bones of Christ's very disciple, Andrew, from Patras in Greece. Why five bones. he thought, and even more why had sick pilgrims for ages jostled to get near to the dead bones of a dead saint in order to be helped, when the help of the living God was nearer than hands or feet? The Holy Spirit infused his own old tired, bones, as he felt the near presence of the Holy One, and shivered, but not with the cold. He turned to retrace his footsteps to his house in St Leonard's Priory, where he lodged with his fellow Reformer, John Winram, to be met by Richard Bannatyne, his worried servant, at the door.

"Where have you been, master? You will catch a rheumatic fever without your fur overcoat!"

"Och, dinnna fash yourself, Richard! I'm no' bruised reed, man! A man has to be alone wi' his God at times. Go, heat me some good claret and rabbit stew and stir up the embers there, for my bones are not what they were." When he thought of claret, there came to his mind the great port of La Rochelle, the chief town of the Huguenots, the faithful French Protestants, from which Scotland's supplies of claret were shipped, and where he had stopped for a day and a night on his European journeys. There he had baptised a child in the midst of a thriving Scots Protestant congregation, and had made the remarkable prediction against all the odds that he would be preaching in St. Giles within a few years. So he had, and so, God helping him, he would again, despite all that that foolish Kirkcaldy of Grange and his accomplices could do. His thoughts returned to the present, for he had hardly settled down, when a tentative knocking at the door alerted Bannatyne to answer it.

"It is Archbishop John Douglas," he announced hesitantly. John Knox stiffened, for, although he was not actively against Episcopal authority, he had been most displeased at the decision of the now Regent, the Earl of Morton, to appoint the Archbishop as Rector of St. Andrews University, and had refused to take part in the ceremony of the installation of Douglas, and Knox's fellow Reformer, John Winram, Prior of St. Serf's Inch, Lochleven, had installed the Archbishop. To the man of Haddington, it was impossible and wrong to try to fulfill both posts. Yet he felt no personal animosity towards Douglas and rose to greet him despite his creaking bones.

"Greetings in Christ, Archbishop. What has brought you to seek my audience, a desire for wisdom?" John could never resist a vein of irony, when the opportunity presented, He had suffered so much of such against himself." I pray you were not offended that I left your induction as Rector of the University to John Winram. I believe that the spiritual and the academic worlds, while they go hand in hand, must not become the same."

"But did you not insist at the Reformation Parliament and in the First Book of Discipline that there should be clear and total provision for education of our youth in every parish and Burgh of our land? Do you think that I do not take my post at this, the oldest University of the land and the third in the whole English-speaking world, seriously?" Douglas retorted indignantly. The Rector of St. Andrews University was not going to surrender easily to the minister of St Giles on any point.

"God wants a literate people, who can read the Scriptures freely, but a man can only do one job well! We want nae tulchan bishops, Rector, or is it Archbishop?" Douglas squirmed in embarrassment at the accusation. It was put in true Scottish humour, noted for its cutting power, for tulchan bishops derived from the practice of putting a stuffed calfskin, or tulchan, underneath a cow in order to induce it to give milk. This was the Scots irony for the Act passed by the Privy Council in agreement with the new Kirk that the nobles could have the income from the former bishoprics, as long as they appointed Protestant ministers. This artificial arrangement stank of hypocrisy and private greed to Knox, who had opposed it, and with others had nicknamed the appointees" milking cows" or "tulchans". Archibald Douglas could not gainsay the truth of the barb.

"Whatever, Master Knox," he answered gruffly," But it is something else I have come to discuss with you, the anger of a student, Archibald Hamilton, at your preaching that all Hamiltons are murderers. He wishes an apology. Remember that he is a relative of the Earl of Arran!" Knox snorted and his bones became suddenly animated, as in the pulpit.

"Which Arran, the father or son? The son is a complete madman, whom Chatelherault has had to keep under arrest for his own sake, for his mind has gone. As for his father, Chatelherault's authority has now gone, I am afraid. Archbishop Hamilton has swung in the wind outside Stirling as a traitor! Do not talk to me of Hamiltons, when one, who was shown, mercy after Langside's Battle by the beloved Earl of Moray, returned that mercy by murdering James Stuart treacherously!"

"Do you not know that you have already divided the town, and that two colleges, St. Mary's and St. Salvator's are sympathetic to the Queen's party?"

"St. Mary's!" John Knox snapped his fingers dismissively." Did not their minister, that other Hamilton, slanderously accuse myself and the cruelly assassinated Earl of Moray of plotting to murder that foolish Darnley? How incredible, when even the simpletons in the street and the cats in the sheugh of Edinburgh know that greedy adventurer and cowardly murderer, Bothwell, committed the dastardly deed, as if it had been alone in the broad daylight."

"Richard Hamilton has since denied it."

"Aye, only when I threatened to sue him for slander!" countered John Knox." As for St. Andrews, I have the support of St. Leonards College. Why, every day I sit in the courtyard and talk with the many young students, who come to seek my advice and words of knowledge. Even my brother William's son, Paul, my very own nephew, is studying there. Sometimes I sit over the grating of that deep and ancient well". The deep things of God and His Christ had often echoed down its dark depths too. Surely one day, as the Lord once said, even the very stones would cry out praise to Him?

"They always try to be best," he said, pointedly, remembering the University's Greek motto, inscribed above the doorway of St, Leonards, "*Aien aristeuein.*" They ask me of Geneva and the Continent and all kinds of thorny questions of theology. So I am not short of support, Archbishop, and need no petty Hamilton! Forby, I will; not be told by you what to do. The Church must be preserved from the bondage of the Universities!" The old fire had returned to Knox and the poor Archbishop shrank back.

"I meant no offence, Master Knox," he stumbled out.

"There is none, man; take some claret before you go, for it is cold out there." The Reformer's ire had died down as quickly as it had risen.

But the prophetic fire had not lessened by the following Sunday when preaching in the parish Kirk, with many students present, their minds and hearts like tiny birds seeking fresh sustenance and guidance. With no doubt prominent in his mind a satirical play put on a few days prior by the imaginative students of St. Leonards in which the Castilians in Edinburgh, supporting with misplaced loyalty the absent Queen Mary, ended with them all being hanged. John Knox suddenly lent over the pulpit, as if about to take very wings out of its structure, with an otherworldly light in his eyes.

"I predict that Edinburgh Castle, held by our enemies will burst like a sandglass, and spew that traitor, Kirkcaldy of Grange, over the wall, and from it he shall be hung and die a traitor's death." The congregation was transfixed, as people always are by prophecy. Genuine predictive prophecy conveyed a powerful and authoritative message like no' other and produced a complete sense of awe in its hearers. God was providing evidence that He is the true God and that His words can be trusted." The Lord kens all of history, the past, present, and future. Seek ye the Lord, while He may be found; call upon Him while He is near! The arrogant heart of William Kirkcaldy of Grange has hardened against the still small voice. God, who knows his eternal destiny, have mercy on him! Remember that one man with God on his side is in the majority."

The congregation gawped at this original statement of faith, apart from the widespread belief that Kirkcaldy and the Castilians were impregnable in that mighty fortification on Edinburgh's ancient rock." The prophet Daniel, unlike the wise men of Babylon, had the secrets of Heaven revealed to him, for he did not contaminate himself with the rich meat and wines of King Nebuchadnezzar, but confined himself to plain pulse and water and the King was at the last reduced to acknowledge the greatness of the God of Israel as the true God by his prophetic voice, which the Ancient of Days revealed of the Kingdoms of this world in the great image of gold, silver, brass, iron and clay, which would be brought low in due time. The proud Emperor of ancient Babylon, the mother of mystics and dark secrets, had to bow the knee and recognise that Daniel's God was the God of gods and Lord of Kings, and the revealer of secrets! He made Daniel ruler of the whole Province of Babylon and chief of the governors over the wise men of Babylon.

Then for the evil Belshazzar of the Chaldeans the writing was on the wall that he was weighed in the balances and found wanting, and that night when he feasted with all his Lords, forgetful of God, came into judgement and Babylon fell to the Medes and Persians. So it was that Daniel, the prophet of God, in his gift of God transcended the pagan Empires of men, for under Darius and then Cyrus of Persia Daniel was made great in the Kingdom when the Lord miraculously delivered him from the lions' den. Many were the visions he revealed of the Last Days, but when Daniel asked the figure in white linen standing upon the waters of the river when there would be an end of these wonders, he was told that the words were closed up and sealed until the time of the end. He sware by Him that lives forever that it shall be for a time, times, and a half. Before that great and terrible Day of the Lord, *Dies Irae*, the Anti Christ will come!" The people of St. Andrews Kirk gazed in awe and perplexity at this man, who preached on mysteries, which would cause scholars to argue over for centuries to come.

"The hidden things belong to the Lord, but the secret of the Lord belongs to those who fear Him. They shall keep His Covenant!" Knox paused and drew breath, as if about to embark on a new tack.

"As for that Church of Rome, which we have banished from this land, we hear that a new Counter Reformation has begun. I know as much as any of the lives and laws of Popes and cardinals and the writings of the Early Fathers, such as Augustine. So from Scotland there is an answer to the upstart Jesuit who jeered at me, 'Where is your eight year old Kirk compared to the fifteen hundred years of the Church of Rome? 'In answer to that man, we are part of the one Catholic and Apostolic Church! Why, did we not receive a letter from the churches of Geneva, Berne, Basel, and the other Reformed Churches of Germany and France, containing their Confession of Faith and desiring to know if we in Scotland agreed with their doctrine? And did we not here in very St. Andrews at a Conference of our learned Scottish churchmen find that in nothing we differed, except that they keep a number of Festal days and we keep only the Sabbath?"

He looked round for the affirmation of silent nodding of heads, as the people were too awed almost to murmur even in agreement with this frail figure, who, when he entered his true home, the pulpit, grew into a giant of spiritual authority and even physical strength before their eyes." I say that our entrance into history came not now but that fifteen hundred years ago our Kirk was in Jerusalem, in Samaria, in Antioch, and wherever Christ Jesus was truly preached in power, and his blessed and glorious Evangel obediently received, whether it was amongst the Jews or the Gentiles. There we say was our Kirk, which is not bound to any one place, but is dispersed upon the face of the whole world; having one God, one faith, one baptism, and one Lord Jesus, Saviour of all that unfeignedly believe!"

A gasp went out from the hushed congregation at the astonishing, revolutionary, words, for they were a people only newly released from the trammels of Rome's controlling power and still not accustomed to the world wide liberty it meant for all the peoples of not only their island, but a Continent beyond. This was a world vision by a man who saw far beyond the smallish confines of Scotland and justified by theology and history the cataclysmic effect of the Protestant Reformation for the freedom of the individual soul to come boldly to God." We further boldly affirm that if ever God is pleased to bring the Kirk of Rome back to her original purity, so that she shall not be ashamed to reverence the pure Kirk of Scotland as her dearest sister, and resembling her in all things before pride and avarice corrupted her ministers and the inventions of men were preferred to God's simple truth. We say yet again that if ever the Kirk of Rome is reduced to the estate in which the Apostles left it, be assured that she shall vote in favour of our Reformation."

He paused once more for effect after this profound statement." As for those who say there is schism and sectarianism in Protestant countries, let me say this, that, although in all ceremonies there is not uniformity, yet we will not break brotherly concord, on condition that we agree in the principals."

The irony struck him of the division between Scotland and England in their Protestant forms of Church, for, if he had got his way, a joint British Church would have been hastened. As to the vexed question of Apostolic succession, God does not send his afflicted Kirk to seek a lineal succession of any person, saying it has been handed down from Peter, before He will receive them. But with all gentleness He calls his sheep unto himself, and says, 'Come unto me all you that labour and are heavy laden, and I will ease you. All that the Father gives me shall come to me. Him that comes to me I will not cast away.'

The false claim of Rome that Peter was the first pope, and the Rock instead of Christ, the Chief Cornerstone, had been blasted into pieces by the Biblical expositions of Luther, Calvin, Zwingli and such. It had been exposed simply as a religious claim to control the spirits of men, but where the Spirit of the Lord was, there was liberty. If it was not in the Bible, he did not believe it. All works or ceremonies were man made, unless found in the Bible. He loved to quote Isaiah, Jeremiah, his favourite prophet to the end, and the Psalms. With that Knox started down the steep pulpit steps, and, though he still gripped his long staff tightly. When his faithful Richard Bannatyne began to offer his arm along with that of Jamie Campbell, another servant, the reinvigorated Reformer refused with a vibrant shake of his head. When they had walked slowly from the Abbey to St. Andrews parish, Bannatyne's help had been necessary to support his master's left oxter, for his weak frame shuddered in the cold North wind. His coat with pine marten fur trimming the neck stood him in good stead. But now a completely renewed person stood before them. The words of God were literally the words of life to John Knox, as though fresh blood flowed through his veins.

"It will soon be time to return to the capital, Richard, I feel it in my bones," he said quietly to his good servant. But he was sure his end was near, and would prefer to be in the ancient capital. More and more, he was confined to bed.

But on the last day of July, a message came that Edinburgh was safe. that the King's and the absent Queen's party, under pressure from France and England, who felt scared of the danger of a Spanish invasion, had come to an understanding.

"Time to go home, Master," said Bannatyne.

"Aye, Richard," John's voice was low and weak. The effects of the stroke the year before were still with him. Knox felt happy to go back to Trunks Close, his lodgings on the Royal Mile, a splendid house, formerly owned by James Mossman, a wealthy goldsmith, confiscated from him when he supported the Castilian traitors." They tell me that my Colleague at St. Giles, dear Master John Craig, is too neutral for the liking of these Lords of the Congregation. There is no pleasing them! P-sst!" The preacher showed his disgust." I doubt if they will find me any better, for my strength is failing,

Richard. I must write a farewell letter to my faithful friend, Christopher Goodman, for he has indeed been one. I do not blame him for retiring to a country parish."

Seven years before his colleague in Geneva had taken refuge from the strain of the front line in Scotland to become a vicar in the north of England, just as his other bosom friend, John Willock, had also retired to the relative quiet of Loughborough. Knox had been left to man the bulwarks alone almost, but he did not judge them harshly. God knew those who could bear the brunt. The Lord would deliver him from the rage of his enemies, and the disloyalty of his one time friends or pretend friends, like Kirkcaldy of Grange and Maitland of Lethington.

"I shall write that I fear that Pastor Goodman and I shall never meet again in this life, Richard. For I am a poor, unco frail, hirplin, creature."

"Shsh, master! Dinna say sic things," Bannatyne soothed him.

But, nevertheless, John did write such sentiments to his old fellow minister in Geneva and Frankfurt, and thanked him deeply for his close fellowship in the work. He felt the loneliness of his separation from Goodman. Tears came easily and freely in the privacy of his study, as he penned his farewell. It was now time to return to the centre of the spiritual battle in Edinburgh, and the end. But first he must pen a return letter to the St. Giles congregation who had written, begging him to come back, and not to pull back from laying down the condition that he could speak freely in judgement on those who still held out in Edinburgh Castle. His uncompromising spirit had not weakened, if his body had.

But when he got back to his beloved Canongate, where he seemed to know every single cobblestone, his frame was so rickety that it was decided that Knox should preach only in the smaller and nearer part of St. Giles, the Tolbooth Kirk. His voice was now cracked and feeble. For three days he was confined to bed in his Trunks Close lodging with a racking cough. When he recovered, John realised how much he missed the familiar outline of Edinburgh's High Street from the Palace to the Castle. They were imprinted on his heart and his mind. His first priority was to seek permission from the Assembly to call James Lawson of Aberdeen University as his successor. Much to his relief, it was given promptly, and he at once composed a heartfelt missive to the man God had told him would take over his post.

'Beloved brother, seeing that God in His mercy has, far above my expectation, called me back to Edinburgh once again, but since I feel so decayed in my body, and even decaying more every day, so that I don't expect the battle to continue long, I gladly open my conscience to yours, and long that we may confer together in the things of God. So we invite you to take over the great responsibility of St. Giles pulpit and ministry, for on earth there is no other stability than the Kirk of Jesus Christ, always battling under the sign of the cross. To the mighty protection of the cross of Christ I commit you with all my heart.
Make haste lest you come too late!

John Knox

But before Lawson could respond with his acceptance, at the end of August, barely a month since his return, a thunderclap fell with terrible news brought by the

English Ambassador, Sir Henry Killigrew. There was something of the pirate in this Cornishman, with his dark glinting eyes, moustache, and beard, and the spirit of the bravado about him. This was nearer the truth than might have been guessed in a person with the dignity of an Ambassador of Queen Elizabeth, for in fact when exiled in Paris as a Protestant in the reign of Mary Tudor, Killigrew was regarded as a rebel and with his brother had engaged in piracy from a base on the French coast.

In the complicated twistings of European politics then, Henry Killigrew had even fought at the Battle of St. Quentin in northern France in the pay of the Spanish forces in defeating the French. But returning to England on the demise of Mary and the safety of Elizabeth's reign, he had been often employed by the Virgin Queen as a diplomat in Scottish affairs, yet even he knew the need of the greatest requirement of sensitive diplomacy at this point for there had been a deed done in Paris beyond the wickedest imagination for horror and atrocity. Sir Henry Killigrew was a Cornishman of great boldness, a boldness bordering on impertinence, and an air of secrecy about him.

"I have terrible news, Master Knox, which I hesitate to announce." Knox nodded from his couch to proceed.

"There has been a horrific massacre of the Huguenot Protestants of France in Paris, some say 30, 000, at the hands of Catherine de Medici and her puppet son, Charles IX, without the slightest warning or the slightest mercy. She has been brought up in the school of Machiavelli and could wait her time. It took place on St. Bartholomew's Eve."

The features of John Knox were white with shock and anger and words were near impossible, as his emotions shook within him. A silence reigned, while the hand of Richard Bannatyne gently touched his master's shoulder.

"It is ever so with evil, it will choose what are called sacred days to perpetrate its works. It is the work of that wicked witch of a de Medici!" At last he spoke, restraining barely his volcanic rage.

"They, who sow to the wind, will reap a whirlwind. Judgement will come on France, mark my words!" A prophetic spirit was in his eyes and voice." How did it happen?"

"It was carefully planned beforehand. To distinguish themselves in the darkness the perpetrators wore a white badge on their left arm and a white cross in their hats. At two o clock the great bell of the church of St. Auxerrois was struck for early prayer and the die was cast. The first pistol shot was heard and the massacre of St. Bartholomew's Eve began. The royal guard rushed into the streets, crying," For God and King", the hypocrites. ! Brave Admiral Coligny was stabbed to death and his body flung down into the courtyard, and the great man's body brutalised, I 'm told.

One by one the officers of Henry of Navarre were marched out into the quadrangle before the Louvre and hewn down before the very eyes of King Charles IX. That was only the beginning of the widespread slaughter of innocent Huguenots throughout the streets and houses of Paris, men, women, and children. A more perfidious butchery has not been recorded in history, I swear, Master Knox. The pavements flowed with blood. The killings have spread even through much of France, in

Dieppe, Havre, and Rouen. Some estimate near 100, 000 have died. One light is that the brave inhabitants of La Rochelle are holding out with strength and faith, throwing back the King's soldiers,"

"Enough! Enough! I can bear no more! The brave Huguenots, I have no doubt sang their special psalm of battle! May the Lord arise and His enemies be scattered!" Knox lifted his arm sternly, pointing at Killigrew with a furious finger." What is France's loss will be others' gain! One day France will have great cause to deeply sorrow this heinous act, especially the nobility of that land," he said quietly, but prophetically, his anger subsiding, and he looked pointedly up at Sir Henry Killligrew." But what is your real purpose in coming here?" The English Ambassador blinked in surprise and swallowed quickly. Clearly there was more to this Scots preacher than he had thought, and his bodily weakness had not affected his acuity of mind." E-e-rr, it was with regard to the exiled Queen, Master Knox," he stammered ever so slightly." Her Majesty wishes to know what would be the feelings in Scotland, if her cousin was sent back, for with an open heart I tell you Elizabeth finds her royal cousin an embarrassment to know what to do. To execute a monarch is a terrible thing."

The Ambassador hesitated." I have been commissioned to find out what the King's Lords of the Congregation would think of putting Mary on trial in Scotland?" The question was in the air, if not in the words. Tension hung in the atmosphere, as the old preacher felt the pull of his lower nature, that part which afflicts every man, even the true believer in Christ, to yield to its demands. To have that Queen in his hands again to have her punished for all she had done to the good ship of Scotland and the Reformation to put them on the rocks, appealed to that lower nature. But Knox resisted.

"It is not for me to decide. You must ask the Regent and the Lords themselves," he answered quietly.

But nothing was ever decided upon, with shilly-shallying amongst those in power during young King James's minority. Not least it worried them what the reaction of the future King would be, if anything drastic as done to his mother. It might return to haunt them, and so happily the question faded out from the people of Scotland's vista and troubled them little now. But they did hear in no uncertain terms Knox's fierce anger at the French monarchy and Roman Catholic nobility for the devilish horror of their wholesale massacre of the Huguenot Protestants. France had washed its very streets in blood. It was a deed that would haunt France for centuries to come in the huge loss of a skilled middle class who might conceivably have saved their land from a similarly terrible bloodshed two hundred years later.

Knox had crept up the High Street, leaning on the arm of Bannatyne, but again in the pulpit he was transformed and ravaged the perpetrators, Charles IX and his evil mother, Catherine di Medici.

"God is not mocked! They that sow to the wind will reap a whirlwind. Righteousness exalts a nation, but sin is a reproach to any people. The evil rulers of France who have planned and ordered this satanic deed will have the curse of God on their lives! The name of Medici will be linked with treachery though history. The she - witch, Catherine de Medici, the spawn of the man of sin, like a poisonous spider, will be burned up by the fire of God!" The French Queen mother was in fact the niece of the Pope Pius IV.

"The faith of Christ will be lost in France for long years to come." So he continued to denounce the land which once had been a sister to Scotland. The French ambassador had been present in a rear alcove, and was so outraged that he demanded an apology from Regent Morton, and when that was outrightly refused, he immediately left Scotland.

As the autumn slowly gave way to the winter chills and winds coming in off Arthur's Seat, the old warhorse more and more was by necessity confined to bed, and a fearful cough seized his frame, so that he had to give up his usual daily Bible reading, which was some chapters of the Old and New Testament and some psalms, so that he usually in his last years read through all King David's songs in a month. His loving Margaret and faithful Richard instead read to him. Even though he had been fifty and Margaret Stewart of Ochiltree a mere maiden of seventeen, a third of his age, theirs had been a marriage of deep affection, and their three daughters, Martha, Margaret, and Elizabeth toddled round her ankles as she lovingly served her husband. By now she was not only his nurse but his secretary. Being of noble blood, her scholarship was of the best.

"Dinna neglect the wee ones, Margaret," he croaked," tae attend tae this broken down body."

"Shsh, dear one, and dinna strain yersel'." She soothed his brow and stroked his hair, still streaked with grey, stubbornly refusing to go white. From a strongly Protestant family, in the eyes of her and her father, Sir Andrew, she had married the hero of the age, who had rid Scotland of Catholicism.

"Read me ince more the great prophet, Isaiah, frae chapter fifty three, and then ma' favourite, John seventeen, noo that I am faur ben." He intoned fainter, his Scots coming to the fore, as his earthly role became played out, and the French and English intonations that had influenced his speech were forgotten.

A few days before he had preached in his successor, James Lawson, but his voice was so faint that he could just be heard by a grieving congregation, who hung on his words, and strained to hear him. They could not believe that this human firebrand was burning out.

"The duty of a minister and his successor too is to preach the whole counsel of God, missing nothing out! I am now making a marriage between Mr. James Lawson and you, my people I praise God with all my heart that he has given me such a one in my place, now I am too weak to go on. I pray that God will augment his blessing a thousand fold above all I had." He intoned in a low voice the common blessing, and to the massed indrawing of breath, John Knox stumbled down the pulpit's steps of St. Giles. A great soul had handed over the reins. James Lawson, in tears he had held back in vain, was left alone in the wide pulpit. The great congregation followed the stooped figure, as he walked slowly down the Royal Mile; leaning on his staff, for he was too proud to seek the support of Bannatyne's shoulder on' this occasion, like, for all, Moses leading his people in the wilderness.

By mid November it was now the last week of his life, John Knox sensed, and he ordered his coffin to be constructed. But he continued to think of others.

"Margaret, settle the servants' wages, and call Jamie Campbell to me, for Richard knows what I owe him. Then help me up, for I must preach on the Resurrection today."

"No, no, dearest, it is only Friday, not Sunday!"

"Ach, my mind's awa' but, praise God, my spirit has great clarity! Oh, have Jamie bring up that hogshead of wine from the cellar below. I want it pierced for the consumption o' the ministers o' Leith who are comin' the morn', for I winna tarry till it is drunk." The tiniest hint of humour came through. A hogshead of fifty four gallons normally would have lasted them many months, not to forget the extra pints that were allowed over the limit.

"Oh, may the guid Lord put a guard on your lips, dearest, or hasten the eternal gates! God spare you for years to come." When his servant Campbell came with the barrel of claret, Knox's words were short and direct.

"Here is your money for your services, my man, with twenty shillings above the agreed wages. You will get no more of me in this life," He added, as the humbled man grunted his thanks.

"Gentlemen, be my guests to a new hogshead of claret just opened. Drink freely o' it, for I will not live to finish it." The Saturday saw the assembled ministers of the old port crowded round his armchair, for he had arisen for them. Their mouths fell open, for not only did they not know the revered Reformer was so ill, but surprised that he should celebrate it. Deer bone cups were brought and the dying preacher joined them, to quaff God's health to all. The deep joy of the Lord was present in their midst.

"Aye, it's the fast day tomorrow proclaimed for the French massacre, so make the most of it."

"No, no, Master John!" Rev, Fairley, the minister of Braid, on the outskirts of Edinburgh, reassured him.

"It's not yet the Fast Day. Please take a little meat for your sustenance, Master John."

Before he passed to his reward, the great Reformer was to receive a visit from the 4th Earl of Morton, now the Lord Regent of Scotland on the death of Mar. John had never felt totally comfortable in the presence of Lord Morton with his long beard of fierce red hair. He secretly surmised there was a ruthless streak about James Douglas, which was only recently brought out in no small way when he invented the maiden, a primitive but deadly guillotine, as a weapon of public execution. The man of Haddington had felt there was something ominous for Morton himself, when he heard he had contrived such a dreadful instrument of death. Morton had a powerful, aggressive, face. But he could not hold his gaze firm when the frail preacher turned his gimlet grey eye upon him. They were alone.

"I thank you, my Lord Morton, for holding loyal, when our Reformation cause was in jeopardy against the two in the castle who have played the traitor. But I want to ask you one question. Were you involved in the plot to murder Lord Darnley?" Knox fixed him with an unwavering, searching, gaze." I have heard rumours." James Douglas paled imperceptibly, but quickly regained his equilibrium.

"I swear by all that's holy that I had no foreknowledge of that terrible affair and was as shocked as you, Master Knox."

"Do not swear by anything, my Lord!" Knox's eyes sparked fiercely.

"I knew nothing of it, but was at the wedding party of the Queen's page, Bastian, that night. But I had always suspected the rogue, Bothwell."

"Aye," grunted John non committally, and long after the Regent had departed, continued to stare into space. How subtle were the ways of men.

But as the end drew near, it was his beloved Glencairn, and other faithful noblemen, that he wished at his bedside, along with Lawson and the St, Giles elders. Taking the opportunity, he plucked weakly at his successor's serge sleeve.

"Carry a last appeal from me to the Castle to William Kirkcaldy, will ye? Tell him that his soul is dear to me, and I would not have it perish, if I could save it!" As always, his heart was in his voice, and his een glistened. But it was after psalms were sung heartily and prayers wrenched from their whole souls that his followers all departed in tears, much to John Knox's embarrassment.

As his last days approached, he interviewed many at his bedside, including Lord Boyd, who craved the preacher's pardon for offending him in many things, most of all taking the foolish Queen's part in the Battle of Langside, which was readily given of course. 'Lord Lyndsay and the Bishop of Caithness also came, but most often his faithful old friend, the Earl of Glencairn.

"How sad I am that Kirkaldy of Grange has rejected my last appeal, Glencairn, for I prophesy that his body shall hang over the walls of Edinburgh Castle, facing the sun." Even the tough Laird of Finlayston shivered at the starkness of the prophecy, but like those of all true prophets, it came to pass, and the man once known by the secret cypher of *Corax*, the raven, when an agent in France, had the ravens pick his bones when hung from the Castle walls a year later.

"You have been a watchman for Scotland, Master John," Glencairn squeezed Knox's thin hand with deepest affection. Barely able to answer, his friend sighed happily, for there was no doubt the great man was at peace, despite sleeping little, for he spent his last hours in prayer and profound meditation. Limited in breath, he would break out in short bursts of beseechings.

"Live in Christ! Lord, grant true pastors to thy Kirk! Lord, I commend my spirit, soul, and body, and all, into thy hands!"

On the Sunday he passed on quietly to an elder, whom he trusted, a personal communication.

"I have been in meditation this last twa nichts for the troubled Kirk o' God. I have called tae God for it...and have prevailed!" His voice rose." I have been in Heaven, and have possession of it, and I have tasted of these Heavenly joys, in which I presently am dwelling."

The elder was silent and awed." Let us say the Lord's Prayer the gither." At the end with a sigh John Knox said," Our Father which art in Heaven. Wha can pronounce sic holy words!"

And so to his last day on earth, Monday 24th November, when he insisted to Margaret on rising and putting on his doublet and hose. He sat in his deep armchair for half an hour, then returned to bed. Kinyeancleuch, a friend, sat near, and lowered his head close to his.

"Do you have any pain, John?"

"It's not a painful pain, but sic a pain as shall, I pray, put an end to this battle." he whispered, making sure his young wife never heard." I maun leave the care of my wife and bairnies tae you."

His confidante nodded slightly. Knox turned to Margaret, pointing to the book, which had been his mainstay." Dearest wife, read me from First Corinthians fifteen, dealing with death and resurrection." After she had recited it with tears, her husband commented gently." Is that no' a comfortable chapter? Now, for the last time, I commend my soul, spirit, and body unto Thy hands, O God," and he ticked off the three graphically on his fingers. But by five o clock he requested his Margaret for a last reading.

"Go read, where I first cast my anchor." She knew intimately where to go, St. John eighteen, the story of Gethsemane.

"Glorify Thy Son, that thy Son may also glorify Thee. And this is life eternal, that they may know thee, the only true God, and Jesus Christ, whom you have sent."

A strange silence reigned in the room and along the Royal Mile, during the rest of the dark November day. Bannatyne wetted his master's mouth with some weak ale, but suddenly John Knox gave a long sigh and sob, and whispered "Now it is come!", and passed to the other side of Eternity, but not before Richard Bannatyne had thrown himself headlong down by the bed and called for a sign from his beloved master.

"Make us some sign, Sire, that you know the promises of our Lord and Saviour Jesus Christ."

Knox raised one hand, then slipped away. So died a great Scotsman. His name was to go down for centuries to come as synonymous with whenever freedom of religion and personal worship of the Christian God is talked about and honoured throughout the world. Wherever Scots men and women live throughout the world, the name of John Knox will live also. John Knox's name would be remembered in towns, streets, monuments, colleges, institutions, and churches throughout the Presbyterian and wider world for generations to come. His grave in St. Giles contains only his mortal remains. His spirit lives on. Forever after John Knox's name would be synonymous with the Heavenly vision and a determination never to give up, and his great prayer would echo down the corridors of time,

"Give me Scotland, or I die."

THE END